Arc

Book 1: Arcane Magic

BY: MashtonXX & MashtonXY

Table of Contents

CHAPTER 1 — "Blue Grass?"

Sam yawned as she sat up, rubbing her eyes, *"Man, what a good night's sleep! I don't remember sleeping that good in...forever."* Opening her eyes, she looked over to see what time it was and, "*What the hell?*

Where there should have been a phone on her bedside table was grass, blue grass to be exact. Her sleep-addled mind took way too long to process this as she stared blankly at the grass in question for a full thirty seconds before finally speaking her thoughts, "What the fuck?"

Jumping to her feet, Sam looked around franticly, her thoughts chaotic, *"Last night I went to sleep in my bed, in my apartment, an apartment that had walls...and a ceiling, right? Today is Sunday, my day off, so I slept in,"* by now she was trying not to hyperventilate, but it was difficult, *"this is just a weird dream; it has to be."*

Except it wasn't a dream. As she looked around, Sam felt the panic intensify. Checking her surroundings, she was apparently in a clearing roughly the size of her small apartment and surrounded by a dense dark forest that was eerily quiet. Looking at the grass under her bare feet, she thought, *"What forest has blue grass? Wait, is that really a thing...not just a genre of music?"*

"Okay, you got me; you can come out now," she spoke loudly into the quiet forest; even her voice sounded muted in the oppressive silence. She had no idea who or what she was talking to, "*kidnappers, maybe?"* Nothing, not even the sound of insects, could be heard. The silence of the forest was starting to creep her out, that and the fact she was here in the first place, *"wherever 'here' is."*

"Hello, can anyone hear me? Hello...umm...kidnappers? I don't know who you think you have, but I can assure you I am not that person." She waited, hoping for a response, but no sounds came.

"This is bad," she thought and then had an idea. She pinched her arm as hard as she could on the off chance she was dreaming. The pain made her grunt, but she didn't wake up, *"nope, not dreaming."*

That's when Sam saw something looking strangely like an icon of herself with three horizontal bars next to it fade into view in the upper left corner of her vision. The top red bar flashed around its border for an instant, and a -1 appeared floating up from the bar before fading away. Then, the image and bars faded from her view like they had never existed.

That's when Sam thought it was as good a time as any to freak out, and she started hyperventilating. This place…it wasn't normal. None of this was normal! She was standing in a scary forest while hallucinating strange blue grass that looked like plastic but was incredibly soft under her feet, along with strange icons of herself floating in her vision. To top it all off, she was still in her night clothes, which consisted of nothing but an old brewery shirt that was threadbare and had holes everywhere, also known as the perfect sleepy-time shirt.

Starting to feel panic welling up inside her chest, Sam did her best to control her rapid breathing and start thinking clearly. After several deep breaths, she managed to calm herself a little. Speaking aloud she said, "Okay, I need to think about this logically. I know I'm not crazy, at least not the last time I checked anyway. So, where am I? Let's see strange blue grass, check. An oppressively silent, dark, and scary forest, also check. I could have been sleepwalking," she looked at the forest around her. There was no forest this dense anywhere near where she lived, "maybe sleep-driving then…no, that's ridiculous! Maybe I was abducted by aliens or hooked up to some super advanced hyper-realistic VR module as an experiment?" She sighed; not only were those ideas also ridiculous, but "who would experiment on a random attorney living by herself in an average apartment? Probably no one," she concluded to herself. So, what then? Try as she might, Sam could think of no plausible scenario where someone could go to sleep at home, in bed, and wake up in a random forest.

Sam looked closely at the trees around her, *"am I even in America?"* She didn't recognize any of the trees bordering the clearing, and she knew most of the tree species in North America, but she couldn't think of any books she had read that mentioned black trees with grey leaves, *"is this even Earth?"* Looking up at the sun high overhead, it looked normal enough, maybe bigger? "*I haven't invested much time staring at the sun, so I'm unsure if it's different. At least it's daylight. Although I've never seen a forest as dark as this in the middle of the day."* It was as though the canopy barely let sunlight through; from where she stood, Sam could only see possibly five small patches of sunlight peeking through breaks in the thick canopy deeper into the forest. "*What trees are these? They look like cypresses, but I've never seen this color, and the bark is all wrong. And what is up with this blue grass? It looks fake."*

Sam's thoughts were interrupted by a low rustling behind her. Her whole body went stiff with fear. She slowly turned around and came face to face with a, *"What the hell is that thing?"* She asked herself.

Stunted Imp: [Level ??]

'Bing' Congratulations! You have learned the general racial skill: Identify.

The chime, which sounded similar to a phone notification, resonated in Sam's head along with lines of text floating across her vision, which she could barely register because she was suddenly making eye contact with a small terrifying creature in front of her, standing a meter or so outside the clearing within in the shadows of the trees. It looked like a grotesque cross between a chubby cherub and a terrifying demon. Loose pale gray skin covered the creature's body in direct contrast to the dark claws on its hands and feet. It had tiny dark-grey wings that didn't look to Sam as flight-capable and a pair of short stubby horns protruding from its forehead.

Sam took an involuntary step back, and the creature smiled, revealing rows of razor-sharp teeth in a too-wide mouth. Her eyes were drawn to a small sphere of blue flame hovering a few centimeters over the Imp's open palm. Seeing the fire, Sam's fight or flight instincts kicked in, and 'flight' instantly won out. Taking off at a dead sprint, trying to put as much distance between herself and the horror show behind her as she could, Sam's mind was in full panic mode as thoughts were racing through her mind as she ran, *"What the actual fuck is happening? What kind of a creature is that? Did that thing have fire in its palm? Focus, Sam, flee first, then freak out!"*

Sam only ran two steps out of the clearing when a blast of searing heat slammed into her back, right between her shoulder blades! Her whole world went white as the pain hit her. It felt like she had just been splashed with a frying pan full of flaming grease. The scorching pain flared across her back and down her butt and legs as the liquid fire quickly burned through her nightshirt and flowed down her back and legs, her skin sizzling as it did. The pain was more than she could manage, and her mind went numb, utterly overloaded with pain. The smell and sound of her skin and muscle burning made a sickening crackle as she was roasted alive. Her vision blurry from intense burning, Sam only made it one more step before she tripped and fell; an ear-splitting scream ripped from her throat, her vision narrowing to a pinprick. Too disoriented to catch herself, Sam hit the ground hard. Rolling onto her back, still screaming, she tried to smother the flames, somehow remembering, through the agony, the stop-drop-roll technique she had been taught as a child. Trying to wipe off the flaming blue liquid from her legs, she only managed to transfer it to her hand instead, which she quickly wiped onto the detritus of the cool forest floor.

As the flames died down, so did any remaining energy she had left. Sam knew she should keep running; the Imp was only a few meters away and probably preparing another one of those liquid balls of death to end her life. But try as she might, Sam couldn't move. Her world was nothing but agony as her vision narrowed until she could see almost nothing, but despite all of this, and to her dismay, she did not blackout from the pain as she hoped.

***

Sam lay on the forest floor for what seemed like hours but was, in reality, only a few minutes. She stared at the red bar in her vision slowly ticking down. It had not taken her long to realize the red bar represented her life force as she watched it drop slowly even after the fire burning her died out. The bar finally stopped reducing, leaving the tiniest sliver of red remaining. The border around the bar was flashing emergency red. The crippling mind-bending agony was, thankfully, beginning to numb.

"Probably burned away all my nerve endings," Sam thought as the pain faded, then a frightening thought hit her, *"How long have I been laying here? Shit! Where's the fucking Imp?"* Still too exhausted to move, she called out, "What the fuck are you waiting for?" Her voice was raspy from all the screaming. She heard nothing, and then a message popped up in her vision.

'Bing' Congratulations! You have learned Heat Resistance [Level 3]: Bathing in liquid fire while practically naked has tempered your body to resist heat. You will now receive less damage from heat-based attacks. Pain from burns is also reduced slightly.

There were other notifications, but Sam ignored them momentarily, thinking, *"What is up with that description? It's not like I intended to bathe in fire."* She decided she had more pressing concerns at the moment Sam lifted herself to look for the Imp, and then she froze. The Imp was staring right at her just inside the clearing opposite the side she was on, its red eyes staring into her own as it hovered in midair on its leathery wings that still looked too small to fly.

After staring for a moment, she realized, *"the wings aren't moving!"* Looking closer through still blurry eyes, Sam could see the Imp wasn't moving at all; it was like the little creature was frozen in place. She couldn't even tell if it was breathing from where she was. She had no idea what was happening and thought, *"Should I try to run now? No, if it gets free, it can firebomb me to death instantly! I already know I can't outrun it. I have no idea what is happening, but I need to take care of that...thing...before it gets free."*

The pain from the burns was nearly gone, which made Sam worry a little about how much damage had been done to her back and legs. *"I bet my back and ass look like fried pork belly. Am I going to be permanently disabled? Can I even move properly? How will I survive in this forest if I cannot even defend myself? I guess it's not like I could before...but there is no telling how far it is to civilization if there is even any civilization to get to in, wherever this forest is."* Her disjointed thoughts were interrupted by another notification.

'Bing' Natural healing and recovery detected. Your body's ability to metabolize stored compounds and use them to heal itself has been analyzed. Mana has been added as a metabolic component to passively speed your natural recovery ability.

'Bing' Congratulations! You have learned the passive racial skill Recovery [Level 1]: Your natural healing ability was rudimentary at best, but with the addition of mana, you can now recover from all wounds, no matter how severe, given enough time. Although passive, this skill can be enhanced by adding your personal mana to it.

'Bing' System Quest received: You have been summoned to a System-controlled world through an unknown means. The System has recognized this and has granted you a timed quest, offering mana channels and a class option. Return to the nearest System-generated temporary safe zone to receive Mana Channels that will grant you the use of your personal mana and unlock your class options. The closest safe zone is 1.7 meters. Time remaining to complete quest 147 seconds, 146 seconds, 145 seconds…

"M*ana? As in magic energy from fantasy stories? This is like an extremely painful and terrifying game similar to the RPGs back on Earth I played occasionally. I suppose the 'magic' thing shouldn't be too surprising, considering I was just blasted by a freaking fireball-flinging demon cherub! What's weird is not even this 'System' knows how I was summoned here, wherever "here" is. And if I am reading this right, it sounds like this isn't the only world the "System" controls,"* Sam mused, then she mentally slapped herself, *"shit! You idiot, stop thinking and get to that clearing! Time is running out!"*

Sam assumed the safe zone was the clearing by the Imp being frozen in place, which made it safe, right? She hoped so. With an effort of will she didn't know she had, Sam started crawling back toward the clearing. Regeneration or not, she was nowhere near fully healed as she noted the red bar in her vision as proof. Every motion opened her burn wounds, causing fresh waves of pain to wash over her as the exposed raw muscle tissue flexed under the strain of her slow crawl. The quest timer counting the seconds was an excellent motivator to keep moving. Sam fought through nausea and pain, dragging herself, agonizing centimeter by agonizing centimeter, ever closer to the blue grass of the clearing and, she hoped, to safety.

Entering the clearing with fifteen seconds remaining on the timer, Sam collapsed to her stomach, breathing like she had just finished a hill sprint. Looking at the timer, she realized it hadn't stopped ticking down...14...13...12...11...realizing her legs were still outside the circle of the clearing, she summoned the last of her strength to drag them into her chest, rolling to her side and curling up into a fetal position. Her feet and legs were finally inside the clearing. She looked at the timer again; it had stopped at three seconds. "*Way to play it down to the wire there, Sam.*"

'Bing' Quest Complete: You have arrived at a System-generated safe zone within the allotted time limit. Would you like to receive your reward now? Yes/No

Sam focused on the floating text with the words Yes/No that followed the notification. She tried mentally highlighting the word 'Yes', but nothing happened. She spoke out loud, "Yes, give me the reward!" Still, nothing happened. Getting frustrated and a little worried, Sam closed her eyes, focused mentally on the somehow still visible text, and thought, *"Yes,"* the word highlighted, and the text faded from her view. Sam's body was instantly yanked violently upward and sideways to hover suspended over the center of the clearing, facing down slightly. She screamed from the pain of her wounds and the shock of an unseen force suddenly grabbing and jerking her around like a rag doll without warning.

Hanging suspended the way she was, Sam watched as a small patch of blue plastic-like grass began to grow upward, moving toward her like sharp little vines snaking through the air. The grass blades started splitting until she felt dozens of them reach the tips of her fingers and toes, where they paused for a second before pushing inside her body!

She tried, she really did, but try as she might, Sam could not hold back her scream as the thin blades of grass burned their way under her nails, through her fingers and toes, past her hands and feet, and into her limbs. She was tired of screaming, tired of what seemed like constant pain since she had woken up just a few short minutes ago, but no pain relief came. She couldn't move a single muscle, the unseen force holding her suspended in place, not allowing any movement. The agony of each blade of grass burning new paths into her body was almost unbearable. Then, through bleary, tear-filled eyes, she saw what was coming next, *"no, no, no, please, no,"* she thought in horror as two blades of blue agony rose in front of her face, level with her eyes. Each of the blades split into hundreds of tiny tendrils as they extended closer to her eyes, which were held open by the force suspending her in the air, forcing her to watch as the blades grew ever closer. Without slowing, the tiny blue needle-like tendrils of pain entered her eyes, nose, and ears simultaneously. Sam felt the torture as new pathways were burned into her optic nerves, barely aware her health bar started blinking red again as more pain exploded in her mind. Mercifully, Sam blacked out moments later, her mind and body no longer able to withstand the brutal agony.

CHAPTER 2 — "Why Does that Read Like an Advertisement?"

Sam awoke lying on the blue grass of the clearing for the second time that day, "That fucking sucked!" She said to no one as she sat up with a groan. Looking at the flashing text in her vision, which she now knew were system messages, she mentally selected one. She was about to read it when she caught sight of movement to her left. Surprised, Sam dismissed the message with a thought, and it thankfully disappeared from her view. Jumping up to her feet, she saw a long, sleek, black, panther-like creature with six legs stalking around the perimeter of the clearing. It seemed wary of the blue grass as it paced around, always keeping at least a meter away from the grass, like it was a threat, *"if what the freaking grass did to me is any indication, it's most definitely a threat!"* She thought, remembering the unbearable pain she went through a short time ago.

Tracking the large, lithe cat as it paced around the clearing, she thought, "*Smart cat, if it's avoiding the grass on purpose…also an enormous and scary cat. The damn thing could probably eat me and still ask for seconds!*"

Focusing on the frightening cat the same as she had the Stunted Fire Cherub of Death, "*or whatever it's called,*" Sam's reward was a message directly into her mind.

Blade Tail Panther [Level ??]

Which was followed by a subsequent message:

'Bing' Identify has leveled up to level 2.

The cat, or Blade Tail Panther, didn't seem to see her and was instead focused on the Imp that was still frozen in the clearing as it paced around the perimeter. Sam even tried waving her hand at the panther to get its attention, but it never looked her way.

"Huh, I guess it is a safe zone after all," she thought, keeping her eyes on the panther, *"I wonder what will happen if it attacks the Imp?"* Looking closer at the cat, she realized a discrepancy between the description and reality, *"Hey, there's no blade on its tail! What's up with that? Its name plainly says Blade Tail! I don't see any freaking blade on its tai—oh, there it is."*

The panther had circled until it was behind the Imp, and a glistening black blade as long as her forearm slid out of the tip of the panther's tail, the deadly sharpness of the blade reflecting the waning sunlight. Sam continued watching. For some reason, she wasn't even frightened by the new development; that realization bothered her a little. However, she decided to unpack that issue later as she was too interested in what was happening in front of her to care.

The panther shifted its body ever so slightly, and it took Sam several seconds to realize it had whipped its tail blade directly at the Imp's exposed back. The motion was so fast Sam's eyes couldn't track it; the tail with a dagger-like blade sticking out of it was there one second, and the next, it was in the Imp's back.

"Wait! It isn't in the Imp's back; it's a millimeter away from going in!" Sam wasn't sure who was more surprised at the turn of events, her or the panther, when the blade stopped, suspended in its flight. But the blade stopping was just the start of the weirdness. As soon as the System stopped the Blade Tail's attack, the clearing expanded outward to encompass the panther's three-meter body, blue grass and all! What freaked Sam out the most was how the trees surrounding the clearing hiding the panther vanished, as in, one second, the panther was hiding in the forest with its tail stuck, frozen about a meter into the clearing. The next second, the clearing was around the panther, and the trees it had been hiding in disappeared, replaced with a level patch of blue grass.

Before Sam could freak out, a notification popped up in her vision.

Warning! Hostile action detected. A non-sapient creature is attempting to enter a safe zone while the current owner occupies the zone.

"Well, that is certainly interesting, but how could the Imp attack me with that fireball? Hmm, maybe it didn't throw it until I was out of the clearing and thus no longer protected? Either that or it wasn't a safe zone. Maybe we were both out of the safe zone when it threw the fireball, and it tried to attack again when it entered the clearing?" Sam didn't have time to think about it longer as more notifications came in.

Attention: The current safe zone owner [S.AM.] has the right to decide the fate of the two hostile entities trapped inside. As the owner of the safe zone, you have the right to punish the entities with any form of discipline you deem acceptable, leading up to and including execution, as the intent of the invading entities is determined to have been lethal by the System. As the owner, you must decide their fate within 48 hours, at which point the System will remove the safe zone. Note: if the owner exits the safe zone for a period greater than 10 minutes, the safe zone

will be considered abandoned, and the System will remove all protections, including releasing all occupants.

Sam wasn't sure what she had been hoping for but leaving the clearing in search of food and water for more than ten freaking minutes would have been nice. But that ship had sailed. There was no way she was going to try to dash through the forest for a few minutes in search of sustenance before having to run back to the clearing so the System didn't release two deadly creatures that would almost certainly track her down and kill her if she didn't make it back in time. Looking at the two suspended creatures, she sighed and asked, "What the hell am I supposed to do?" When the Imp and Blade Tail didn't answer, she sighed again and plopped down in the middle of the clearing, trying her best to ignore the two hostile creatures in there with her.

"At least I'm not in pain anymore. Might as well check my notifications while I try to figure out what to do with those two." Simultaneously with the thought, the list of notifications Sam previously ignored popped back up into her vision.

'Bing' Congratulations! You have received Crystal grade mana channels: The System has recognized you have been brought to this planet against your will by an unknown means, and instead of destroying you, the System has rewarded you with Purified Crystal Mana Channels. Purified Crystal Mana Channels: All mana-based functions are 200% more efficient. Your mana channels cannot be destroyed and will regenerate in the event of lost body parts, chance for mana poisoning or channel burnout reduced to 0%, entropy reduced by 200%, reducing the cost of all mana-based actions by the same percentage.

'Bing' Your Crystal Mana channels are fully integrated, and Soul Link is established.

Sam whistled to herself and told the two monsters, "Wow, I'm not a hard-core gamer, but even I know those are some impressive bonuses!" Having played RPGs on and off through the years, Sam knew that 200% of anything was an amazing bonus. Hell, it was almost a cheat to have that kind of bonus, considering this new world seemed to have similar mechanics as the games she used to play back on Earth with the notifications and monsters with levels. Sam knew she had just hit the holy grail of upgrades, assuming everything else in the world didn't receive the same thing at birth, of course. She admonished herself, "*I'm operating on a lot of assumptions here. I shouldn't get too excited just yet."* She continued scrolling through her notifications.

One racial skill detected: Recovery [Level 1]:

Skill 'Recovery' has been integrated with your mana channel upgrade and is now 200% more effective: Lose a finger, no problem, grow it back! Lose an arm, quick, reattach it, or grow it back! Lose your head; well, you better act fast!

"Surely that's a joke, right? Heal a decapitation?" Sam was a little skeptical, *"I hope I never find out if that's for real, that's for sure! Anyway, moving on,"* she checked the following message.

'Bing' Congratulations! You are now a System Interface User:

Designation: Samantha Alecto Moura [S.A.M.]

Origin: Earth [location unknown]

You may now choose a class from the available options or wait and choose later. Note: once a class is selected, you cannot change it easily, so choose wisely.

Wondering how the System knew her name and that she was from Earth, for a brief moment, Sam dismissed the thought, assuming she would eventually find out. She thought to herself, "*Class Options*," and a list popped up in her vision, prompting her to exclaim, "Hey, I'm figuring this stuff out!" She said to the two monsters in the clearing, frozen in stasis. Shrugging when they didn't answer, she eagerly looked at the list of classes that appeared and was disappointed immediately; it was a short list with only two options:

Class options:

Option 1: [Healer]:

Receive two free attribute points per class level, two attribute points in wisdom per class level, and one attribute point in intelligence per class level.

Healer Description: The Class 'Healer' is integral to any successful adventuring party but is rarely selected as a class choice by individuals due to the inherent drawbacks associated with the class. As a healer, you can boost your already impressive regeneration ability to the point where re-growing limbs will take minutes. You can heal almost any wound and may even develop the ability to revive the recently deceased

at higher levels in the class, as long as your mana pool holds out. These abilities will make you extremely difficult to kill and one of the most sought-after members of any serious adventuring party. Wealth and fame will be within your grasp if you survive, that is. The Healer is a support class that relies heavily on others to protect them because they are limited in offensive abilities. As a Healer, you will be the primary target in every conflict. Almost all enemy combatants will try to create opportunities to remove you from the battle first, above all else.

Choose Healer as your class. Yes/No

"Nope! I have been single and independent my whole life for a reason. I will not be choosing a class that forces me to seek protection from others! Like needing to be protected by some weird, overconfident alpha character who thinks I owe them something, 'extra,' for their protection...in the creepiest of ways. Besides, I have no idea how far it is to the nearest humans...at least I assume they will be human...what if the nearest sapiens are like lizard people or something?" That thought set Sam back for a second. She had no idea what the indigenous residents of this planet might be or even what they may look like. "*Huh, I guess there's no point worrying about it now when I haven't made it more than five meters from where I started,"* she thought morosely. Shaking the thought off, she checked the next class option and smiled to herself, *"now this is more like it!"*

Option 2: [Arcane Pathfinder]:
Receive ten free attribute points per class level, plus 1% to all base attributes every ten levels.
Warning! Arcane Pathfinder is a System curated class. Due to your unknown origin and after analyzing your memories, the System has marked you for study. It has created a class option unique to you.

Arcane Pathfinder description: you have traveled, mostly naked, through the void and possibly dimensions to arrive here; it is only fitting your class reflects the unique nature of your arrival on this plane of existence as well as the path(s) you traversed along the way. As an Arcane Pathfinder, you will forever be a wanderer, never able to settle for too long in any one place. You will find the call of adventure increases over time if you pause your exploration for too long. Although not prevented by your class, companions will be challenging to keep due to your class-enforced wandering soul. As an Arcane Pathfinder, you will find yourself alone for long periods, traveling companions coming

and going along your path, likely only staying for a short time. Still, you will also see and experience many wonders others will never have the opportunity to see, making the class both solitary and rewarding. This class is not for the weak or faint of heart and will be filled with wonder and danger in equal measures. This class is designed for you, a strong individual who only needs herself to survive.

Warning! Selecting Arcane Pathfinder will remove all other class options permanently! You will not be able to learn spells or skills from books, scrolls, or any other accelerated means; all spells, abilities, and skills must be created by you, either consciously or otherwise. To compensate for this, you will be provided with a curated set of abilities to aid you in your journey, but no skills or spells. Racial skills, spells, resistances, and occupations will remain available.

Choose Arcane Pathfinder as your class. Yes/No. Warning! Selecting 'No' will permanently remove this class as an option.

"Holy crap, this class is amazing, but do I really want to never settle down? To top it all off, the freaking System read my mind and thinks this is what I want. At least that explains how it knows I'm from Earth... Don't get distracted; this is what the System thinks I want. Is it what I want?"

Sam searched her emotions, trying to find anything that might prevent her from wanting the life the Arcane Pathfinder offered. Did she want to settle down? No, she had never had that desire and didn't expect it to change; it just wasn't an urge she had ever felt, and watching how utterly miserable the people she had grown up with had become once they settled down and started their family only solidified her not wanting to even more in her mind. One of her favorite sayings was, "People with kids are the best birth control ever."

"But do I never want to settle down with someone once I feel like I have done and seen it all?" Sam thought about the wording of the class description, *"It says I will be forced to wander from place to place for the rest of my life. The message doesn't say how long I will be able to stay in one place, and by one place, does it mean a city? A country? A planet? No, that's ridiculous; it couldn't mean a planet...is it that ridiculous, though? I mean, I'm standing, well, sitting on an alien planet right now...so...,"* she slapped herself lightly on the cheek, *"stop it, Sam! Get back to the real question! Do you want to wander for your entire life or not?"*

Focusing, Sam thought hard about the question. She could not find anything wrong with the idea of having to explore for the rest of her life.

Back on Earth, Sam had always forced herself out of her comfort zone by traveling to and exploring different countries alone without the need for a traveling companion. She also loved hiking and exploring state and national forests. Camping in the backcountry was her guilty pleasure, which she found to be a peaceful reprieve from her high-stress job. As far as companionship was concerned, she had never truly felt the need for it. She had never been interested in someone enough to pursue a relationship apart from a quick fling on occasion. Sam enjoyed being single. She was still young and suitably attractive. If she ever felt the urge, she only had to wear something revealing and visit the local club to satisfy her needs.

Yet somewhere in the back of her mind, Sam had always held out hope someone would one day sweep her off her feet, and they would live happily ever after. So, it was annoying that one of the first significant decisions facing her in this new world was guaranteeing that would likely never happen.

After searching her soul for a reason, she should not choose Arcane Pathfinder as her class and finding nothing, Sam made her decision. Without any more hesitation, she selected 'Yes' and tensed for the inevitable pain to follow.

A warm blue glow enveloped Sam, and once again, she was carried by an unseen force to the center of the clearing and was suspended off the ground. But there was no pain this time, and the System was gentler with her. That didn't stop her from looking at the grass in fear, thinking she was about to be probed again, but to her relief, no blades grew to meet her; the grass remained inert. Instead, the blue glow surrounding her turned into a mist and started siphoning away from her body, forming a replica of her, that is, if she was colored blue and translucent. Sam watched in fascination as tiny threads ranging in color from a vibrant dark purple to a silly light pink formed in the blue body before her. "*Those are my nerves; they must be. But what is the other stuff?"*

Along with the representation of her nervous System was a network of what she could only describe as purple circuitry. However, unlike the circuits on boards she remembered seeing, these were three-dimensional and much more numerous than her actual nerves. Sam was taken aback by how many were in her brain and eyes, "T*hose must be my mana channels. No wonder I blacked out when they burned into my brain! I'm lucky I don't have permanent brain damage!"*

All the mana channels originated from two places in her body. One was a small purple sphere about the size of a golf ball at the base of her brain, where it connected to her spinal cord. The other was a slightly larger softball-sized sphere in the center of her chest. The two orbs were joined by a dense cluster of circuitries pulsing in time together and flowing out to her extremities with each pulse. Watching the pulses, she thought, "*I am lucky I don't have brain trauma from what I assume is a golf ball-sized mana battery placed in my brain.*"

Both spheres continued to pulse in synch with each other with less time between each pulse. Each pulse sent more purple energy flowing down Sam's mana channels, and she began to feel the energizing pulses in her body as the magical energies increased. Sam realized this wasn't happening outside her body but was only a visual representation of what was happening inside her.

The pulsing light show continued for another hour, with the pulses eventually becoming so fast there was virtually no perceptible time between them until, finally, the pulses stopped. Sam stared at her mana channels; they were now glowing a bright, deep purple, and she could feel they were intensely charged with energy. The three-dimensional representation of her body turned back to mist, which siphoned into her chest. The invisible power keeping her suspended gently lowered her to the ground and released its hold once she was steady on her feet.

'Bing' Congratulations! You have gained the class Arcane Pathfinder [Level 1]; you have received:
10 free attribute points
New abilities:
Mana Manipulation
Loot
Spatial Inventory
Cartography
Linguistics
Mana Sight [Level 1]

Sam was grinning ear to ear, "I know magic!" she whooped and did a little jump in the air, pumping her fist, "And to think, Healer was the only other choice."

Sam felt the powerful purple energy flowing inside her body, and it felt good! After a quick self-assessment, she found there was not even an inkling of pain anywhere in her body, not even a mild backache. Clapping her hands excitedly, she said, "Now, how do I view my new abilities, allot my free points, and check my status? Hmm, maybe not in that order."

Sam tried to clear her mind and thought, *"status,"* nothing happened. Frowning a little, she tried again, this time focusing on her caricature floating in the corner of her vision and thinking, *"status."*

A semi-transparent window popped up, obscuring her vision slightly.

Samantha Alecto Moura [S.A.M.]
Race: Human; Mortal [Level 0]
Class: Arcane Pathfinder [Level 1]

Health: 46
Stamina: 93
Mana: 219

Attributes:
STR – 5
VIT – 3
END – 6
AGL – 7
INT – 10
WIS – 7
Free Attribute Points – 10

Abilities:
Spatial Inventory
Loot
Linguistics
Cartography
Mana Manipulation
Mana Sight [Level 1]

Class Skills:
None

Racial/General Skills:
Identify [Level 2]
Recovery [Level 1]

Class Spells:
None

Racial/General Spells:
None

Resistance(s):
Pain [Level 5]

Heat [Level 4]

"Not exactly as epic as I initially thought. Also, why the fuck are my initials an acronym used to identify me, and why are they in brackets? I guess I'll figure it out in time...maybe. I'll check the descriptions of the abilities; that might give me a better understanding of what I am capable of. If they even have descriptions."

Focusing on Spatial Inventory, Sam tried to will more information from the ability, and it worked, "Yes!" she exclaimed to the clearing, "This is getting exciting!"

Spatial Inventory:

While spatial storage isn't new to the multiverse, you are the first to have the spatial link etched onto your very soul; lucky you! Backpacks and coin purses can be lost or stolen. Banks, countries, worlds, and empires can collapse, and for an eternal traveler, this can be devastating. But not if that traveler is a Pathfinder with access to her own pocket dimension! Which, you guessed it, you now have! With your Spatial Storage ability, you can store items, weapons, living non-sentient life forms, and trade goods, among many other things you will encounter on your travels. The weight of all stored items will be drastically reduced. Stored items can be retrieved to appear anywhere within a three-meter radius of your body.

"Why does that read like an advertisement?" Sam thought when she finished reading the message, "*Please tell me the System doesn't think this is how I want to be addressed just because of all the targeted ads it must have seen when it read my memories,"* she was not sure she liked that idea but waved the worry away, *"I don't care about that now. I have, no, I am, a freaking bag of holding! Screw you, inventory control...at least I hope I can hold more than a backpack worth of items...the description does mention trade goods, so surely, I can hold enough to turn a profit if I become a trader? I'll just have to try it out later."* She thought about another part of the description, *"I'm not too excited about it being 'etched' on my soul, but I'm pretty sure there's nothing I can do about that now."*

Sam chose to read about her Loot ability next, moving down the list.

Loot:

The ability to assimilate defeated foes instantly using the ambient mana from the atmosphere and the residual mana from your defeated foe. Please note looting will not destroy the body but only remove a

certain percentage of usable parts from the target. At the same time, the ambient mana used will also synthesize a replica of some parts and possibly create random items. The replicating effect is to prevent users with the loot ability from disrupting the ecosystems they visit by robbing local scavengers of their sustenance. Looted monsters may still be harvested for additional parts once looted. The Loot ability is synergistic with Spatial Storage.

That was a straightforward explanation, less like an advertisement than Spatial Inventory had been. Still, Sam wondered what "synergistic with spatial storage" meant. The description didn't say, though, so she figured she would just have to wait and see. She skipped over Linguistics and Cartography, not checking either of them, already assuming she knew what they meant, *"I will be able to communicate with races I encounter and will be able to map my way with the mini-map I can already see in my field of vision."* A small full-color map in the top right corner of her vision showed her standing in the center of the clearing. Waving her arms, she watched as the map displayed her motions in real-time, *"Nice."*

Sam looked at the ability description she was most interested in, Mana Manipulation.

Mana Manipulation:

Have you ever wanted to harness the power of mana, creating, changing, or destroying the reality around you at will? With the mana manipulation skill, you can do just that! Mana Manipulation is an advanced skill that allows competent users to 'Manipulate' their mana and sometimes the mana around them. The only limitation is the user's power, mana reserves, and mental abilities. This skill will allow the creation of spells once the user has created and used skills with mana manipulation enough to etch the pathways to their soul. Spells created will be more efficient than the specific skill(s) used to create them.

"Either the System is slightly unhinged, or someone is messing with me with some of these descriptions," Sam was leaning toward the former, *"I guess that only leaves Mana Sight; let's see what I got."*

Mana Sight [Level 1]:

Synergistic with Mana Manipulation. By infusing your eyes with mana, you can view the mana in your environment. Higher levels will add additional effects and strength to this skill.

"That was short, but at least it was informative."

Sam sighed; she knew she was just putting off the inevitable, so, dismissing the screen from her vision, she looked at the Stunted Imp and Blade Tail Panther with another sigh but resolve in her eyes. She didn't want to kill them, but she knew deep down that if she waited or tried to run, they would very likely hunt and kill her once they were freed.

Closing her eyes, Sam calmed her breathing, relaxed her body, and reached out to her mana with her senses…nothing happened. *"Um, maybe if I focus on the mana sight skill, how do I do that again?"* When nothing popped into mind, she started saying things like, "Mana Sight! No, that didn't work. How about Manipulate! Hmm, nothing. Maybe I need to meditate or something?"

Sam sat in a lotus position and did her best Buddha imitation, "*Focus your thoughts. You want to manipulate mana, to see mana, to be mana. Wait, no, that last one was silly. Focus, Sam, your life may very well depend on it!"*

Sam sat and simply meditated, feeling the grass beneath her naked backside, the cool breeze on her skin, the rustling of the leaves in the breeze…

'Bing' Congratulations! You have learned the General skill of Meditation: By clearing your mind of unneeded thoughts and focusing inward, you have achieved a meditative state. While in meditation, all recovery speeds will be increased by 50%.

"That was not the notification I was hoping for." Grumbling a little, Sam opened her eyes and realized she had been meditating a bit longer than she thought. The sun was long past its zenith, and the shadows from the trees were becoming longer by the second. Two moons were visible in the dusky sky when she looked up.

"Two moons, huh? One is small and blue and the other is green and looks similar to Earth's moon in size. I guess that solves the question as to whether or not this is Earth."

Standing up and stretching, Sam brushed off her bare butt, and looking to the sky, she asked anything that cared to listen in annoyance, "Would it have killed you to give me some clothes? You even mentioned I traveled mostly naked across dimensions or some shit. Did it occur to you that may not be how I prefer to travel?" There was no response, not that she had expected one.

Taking off her T-shirt, Sam inspected it. It was a goner; the entire back of the shirt was burned away except around the collar and shoulder areas. *"This won't even be useful as a blanket."* The shirt still carried some sentimental value, though, so she wanted to keep it, deciding to store it in her inventory for safekeeping.

"I hope this works," Sam focused on the shirt in her hand and imagined it going into her inventory. Instantly, the shirt disappeared.

As soon as the shirt disappeared, Sam realized she was completely naked with no idea how to retrieve her only possession from the freaking pocket dimension she had just put it in. She slapped her forehead, *"God, I can be an airhead sometimes! Now, how do I check my inventory? Uh, inventory?"* As soon as she thought it, a massive empty space opened in her mind's eye. "*This is way bigger than I imagined. It must be at least—"* Something caught her attention, and Sam facepalmed at the sight. There floating in front of her in the infinite void was her T-shirt, and right next to the damn T-shirt was a large hiker's backpack, complete with a bedroll strapped to the top. Shaking her head, she mentally summoned the pack out of her inventory by imagining it on the grass in front of her. It appeared exactly where she wanted it instantly, much to her relief. "*Thankfully, that was easier than trying to manipulate mana."*

With curiosity, Sam started rummaging through the backpack, noting the items as she went, "Let's see…rope, bedroll, a little cook pot. Hey rations, nice," setting the items to the side as she pulled them out, Sam came to a set of clothes and did a little fist pump when she pulled them out of the backpack, "yes! Thank you, System! Sorry for ever doubting you," she wasn't even upset about the System not telling her about the backpack, it probably had in one of the dozen messages she had skimmed over but even if it hadn't Sam figured the System had more important things to worry about than reminding a weak little Earthling to check her inventory. Sam held up each item of clothing and inspected it, her Identify skill kicking in after a second on each one.

Plain leather trousers
Plain leather shirt
Plain leather gloves
Plain leather boots

There were no undergarments in the backpack, but that didn't bother her; she wasn't accustomed to wearing underwear anyway. She just hoped the leather didn't chafe. Putting the forest green leather clothes on, she realized she shouldn't have worried. Plain or not, the leather was as soft as velvet against her skin, and everything fit her perfectly.

"Stands to reason, I guess; they were made specifically for me. Damn, I feel better already; it's amazing what something as simple as plain clothes can do for my mental state."

Dressed and feeling less, well, naked, Sam continued rifling through the backpack, "Flint and steel, hmm, it's no ferro rod, but I think I can figure it out. What is this?" She pulled out what looked like a bundle of neatly folded leather straps that unfolded as she pulled it out of the bag, revealing:

Leather Harness
Iron Dagger x 6

"What the hell am I supposed to do with these? Trip and fall, accidentally stabbing myself to death?" Pulling one of the daggers out of its sheath on the harness, Sam slowly turned it over in her hand. She glanced sideways at the Imp, where it hung in suspended animation, "I guess there are worse ways to die," she said. Walking the short distance to the Imp, she held the knife to its throat and said, "This is for trying to fry me alive, asshole," as she drew the blade across the Imp's throat. She braced for the spray of blood she expected to come. Nothing happened. She tried again, but the dagger didn't even leave a scratch on the Imp's skin where the blade slid across it. Confused, Sam stabbed the knife into the Imp's eye, throwing caution and her own queasiness at killing something aside. Nothing. It was like an unseen barrier was in place, protecting the little demon cherub from her attacks. Sam went to the panther and tried to cut and stab it with the same result. "What the hell? What am I supposed to do, smother them?" She looked at the two monsters closely, "*Are they even breathing?* She leaned in until her nose was a centimeter from the Imp's, "*Nope, not breathing.*"

Sam turned back to the backpack, frustrated at her failure. Looking at the grass next to the pack, she noticed a small blue leather-bound book neatly camouflaged by the blue grass of the clearing. "*It must have fallen out of the pack when I pulled other items out. Either that or it was always there, and I didn't notice it."* Picking up the book, Sam identified it.

A Beginner Guide to Manipulating Mana

Looking up at the sky again, she said, "You're laughing at me, aren't you," before looking back to the small book in her hands. Sam opened the book to a random page and braced for something to happen. When the 'something' never came, she shrugged, *"I guess it was too much to hope for the book to just download its information into my brain magically, like in a game, I suppose."*

Flipping to the first page, Sam realized the book was written in some sort of alien text like nothing she had ever seen except, maybe in movies, *"I can't read this!"* but that thought had no more popped into her head when the strange characters on the page suddenly started to make sense. They didn't transform into English lettering; no, she could read the text as it was written! *"I can read this! Thanks Linguistics!"*

Sam eagerly started reading like her life depended on it, which was, in truth, the case. The moons light were bright enough for her to read well into the night, her head resting on the backpack as she lay on the bedroll, learning how to become a genuine magic user.

CHAPTER 3 — "Okay, now for the scary part."

With a groan, Sam stretched, the light of the new day stinging her closed eyes as it penetrated her eyelids. She had passed out while reading the short book about halfway through the night. She had read the 'Beginner Guide to Manipulating Mana' cover to cover twice, trying her best to understand concepts about magic that were utterly foreign to her. The book read more like mystical teachings, an order of space wizards would have written rather than an actual textbook.

After rereading the book, Sam's best guess was that every individual under the System's control felt and used mana slightly differently. A few classes couldn't even use mana, instead relying on stamina or even, in some rare cases, vitality to activate their skills and abilities. A lesson that stood out to Sam said that to truly understand how mana affected each individual and the world, the individual had to 'experience' the mana flow around them and how it interacted with reality. The book assumed this would have already happened to the reader as a child, using the example of watching an injury slowly heal, aided by mana, from a scuffed knee. The author suggested that a simple act, even if the individual couldn't actually see the mana but only how it interacted with the body, would be enough for the individual to activate the manipulation ability and have the Mana Manipulation option granted by the System. Apparently, everyone had the potential for Mana Manipulation, but only some learned the ability because of a lack of Mana Sight; even those few that were given the option usually turned it down because the System enforced class restrictions on Mana manipulators. Most individuals, when given the option to have a mana manipulator class, opted for a more standard class instead, choosing to learn spells from skill books and teachers as opposed to the difficult task of having to create their own spells, which, for some, could sometimes take decades, or in rare cases even longer.

Sam had one skill she knew used mana automatically: Recovery. She didn't like the idea but knew she would have to cut herself and observe the skill through her Mana Sight, which she kicked herself for not activating yesterday. Apparently, all she had to do was focus on the skill mentally, which would activate it; it was no different than how her spatial storage worked; everything seemed to be activated mentally with this System. Thinking about it, Sam realized she never had to speak out loud when using her abilities, so it made sense to her. Still, for some unknown reason, Mana Manipulation needed a kickstart.

Not putting it off, Sam got up, and after a sip of water from the canteen she found in her backpack, she stepped out of the clearing. She noted a countdown timer began ticking down in one corner of her vision when she stepped out of the circle of blue grass. She was worried about what would happen if she harmed herself while in the safe zone and didn't want to take any chances, so she planned to cut herself for her experiment outside the clearing. *"Don't want to get trapped like those other two just because the system sees me as self-harming."*

Sam psyched herself a little, *"Okay, you must do this to survive! Don't chicken out; it's just an experiment! A really painful and gross experiment...crap, this is going hurt, isn't it...I hope it works. Well, no use delaying it any longer."* Placing one of the daggers on the back of her forearm, she gritted her teeth and cut deep; the dagger was so sharp she barely felt the cut, which went much deeper than she had intended. "Damn, that was stupid," dropping the dagger, Sam grabbed her arm above the deep cut as blood started pouring from the wound. She gritted her teeth, but the pain was surprisingly tolerable, *"I guess when compared to getting nearly burned to death, most things are less painful,"* she thought wryly and was surprised when the blood stopped flowing from the deep gash almost immediately. Looking closer, Sam could see the wound started visibly closing. Quickly activating Mana Sight with a thought, she instantly saw her mana flowing down her arm and into the wound. Purple threads that were so numerous they looked like cobwebs were slowly closing the wound. Watching in fascination, Sam realized the mana was eating away at damaged muscle and nerves and then replacing them anew, *"So it is not so much healing as repairing and replacing damaged tissue, interesting, I think I understand now."*

Sam tried again to activate her manipulation ability. Now, she was sure she understood how her mana interacted with her body to "repair" the wound. She was elated when she felt the ability activate in her mind and could instantly sense her mana pool inside her body. Tentatively, Sam, remembering the book's instructions, reached out to her mana in her mind's eye and 'pushed' her mana using her will while visualizing her wound closing. She felt a strange feeling of something flowing through her body toward her wound, and it sealed shut almost instantly. A wave of vertigo washed over her when the wound closed, and her mana reserves dropped by half. She also noticed a large amount of mana had puffed out into the atmosphere and dissipated when the wound closed.

Once she recovered enough from the light attack of dizziness, Sam analytically thought about what she had just done. "*So, I need to regulate the amount of mana I push into a wound; otherwise, it will be wasted. Also, it seems I need to keep from using so much mana at once, or I will get dizzy. Was it the amount of mana I used or my speed that got me dizzy? Something to experiment with later. But for now—"* Sam did an excited dance, singing,

"I can use magic, I can use magic, I can use magic! Who can use magic? Me! I can use magic!"

With her celebration complete, Sam turned off her Mana Sight and checked her mana pool using her System interface. It was refilling slowly, and she watched the numbers climb for precisely one minute, noting that her mana had risen 44 points in that one minute, around one-fifth of her max. She started doing math in her head, "*Hmm, 44 points per minute...if that stays consistent, then I recover around 2640 mana per hour? However, with meditation active, I can increase that number to 66 mana per minute, which would be 3960 per hour; that's over one point per second!*" Sam wasn't sure, but she assumed her crystal mana channels probably assisted in her mana regeneration. "*I am definitely overpowered!*" She thought. Even though she had used over a hundred mana to heal herself. Sam estimated she had wasted at least half of it, if not more, by the density of the purple mana cloud that escaped her wound. However, her mana pool was almost back to full capacity after only a few minutes.

"*If I learn how to control my mana output better, I will be able to heal from some serious injuries rather quickly,*" Sam mused as she stepped back into the clearing after scooping up the knife she had dropped, happy she was now able to use her Mana Manipulation ability.

***

"*Okay, now for the scary part,*" Sam thought, staring at the suspended Imp and Panther. She began figuring out how to use her manipulation ability to kill the two monsters before her. She activated her Mana Sight again and was at once blinded by the bright blue glow of the seemingly inert grass; it was impossible to see anything else. Although she wanted to, Sam didn't deactivate the skill. The book instructed the reader to "*look past the things you wish not to see,*" which Sam understood meant 'try to deselect the shit that is blinding you'. To Sam's surprise, it was much easier than she had expected. Within a few minutes, she was back to staring at the two other occupants in the clearing with her mana sight. Without the annoying blue glow from the magical grass, it was easy to see what was happening with the paralyzed monsters. What Sam could only describe as a spring of dense mana was tethering the two creatures in place. The spring of mana rose from the ground under each of them, like water from a fountain, and completely enveloped the two beings, creating a skintight bubble around them.

"*No wonder I couldn't harm them. I bet that bubble keeps me out just as much as it keeps them in,*" Sam thought as she stepped up to the Imp, readying one of her daggers; its weight in her hand felt heavy, the reality of what she was about to do created a sense of dread, "*this is going to be gross isn't it,"* pushing past the thought she began coating the dagger in her mana making sure to carefully regulate how much she used careful not to waste it.

It took a little while to get her mana to react as she wanted; envisioning the dagger coated in her mana didn't work like imagining her wound closing. After struggling, the blade finally began to glow slightly purple in her Mana Sight. She finally succeeded when she traced a wire frame around the blade of the dagger in her mind, imagining she was creating a model framework for a sculpture; she then connected the 'wires' of the framework with a thin layer of mana between them to 'form' her sculpture. *"Hmm, my way of manipulating mana requires me to visualize the form it will take first, outline it, and then fill it in. It makes sense; that's what I usually did when sculpting with clay in my free time back on Earth. But it could also be I'm subconsciously trying to restrict how much mana I use so I don't overexpend myself again like when I healed a minute ago, and this is the best way my brain can think of to do it...time will tell,"* promising herself she would focus on it later Sam turned her attention back on the dagger and decided the blade was ready when the construct she had formed around it started leaking mana into the atmosphere indicating her construct had reached a limit of sorts.

Before she could lose her nerve, Sam quickly drew the mana-coated blade across the Imp's throat. She felt little resistance as her mana-coated blade sliced through the blue mana, holding the Imp in place easily before digging deep into its throat with a revolting tearing sound. Hot black blood started spraying Sam's hand as she cut; not letting up, she followed through, cutting open the ugly creature's throat. She was leaning in too close, and blood sprayed into her eyes, causing her to stumble back in shock and revulsion, wiping her eyes while trying not to vomit from the terrible taste and smell of the fetid black blood.

Clearing her vision, she watched as the mana holding the Imp in place dissolved, and the Imp fell to the ground with a wet thump, landing in a pool of its blood. But instead of lying there and bleeding out on the grass, as Sam expected, the Imp stood slowly to its feet, glaring at Sam with unbridled rage. Locking eyes with a terrified Sam, the Imp put a hand to its neck. Sam could hear sizzling and smell burned flesh as the Imp cauterized the wound in its own throat with a look of pure evil in its eyes.

Shit, shit, shit! What do I do? Do I run? No fuck that! The little demon cherub will blast me in the back, and I refuse to take another one of those fireballs to the back again!

Sam watched as the Imp's Mana flared in her mana sight. A streak of red magic flowed to its free hand and formed a sphere. An evil grin lit the little creature's features as it prepared another fireball for attack.

Sam realized with surprise that she was much calmer than the situation demanded. She wasn't the same person this little fucker attacked yesterday; she was an Arcane Pathfinder now, and that realization had changed her whole outlook on what was happening in front of her. Her only thoughts were, *"This little asshole tried to kill me without provocation yesterday. Well, it's payback time, you little shit!"* Sam quickly thought of a plan, and now it was her turn to grin wickedly; dropping the bloodied dagger, she dashed forward. She had an idea.

***

The Stunted Imp stared at the pathetic creature that had attacked him, *"Stupid human, level 0, how is that even possible? It matters not; she will burn as all the others before her. But how is she standing before me now, though? Didn't I burn her a moment ago? And how did she get close enough to cut my throat—"*

The Imp's thoughts were interrupted when the level 0 human grinned at him, her purple eyes beginning to glow. His confusion only deepened when the foolish human dropped the dagger in her hand and charged weaponless toward him. Why she did it mattered little, though; the stupid human had just made killing her that much easier.

Finally, his fireball finished its charge, and he threw it at the stupid human to melt that grin off her disgusting face.

***

Sam was thinking in overdrive. She knew she had to act fast if she was going to have a chance of surviving this encounter. The little demon cherub seemed intelligent but overconfident. She knew she had just drained at least half of his blood, and even though he had stopped the external bleeding, it didn't mean the internal damage was healed; at least, that was what she hoped. When she looked closely, Sam could see how dim the mana flow was going through his small body; using her mana sight, it was nothing compared to her mana flow. So, she devised the desperate and insane idea of going on the offensive.

Sam was betting everything on the Imp's magic being weaker than hers, hopefully allowing her to block the fireball with the shield construct she franticly created in her left hand as she leaped toward the Imp. She had dropped the dagger because she didn't need it. Her mana sight had told her earlier that the dagger had been something to form her mana frame around. She hadn't infused the dagger with the mana, nor had she used the blade to cut; instead, she had created a shell of mana around it using the blade as a template to form the initial framework of her construct. It hadn't been the dagger holding the Mana but the Mana holding the dagger. Back on Earth, she enjoyed sculpting in her free time, so creating a tangible piece of art out of a formless block was second nature. So, using her experience as an artist, she made a weapon of pure mana in her right hand as she lunged toward the Imp, going entirely on the offensive. Her smile never faltered. Sam thought randomly, *"Why am I enjoying this? I should be terrified."* But there was no more time to think, only act.

Sam didn't have the first idea of how to fight with a dagger. She instead formed a twenty-centimeter-long spike of mana at the end of her right fist, *"Let's see how you like a mana spike in the face, you little shit."* Sam swung her fist, punching at the Imp's face.

Before her blow could connect, the Imp launched its fireball at her just a moment before her mana spike hit him. Sam was prepared; pulling back her right hand, she swung her fully formed shield of mana in her left hand in front of her face to block the attack as it hurled toward her. She nearly didn't react in time even though she was prepared for the attack, only getting her shield in front of her at the last second. The fireball hit her shield with an impact so hard it arrested her forward momentum and threatened to knock her off her feet like getting hit with a water balloon launched from a cannon. The flame splashed across her shield, and she stumbled back from the impact, instinctively pushing the mana, infusing her shield outward in a short blast of force. The fireball exploded in a shower of flames, throwing it back toward the Imp. Some of the flaming droplets landed on her exposed arms, burning through her leather shirt. Still, thanks to the adrenalin and new resistance, Sam remained steady on her feet and barely felt the sharp spikes of pain as the burning rain fell.

When the flaming rain splashed back, it surprised the Imp and caused him to shield his face with his arms. Sam didn't give him time to recover from his surprise and quickly closed the gap between them again, running from where she had been pushed back by his attack, getting in range with a quick lunge. She switched her attack from his covered face to his chest and thrust the spike of hardened mana on her fist into his chest right at the point where his mana seemed to originate. Her only thought was, *"I hope this is something vital."*

The mana spike, shaped like a thin bayonet, hit resistance as it touched the surprisingly dense flesh of the Imp's chest. Nevertheless, it slowly penetrated deeper into his body as Sam pushed with all her strength. She hadn't been idle with her shield hand either; she released the mana holding the shield together. Instead, she formed vicious claws of purple mana at her fingertips, using them to rake at the Imp's cauterized throat where she had cut him only moments earlier. The wound in his neck reopened quickly as her fingers dug into the small throat, her claws sinking deep into the recently cauterized flesh. She was thankful the Imp wasn't immune to its own fire, judging by the fact it had shielded its face with its arms, presenting her with the opening she was currently exploiting. Distracted or not, the Imp quickly reacted when she stabbed it and removed his hands from his face, using them to lash out with his clawed hands at Sam's face.

Jumping back, Sam tried to avoid the black claws but still managed to take a swipe across her face, leaving streaks of burning pain in her cheek and a renewed scent of burning flesh from the Imp's claws, having been coated in flame when they hit her. The two stared at each other with caution when they disengaged. Sam could feel the skin on her cheek burning from the liquid fire on the Imp's claws. A few tense moments passed as they calculated their next move. Then, to Sam's relief, the Imp, still bleeding from the reopened wound in his throat and the new wound in his chest, collapsed to the clearing floor, staining the blue grass black with more of his fetid blood. Seeing this, Sam stopped channeling her mana and allowed her constructs to dissipate as she watched the Imp twitch several times and then lay still.

'Bing' You have defeated Stunted Imp [Level 16]. Bonus experience has been granted for defeating an enemy at least 10 levels above your own.

'Bing' Race Human has leveled up to Level 1, 5 free stat points received.

'Bing' Race Human has leveled up to Level 2, 5 free stat points received.

'Bing' Race Human has leveled up to Level 3, 5 free stat points received.

'Bing' Class Arcane Pathfinder has leveled up to Level 2, 10 free stat points received.

'Bing' You have learned a new skill, Mana Crafting [Level 1]: you have learned how to craft crude tools from your mana using Mana Manipulation. When channeling the Mana Crafting skill, all created constructs will require less mana to create and maintain.

"Dumbass!" Sam slapped her forehead, "Stat points; I forgot to assign my free points last night! I need to be more careful in the future!" Her self-admonishment was complete; Sam felt better and started to calm down.

"Okay, deep breath, first assign my points, then recover before moving to the Blade Tail Panth— shit, where is the fucking panther!?"

***

A sick feeling of terror filled Sam's stomach when she realized the large black panther was no longer held in place by the System mana. "*Did some fire splash on it, causing the system to recognize it as an attack and release it like it did the Imp?"* She didn't know and had no time to think about why the panther wasn't there, only that it was free now.

"Where is it?" The motion to her left caught her attention; turning quickly, she saw the panther crouched within lunging distance, eyeing her with a hungry gaze. It had apparently been trying to circle behind her the way it had with the Imp the day before, and she had turned just in time to catch it before it attacked.

Sam was now entirely out of her depth; keeping eye contact with the panther, she thought, *"Okay, so now what do I do?"* Thinking fast, Sam kept her eyes locked on the creature. It was apparently treating her as a valid threat since she had just killed the Imp and didn't seem inclined to attack her as long as she stared at it. A quick check of her mana reserves showed them down to less than half, *"200% efficiency, my ass, I just made a couple of little constructs, and it took that much mana? I was being careful, too! I guess I did feel a drain when the fireball hit the shield. I didn't regulate when I reacted and pushed the fire back at the Imp…but still, that took a lot of mana for someone with zero entropy and crystal mana channels… at least, I assume it was a lot of mana. It doesn't matter right now; I need to focus on how to kill this panther."*

After the quick mana check and her inner monologue, the panther still didn't strike. Sam took a risk and pulled up her stat sheet while still trying to stare down the big cat to keep it from attacking. Without time to think it through, she quickly assigned her free attribute points. 10 points into intelligence, 10 points into wisdom, 5 points into agility, 5 points into vitality, and 5 points into strength…nothing happened. *"Shit,"* risking a quick glance at why nothing happened, Sam saw a flashing text box floating in her vision.

Assign Points Yes/No

"Yes!" she mentally shouted. The word "Yes" was highlighted in her vision, and the box disappeared. A feeling of pure power and mental clarity she didn't think possible washed over her, infusing her entire body with euphoria.

***

Sam's decision may have been hasty, but it was logical; she owned her own law firm back on Earth and was the firm's best trial lawyer. Fast, logical decisions were her bread and butter. Her thought process had been simple in choosing where to assign her free points. However, she had also based everything on the risky assumption this world operated on similar mechanics as the RPGs she had played in the past. Intelligence and wisdom received the most points because of her mana-based class. Those two attributes would influence her mana abilities the most, with intelligence increasing the power of her magical abilities and wisdom expanding the size of her mana pool. Her book from the System said that much, at least. Agility had received points because she wasn't able to even see the blade tail move when it attacked the Imp the previous day, so she would need to increase her reaction time if she had any hope of surviving an attack from the beast; *you cannot block or dodge what you cannot see after all*, she hoped 5 points would be enough. Vitality was obviously her life force, which was dangerously low compared to her mana, so that needed some points. Finally, strength needed a boost because of how hard it had been to penetrate the Imp's body with her mana spike just a moment ago; it was like she was stabbing a block of rubber instead of a flesh and blood body. Sam also hoped strength and vitality together would help her resist physical damage from things like the blade tail that was now darting toward her almost faster than she could track.

***

Sam's purple pupils dilated as she tracked the blurry image of the black blade streaking toward her chest. The Blade Tail had reacted as soon as she had selected 'Yes,' probably realizing what she had done and wanting to stop her as quickly as possible. But the creature's attack was too late. Sam's crystal mana channels made the level-up transition 200% more efficient, and her body changed nearly instantaneously.

Sam jerked her body back and to one side, spinning out of the path of the blade tail. Although superhuman compared to what it had been only a second ago, her reaction speed wasn't quite fast enough to avoid the blade. Still, it was enough to miss hitting her vitals, instead cutting a deep gash in her left side as the blade skipped off and cracked two ribs from its impact. Sam focused; everything seemed to be moving in slow motion. Thinking faster than she ever had, she formed a blade of mana extending from her hand as the tail whipped by her. Using the blade, she sliced down onto the tail as it traveled past, using all her strength to sever the tail completely. Her blade didn't cut all the way through the tail, which was nearly as thick as her wrist, unfortunately stopping when it hit something hard. However, her strike was accompanied by a satisfying crack and a yowl from the beast as it yanked its tail back, spraying red blood across the blue grass of the clearing.

***

Taking a step back from Sam, the cat looked back at its tail, the blade tip now hanging limply, Sam's attack having broken something internal. As it viewed the damaged tail, it let out a deep, menacing growl. Turning back to its prey, the cat stopped growling. Sam was right in front of it, punching directly at its face.

***

Sam knew she didn't have much time; she was running out of mana and was starting to feel woozy from the gash in her side, which was gushing blood. So, as she had with the Imp, she went on the offensive and dashed toward the panther when it looked back at its tail. Dismissing her blade, she formed a mana spike on her fist again, intent on plunging it into the creature's brain through its eye socket. The second she was close enough, the panther looked back toward her. Seeing her opening, she put everything she had into a punch with the mana spike aiming at the panther's eye just as it turned its head to her, *"I hope this works; I don't want to be cat food,"* she thoughtfully committing to the attack putting the weight of her entire body into the punch.

It didn't work. Seeing Sam's attack, the blade tail opened its mouth and lunged, swallowing Sam's arm up to the elbow before clamping its massive jaws shut, its fangs sinking to the bone. The big cat's eyes widened when the spike hit its throat, but it clamped down harder when it felt the mana spike stab into it, the pressure of its bite wrenching a pained scream from Sam. Even through the pain, Sam managed to form mana claws on her left hand and dig them into the monster's throat, holding herself in place as the big cat shook its head back and forth, trying to sever her arm. Sam held on long enough to summon the last of her dwindling mana into the hand buried in the panther's mouth and use it to blast the spike off her fist, launching it deeper into the panther's throat. The mana blast caused the panther to bite down even harder. Sam heard a sickening pop, and suddenly, she was free of the creature's grasp, her arm now completely severed just above the elbow.

Releasing her grip with her other hand, Sam stumbled back a couple of steps before collapsing onto her back; the trauma of having her arm bitten off and the exhaustion of completely emptying her mana pool left her on the verge of passing out. She stared at the panther through bleary eyes. It had fallen to its stomach, its head lolling to one side on the ground; dark red blood was oozing from its throat where her mana claws had dug deep furrows in the softer flesh. Blood was pooling in the blue grass from the wound in its throat and its open mouth as its breath came in ragged gasps. "*What the fuck? I didn't do nearly enough damage to bring that thing down,"* Sam thought as her head swam.

Sam was in a bad way; her health was less than 1% for the second time in 24 hours. However, thanks to her accelerated natural regeneration, she had already stabilized; even the bloody stump of her right arm had stopped bleeding. Thinking about her arm made her look at it; she vomited at the sight. Her flesh and muscle were hanging down in ribbons from the severed limb, and she could see some bone exposed, the white of the bone stained red with her blood, "*Or is that the panther's blood? Does it even matter? I'm so fucked; no way will I ever survive alone with only one arm in this freaking fantasy land filled with monsters.*" Tears welled up in her eyes. This wasn't supposed to happen. She was supposed to be an explorer, an Arcane Pathfinder exploring worlds, forging new paths to places forgotten by time. She was now a crippled and helpless girl who would likely be killed within her first few days of exploring her new reality. "*What was I thinking?*" The hard thoughts came, *"I'm no warrior, no fighter. I'm just a single female in her late twenties whose only fighting experience was a few martial arts classes I took every now and then; hell, even that was more for exercise than anything else...well, exercise and the cute instructor... Meh, who am I kidding? I only took the classes for the instructor, but I did get exercise too!"*

As a distraction from her current situation, Sam argued with herself about the real reason she had taken martial arts, as she thought back to the 'private' lessons she had received from Kate, the beautiful redhead instructor who so enamored Sam with her strength and confidence, brought a smile to her lips. *What would Kate say about my situation now? She would say something like, "The only true failure is not trying in the first place," or something sappy like that.*" The thoughts helped Sam get over the terror of the giant panther lying a few meters away. She sighed through her pain and tears, thinking, *"Kate was always right about one thing, though, people will never know what their true potential is until they get off their ass and try."*

The thoughts of Kate helped pull Sam from her self-pity, and looking at the stump of her right arm again, she decided, *"I have to get it together! I have freaking magic! I'll make a new arm if I have to, I'll—"* Her thoughts trailed off as she stared at the bone of her arm; it was ever so slowly regrowing. "*I'm a fucking idiot! I just healed from being nearly burned alive less than twenty-four hours ago; of course, my limbs will regrow...seriously though, there was no way I could have really believed that.*" Channeling a small amount of her recovered mana into her bloody stump, Sam was rewarded with a centimeter of rapid growth. First, her bone regenerated, closely followed by her muscles and skin. Her mana dropped back to zero, and the splitting headache of mana depletion hit her, but Sam barely registered the pain now that she knew there was still hope. "*I can do this; I can repair lost limbs! Why didn't I think about that earlier? Probably because it should be impossible. I had just gotten my arm bitten off by a panther right after fighting off a freaking flame throwing Imp. That is not something I was taught to handle growing up in suburban America.*" Laughing out loud, Sam couldn't help but feel giddy; she would survive this. "*Now get off your ass and kill that stinking cat before it kills you!*" She told herself with determination.

Blinking her tears away, Sam was glad no one was around to watch her little breakdown. Struggling to her feet using her one good arm, she shuffled over to the panther slowly, still a little dizzy from the blood loss and physical trauma. She only took a step when she kicked the backpack she had left out as a pillow. Stumbling to her knees next to it with a grunt of pain, she heard the clinking sound of glass, "w*hat was that?*" Looking at the backpack, Sam saw a small vial with a dark green liquid inside that had fallen onto the grass; it looked like a test tube with a stopper on the top. Picking up the vial, Sam examined it with Identify.

Small Stamina Potion: Restores a small amount of stamina.

"Yes! Please have a health and mana potion in there too!" Sam grabbed the backpack with her left hand and tipped it upside down. A small hard leather case fell out of the backpack. Its top was open, the securing cords holding it closed having come undone, and it spilled several more vials out as it struck the grass. "*Man, I really suck at this adventurer explorer thing. I'm pretty sure anyone else in their right mind would have assigned their free attribute points immediately and gone through this bag with a fine-tooth comb before doing anything else.*" Despite her frustration at herself, Sam was still elated as there were vials of red, green, and blue liquid; each color corresponded with the colors of her health, stamina, and mana in her HUD. She picked up a red and blue vial and identified them.

Small Health Potion: Restores a small amount of health.
Small Mana Potion: Restores a small amount of mana.

Sam popped the stopper from the red vial with her teeth and brought the rim of the vial to her lips. She stopped herself with a thought, "*What if I can only drink one potion and then have to wait an hour or even a day before I can drink another?*" This thought made Sam pause. She had read something like that in a fantasy book years ago, and although she knew it had been fictitious, the similarities between the fantasy stories back on Earth and what she was currently experiencing were too great to dismiss out of hand. "*The System said I'm the first one here from Earth, and it doesn't know where Earth is, but did someone from here go to Earth? There are too many similarities between how this System works and the RPGs back on Earth for there not to be some connection.*" Sam returned to the moment, intent on exploring that line of reasoning at a future date, "*I have to survive the next five minutes first, then I can get lost in thought once I'm safe.*"

Sam put the health potion down reluctantly. She really wanted her arm back, but she knew what she needed to do, and that was to take care of the panther. Having her arm wouldn't help much if she was still bottomed out on mana. Without further delay, she grabbed the mana potion, popped the stopper, and knocked it back like a shot of tequila. "*Yum, tastes like blueberry, nice,*" she enjoyed the taste almost as much as the sudden rush of energy that came with her mana reserves replenishing. Her mana headache instantly disappeared, to her relief, and she regained her clarity. She was tempted to regenerate her arm using her mana. Still, she resisted the urge and instead made sure the wound wasn't bleeding anymore and closed the wound in her side that was still oozing, realizing almost too late the hit to her side had been a lot worse than she initially thought, "*either that or the blade on that tail has an anticoagulant property.*"

Struggling back to her feet, Sam approached the still-motionless feline. She noted it had also stopped bleeding but, thankfully, was still lying in the same place motionless. This made her even more cautious. "*What kind of game are you playing, little kitty? Will you ambush me as soon as I get in range?*" As she drew closer to the panther with slow, cautious steps, she finally realized why the panther wasn't moving. "*Oh, you poor unlucky bastard,*" she thought, looking at the cat. The mana spike she had launched off her hand before the panther had bitten through her arm had exited out its neck right in front of its shoulder blades, completely severing its spine. She could see where the bone was pushed outward from the impact. Some of the panther's wounds may have healed, but its spine had not repaired itself. "*I'm not sure if it will ever actually heal from that, but I am definitely not going to find out.*"

Sam knelt beside the Blade Tail's basketball-sized head, listening to its labored breathing and seeing the fear and anger in its eyes as it stared at her. She whispered quietly to the large animal, "I'm sorry for this; I know you were just following your instincts, but so am I," not wanting to use too much mana, Sam summoned one of the iron daggers gifted by the System into her left hand and placed the tip of the blade at the opening of the panther's ear while building up a small ball of compressed mana in her palm at the hilt of the dagger and releasing the mana as she stabbed the dagger into the panther's ear. The boost from the mana blast in her palm and her newfound strength buried the blade of the dagger in the panther's brain with a nauseating pop. Sam watched the life fading from the creature's eyes and felt the tears well up in her own again. She shook her head, angry at herself, "*None of that, Sam! Either you toughen up, or you fucking die! That panther was going to kill you. Now snap out of your freaking self-pity!"* Sam felt something fall into place at that moment. She realized she desperately wanted to live, explore this new world, and escape the freaking clearing for god's sake. With a new resolve, Sam stood up, checking her notifications.

You have defeated Blade Tail Panther [Level 15]. Bonus experience earned for defeating an enemy at least 10 levels above your own.
'Bing' Race Human has leveled up to level 4. 5 free attribute points have been awarded.
'Bing' Class Arcane Pathfinder has leveled up to level 3. 10 free attribute points awarded.
'Bing' Class Arcane Pathfinder has leveled up to level 4. 10 free attribute points were awarded.

Sam distributed her free points right away, not wanting to make the same mistake of forgetting about them. She thought hard about what to do with her points before deciding to keep her stats as even as possible while still focusing on her magical abilities the most, seeing as that was to be the focus of her class. She knew from her class description that she would rely on herself more often than not, so she would have to be balanced with strength and endurance. So, she added 2 points each to STR, VIT, and AGL. Then a whopping 7 points into END. Lastly, she added 5 points to INT and 6 points to WIS. She kept one point in reserve just in case. Accepting the changes, Sam reveled in the feeling of clarity and power as it washed over her. *"I could get used to this,"* she thought, *"this feeling is better than an orgasm!"*
Sitting on her butt next to her defeated foe, Sam checked her status:

Samantha Alecto Moura [S.A.M.]
Race: Human; Mortal [Level 4]
Class: Arcane Pathfinder [Level 4]

Health: 23 / 158
Stamina: 68 / 207
Mana: 37 / 767

Attributes:
STR – 12
VIT – 10
END – 13
AGL – 14
INT – 25

WIS – 23 [46]
Free Attribute Points 1.

Abilities:
Spatial Inventory
Loot
Linguistics
Cartography
Mana Manipulation
Mana Sight [Level 2]

Class Skills:
Mana Crafting [Level 1]

Racial/General Skills:
Identify [Level 2]
Recovery [Level 2]
Meditation [Level 1]

Class Spells:
None

Racial/General Spells:
None

Resistance(s):
Pain [Level 6]
Heat [Level 5]

Satisfied with what she saw, besides her low health, Sam looked at the stump of her arm, "*Okay, now to heal this arm.*"

***

Regenerating her arm went surprisingly fast to Sam, which is to say, it only took around two hours instead of...well, never. She had gotten the hang of it quite quickly, learning to 'push' the mana from her natural regeneration and using a little extra from her reserves to speed the healing process. There was a limit to the amount the repair would accept, and any extra mana she tried to pump into it dissipated into the atmosphere. She didn't use a healing potion, wanting to save her potions for an emergency, so she was forced to stop and meditate twice during the repair process when her mana dropped to less than ten points, causing a headache. Each time she meditated, Sam quickly refilled her meager reserves with her bonuses on top of the meditation bonus. In the end, she received two levels in meditation.

Once healed, she turned her attention to the corpses in the clearing, no longer able to stand the smell. Beginning with the Imp, Sam walked over to it and gagged. It had defecated itself when it died, and the smell of blood mixed with fecal matter was almost too much for her stomach to handle. But she managed, reaching down and touching one of the creature's wings. She thought, *"Loot!"* She was not disappointed.

Stunted Imp items:

1-Silver; 15-Copper; Monster core [Stunted Imp]; Vial of Imp blood x 2; Imp wing x 2; Imp horns x 2; 10kg Imp meat; Small Health Potion x 1. Take all Yes/No

Selecting 'Yes,' Sam noticed the Imp's wings and horns vanish, but other than that, nothing seemed to change. Checking her inventory, she found everything listed floating in the void of her personal storage. Walking over to the Blade Tail Panther, she looted it as well.

Blade Tail Panther Items:

2-Silver; 47-Copper; Monster core [Blade Tail Panther]; Blade Tail Panther hide [Level 15]; Blade Tail Panther tail; Blade Tail Panther eye x 2; 50kg Blade Tail Panther meat; Small Mana Potion x 1. Take all Yes/No

Selecting 'Yes' again, Sam thought, *"Wow, that was a lot of stuff. I'm just glad my arm wasn't one of the options."* The thought made her snort out a laugh. She wasn't sure how she would have reacted to that as a loot option.

Still chuckling to herself, she started back to her bedroll but stopped and looked back at the panther with a thoughtful expression. She had received a hide, but the panther's hide hadn't disappeared. The tail was missing, as well as both of its eyes, but not the hide. *Does this mean I can double the amount of certain types of loot? If I learn how to skin animals, I should be able to get two hides off everything I kill. Assuming this is the case, this Loot skill is way awesome. Also, what's so special about that thing's eyes? I get why I received the tail because of the blade, but the eyes?"* Looking at the panther, she asked, *"What do your eyes do?"*

Sam looked at the panther, but when it didn't answer, she plucked one of the eyes out of her inventory with a thought. With all the nerves attached, it landed with a squishy plop in her palm. With a squeal of disgust, she quickly dropped the eye on the ground, shaking her hand free of the slimy feeling.

"*Gross, that's disgusting!*" She thought as she watched the eye roll on the grass of the clearing, *"Aww, now it's dirty."* Sighing and picking the eye up with a look of disgust on her face, she examined it.

Eye of a Blade Tail Panther: Consuming this eye will grant you night vision for 8 hours.

Sam had no intention of putting the thing anywhere near her mouth but realized she might be able to sell or trade the eye, *'It could be valuable to someone desperate enough to eat an eye so they can see in the dark. Well, assuming I ever get out of this forest and find someone to trade with, that is,"* she thought sullenly before shrugging it off. Putting the eye back in her inventory, she had an idea. Reaching down and touching the panther again, she tried to put it in her inventory, and it worked! Running over, she did the same with the Imp's body. Waste not want not after all, plus it remedied the smell of gore and death permeating the air of the clearing.

With her attribute allotment, healing, and looting complete, Sam looked up at the sun; it was already past its zenith high overhead. While healing herself, she had decided to wait until the next day to leave the clearing. The Safe Zone timer still had over 24 hours on it, so she intended to take advantage of the safety while it lasted. The backpack had rations, and a canteen was hooked to it, so she wasn't in immediate danger of running out of water or food. Plus, she had those 50kgs of cat meat sitting in her inventory after all; there was no way she would eat the Imp meat, though, not after how its blood smelled. Staring at the canteen she had just taken a swig from, she mumbled to it, "I better start rationing you though; I have no idea where or how far the nearest water source will be," she started to put the canteen back into her inventory when she stopped and identified it on a whim.

Cold Spring Canteen [Rare]: An enchanted canteen that will never run dry if you have enough mana.

Huh, it seems the System didn't want her to die of thirst or starvation, only deadly monsters, "*Well, that's reassuring,*" Sam thought, taking a long drink of the cold refreshing water, looking at the canteen with Mana Sight active. The canteen's sides lit up with glowing runes in her sight, and after a couple of tries, she could push her mana into the runes. The water in the canteen replenished and started overflowing, splashing over her hand, and, to her delight, as long as she kept her mana channeling into the runes, the water kept coming.

"Yes!" Sam shouted, pumping her fist in the air and stripping off her clothes. She tipped the canteen over her head; the water was ice cold, but she didn't care as long as she got clean. She did her best to rinse the blood and grime off from the past day with one hand while the other held her canteen. Once she felt sufficiently clean, she looked at the clothes the System had provided her and held up her leather shirt with a sigh, "That didn't last long," she said to herself while looking at the burns from the Imp and the cut in the leather left by the Blade Tail, *"Maybe I can repair it later."* With that thought, she dug through the backpack, hoping to find some repair kit she may have missed, but she found nothing. She continued cleaning her clothing in silence.

Sam lay on her back on the bedroll that had been spared from blood splashes while she waited for her clothes to dry in the warm sun. She investigated the surrounding forest. It seemed slightly less scary than it had before. Maybe it was because she felt much more powerful than she did just a day ago, she had, after all, fought and survived a fireball-throwing Imp and a freaking panther with a blade coming out of its tail. One thing she was sure of was her desire to feel the power of those added stat points from leveling again. Those points had improved her body and mind enough to let her kill a creature she knew she had no business fighting. She closed her eyes and thought, *"I think I'm going to like this new world. Having magic sure doesn't hurt, either. I am worried I will become addicted to this feeling of power, though; I'll have to be careful not to let it go to my head."*

After resting for a little while, Sam spent the rest of the day preparing for her upcoming journey through the forest and, hopefully, to civilization. She spent her time storing everything in her inventory, including the empty backpack, and gathering any dead wood lying around the area just outside of the clearing. As she worked, she kept her mana sight active and did not stray too far from the clearing for too long, just in case more monsters lurked nearby.

Before dusk, Sam climbed the tallest tree that bordered the clearing, staying within the ten-minute timer that started in one corner of her vision every time she walked out of the safe zone. Scanning her surroundings from as high up in the tree as she dared to climb, Sam realized this forest was immense. To the south and east was more forest, although she thought there may have been what looked like the beginnings of grasslands to the east; she couldn't be sure. There was a mountain range that looked like it began in the distance to the west and continued to the north, the peaks getting progressively taller the farther north they went, with the tallest ones due north disappearing into the clouds. There was a winding river to the west, maybe halfway between where she was and where the mountain range began in the southwest. It likely found its origins in the mountains to the north. She decided following the river south would be her best bet if she wanted to find civilization.

While she was in the tree, Sam found out her mini map turned out to not be just mini; she could make it fill her entire visual range by focusing on it in her mind and willing it to expand. It acted like a map application on her cell phone with options to zoom in and scroll around. There weren't actually 'zoom' or 'scroll' buttons, so it took a little bit to get used to moving the map with her thoughts. Most of the map was obscured; even the areas she could see from her perch in the tree needed to be more detailed when she zoomed in on the map. That is except the area around the clearing, where she could zoom in and count the blades of blue grass if she wanted to. She figured that meant she needed to be physically near an area for the map to get its details updated, which didn't bother her much as the map was a fantastic tool, and she was glad she had it. After playing with the map for a while longer, she found no other functions, so minimizing it with a thought, Sam climbed out of the tree, returning to the safe zone with less than three minutes to spare.

Sam decided not to leave the safe zone after that, having already picked the river to the west as her destination for the next day and prepared as much as she thought possible for her upcoming journey. There was only one thing left to do. She needed to figure out how she truly wanted to continue to assign her stat points as she progressed. She had been thinking long and hard about this as she prepared to travel. And settling down for the night, she started thinking through her thought processes as she lay on her bedroll. "*My class is obviously mana intensive, but it also requires me to be a wanderer, likely a loner most of the time. That means I will have to be strong enough to fight by myself, and if the creatures in this forest are the norm on this planet, I will need every attribute I have as high as I can get them. I need to bolster every weakness. In gaming terms, I will have to be a warrior, rogue, mage, ranger, and healer all in one to truly survive on my own in what I assume is going to be a medieval game-like world,"* Sam shook her head a little at the thought, "*There is really no way to know that this world is medieval, apart from the leather clothes and daggers which seem to be positive clues this world is medieval in nature."* She had noted she hadn't heard a single mechanical noise since she arrived, no cars, train horns, or airplanes, not a single sign of modern technology, which helped solidify her assumption of the planet's medieval or at least non-mechanical nature. It went against her inner gamer to continue distributing her points as she had been with a focus on mana but keeping all her stats moving up steadily so nothing fell too far behind; "*I really want to dump everything into intelligence and wisdom and see how much power I can wield...I mean, I've only put 31 out of the 60 free points I've received into those two attributes, and my mana has gone up to…"* she checked her status screen, "SEVEN HUNDRED SIXTY SEVEN!" Sam screamed out loud. "What the actual fuck? I'm only level 4 in both my classes. I'm regenerating," she did some quick math, "nearly two mana per second with meditation active."

Before she could get too excited, though, Sam checked her health and stamina and cringed at the numbers. Apparently, her mana channels didn't assist with those attributes, with health being at a paltry 158 points and stamina barely any better at 207 points. "Okay, that decides it. I definitely have to focus more on vitality the next time I level up," she mumbled, "otherwise, I'll wind up overpowered but underdefended. Hell, that damn panther could have easily one-shotted me if I hadn't managed to dodge that blade in time."

Thinking about how there were no automatically added attribute points when her class or race leveled made her wonder if it was like this for all individuals in this verse, "does everyone have to manage their level progression themselves, or is it just because I am a System experiment? No, the healer class description said it automatically added points to some attributes. My class should have been called Jack of All Trades or Jill of All Trades. Laughing at herself, Sam looked around and, seeing nothing else to do, she tried to get some sleep. *"Maybe I'll find someone to ask soon,"* was her final thought before drifting off to sleep.

CHAPTER 4 — "Apparently this is a potion."

Sam woke before dawn and ate a healthy breakfast consisting of cold water from her canteen and the extremely bland and dry rations the System had provided. "*They are like dry oat cakes I used to bring hiking back on Earth; I wonder if the System designed them for me from one of my memories?"* She thought while absently munching. Having slept in her clothes and stored everything else she had in her inventory the previous day, all that was left to do was to store the bedroll and relieve herself before beginning her journey into the forest. Sam didn't bother digging a hole or hiding behind a tree when she heeded nature's call and was grateful for the endless water from the canteen to keep herself at least relatively clean and scent-free before venturing out into the forest, *"Probably still smell strong enough to paint a rather large target on my back though,"* she thought morosely, *"well, I've done the best I can I suppose. I'll have to stay vigilant."*

Taking one last look at the clearing before she left, Sam took in the scorch marks, blood, and viscera covering the blue grass and felt mixed emotions. A smile finally tugged at the corners of her lips as she looked at the last signs of carnage. This new world may be brutal, but she could see magic and construct blades out of thin air now. Her new powers had allowed her to kill monsters way above the level she should have been messing with if Earth RPGs were any point of reference. The explorer in her yearned for more; she wanted, no, she needed to go out and experience all this world had to offer, and she knew it wasn't just because of her class. It was the innate desire to explore she had always felt. Even as a child, Sam had always wanted to explore and experience new places and never stagnated in one location for too long throughout her life. One of her favorite memories was when she was only six years old; she had gone missing from the orphanage she grew up in, causing quite a ruckus in the small town where it was located. After frantic searching by the townsfolk, they found her three days later, camping in a forested area just outside town, quite content with her surroundings and seemingly no worse for wear.

Shaking her head at the memory of her youthful shenanigans, Sam oriented herself using her map and set out toward the river. She knew the safe zone timer for the clearing still had several hours remaining, but she wanted to get an early start this morning. The river looked nearly twenty kilometers away by what she could tell from her tree climb the previous day, and she wanted to reach it before dark.

Turning on Mana Sight, Sam began moving quickly through the dense forest, relying on the magical sight to warn her of any danger as she focused on her footing; both the panther and Imp had been plainly visible to her when her sight was active the previous day. She hoped it would be the same for all the creatures this forest had dwelling in it. Traveling through the woods with Mana Sight on was…interesting. With her eyes open, the forest mainly looked normal; most of the trees were inert, that is to say, they didn't have any appreciable mana glow to them, with the only glow being almost invisible lines of green energy slowly traveling up and down the tree from the roots all the way up the trunk to the leaves. Closing her eyes as she walked, however, she found it wasn't only mana her sight could detect but also the absence of it. The ground, some trees, and even the sky were visible with her eyes closed; it was more like walking around in the dark with the outlines of trees faintly visible but not distinct. Sam soon got used to walking in the forest with her eyes closed, relying solely on her Mana Sight. Granted, she did walk into more than one tree while she was adjusting to moving through a dense forest with her eyes closed, but she felt the effort she made was worth it, *"I'll be able to move around and, more importantly, fight or flee when it gets dark if I can get good enough at this skill. I am glad no one is around to see me walk into trees like an insane woman, though."*

Sam encountered a tiny blue flower glowing brightly a few kilometers into her hike. The flower's glow was so bright Sam had to turn off her Mana Sight to see it. Looking at the little blue flower, Sam was so excited about finding something cool that she instinctively bent to pick the flower. Still, she stopped herself with a jerk, *"What am I thinking? Am I trying to get myself killed? Go ahead and pull the glowing blue flower, Sam; what could go wrong?"* Sam admonished herself and identified the small flower instead.

Cyan Death Blossom

There was no description other than the name. "*Well, that's not helpful, but it does have the word 'death' in it, so… hard pass."* Sam thought as she stepped slowly away from the flower.

The only creatures Sam saw were a few packs of small raccoon-like animals with six legs and bushy tails. She tried to identify them, but they seemed to sense her presence when they were at the edge of her Mana Sight and quickly scurried away. Sam did notice once she saw the little creatures, even if it was for the briefest of moments, they would show up on her mini-map, represented by a grey dot, for a short time, even after they were out of her direct line of sight. She also learned she could keep Mana Sight up indefinitely. Even though her mana would slowly creep down as soon as she turned the sight on, her regeneration quickly kicked in and topped her off again. She continued like this for the rest of the morning, making surprisingly good time and thankfully not walking into too many more trees as she traversed the forest with her eyes closed.

Sam arrived at the river quicker than expected, her enhanced body being much more resilient than it was back on Earth, giving her what seemed like infinite stamina, at least at the medium pace she was moving. In fact, her stamina wouldn't even go down if she was walking, and it barely ticked down when she ran. "*Maybe I don't need to focus too much on stamina, which I believe would be my endurance and maybe agility attributes.*"

Making it to the river felt like a personal victory to Sam. She walked to the bank of the slow-moving river and stared at the murky water, turning off her mana sight to better take in the scenery. Looking closer, she could see the water was clear but stained a dark brown, almost black; it reminded her of the 'cypress tea' color of the bayous she had enjoyed canoeing down on occasion. The only thing missing from making it a perfect 'bayou' was Spanish moss hanging off the trees along the river's edge. The river was small, barely twenty meters across at its widest, and moving slowly. Listening to the light gurgle of eddies along the bank, Sam relaxed, realizing how tense she had been hiking through the dark, quiet forest.

Plopping down on a grassy spot at the water's edge with a sigh, Sam examined her surroundings, first with and then without Mana Sight active. There was nothing she could see to suggest the river was traveled by people; no signs of civilization could be seen along the stretch of the river. She hadn't really expected to see any indigenous people. Still, she had hoped for some telltale signs, like the remains of campsites or maybe skid marks from canoes or barges where they had been pulled onto the bank. Seeing no indication that sapient life used the river, she decided to follow it south mostly because she wanted to avoid going toward the massive mountains to the north with their snow-covered peaks reaching into the clouds. The mountains looked ominous and too cold for a southerner like her, so the south seemed the better choice.

The forest was thinner along the riverbank, so Sam ran for a while instead of walking. She made it two more hours, traveling downstream parallel to the winding waterway without seeing another living creature before the stamina drain finally forced her to stop. "*Where are all the animals? Hell, where are the monsters? Were the Imp and Blade Tail only attracted to whatever energy brought me here? Also, why am I disappointed I haven't encountered a monster? Have I lost my freaking mind, what's gotten into me?*" Sam shook her head; she had no idea why, but the thought of encountering another Blade Tail or even an Imp excited her more than it should have. "*Is it my class craving excitement, or just me craving power?*" The thought was sobering; Sam didn't want to become a power-hungry battle maniac who hunted and killed simply to feel the rush of leveling up.

Still lost in thought, Sam wandered up to the bank of the river and absently kicked a small stone into the water, blankly staring as it plunked in with a small splash and drifted out of sight into the murky depths. Her stamina was regenerating rapidly, and she figured she could continue for at least three more hours before stopping for the night. She looked around, "*Maybe I should cross the river; the forest seems less dense on the other side. I could make better time if I—*"

Sam's thoughts were cut off when a tentacle shot out from the water at the river's edge and wrapped around both of her legs. Before she could react, the tentacle yanked her feet out from under her, dragging her toward the river's murky depths. Grasping frantically around her, trying to find anything that she could get a grip on, Sam managed to get one hand on a small sapling at the river's edge, stopping her momentum right before the unseen creature could pull her entirely into the water, with only her legs submerged beneath the cold surface of the river.

Sam's arm muscles bulged from the strain of gripping the sapling; it felt like something had wrapped barbed wire around her legs, tied the loose end to a car, and pushed it off a cliff. Hooks and barbs from the tentacle dug into the flesh of her legs, threatening to shred her muscles from the strain as she slowly inched her other hand toward the sapling she was holding onto with a death grip, trying desperately to get both hands on the small tree so she could use her newfound strength to pull herself away from whatever it was trying to drag her into the river.

With a primal scream, Sam heaved with all her strength and managed to get both hands on the sapling, her fingers griping so hard she could hear the creak of the wood being stressed as she pulled her body slowly forward, away from the river; dragging herself and the mysterious owner of the tentacle with her. *"Just a little bit more!"* She thought desperately, pulling her legs out of the water a centimeter at a time; she could hear and feel her muscles and skin tearing as the hooks in the tentacle started to loosen and rip out of her legs one by one. Then the unthinkable happened: the sapling snapped from the strain, and the tentacle's tension slingshot her backward into the river. Sam's fingers dug deep furrows into the Earth of the riverbank, trying to stay out of the water, but she was quickly sucked beneath the river's surface.

The only sign of Sam's frantic struggle against the creature was the broken sapling and deep furrows left by her fingers in the soft sandy soil of the quiet riverbank. The water's surface was once again calm, and the forest resumed its ominous silence; no creature dared venture near the river for fear of meeting the same fate as the foolish Earthling.

***

Feeling the cold water rush around her as she was pulled by the tentacle, Sam struggled, but it was no use; she still felt herself being dragged down quickly, far too quickly, into the darkness of the river by the yet unseen foe. All she could think as she was dragged down was, "*At least I took a breath instead of screaming when the damn thing dragged me under; who knows, maybe I am getting the hang of surviving this world? Not panicking and losing my shit every time a monster tries to kill me seems to be a good starting point for survival.*"

Sam activated Mana Sight, doing her best to be logical about what was happening and trying to remain calm. She was already too deep for light to penetrate the murky water, limiting her visibility to nothing. As soon as her sight activated, the outline of the creature attacking her illuminated. It was a massive octopus-like creature with too many tentacles and at least four eyes in the darkness. Yanking her toward its mouth by the tentacle holding her legs, a sizeable wicked beak in the lower part of its bulbous head was open wide to, no doubt, bite her in half. Sam relaxed slightly as she watched the creature's open mouth draw closer. Instead of terror, she felt calm, calculating how to counter this creature and survive the encounter. "*Why am I not afraid? Is it because I have no other choice but to survive? Maybe it is a hidden perk of my class?*" Everything currently happening should undoubtedly be terrifying, to be sure, but not to Sam. Even she didn't understand. Looking at the sizeable aquatic creature that was, for all intents and purposes, about to eat her, Sam's only thought was, "*You're going to be worth a lot of experience points, you big dumb asshole.*"

Sam waited until just before the creature would bite down on her legs with its large beaklike mouth before acting. Right before her legs were about to disappear into the creature's mouth, two-meter-long blades of mana shot out from the soles of her boots, where she had conjured them, shooting straight down the creature's throat! Simultaneously, Sam summoned tiny mana spikes around her legs where the tentacle was wrapped, puncturing the soft flesh of the tentacle holding her. The octopus creature released its grip on her legs when her spikes penetrated its flesh and her blades lodged in its throat. The beast's tentacles began thrashing about in all directions as if to ward off any further attacks, and a gout of blood came out of its mouth. The blood from its mouth and bleeding tentacle looked like a cloud of darkness in her magical vision.

Taking advantage of the distraction her attacks had caused, Sam started swimming upward toward the surface; she needed oxygen badly. The light of the river's surface came into her view, and she swam even harder, desperate to get a breath into her starving lungs. Her head had barely breached the surface when a tentacle wrapped around her throat from behind, crushing her windpipe. The breath she desperately needed never came as she was sucked back under the water, disappearing again beneath the surface.

As she was dragged backward through the water by her throat, Sam could not see the monster, which she expertly deduced was not good. It took a second before she could shut down the rising panic she felt when she couldn't take the much-needed breath. Instead of panicking, she focused on forming short mana spikes in her palms. She grabbed the tentacle around her neck, squeezing with all her strength, forcing the spikes deep into the tentacle, choking her. She felt the grip of the tentacle loosen slightly as her grip tightened, but the damn thing didn't release her throat. Getting more desperate now, she formed mana claws on her fingers. She began raking them across the soft flesh of the tentacle around her throat, cutting deep bloody gashes into the suffocating appendage, forcing it to finally release her. The instant she was free, she turned back toward the surface. Before Sam could start to swim upward, another creature's tentacles wrapped themselves around her chest, crushing out what little air she still had out of her lungs and yanking her back toward the deep black depths of the river.

Desperation clawed at Sam's mind as her body screamed for oxygen. Panic finally took control of her, and not knowing what else to do, she coated her whole body in a thin layer of mana, using most of her reserves, and then pulsed it outward, spending a full sixty percent of her mana pool instantly. The result was worth the mana headache when the tentacle around her chest and another that just latched onto her legs were forcibly blown away from her body. The tentacle around her chest even tore apart into several pieces from the violence of her mana's rapid expansion, creating a circle of torn flesh and blood around her. Sam noted absently in the back of her panicking mind, as she floated suspended in the dark water, that a lot of the flesh floating around her was her own, torn from her body by the wickedly sharp hooks in the monster's tentacle.

Looking up in a daze, Sam could see a pinprick of light; it looked so far away to her oxygen-deprived and pain-addled brain, *"Just how deep is this freaking river?"* Dismissing that thought, she used all her willpower to focus and formed a layer of mana on the soles of her boots. Using every last bit of concentration she had in her oxygen-starved mind, she pushed the mana out from the bottom of her feet in a controlled manner, propelling herself upward through the dark water far faster than she could swim. She wasn't sure she would make it; she was developing tunnel vision, and her lungs involuntarily convulsed, jerking her whole body as she fought herself from taking a breath as she sped toward the river's surface.

Just as she was on the verge of blacking out, the darkness closing in on her vision stopped. *"What is up with not being able to pass out? Am I—"*

Sam finally broke the surface of the river as her momentum propelled her body clear of the river and onto the far bank, opposite where she had begun the dance of death with the monster from the depths. Flying five meters through the air into the forest, there was a loud crack when she landed on a protruding root, followed by a fresh wave of pain. Sam somehow knew she had just broken an arm and at least one rib from the impact.

Not knowing the range of the octopus monster, which she had yet to identify, Sam struggled to her feet and managed to stumble farther into the forest, finally settling behind a large tree and collapsing against it. She slowly slid to her rump, resting her back against the tree's rough bark, and began to gasp in great, painful breaths of air.

Sam was surprised to see her mana was hovering around thirty percent. Apparently, propelling oneself through the water was less mana-intensive than blasting a tentacle off; who knew. She was tempted to drink a mana and health potion just in case the creature pursued her on land. Still, she refrained when she peeked around the tree and saw the monster wasn't coming after her. Once she was certain the creature wouldn't leave the water, she sat against the tree again and activated her meditation skill. Sam began repairing the damage to her body when she felt the boost from Meditation kicking in and using her rapidly regenerating mana to boost her healing ability; she started healing her throat first because it had the worst wound. One of the hooks had apparently torn open her jugular when it was ripped out, and only her regeneration had kept her alive. Considering the amount of blood she had lost, she figured she would have died twice if she had still been an average human. Sam wasn't surprised to see her health was at less than two percent...again. "*How many times have I been seconds from death since I arrived in this world? It has only been a few days since I woke up here, and it must be at least three now! And why didn't I pass out from oxygen deprivation?"* Dismissing her thoughts and focusing on healing, Sam tried to control her breathing and relax her body and mind as best she could under the circumstances. Once her throat was healed, she started on the rest of her wounds; she winced as each of her broken ribs snapped back into place as they healed. Apparently, she had broken four ribs when she hit the root.

Sam managed to get her health back up above half before her mana dropped to ten percent, and she had to stop actively healing herself to let her reserves refill. As she healed, she thought about the fight, trying to determine what she did right and what she needed to work on in the future, "*I don't think the creature was solely responsible for my less than two percent health; I actually think it was when I blasted the tentacles off my body, tearing out all those hooks, and when I launched myself out of the water so high I broke my arm, and my ribs which punctured my lung. All of that pushed my regeneration past its limit, I think,"* Sam looked at the wounds on her chest and legs, which were still healing, *"I really can't believe I survived this kind of trauma to my body again. I have to get a better handle on my magic abilities soon; they're almost too powerful for my body to handle physically,"* she sighed at the thought, knowing what she needed to do, *"I guess that means I need to focus on building my strength when I level up. I need to, at least, get it to the level so my body can handle the raw power of my magic."*

Sam continued for another hour before she was fully healed and topped off with mana again. She was pissed,*" Ambush predator, huh? Let's see how you like being ambushed,"* she had devised a plan as she healed herself and was anxious to put it into motion. There was no way she would let that creature get away with nearly killing and trying to eat her, and it hadn't even been in that order! Plus, she really needed the experience to improve herself to a point where using her skills didn't nearly kill her. Her plan was simple, and once she had confirmed she could indeed see through the water using Mana Sight, observing several tentacles right below the surface of the river waiting motionless for unwary creatures to come by for a drink, she knew her plan would work. "*Oh, do I have a surprise for you, asshole."*

Sam used Identify on the tentacles.

Deep Hunter Level??

'Bing' Identify has leveled up to level 3. Additional information may become available depending on the level of the subject being identified.

Taking the notification as a challenge, Sam identified the Deep Hunter a second time.

Deep Hunter Level?? [Hostile]; Affinity: Dark

"No shit, it's hostile, but I suppose I would have thought it had the water affinity, so there's that." Sam mused aloud. She also checked her notifications from the fight. She was surprised her class had gone up a level, "*I guess my class can level from using my abilities and skill as well as from the experience I gain from defeating enemies; that stands to reason; how else would a crafter class or healer class level if they don't have any offensive skills or spells?"* Continuing through her messages, she found her Mana Crafting and Mana Sight had both leveled up, reducing the mana cost, which was a welcome discovery. She expeditiously distributed all 11 free points she had to spend on strength and vitality, the two attributes that would help her body adapt to her magic power and, hopefully, keep her alive longer. Vowing to herself, she would focus on her endurance and agility next to increase her stamina and reaction speeds. Now, all she had left to do was execute her plan, picking a tree near the river Sam began to climb.

***

Six daggers hovered three meters above the slow-moving water of the river; they looked to be suspended in midair by an invisible force to a casual onlooker. The daggers only hovered above the water's surface for a few moments before each shot into the water with incredible speed, one after another, each barely making a splash as they disappeared beneath the surface. Seconds passed as the water's surface once again became calm and smooth. Then, only moments later, the water began roiling, turning a deep crimson as blood began bubbling to the surface. The water-churning bloody bubbling continued for a full minute, and after another minute passed, part of a tentacle floated to the surface with a dagger protruding from it. The dagger looked like it was trying to pull itself out of the tentacle, jerking back and forth but without success. Then, two daggers that had plunged into the water resurfaced, hovering for a moment before plunging back into the bloody water again. The daggers were followed into the water a moment later by a naked human female with glowing purple lines resembling lines on a circuit board covering her body. "Oh no, you don't!" Sam yelled as she dove headfirst into the roiling mass of blood and flesh leaping from the tree bordering the river. Diving smoothly beneath the surface, she disappeared.

***

Sam hit the water, cutting into its surface with barely a ripple. She formed a spear of mana around her body to help her move through the water more swiftly. Once submerged, Sam didn't waste a second, knowing she was burning mana at a prodigious rate and would need to end this fight swiftly. Sighting in on the Deep Hunter, she used pulses of mana to propel her toward it, aiming for the creature's center mass with the pointed spear surrounding her body, intent on preventing its escape. A tentacle snaked toward her, trying to knock her off course. She stopped it with one of the two remaining free daggers she had control of, stabbing the dagger into the appendage and pushing it out of the way with her mana thread.

"Come on! Only ten meters...eight meters...six meters," the beast stopped its retreat and started turning toward her, *"five meters,"* another tentacle tried to block her path but was stopped by her last free dagger, "t*wo meters,"* the beast had now fully turned toward her opening its beak preparing to snap her in half.

The instant the creature opened its beak, Sam blasted the spear of mana forward off her body, sending the sharp mana construct down the Deep

Hunter's throat. Once she launched the spear into the Deep Hunter's mouth, she used a directed mana blast to change her trajectory, clearing the monster gliding through the water just over its head. Quickly forming a mana blade in her hand, Sam thrust it into the soft tissue of the Deep Hunter's head, cutting a deep gash in its forehead as she went past. The Deep Hunter let out a strange warbling cry she could hear even deep underwater as it released a cloud of black ink around them. The mana spear must have done an incredible amount of damage, judging from the obscuring ink it released to cover its escape.

Sam took a deep breath; she had formed a bubble-shaped helmet around her head before diving into the river, trapping a small amount of air inside. The helmet wasn't much, barely enough for a few breaths, but it allowed her to remain in this fight much longer without needing to surface for air. The ink from the Deep Hunter had completely obscured her mana sight by clouding the water with dark mana. The Deep Hunter used the distraction from the ink as a chance to flee and darted away from her hurriedly. Still, it only took seconds for Sam to deselect the mana from the ink to see through the obscuring cloud. She found it much easier to ignore the ink in her mana sight than the blue grass of the clearing. The Deep Hunter was already a few meters away, still trying to flee; plumes of mana-rich blood were pouring out of its body as it swam. It was moving slowly now, with only one unharmed and fully functional tentacle. All the other appendages in various states of mutilation were haphazardly flopping around as it swam away. The damaged limbs were hindering more than helping the Deep Hunter's movement as it fled.

Determined not to lose her advantage, Sam channeled Mana Crafting and formed a two-meter harpoon in her hand, attaching all six of her mana threads to the butt of the harpoon, twisting the threads together, making a mana rope. Using the newly formed mana rope, she launched the harpoon into the Deep Hunter's body as it fled and was yanked forward through the water when the mana rope went taut. The Deep Hunter didn't even acknowledge her as it continued trying to escape, dragging her through the water as it fled.

Hanging on her mana rope with all her strength in the water, Sam realized the Deep Hunter wasn't nearly as exhausted as she had hoped. Desperate to end the fight, which had been going on for far too long, Sam started constructing and firing mana spikes at the monster's back with her left hand while holding on to the mana rope with her right. The spikes cut smoothly through the water with a push from a controlled blast of her mana. "*I always knew being ambidextrous would help me defeat a giant octopus monster,*" she thought wryly, unable to hide the slightly manic smile that played across her lips despite her situation. Getting serious again, "*Okay, big guy, let's see how you like being perforated...repeatedly.*"

Every mana spike that struck the Deep Hunter slowed it ever so slightly. Still, as they continued their battle of attrition, the spikes started growing smaller and smaller as Sam's mana got lower with each attack. After five minutes of constantly assaulting the Deep Hunter, Sam was out of oxygen and nearly out of mana. She was about to release her mana rope when the sweet sound of victory played in her mind, and a welcome notification popped up in her vision.

'Bing' You have defeated Deep Hunter Level 36. Bonus experience earned for defeating an enemy at least thirty levels above your own.

"Level 36! This fucker should have annihilated me!" Sam thought as she propelled herself to the dead creature and, with a thought, put it in her inventory. "*Oxygen first, then Loot,*" with that decision, she swiftly shot to the river's surface, gasping in a deep lungful of air as she breached the water.

Sam didn't immediately swim to shore. Instead, she trod water while she scanned both riverbanks, the river itself, and the surrounding forest. If she had learned anything by now, it was not to trust the relative quiet of the forest, which seemed full of high-level ambush predators all wanting a taste of tender Sam flesh. Finding no apparent threats, none she could tell anyway, Sam swam to the west, the closest riverbank, and crawled out of the water. Flopping to her back and staring into the dusky sky, she was more exhausted than ever. "Definitely have to increase my stamina," she told the empty air as she got to her feet with a grunt.

Moving farther into the forest, Sam found an open area partially protected from the elements by several large moss-covered boulders that formed a semi-circle around a clearing. She noticed the terrain becoming rockier the farther southwest she traveled, suggesting she was getting closer to the most miniature mountain she could see to the west. Sam could tell that the small mountain signified the beginning of the large mountain range that stretched to the north. She figured the mountain range must be shaped like a crescent, cradling the forest inside its half-moon shape. Moving out sticks and small stones from the clearing she intended to camp in tonight, Sam decided to aim for the small mountain. Sam thought if she couldn't find a village or town along the river tomorrow or the next day, "*Maybe I'll get lucky and find a mining town. If the river runs close enough to the mountain range to provide transportation, there may be a trade route or something...but that is a worry for tomorrow. Tonight is for rest and recovery.*"

Sam got to work, in earnest, setting up her campsite. An avid hiker and wilderness camper in her past life of three days ago, she soon had a sturdy lean-to assembled. The lean-to was facing one of the boulders bordering the clearing. She dug a fire pit between her sleeping arrangement and the boulders so heat from her fire would be reflected at her and the light from the campfire would also be partially hidden. Using the flint and steel the System provided, Sam started an ember in the small bundle of kindling she had gathered as she had set up her camp. Placing it in the fire pit she had lined with gathered stones, she carefully added larger and larger sticks until the fire was sufficiently large. Sam watched for a while until she was sure the fire had taken hold and wouldn't go out before moving on with her preparations.

Happy with her setup, Sam walked back toward the river so she wouldn't ruin her campsite with gore when she pulled the Deep Hunter out of her inventory. Once far enough away, she unceremoniously dumped the corpse of the Deep Hunter onto the ground with a giant squishing plop, speedily looted it, and stored it back into her inventory space to avoid attracting the attention of predators with the smell of the carcass. Sam had tried looting it while it was in her inventory, but that try had sadly failed. She reviewed the loot in her inventory.

Deep Hunter Items:

1-Gold; 37-Silver; 28-Copper; Monster Core [Deep Hunter]; Vial of Organic Ink x 2; Deep Hunter Tentacle x 8; Deep Hunter Beak x 2; Iron Dagger x 4; Mana Potion x 1; Health Potion x 1; 200kg Deep Hunter Meat.

"Yay, I got some of my daggers back!" Sam did a little hop with a fist pump. She walked back to her campfire and sat down on the soft moss she used to line the floor of her lean-to. Staring absently into the flames, she wondered if the fire would deter or attract monsters. She worried she had mistakenly built a campsite and fire instead of hiding in a tree. Looking around and hearing no sounds from the dark forest around her, she looked at the dark, creepy shadows of the campfire's light. She thought, *"Did I sign my death warrant by building a fire in this forest?"* Her question was soon answered when a notification popped up out of nowhere.

'Bing' Temporary Safe Zone recognized. This campsite meets all requirements, albeit barely, to grant the user temporary System protection for 8 hours unless the fire is doused. Protection level: All sound, scent, mana, and light the occupant(s) create inside the perimeter

will be obscured from all creatures with hostile intent during the 8-hour period this safe zone is in place. Hostile creature(s) will not be prevented from entering the safe zone accidentally. No System action will be taken if a creature(s) attacks the occupant(s). The occupant(s) will be notified if a hostile creature(s) breaks the border of the safe zone. Attacks inside the safe zone will remove the obscuration effect for 5 minutes, beginning after aggression has ceased. The safe zone diameter is 20 meters.

After reading the message, Sam threw another piece of wood on the fire, *"It isn't as good as the blue grass clearing, but at least no hostile predators will be able to see me or my fire, and I will be warned if something accidentally stumbles into my camp."* Her dilemma of how to rest peacefully in the forest of doom (as she began calling it) was resolved, and she decided to go over the rest of her notifications from the fight with the Deep Hunter.

'Bing' Race Human has leveled up to level 5. 5 free attribute points awarded.
'Bing' Race Human has leveled up to level 6. 5 free attribute points awarded.
'Bing' Race Human has leveled up to level 7. 5 free attribute points awarded.
'Bing' Class Arcane Pathfinder has leveled up to level 6. 10 free attribute points awarded.
'Bing' Mana Sight has leveled up to level 4. Mana cost is slightly reduced. Range is increased.
'Bing' Mana Crafting has leveled up to level 5. Mana cost is slightly reduced. Your mana constructs can now last slightly longer without your direct contact.

"That makes sense; I did notice my constructs dissipating fast once I stopped infusing them with my mana." Laying back on her bedroll, Sam enjoyed the soft crackling of the fire as she assigned her free attribute points.

Resisting the urge to dump all her free points into wisdom, vitality, and intelligence, she spread them out across all six attributes, making sure not to neglect any of them. She knew if she had just been a little stronger in the fight, she would have been able to pull herself closer to the Deep Hunter along her mana rope when it was dragging her as it tried to escape. She may have been able to end the fight swifter with a decisive blow from another harpoon or spear or something if she had managed to get closer. She thought back to how exhausted she had been. There was no way she would have survived another fight. If another monster had been close enough to hear and investigate the disturbance, there would have been no way she could have fought it, so she needed more endurance. As far as agility was concerned, she could dodge the Deep Hunter's tentacles and beak with her current level in the agility attribute. Still, suppose her agility had been higher during the fight. In that case, she may have found an opening in the Deep Hunter's attacks she could have exploited to make a killing blow. Sam knew what really won the day, though, *"Of course, it was my intelligence and wisdom attributes that won out in the end. Without them, I am just a strong, agile human with no real fighting experience or skills,"* looking at her status window she thought, *"Choosing what attributes to increase is hard, I guess I really do need them all though but how awesome would I be if I just dumped everything into intelligence and wisdom?"* She knew the answer, though, *"I probably would have ripped my body apart trying to do something stupidly powerful with magic by now."*

Sam somewhat reluctantly bolstered her strength and endurance, followed by vitality and agility, before shamelessly dumping the rest into intelligence and wisdom. Selecting 'Yes' to finalize her choices, she let the addictive energy surge wash over her. It was like a shot of adrenalin straight to her brain that, even after the initial rush, still had residual effects that lasted for over an hour. *"I have to be cognizant of this feeling and how it affects me,"* she told herself, but deep down, she already knew she was hooked on this new life and eagerly anticipated growing more powerful each day. Her class and this world catered to all her favorite things: creating, exploring, camping, and the excitement of experiencing new things. The absence of any real responsibility was also a wonderful thing; there were no deadlines, no coworkers to avoid or discipline, no friends showing her endless pictures of their children doing mundane tasks for the first time, and best of all, no one was telling her how to live her life. Being single, successful, and child-free into her late twenties, Sam had been the victim of more than one elderly lady or a stay-at-home mom trying to tell her she was missing out on the wonderful life of servitude and dependence on some man, along with endless the bliss of being a baby factory for said man. *"No thanks, and fuck that shit!"* Sam valued her freedom above all else and decided that should she ever wind up in a relationship, she would never lose her freedom and be forced to rely on the person to survive. The need for self-reliance is why she got her law degree, to ensure she could always support herself no matter the circumstance. She didn't judge other women for settling down and having kids with a few ex-husbands, so why did they always seem so insistent on judging her for not going that route? Was it a misery loves company thing? Sam smiled, thinking back to the women who looked down on her for not conforming to their ideal societal norms, and thought, *"I would like to see some of those stuffy bitches survive what I've been through the last few days."*

Enjoying the fire as she let her thoughts wander, Sam checked her reserved energies. Her health was 310, her stamina was 310, and her mana was a whopping 911. She whistled, "Gotta love those crystal mana channels!" Sitting up and after some indecision, Sam pulled out a portion of the panther and octopus' meat. She had been afraid she would have to pull the entire amount of each from her inventory to cut off the pieces she wanted. To her relief, the meat had already been sorted into one-kilogram chunks. The cat meat looked like a juicy steak, while the Deep Hunter's meat appeared as a cube of white rubbery meat resembling tofu.

Sam set the octopus meat to boiling in her cookpot with some water from her canteen and skewered the panther meat on a stick she had picked up and sharpened just for this occasion. The smell of delicious meat roasting soon filled the air, making Sam's mouth water and her stomach grumble in anticipation. Taking her first bite of the panther steak, she moaned as the delicious juices dribbled down her chin, "It's so good, and it isn't even seasoned with anything!" She said to no one. The meat was tender and juicy, nothing like what she had expected from a wild animal. Chewing and swallowing the delicious bite of cat meat, Sam stabbed the Deep Hunter meat with a dagger, cutting off a slice of the cube with another dagger; she used it to pop the meat into her mouth, *"Hmm, not fishy at all. It's kind of like an octopus—"* Every muscle in her body stopped responding to her signals; she could not move.

'Bing' You have been poisoned with Deep Hunter toxin: Although Deep Hunters have no toxic attacks or venom glands, their flesh contains a potent toxin. -5hp/sec for 420 seconds; paralysis for 120 seconds.

"Why didn't I identify that? It's enough to kill me three times over!" Sam's first instinct was to pour her mana into her natural regeneration. She stopped, though, realizing she was panicking, and calmed herself. She could only survive this by carefully regulating how much mana she used to heal herself until the paralysis wore off and she could get to her potions. She still wasn't entirely sure they would be enough, but she hoped they would; she had to stay positive, after all. Unable to close her eyes or even breathe, she was hit with a weird thought, *"How is my heart beating? Is it beating?"* She quickly check*ed, "Nope, my heart isn't beating? What the hell, man, how is this even possible? Stop it, Sam!"* She admonished herself, *"Focus on the immediate problem!"* Despite the paralysis, Sam could enter meditation, even though she couldn't control her breathing or

relax her muscles. She calmed her mind, increasing her regeneration speeds. She then focused all her mana on destroying the foreign toxin from her body as she counted each second until the paralysis wore off.

Sam managed to slow the health loss from five points a second to three; that alone wasn't enough to beat the paralysis timer, though. Fortunately, her regeneration shortened the duration of the paralysis because, with less than 15 health points left after 100 seconds, she could move the tips of her fingers slightly. "*Still can't move enough to drink a potion, can I?*" She managed to open her mouth slightly and summoned a small health potion directly between her teeth from her inventory. She bit down as soon as she felt it appear in her mouth. Ignoring the glass shards cutting into her gums, she swallowed the red liquid and the broken glass. Her health jumped from 9 to 109 before steadily declining from the still-active poison. This gave her time to think as the paralysis finally wore off.

Able to finally move, Sam pulled all her potions out of her inventory while spitting broken glass out of her mouth. Putting the useless stamina potions to one side, she did some quick math, sketchy at best, as she had no idea how much the regular healing potion from the Deep Hunter loot would recover. Downing her final small health potion to give herself more time, she continued pushing the maximum amount of mana she could into her regeneration. Now her mana was taking a hit, even though Sam was sure she was recovering over four points per second with meditation active. She only had two mana potions left. "*Think Sam, think...Identify, it's leveled up!*" Using her ocular skill on her remaining health and mana potions, Sam frowned.

Health Potion: Instantly restores 300hp.
Small Mana Potion: Instantly restores 50mp.
Mana Potion: Instantly restores 300mp.

"So, do my mana channels work on all potions, doubling their effectiveness? Assuming the small health potions I drank restored 50hp normally like the small mana potion does...this will be close." A quick glance at the small stamina potions showed her they also restored 50 stamina points. *"This is going to be close,"* Sam thought as she waited until she only had 2hp, the border around her health bar flashing and emergency red, and drank her last health potion, chasing it with her only regular mana potion. All she could do now was focus solely on keeping her mana flowing into her recovery at a near-perfect rate to not waste a single mana point. The countdown timer ended at 238 seconds, her stats apparently reducing the effects of the toxin ever so slightly.

Breathing a sigh of relief, Sam relaxed; her health was at 3 points when the timer stopped; as usual, her health pool was at less than two percent, but at least it was no longer going down. With meditation active, she was recovering quickly. She started putting her remaining potions back into her inventory when she noticed the two vials of black ink next to her. She had only thought 'potions' when she summoned them from her inventory earlier. *"Apparently, this is a potion,"* Sam thought as she picked one up and identified it.

Organic Ink [Uses 12]: The organic compound found in a Deep Hunters ink sack. The Deep Hunter uses its ink primarily in defense to confuse potential predators, allowing the Deep Hunter a chance to escape. Potion Effect: When consumed, the ink negates the toxic effects of the Deep Hunter meat.

Had Sam not been in a System-enforced safe zone, her scream would have woken the entire forest.

CHAPTER 5 — "Holy crap, I could ride that thing!"

Sam woke the next day with the sun illuminating the forest on her side of the river. She noticed the woods on the west side of the river had become considerably less gloomy as she progressed farther down the river. At the same time, the gloom remained almost unchanged on the side of the river where she had fought the Deep Hunter. It was almost like the river was a border between two distinct forests.

It took Sam nearly an hour to get over her initial fury and frustration at herself over not identifying the vials of ink in her inventory the previous night. An act that would have saved most of her potion supply from being consumed. Even now, she was still kicking herself for not checking the ink vials in her inventory, which were the cure for the Deep Hunter toxin. Reading her notifications after her initial anger helped her calm down, especially the message explaining she had gained poison resistance and leveled it up to level 3, which was reassuring. As she yawned and stretched in the morning sun, she went back over her notifications from the night before to make sure she hadn't missed anything.

'Bing' Congratulations! You have gained Poison Resistance [Level 1]: You are now slightly more resistant to poison due to your willful consumption of a highly toxic substance. Good job?

'Bing' Poison Resistance has leveled up to Level 2: You are slightly more poison-resistant.

'Bing' Poison Resistance has leveled up to Level 3: You are slightly more poison-resistant.

"Not surprising when you eat something that can kill you three times over. That notification was just ridiculous, though, 'Good Job,' really? Fuck off System." Sam couldn't tell if the System was being snarky on purpose or if it genuinely thought that's how she wanted it to sound…she was still leaning toward the System being a general dick though.

That particular notification hadn't been the one that got her out of her bad mood last night. However, the following notification of a new skill had her perked up. She pulled that notification back up to ensure she had caught everything it said the previous night; she hadn't exactly been in her right mind when she read it after all.

'Bing' Congratulations! You have learned a new skill, Mana Repair [Level 1]: By repeatedly using your mana to supplement your natural

regeneration efficiently and in a controlled manner, while under duress, you have developed the skill Mana Repair. All mana costs for healing will be decreased when using this skill. Channeling mana into this skill will recover your health and/or stamina. Channeling stamina and/or health into this skill will recover mana. Warning: The user can completely exhaust all health points (HP) with this skill; use wisely.

"So basically, I can burn mana until my stamina is full while also healing myself, then switch to stamina to refill my mana reserves and continue healing and building more stamina," Sam tapped her chin. Now that she wasn't still furious, she understood the implications of the skill, *"what's the catch? I wonder. It can't be that easy. I bet it's not a 1:1 ratio."*

Sam decided to test the Mana Repair skill before doing anything else now that she was fresh and could focus on what she was doing. Quickly creating a blade construct, she cut her arm, exactly as she had done outside the blue grass clearing, and activated the Mana Repair skill to heal the wound. She immediately noticed how much less mana it took to heal herself; she also felt or rather sensed a detailed understanding of what part of her body was damaged and how to heal the wound most efficiently, *"well this is interesting,"* she thought as the shallow cut on her arm closed almost instantly using virtually no mana. Checking her mana reserves, Sam cursed quietly to herself, "shit, I'm already full again; this skill is way more efficient than I expected! And I am not complaining about that!"

Next, Sam checked the transfer ratios of her new Mana Repair skill by burning a prodigious amount of mana using several gigantic shield bubble constructs to expend almost all her mana reserves. Once her mana was mostly depleted, she refilled some of her mana reserves by converting her stamina first. After refilling her mana by channeling her stamina, Sam found it to be a 3:1 ratio, stamina to mana. She had to stop channeling when she started to feel so exhausted she was afraid she would pass out. She looked at the mana she had recovered and thought, *"So I can get a little over 100 mana from my current staminal pool; not great, but I guess it's better than nothing. I'm not sure I would use it in battle, though; it felt like if I had kept going, I would have passed out from stamina exhaustion."* During the transfer, the feeling had been weird, as she had channeled her stamina into mana; Sam felt like she was getting more exhausted by the second, like when she used to run at a dead sprint uphill when she trained for marathons in college. Refilling her stamina with Mana Repair resulted in a 3:1 ratio of mana to stamina, which didn't surprise her. She wasn't disappointed either, *"I can fully refill my stamina if my mana reserves are high enough. Hmm, it could help if I'm running away and need the stamina more than mana."* She decided she was pleased with the stamina and mana transfers her new skill offered.

"Okay, so let's see what the health-to-mana ratio is," Sam burned a little more mana. With a thought, she started channeling her health, converting it to mana but immediately stopped letting out a scream as soon as the skill activated, falling to her knees, her hands clenched so hard her nails were digging into the skin of her palms. Sam collected her thoughts to get her panicked breathing under control. *"What the fuck was that?"* The second she had activated the skill, her vision had gone red around the edges, and she felt something very wrong had just happened to her. It was as if her entire being had rebelled against what she was doing, *"was I just draining energy from my soul?"* Sam wasn't sure what the feeling was, only that it was telling her what she had done was hurting her in a way that wasn't natural. And she should never ever even think of doing it again. She almost decided to call it quits, too, but it was a skill she could use that may very well save her life someday. So, hoping the System wouldn't give her a skill that could cause permanent damage if she used it, and after a short mental struggle, she decided she had to know how the skill worked and resolved to try it one more time to get the ratio. *"At least this time, I'll be prepared for it,"* she thought, but being mentally prepared as she was, the feeling wasn't any easier to manage. What she felt when the transfer of health to mana started wasn't pain; it felt…wrong…like she was taking something from her soul that was not easily replaceable. She got the transfer ratio by gritting her teeth and fighting the awful 'wrong' feeling. She was surprised when it wound up being a 1:1 ratio for health to mana, *"still not worth it, though,"* she thought as her breath was coming in short, pained gasps, *"it will have to be some seriously desperate circumstances for me to convert health into mana."* She immediately refilled her health with mana using Mana Repair. Sam frowned deeply when the skill told her exactly what had happened to her, and as she suspected, she found she had indeed damaged her soul, her life force. The thing that bothered her the most, though, was when she instinctively understood the damage; what she had done to her soul could not be healed by any other means than using her Mana Repair skill to transfer the lifeforce back, *"A health potion wouldn't work,"* she thought with trepidation, *"this is a good way to do some permanent damage to my soul, I think."*

She continued channeling her mana into health until she completely repaired her damaged soul. Sighing once she was back at full health, Sam still felt like she had done something terribly wrong to herself even several minutes after her health was fully recovered. She vowed to not do that again unless there was no other choice. Even then, she wasn't sure if she should or would, *"What in the hell did I take from myself when I was converting my life force to mana? Apparently, there's more to my health stat than I realize. It was like I stabbed myself in the soul with a straw and tried to suck it dry...ugh,"* she shivered just thinking about it and blocked the thoughts for the moment. What made the whole thing even worse was the ridiculous 5:1 ratio of mana to health it took when she healed the damage to her soul, "*even more reason to not use my life force for mana!"* She thought empathically.

Overall, Sam was a little disappointed by the results of her tests but figured she couldn't bolster any of her attributes without a potion before, so something was better than nothing, even if one of the transfers came with some pretty severe downsides and the others weren't useful outside of a desperate need. "*Now all I need to do is get Mana Repair leveled up enough to make the ratios better...at least, I hope that's what leveling up the skill will do."*

Deciding to think of ways to use her Mana Repair skill later, as she traveled, Sam moved on with her review and continued scrolling through her notifications from the previous day. Surprisingly, she found she had indeed missed a notification the night before and eagerly read it.

'Bing' Congratulations! Your Racial Skill Recovery has been upgraded to Resilient [Level 1]: You have been on the brink of death more than you can count in the past 72 hours; it has been six times, but who's counting? Someone is, apparently. In every instance of impending death, your tenacity for clinging to life against all odds has shown in your recent experiences! Each time death has tried her best to claim you, you have managed to pull yourself from her grasp! Because you seem to enjoy laughing in death's face, you have received an early upgrade to your racial skill, Recovery to Resilient; good job! Your new skill, Resilient, maintains all recovery abilities at level 10, along with the added benefit of a ten percent bonus to the base value of vitality and endurance!

"I've nearly died six times in three days...holy crap! I guess I am pretty resilient!" She looked at the message again, *"Who is counting? Is the System trying to be snarky, or is there a planetary administrator counting my near-death experiences, or is the System controlling this entire verse counting how many times I nearly die? It would have been nice to arrive with a guidebook on how this 'System' works, maybe titled something like "A User's Guide to Interdimensional Travel."* Sam chuckled at the thought, *"I guess I could write one if I survive long enough to find a pen and some paper,"* the thought of her writing a guidebook about interdimensional travel made her laugh out

loud, "I would title it, The Book of SAM; How Not to Die When Traveling Between Dimensions and Other Fun Facts!"

After a good laugh, Sam cleared her campsite. She tried to put the lean-to directly into her inventory, which worked! Staring at the empty space where her shelter once stood, she said, "Now that is freaking convenient!" She tried the same with the firepit, but unfortunately, she could only add one stone at a time, which she did, *"Oh well, at least I tried."*

When Sam was finished, she checked her map and, with one last look around to ensure she had caught everything, set off down the river.

***

Sam continued traveling, following the river downstream as it made its slow winding path through the forest. Still, even though the trees were getting thinner and spread farther apart, her travels didn't get any easier because the underbrush was getting thicker, in contrast, forcing her to hack her way through in places and, more importantly, limiting her visibility to a few meters. She was always keeping her Mana Sight active now, afraid something would surprise her if she turned it off. Walking through the forest, she noticed it became less ominous. She found with the brighter surroundings she could enjoy the smell of the fresh foliage drifting off the surface of the slow-moving river as she made her way slowly through the dense underbrush.

As Sam was hacking her way through the thick bushes and vines that were becoming more numerous in the thinner foliage of the forest, she looked at the machete she had constructed. It was an exact replica of the machete she had bought herself from an army surplus store and it was working like a charm. She was proud of the machete construct. It had taken her quite a few tries before she had gotten the shape and weight just right, but once she had got it perfect, the construct proved more than sufficient in removing the pesky limbs, grass, and vines of the underbrush in her way. The only drawback was keeping the construct at the exact weight and sharpness required for the work drained her mana at an insane rate. Fortunately, the mana drain slightly tapered once she received two levels in Mana Crafting back-to-back, bringing it to level 7 and lowering the amount of mana she needed to maintain constructs.

As Sam continued making her way slowly down the river, she calculated her route was bringing her to the foothills of the mountain range or at least within a few kilometers of it by her estimation. The farther she moved south and west, the more sounds of wildlife she heard around her, in the form of bird calls and the calls of other small forest creatures. A few deer-like creatures with glowing horns and sporting manes like a horse darted across her path on more than one occasion, none of them even slowing down at the sight of her. She was a little disappointed at this development because she was itching for a fight that would give her a chance to try out some of the higher-level mana constructs she was toying with at her rest stops.

Sam had been creating mana constructs of every shape and size she could imagine as she traversed the forest. She kept trying to imagine using them in a fight against the creatures she had already encountered. She made everything from spikes that protruded from everywhere on her body to magic baseballs she threw at nearby trees; sadly, the baseballs she made didn't explode on impact as she had hoped and only hit the trees with a light thump knocking some bark off before they dissipated. One exciting discovery was any constructs she created would dissipate within three seconds after she stopped channeling mana into them, regardless of whether or not they were in direct contact with her body. Given what she had been through, Sam thought it was good information to have, especially in a fight.

Sam continued following the river, toying with her skills, ensuring she never let her mana fall below half. The last thing she wanted was to get ambushed with low mana reserves.

***

Midday found Sam sitting on a log near the bank of the river, meditating as she munched on some cat steak left over from the night before. She was impressed her inventory had kept it warm and juicy, precisely as it had been when she stored it the previous night. Her Meditation skill was now at level 6, allowing her to perform simple tasks like eating while still being able to actively channel the skill.

A twig snapping behind her got Sam's attention. Instead of jumping up in reaction to the sound, she only stiffened. Not being able to see behind her, Sam had ingeniously created an early warning system out of the six mana threads she could currently control by weaving the threads through the trees behind her like a web of tripwires. It took almost no mana to maintain the threads so long as she wasn't using them for something strenuous. With meditation active, she could keep the threads up and her mana sight on indefinitely. She could 'feel' the area around all her mana threads, which was a feeling she could only describe as 'interesting.' She was surprised when she first used the threads, and her ability to 'sense' the area around them felt almost entirely natural, and acclimatization was swift. It was as if having six extra appendages, and being able to partially see out of them was the most normal thing in the world.

Sensing the area around her threads for threats when the twig snapped, Sam thought, *"I must have been a spider in a previous life. Wait, not a spider; I technically have ten appendages right now...what has ten legs?"* She thought for a while, and when nothing came to mind, she gave up and went back to thinking of herself as a spider in a previous life to amuse herself. Having sensed nothing, she continued listening. Not hearing any other sounds or sensing anything from her threads, she resumed munching on her cat steak and watching the river flow slowly, carrying the occasional branch or leaf litter. She wasn't being careless; snapping twigs and falling leaves were common in the forest. When she had started her journey, she had reacted to every sound or change in the wind with fear and worry. Still, having spent enough time in this wilderness, she felt comfortable enough to ignore what she considered the usual sounds of a forest as they frequently occurred around her. That is until she felt something tug on one of the mana threads behind her. The tug came from the same direction; she had heard the twig snap.

Sam jumped up and whipped around, ready for a fight. "*Ha! You can't surprise me, you little—oh shit,*" she stared open-mouthed at the creature that had touched one of her threads, and what stood in front of her made her suddenly very nervous. The enormous creature in front of her was the largest dog she had ever seen, *"not a dog, a wolf,"* she corrected herself, *"holy crap, I could ride that thing!"* Recovering from her initial surprise, she identified the creature.

'Bing' Great Timberwolf [Level??]; Hostile; Affinity: Earth

"Nice doggy," Sam softly said as she backed away slowly toward the river's edge, holding her hands out in a placating gesture to the enormous beast. "*How is something so large able to be so quiet? That thing must weigh a metric ton!*"

The massive wolf raised its head and sniffed the air, its enormous snout sounding more like a horse than a dog. It then lowered its head and stared right at Sam, "*No, not at me, at my hands,*" that's when she remembered she was still holding the half-eaten steak in her hand. *"Way to go, Sam; just bait the entire forest full of predators straight to you by eating a delicious steak in dangerous monster-filled territory like you're on a freaking camping trip back on earth!"* She berated herself for her own foolishness.

While she was backing up, Sam was weaving all her mana threads between the trees in front of the wolf to create a barrier. Her actions proved useless though because in a single leap, the beast jumped through the woven threads, snapping like they offered no resistance. The sudden breaking of her threads caused a sharp pain in her temple, but thankfully, it wasn't so bad she lost her focus on the wolf. The leap carried the wolf half the distance toward Sam as it lowered its head to glare at her. A deep growl rumbled in its chest as it curled its lips in a snarl, exposing white fangs as long as Sam's pinkie finger.

Sam tossed the steak toward the wolf with as slight motion as possible. The beast wasn't stupid and didn't snatch the steak out of the air, instead letting the meat fall to the ground in front of it, cautiously sniffing the offering before swallowing it in one gulp. The wolf looked back at Sam expectantly.

Sam took the look as a sign and tossed a raw piece of cat meat to the wolf. This time, the wolf didn't hesitate and snatched the juicy morsel out of the air. The motion had almost been too fast for Sam to track, *"It's fast, probably faster than the Blade Tail."* Sam mused to herself. She was calculating her odds of surviving if the beast decided to lunge at her, and she wasn't happy with the results. Given how fast the wolf closed the distance between them and its quick motion to snatch the meat from the air, Sam knew she could not entirely dodge an attack from the animal, not at this distance anyway. When she didn't immediately produce another piece of meat, the wolf began growling again and took a menacing step toward her, causing her to take a step back reflexively, saying, "Hey, I'm not going to give you all my food if you're just going to eat me any way you overgrown house pet." As she spoke, Sam got an idea, "Do you like a fish, big boy?"

Sam summoned some Deep Hunter meat and threw it at the growling beast's muzzle. Like the previous piece of meat, the wolf snatched the offered morsel out of the air, swallowing it whole before immediately beginning to gag and try to hack it back up. It was too late, though; the wolf stopped mid-hack as the paralysis effect from the poisonous meat took effect. *"Now is my chance!"* Not wasting a second, Sam attacked with her four remaining daggers, using them at the ends of her mana threads with two daggers snaking in from each side of the animal's body to strike it just behind its rib cage.

Sam had hoped that feeding the wolf would make it less hostile toward her, but the 'Hostile' tag hovering over its head had never gone away as she fed it, so, knowing there was no way she could outrun the beast, Sam devised a plan to take the wolf down with as little danger to herself as possible. Even as the wolf ate the poisoned meat, she was already acting out her plan, summoning the daggers at the ends of her mana threads, a convenient trick she had learned traveling, stabbing them at the animal's exposed sides even as it tried to hack up the Deep Hunter meat.

Each of the daggers found their mark in the wolf's thick hide. Sam twisted the daggers using her threads as she ran up to the large creature's head, which was thankfully lowered enough to reach its ear, readying a thin mana blade on the end of her fist to attack. Arriving where the wolf was frozen mid-hack, Sam thrust the long, thin mana blade into its ear with all her strength. The blade slid only a few centimeters into the ear before striking something hard and coming to a halt. Putting all her weight behind the blade, Sam tried to drive it into the beast's brain, but it was useless! She didn't have enough strength! Her efforts weren't even causing the beast to move or sway away from her, pushing against it because its body was incredibly dense.

Cursing, Sam abandoned her attack with the mana blade. She ran to where one of her daggers was protruding from the wolf's side and jumped up; she grabbed the dagger's hilt with both hands and yanked it down. It took two jerks with the full weight of her body behind them. Finally, the blade started moving, sliding down through the thick skin and muscle of the wolf's side, opening a large gash in its stomach. A torrent of blood sprayed from the wound into Sam's face.

Sputtering and spitting at the hot, coppery-tasting liquid in her mouth, Sam yanked the dagger free and grabbed the other dagger buried in the wolf's flesh. She tried to repeat the process, but her bloody hands slipped off the dagger's hilt when she yanked down on it. Sam tumbled to her butt but quickly wiped her hands on the ground and jumped back up, grabbing the dagger again. She was running out of time, and she knew it; even her own low level and stats had shortened the time the toxic effects of the meat lasted, so she knew this wolf would feel the effects for an even shorter time. Her theory was proven correct a moment later when her hands wrapped around the dagger's hilt again; she was knocked back and away from the wolf. Flying through the air, she slammed into a tree nearly three meters away with a wet smack and the loud crack of some of her ribs breaking.

Sam rose dazed and unsteady to her feet at the tree's base, her vision blurring a little, *"Shit, that wasn't nearly as long as I had hoped. Damn thing must have poison resistance, or maybe its high vitality helps with poison. I hope I did some damage and the health-draining effect of the poison wasn't fully negated."* The wound on the wolf's side was still bleeding profusely, which gave her some hope, and as it turned to her, she could see it was a little wobbly on its feet, too. She readied herself, *"Okay, now for phase two."*

Sam had no more time to think, only to act. The beast lunged and was upon her in an instant, but thanks to the lingering effects of the poison, Sam could dodge to the side, barely avoiding the jaws as they snapped shut with a loud snap bare millimeters from her body. However, she could not dodge the lightning-fast paw swipe the wolf followed up with when it missed biting her.

Sam again found herself flying through the air; this time, she trailed a red mist behind her from several large gashes in her back. Hitting the ground hard, she rolled to a stop at the river's edge, a few loose pebbles dislodged by her body rolled into the water with soft splashing sounds. It was hard to focus; pain screamed as her many wounds demanded her attention. She knew she didn't have time to process the damage she had just taken, and sensing what was coming through her mana threads, Sam quickly rolled out of the way! The massive paws of the wolf barely missed her head and left a deep indentation in the riverbank at the point of impact. Her roll took her into the river's dark waters, where she quickly sank out of sight. Phase two of her plan was now in progress.

CHAPTER 6 — "I really need better clothes."

Sam channeled her Mana Repair skill as she sank slowly through the water. The skill was working overtime to reset her bones and close the gaping wounds on her back. She found that channeling the repair skill lessened the pain of the wounds slightly, which was good because her current level of pain tolerance left much to be desired.

Swimming under the surface until she was clear of the riverbank, Sam resurfaced, realizing the wolf hadn't followed her into the water as she had hoped. Instead, the Great Timberwolf had backed away from the riverbank and was cautiously eyeing the murky water; it was for good reason, too. The wolf couldn't see what Sam had already spotted with her mana sight; a large Deep Hunter was moving toward her from downstream. She wasn't bothered by the appearance of the Deep Hunter; quite the contrary, she was elated at the development. Her phase two plan hinged on there being a predator nearby in the water. Her plan was simple; if she couldn't take out the wolf while it was paralyzed, she would use the river and, more importantly, her ability to detect the Deep Hunters with her mana sight to her advantage. Now, she just hoped this plan worked better than her initial failure.

"Here goes nothing!" Using her mana, Sam magically propelled herself through the water directly toward the wolf, which was still eyeing her and the river cautiously. She formed a harpoon construct in her right hand, then connected it to the thickest rope she could make using all her mana threads, twisting them together like a braid. Finally, Sam formed another harpoon on the other end of the rope, keeping her hand on the middle of the mana rope so she could channel mana into the constructs to keep them from dissipating. She manipulated the first harpoon out of the water using her mana rope so it was aimed directly at the large dagger cut she had made in the wolf's side. With all the concentration she could muster, she hovered the harpoon up directly at the wound. She sent a pulse of mana through the rope to the butt of the harpoon blasting the mana outward like an explosion that launched the harpoon into the wound. *"Yes!"* Sam screamed in her head when the harpoon penetrated deep into the wolf's side, and a yelp of pure pain could be heard from the beast. Almost instantly, Sam pivoted in the water and launched the other harpoon through the water and into the Deep Hunter's body, tethering the two creatures together. "*Now all I have to do is stay in contact with the rope, so it doesn't dissipate, and I'll be able to, argh—"* Sam grunted when the mana rope went taut and yanked her through the water. The force of the Deep Hunter pulling back against the harpoon and rope, as it was trying to get away from the invisible force attacking it, jerked the wolf back toward the river's edge. The Deep Hunter pulled against the wolf even harder as it struggled to stay on land, the tension in the rope nearly snapping it in half.

Sam ground her teeth as she pumped mana into the rope, trying desperately to keep it from breaking.

Sam had already figured out her constructs were invisible to the naked eye; she noticed her enemies had not reacted to them. It gave her the initial hint: the constructs were difficult or even impossible to detect. She had confirmed her suspicion the day before by making a few different-sized constructs while toggling her Mana Sight on and off. Her mana threads and simple mana daggers were entirely invisible to her without mana sight active. The larger constructs, such as the mana rope and harpoons, gave off a faint purple glow, but she knew the glow was only visible to her because she knew what to look for. She was using this knowledge to her advantage now because it seemed the two beasts had no idea what was attacking them. She was hoping to turn them on each other.

The Deep Hunter gave another mighty surge, trying to escape. The strain on the line became even greater, draining a significant amount of mana from Sam. She flooded the rope with energy to keep it from breaking. The wolf stood its ground, though, and Sam was starting to worry her plan wouldn't work if the rope broke before either creature gained the upper hand. Just as she was about to release the constructs, one of the wolf's paws slipped in a puddle of its own blood when it tried to take a short step, causing it to lose purchase for an instant. That was all the Deep Hunter needed, and with another surge from the Deep Hunter, the wolf was yanked to the edge of the river, its hind legs slipping over the bank and into the water. Working fast, Sam shortened the mana rope, essentially reeling the two creatures closer together by taking up the slack from the wolf slipping. It was quickly pulled the rest of the way into the river by the Deep Hunter.

Releasing her constructs, Sam propelled herself upstream, putting some distance between her and the two creatures. She would have preferred to keep the two tethered together until the Deep Hunter drowned the wolf. But Sam was running low on mana after healing herself and holding the forms of the harpoons and rope for so long. Channeling her stamina into mana using her repair skill, she watched with relief as the octopus monster ignored her entirely and instead swam toward the flailing wolf, which already had half its body out of the water as it scrambled up the river bank, trying to find purchase in the soft sandy bank.

Four tentacles wrapped around the wolf's hind legs, and the beast was dragged back into the water by the Deep Hunter. The wolf tried desperately to tread water with its front legs, but it was useless; water wasn't its natural element. It was pulled beneath the surface within a few seconds, leaving expanding ripples behind when its nose finally disappeared beneath the water's surface.

***

"Okay, time to get to work on phase...wait, is this still phase 2, or is it phase 2.1...maybe it's 3...doesn't matter, or does it? Maybe I'll call it the end phase or something. I should probably wait till this is over before I call anything the end, though." With those less-than-helpful thoughts, Sam propelled herself toward the two beasts as they struggled with each other. She managed to land on the wolf's back, facing backward so she could see the octopus. She gripped a handful of fur with one hand and formed a short spear with her other. In her best rodeo impression, Sam held onto the bucking wolf with all her might and stabbed the spear into the wound on the wolf's side over and over. She held on for dear life as the animal thrashed and writhed in the water, trying to turn its head to bite her. The wolf's teeth came dangerously close more than once. The bites were getting so close that she turned and started poking at its muzzle with her spear construct each time the wolf snapped at her. The entire time, the Deep Hunter was pulling them deeper and deeper into the murky darkness.

***

The wolf managed to bite down on Sam's spear hard enough to break it, the construct dissipating in a cloud of mana. The familiar sharp pain of magic backlash shot through her brain, causing her to wince. As the wolf bit through her spear, Sam heard a muted crunching sound behind her. She looked back to see the Deep Hunter had just bitten off both of the wolf's hind legs and was eagerly putting more of the animal's rear end into its hungry beaklike mouth and crunching down, the cracking of bone muted in the dark water.

"Shit, that's one hell of a bite!" For a moment, Sam wasn't sure what to do, *"Should I stop attacking the wolf and let the river monster take care of it? But then I might not get any credit for the kill, and all this will have been for nothing."* She decided to detach from the wolf, which was now flailing about madly as it was slowly being devoured by the Deep Hunter.

Sam boosted away from the two monsters, formed a harpoon, and shot it into the Deep Hunter's head right between its eyes, causing it to let out the same weird underwater screaming sound and squirting ink like the other one had when she had cut its head open. It released the wolf and started swimming away. Sam was prepared for that and propelled herself toward the retreating foe. She formed another harpoon twice the length of the others she had created at nearly two meters, using most of her dwindling mana reserves to do so. When she got close enough to the creature, she stabbed the harpoon deep into the soft flesh of its head, using a pulse of magical energy to push it in as deep as possible. Several tentacles wrapped around her, their barbs sinking painfully into her flesh. The tentacles pulled at her, tearing at her muscles and skin, creating new wounds and reopening the deep gashes on her back that hadn't fully healed yet. Sam held her ground through the pain and continued pushing the spear deeper. She felt a 'pop' in the monster's head and then another as the harpoon traveled deeper. She hoped the pops were vital organs rupturing, which must have been the case because she received a notification confirming the kill as soon as the harpoon stopped its forward momentum.

Sam mentally sent the notification away, tore off the tentacles latched onto her during the attack, and put the beast into her inventory. Boosting herself upward, she made a beeline to the surface with the last of her mana; her last breath had been minutes ago, and her vision was already tunneling. She had forgotten in her excitement to trap some air around her head with a mana bubble.

***

Just before Sam breached the surface and sucked in a few deep breaths, coughing up the water she accidentally inhaled, the tunneling in her vision started reversing again. She didn't know what that meant, nor did she have time to think about it. Treading water, she looked around for the wolf's corpse. To her surprise, the animal was slowly paddling toward the river's far bank with its front paws and a long trail of blood floating behind it.

"You've got to be kidding me!" she groaned and began slowly swimming toward the, hopefully, mostly dead monster, failing to avoid the long trail of blood it was leaving behind.

Reaching the wolf as it started struggling to climb up the riverbank with its two remaining legs, Sam dragged herself onto its back, her exhaustion making the process painfully slow. Thankfully, the exhausted and exsanguinating wolf didn't seem to notice as she climbed up its fur. Sam figured she was in a little better shape than the wolf, but it was not by much. Her mana and stamina were almost bottomed out. The octopus tentacles had done a lot of damage, taking a large chunk of her remaining health, leaving it, again, at around two percent of her lifeforce remaining, her health bar flashing its usual bright red. She had managed to stop the bleeding from the earlier paw swipe but hadn't closed the wounds fully, opting instead to conserve her mana for offense. Sam now realized this was probably a mistake. She was now in a precarious state because the tentacle wounds were still bleeding. She possibly had enough mana for one more construct and a pulse of magical force to drive it home. Hanging onto the wolf, she thought about what to do, *"Do I heal and then recover some mana before attacking, or do I go all in and trust in my natural resilience?"* Thinking back to how quickly the wolf had shrugged off the poison and its incredible speed, she knew what she had to do, *"it's obviously a much higher level than me. For all*

I know, it could be pretending to still be weak just to get me to let my guard down," she really didn't believe that but also didn't want to give the powerful beast more time to heal, *"screw it, it's all or nothing I guess."* Sam decided to form a crude spike in the palm of her hand, holding it right between the wolf's shoulder blades. A pulse of raw mana propelled the tip into its back and through its spine with a wet crunch, the mana pulse making her recoil from the force.

The wolf went limp beneath her, the kill notification arriving a moment later. Sam collapsed onto the broad back of the wolf, exhaustion and pain finally overtaking her. She closed her eyes and entered meditation, her health still falling. In fact, it was now falling faster than before, the recoil of her last strike having reopened the wounds on her back from the paw strike that had just barely closed. "Man, this really sucks," she mumbled into the wolf's wet fur as she focused on not passing out. She feared what would happen if she passed out and lost her meditation boost.

Sam lay there for twenty minutes, the wolf's body slowly cooling beneath her. Once she was finally healed enough and had refilled her stamina, she crawled over the top of the wolf onto the soft soil of the riverbank. Sam laid a hand on the wolf's nose and deposited its corpse into her inventory. She surveyed the river and forest with Mana Sight and found no indication of threats. Relieved the fight hadn't attracted any more predators or scavengers, she still hiked downstream cautiously to get clear of the battle area. Performing a self-assessment, she found that, although mentally exhausted, she was otherwise fully recovered thanks to her insane regenerative abilities and meditation skills.

***

"I really need better clothes," Sam was examining her shredded leather shirt and pants by the light of the campfire she had dried them over. Sighing, she slipped back into the smoky dry clothes, even mostly shredded as they were. Something was better than nothing. She had continued walking downstream for a few kilometers after the fight before making camp. It wasn't yet dark when she stopped, but she hadn't had the mental energy to stay alert enough to keep moving. She dumped the two new corpses out of her inventory and looted them before storing them back in her inventory. The Deep Hunter had given her much the same as the previous one, and the wolf didn't have any real surprises either, although she was surprised to see it had been level 61.

Great Timberwolf Items:

5 -Gold; 69-Silver; 7-Copper; Monster Core [Great Timberwolf; Level 61]; Great Timberwolf Pelt [Level 61]; Heart of a Great

Timberwolf; Wolf Fang x 4; Iron Dagger x 2; 100kg Great Timberwolf Meat; Large Mana Potion; Stamina Potion.

Thinking back to the loot notification, Sam realized she still needed to check her kill notifications. She had delayed checking them until she was in a safe place; the memory of how close the wolf had gotten to her before she noticed it was still fresh in her mind and made her extremely wary of her surroundings. She had become complacent, thinking her abilities were sufficient to protect and warn her of danger, *"I thought I had covered all my bases with my mana sight and mana threads."* The wolf had proven that was certainly not the case. If she had learned anything, it was her mana threads, and mana sight were not enough to guarantee her safety in this dangerous forest.

Sam resolved to be more cautious and checked the Deep Hunter meat she had roasting on a stick over the fire. Seeing it was done, she dipped the meat into the organic ink she had poured into a concave leaf she had found just for that purpose. Coating a corner of the meat in the ink, Sam took a large bite out of it. She moaned with pleasure as she chewed the savory meat; it really was delicious. She had been dipping the meat in the organic ink and eating it for a while now, and it was amazing! Plus, her poison resistance was going up steadily as the ink took nearly thirty seconds to counter the poison, allowing it to take effect before negating it. She figured it was because she wasn't receiving the full benefit from the ink. She wasn't consuming a complete dose by only dipping the meat in it like a sauce instead of drinking it like an antidote. The ink dipping helped to prevent the paralysis from the meat and shortened the poison timer. Dipping the meat into the 'ink sauce' again, she took another bite, savoring the delicious morsel she excitedly chewed before swallowing with a gulp.

You have been poisoned with Deep Hunter Toxin -1.7hp/sec for 324 seconds; paralysis for 77 seconds. Paralysis negated by Organic Ink.

'Bing' Your Poison Resistance has leveled up to level 9. By all means, continue poisoning yourself to increase its level and effectiveness.

The poison didn't stack, so each bite just reset the timer. Making full use of her Mana Repair skill, Sam wasn't so much healing herself as replacing or repairing her damaged parts. It was fascinating to her because the skill allowed her to sense what it was doing, giving her an idea of what parts of her body were damaged by the poison and how the skill was going about fixing the damage. Apparently, Deep Hunter toxin was magical in nature, as her mana sight had proved, and started working the instant it touched the saliva in her mouth by attacking her nervous system, shutting down her organs, and eating away at her nerves.

Her meditation was leveling up also, making it even more efficient and coupled with her Mana Repair, which leveled up significantly when she healed the catastrophic wounds all over her body, now allowing her to keep her repair skill going indefinitely as long as she meditated and didn't idly make constructs. The effect of the toxin with her added poison resistance was not only negated, but she gained her health right back after the initial drop. All of that aside, she was also really enjoying her meal. It was like having roasted octopus at a nice restaurant.

After Sam finished her third cube of octopus and put a fourth on to roast, she wondered if the amount of meat she was eating would give her some health issues over time but then discarded the idea because her repair skill didn't seem to be fighting anything like scurvy or constipation. "*Come to think of it, I haven't had to answer nature's call since that day, or maybe it was the day after I arrived here. I haven't even had to pee in two days, and I know I have drunk at least ten liters of water while I traveled. Maybe it's the way my new body operates now?*" She decided to ask someone about it when or if she found civilization. Now, with her hunger satisfied, she opened her notifications and, with thought, scrolled back to the fight from earlier in the day.

'Bing' Defeated Deep Hunter [Level 52]: Bonus experience awarded for defeating an enemy thirty or more levels above your own.

'Bing' Defeated Great Timberwolf [Level 61]; Bonus experience awarded for defeating an enemy fifty or more levels above your own.

'Bing' Race Human has leveled up to Level 8, +5 free stat points received.

'Bing' Race Human has leveled up to Level 9, +5 free stat points received.

'Bing' Race Human has leveled up to Level 10, +5 free stat points received.

This went on until…

'Bing' Race Human has leveled up to Level 15, +5 free stat points received.

"Holy shit, from level seven to level fifteen! No wonder I couldn't stab that knife into the wolf's brain through its ear. I'm lucky I could even penetrate its hide. Not to mention how I could penetrate the Deep Hunter's head. It must have something to do with the attributes of the monster. The Timberwolf probably had high vitality, while the Deep Hunter had high agility? Who knows, maybe there's a bestiary somewhere I can check. It could also be the type of mana I use that makes some monsters more susceptible to my attacks or my higher-than-normal intelligence stat making my magic more potent against certain creatures...probably both."

Sam continued checking her notifications.

'Bing' Class Arcane Pathfinder has leveled up to Level 7, +10 free stat points received.

'Bing' Class Arcane Pathfinder has leveled up to Level 8, +10 free stat points received.

'Bing' Class Arcane Pathfinder has leveled up to Level 9, +10 free stat points received.

'Bing' Class Arcane Pathfinder has leveled up to Level 10, +10 free stat points received. Bonus: +1% to all base attributes.

This went on until…

'Bing' Class Arcane Pathfinder has leveled up to Level 13, +10 free stat points received.

Eight levels in my race and seven in my class, that's...," Sam did some quick calculations in her head, "*one hundred and ten stat points! For just one fight! And I finally got the bonus percentage gained to all my attributes from my class every ten levels!"*

Sam continued through the messages before she could get too excited, skipping any she had already seen.

'Bing' Mana Crafter has leveled up to level 10: Mana cost has slightly reduced. You can now make your mana constructs permanent, although at a significantly higher mana cost.

'Bing' Mana Repair has leveled up to level 10: Mana cost has slightly reduced. You are now able to repair other organic life forms at a much higher mana cost than repairing yourself.

'Bing' Resilient has leveled up to level 3: Passive recovery speed has increased slightly.

'Bing' Mana Sight has leveled up to level 7: Mana cost has been reduced slightly.

'Bing' Congratulations! You have learned a new skill: Mana Caster. Level 1: By using your mana to increase the velocity of your constructs and turning your mana constructs into projectiles repeatedly, you have developed the skill Mana Caster. By channeling the skill Mana Caster, you may now create energized projectiles that can last significantly longer without your direct mana infusion. The amount of mana infused into the projectile will determine each projectile's damage.

Sam was stunned. Not only could she heal other organic life forms now, but she would no longer have to use her mana threads to maintain contact with her construct and keep a constant flow of magic to retain them until she was ready to use them. She was almost overwhelmed with the information in the notifications and read them several times to ensure she didn't miss anything.

Sam closed the notification screen, relaxed against a large log she had placed by the fire for that purpose, and started thinking, *"How do I distribute my free attribute points? Do I keep doing what I'm doing, which, if I'm honest with myself, is just winging it, for the most part?"* She thought about her experiences thus far. On the one hand, her nearly constant mana drain was a problem during fights. Still, the more she created new skills and leveled up her current skills, the less of an issue that would become because each new skill and skill level brought with it a reduced mana cost to varying degrees. More mana was always better, though…right? She wasn't so sure.

However, on the other hand, if she had been strong enough, she could have ended the fight with the wolf before it ever really began with a single blow to its brain, or so she assumed. In the end, it had taken a massive blast of mana to get her mana spike to penetrate the wolf's back and spine, *"I'm lucky the mana spike didn't shatter."* Now that she knew the wolf's level, she realized she was extremely lucky. But what if she had thought of that trick at the beginning of the fight? She could have ended it right there with her magic.

"That's two points to more mana and magic power," she thought. Still, there were her constant near-death experiences. Hell, even the System recognized she spent pretty much every fight on the brink of death, if not from the very beginning, certainly by the end, so increasing her health pool should be at the top of her list of priorities…shouldn't it?

"Okay, with the mana manipulation ability, I can create specific skills that will make specific mana manipulation tasks more efficient and easier to perform, thus reducing the mana required to perform said task; even the

description says something about the ability eventually becoming obsolete, although I doubt that will happen anytime soon. The System was right when it said I am only limited by my mental and physical abilities. I need to note it does mention physical abilities," Sam tapped her chin in thought, *"If I had been stronger in both magic and strength, then I could have conserved mana by brute forcing that mana spike into the wolf's brain which would have allowed me to continue fighting with both magic and stamina in the event there had been more wolves present or something land-based had come from the water. But that still leaves out the fact that I only got close enough to the wolf because it was paralyzed. I would have been slaughtered if I had tried to fight it head-to-head, and I would have never been able to outrun it."* Sighing, she knew how she had to distribute her points; she had always known, but the min/max gamer part of her brain was still struggling.

In the end, Sam decided she no longer wanted to be nearly killed by a single hit within the first few seconds of every fight because her health pool was so small. She wanted to be able to dodge those lethal hits, too. Still, Sam made sure to increase her mana pool by adding points to wisdom and her magic strength, which came from intelligence, according to her primer. Having thought about it more, she was now much less worried; she was making a mistake by not focusing exclusively on the caster route. Fear of being killed in one hit by an ambush predator she failed to detect with her magic helped make her mind up. It kept her from dumping all her free points into intelligence and wisdom. Plus, she had no idea if it could happen, but there could be a time when her magic was suppressed, and all she had was her strength and speed. So, with all that in mind, Sam distributed her free points and confirmed her choices. After the wave of power and ecstasy washed over her, she checked her status page.

Samantha Alecto Moura [S.A.M.]
Race: Human; Mortal [Level 15]
Class: Arcane Pathfinder [Level 13]

Health: 861
Stamina: 485
Mana: 2066

Attributes:
STR – 45 [46]
VIT – 43 [48]
END – 26 [29]
AGL – 27 [27]

INT – 45 [46]
WIS – 57 [115]
Free Attribute Points 0.

Abilities:
Spatial Inventory
Loot
Linguistics
Cartography
Mana Manipulation
Mana Sight [Level 7]

Class Skills:
Mana Crafting [Level 10]
Mana Repair [Level 10]
Mana Caster [Level 1]

Racial/General Skills:
Identify [Level 3]
Resilient [Level 3]
Meditation [Level 7]

Class Spells:
None

Racial/General Spells:
None

Resistance(s):
Pain [Level 10]
Heat [Level 5]
Poison [Level 9]

Sam sat back on her bedroll and stared into the softly crackling fire, dumbfounded by her stat increase. In one fight, she went from a weak human with an epic class to a freaking unkillable powerhouse, or at least that's what she hoped she was now. It was difficult to see it any other way when she was now essentially twice as strong as she had been when she had, at her low level of 7, taken on a level 61 and 52, respectively, and survived against all odds. Now, she had more than doubled her level! She was ready to test her new strength. "*I would annihilate a freaking Deep Hunter right now, and I could probably take on another Great Timberwolf without assistance...probably."* That thought gave her pause. She had only survived the encounter with the wolf because she had used the Deep Hunter to weaken it significantly by crippling it and taking it out of its natural element. After thinking about that for a while, she decided she would still be able to win without help if she encountered another wolf, mostly because she knew her magic blades were currently more powerful than the basic Iron Daggers she had been given by the System. She could make them thinner, sharper, and more rigid. She could also use efficient ranged attacks with the mana caster skill. Also, her agility was slightly higher.

Sam sat for a while in silence, simply enjoying the glowing fire and the cool breeze from the nearby river. After a few minutes, she scrunched her brow in thought, remembering her stat sheet. When did meditation and pain resistance go up? *"Oh well, it doesn't really matter. I do need to focus on meditating as often as possible, though; something tells me if I am ever able to meditate and fight at the same time, it will be a game changer."*

Sam couldn't bring herself to, although she wanted to try her new mana-casting skill. She didn't want to accidentally shut down the safe zone her campsite had created. She was already taking enough of a risk by eating the poisonous meat, knowing it would harm her. Thankfully, it didn't count as an attack, but she didn't want to push her luck.

"No more experimenting," Sam told herself, "Just enjoy the fact you're still alive and relax by the warm fire for a while." Taking her own advice, Sam spent the next several hours enjoying the peace and quiet of camping in the little clearing. As she lay on her bedroll, she stared up at the unfamiliar moons and stars as they floated silently across the night sky, watching them absently until finally drifting off, thinking about how peaceful the forest was when it wasn't actively trying to kill her.

CHAPTER 7 — "Is it supposed to do that?"

"What is this? Day five, six? No, it's five for sure," Sam thought as she doused the fire with water from her endless canteen. She broke camp, which consisted of her waving her hand and everything disappearing into her inventory. She had even figured out how to get the firepit to go into her inventory in one piece by using clay dug from the river's edge as a plaster to connect the stones of the firepit together, forming a solid ring. Sam completed her morning routine and walked closer to the river's edge; she would try her new skills before continuing her journey.

Sam started with Mana Caster and began channeling Mana into the skill. She immediately discovered that unlike Mana Crafting, where she could begin channeling the skill and then form a shape, Mana Caster required her to already have the idea of the projectile shape she would form and cast, or the skill wouldn't activate. Once she got the hang of it, she launched roughly one ten-centimeter-long mana spike per second, using around thirty Mana per spike. The mana caster skill significantly reduced each spike's cost and charge time compared to mana crafting; the same spike and charge took nearly twice as long to form, costing over sixty Mana. She could only create and fire one every fifteen seconds, which also took her total concentration also.

Sam continued playing around with the skill, sticking spikes in trees where they sank nearly all the way into the trunks. After a while, having done her part in killing the local flora, she eyed a large boulder near the river's edge. She summoned a mana spike over her open palm, fixating exactly where she wanted the magic projectile to hit as she sent the mana spike flying with a thought. The small missile struck the boulder dead center, within a hair of her bull's eye. The boulder caused the thin spike to shatter as it chipped off a piece of the rock, leaving a slight indentation where it had struck.

The depth of the indentation was to the first knuckle of her pinky finger when she examined it. Sam decided mana caster would undoubtedly be her go-to ranged skill. She only wished she could change the trajectory of the constructs mid-flight, but she couldn't keep the mental connection to them once she released the spikes. It felt like the constructs Sam formed with the mana caster were held under great tension. Once she identified a target, the tension was released immediately, causing connection loss. She didn't think it was too much of an issue at the rate she could fire them. Her best estimate was that and how fast they traveled was that the mana spikes moved faster than an arrow but slower than a bullet at perhaps two hundred meters per second. She wasn't sure she could track them in flight if it wasn't for her higher agility stat. The larger the construct, the longer it took to charge and the slower it traveled. But the additional Mana added weight to the charge, causing a more brutal impact on the target. She experimented with blades, spheres, spikes, and even arrows, each with a different travel speed, impact, and range. She was also limited to how much Mana she could use to create each construct as she could not continuously infuse a construct to make it more powerful like she could with Mana crafting. Each one seemed to have a preset maximum based on its size. Sam hoped that would change as the skill leveled up, allowing her to hit harder from a distance.

Sam spent nearly an hour toying with the Mana Caster skill and then moved on to her favorite skill, Mana Crafting. It was time to make a permanent mana construct! With a thought, she activated the skill, not knowing what to expect, and created a harpoon with her Mana flowing into the framework. This time, instead of the skill slowing her mana infusion rate once the harpoon was formed, a floodgate opened, allowing her to pour more Mana into the construct, making the harpoon as solid as steel. The skill told her she still had a long way to go before the permanent construct would be completed, though.

Sam quickly looked at her mana pool and smiled; this would be a cakewalk. *"I'm gonna eat some fresh fish I caught with my new harpoon tonight!"* She poured her magical energy into the harpoon, feeling the weapon gaining density as the raw power created compact layers of solid mass. 100 mana, 400 mana; she could feel the harpoon increase in density as she watched arcs of energy running up and down its length. But the skill told her she was still far from making the weapon permanent. Scrunching her brows in concentration, she kept pushing Mana into the now hot, brightly glowing construct. 900 mana, 1300 Mana; the harpoon started vibrating violently in her hand and was getting hotter. *"Is it supposed to do that?"* Sam was getting nervous, 1500 mana, 1800 mana. Sam could barely hold the harpoon as it jerked violently. She grabbed it with both hands, using all her new strength to keep it from jerking out of her smoking and sizzling hands. *"Something is wrong!"* she thought as the searing pain and the violent jerking from the harpoon made her lose concentration, dropping her out of meditation. Her skill finally told her when she reached 2000 Mana that something was not just regular wrong but very, very wrong. Trusting the skill screaming into her mind to get rid of the construct, Sam jumped up and threw the harpoon into the river as hard as she could, watching it slip below the surface in a burst of steam. It disappeared swiftly, leaving a trail of bubbles in its wake. Only a wisp of steam was left, floating up slowly from where the harpoon struck the water. Sam waited a few more seconds, holding her breath, but nothing happened.

Sam sighed in relief, "Whew, I guess the water stopped the react—" WUMP! A loud thud sound echoed, shaking the ground beneath her feet. It caused her to stumble slightly as the river exploded in a geyser of pink foam, rising nearly ten meters into the sky around where the harpoon had struck. A pink vapor filled the air before floating with the breeze downriver from the explosion area, now a five-meter-wide circle of pink bubbling water.

Sam stared at the river in awe, "I wonder what I killed," the words had no more escaped her lips when a notification appeared.

'Bing' You have vaporized Piranha [Levels 16-19] x 28. Experience awarded. Due to the complete annihilation of foes, they have been automatically looted and stored in your inventory.

'Bing' Mana Crafting has leveled up to level 11.

'Bing' Class Arcane Pathfinder has leveled up to level 14. 10 Free attribute points awarded.

After reading the notification, Sam smiled to herself, relaxing slightly, *"Okay...so maybe next time, add the mana slower?"* Sam stared at the palms of her charred and black hands, which revealed her bones in places where the skin had burned off. Her mana reserves were entirely depleted, too. Mumbling to herself, she looked back toward her campsite from the previous night, "I'm glad I didn't practice this in the safe zone last night. I wonder if there is a level of attack that permanently stops a safe zone in an area?" She sighed, thinking a little more help with how this magic thing works would be nice because the book the System supplied was extremely vague, which she thought was probably intentional. It was likely so the user could develop magic without another's influence clouding the path. Still, a guide to a few essential system functions would have been helpful. But beggars couldn't be choosers, so she resolved to continue practicing her magic as she traveled. This time, she used smaller constructs to prevent accidentally blowing herself up until she better understood how the new aspect of the mana crafting skill worked. *"I did discover the auto loot function, which is cool. I did wonder what would happen if I ever developed an ability to cause mass destruction; I guess I know now,"* she mused as she continued her trek downriver.

***

For the next three days, Sam continued her slow trek down the river to what she hoped would be civilization. The journey went without incident for the most part. The terrain became rockier the closer she got to her intended destination, along with a higher amount of non-aggressive wildlife, such as the deer, which she had finally managed to identify as a Lightning Cervidae.

She saw raccoon-like creatures, which she now knew were called Ringtail Procyon, and some squirrel-like creatures, which, it turned out, were squirrels of the usual variety with a few exceptions.

The squirrels moved so fast Sam wasn't even sure she had seen anything the first few times she encountered one, thinking her mind was playing tricks on her. She finally managed to identify one of the lightning-fast little bastards on the evening of her seventh day in this new world. She saw it in time to grab it with one of her Mana threads.

Red Squirrel [Level 36]; Neutral; Affinity: Air

Once she was sure the squirrel couldn't get away, she examined its body closely, making sure to keep out of reach of the thrashing animal's claws, *"this little guy is strangely like a squirrel from Earth,"* Sam thought as she examined the terrier sized creature she had trapped, *"well, except for the fact that it is bigger, has six legs, and seven eyes, of course. I wonder if all organic life follows the same basic pattern in the universe, if I am even in my universe, or if this is just a coincidence? The wolf looked almost exactly like a wolf from Earth after all...except for the mane on its back, and it was the size of a freaking SUV."*

The more she thought about it, the more she realized just how many similarities there were between this planet and Earth. Not only were the flora and fauna similar, but the temperature and gravity were roughly the same. She couldn't leap meters into the air and float slowly back down, nor was the gravity so oppressive she felt like she was weighed down when she first arrived in this place. "*Maybe there is more than one System, and the one Earth is in is more basic than this one. Didn't I read something suggesting that our perception of reality was just our brains operating as a basic interface for our true soul to perceive our reality? There may be a System in my universe or verse or whatever it is, but it hasn't developed enough to allow the use of magic. The more I think about it, the more it seems like there must be people or 'things' that have traveled from this universe...verse to mine, there are too many similarities between this world and the fantasy stories and games back on Earth. Did dimensional travelers try to start a basic system in my verse and fail? Maybe they're the true origin of our species? Are they there now, preparing my verse for the coming System through games and books?"* Continuing to think about it for a while, Sam finally had to stop herself before her brain fried, *"Meh, too deep for me right now,"* she shook her head at the ridiculousness of her own wandering thoughts, *"Look at me, trying to figure out the origin of my species using dimensional travelers from another plane of existence as the catalyst, ha!"*

Sam chuckled and released the squirrel as she continued her hike. She decided to start traveling at night on her fifth day in this world after she realized meditation was a more than acceptable alternative to actual sleep. She could keep the skill on constantly so long as she moved slowly, preventing fatigue. Her high recovery stats more than compensated for the energy expended while hiking slowly through the forest as she meditated. After a short mental struggle over the wisdom of her decision, she decided to take her chance at night travel; so far, it had proved to be just as uneventful as traveling during the day. Her mana sight and the two moons' bright light kept the thinning forest well-illuminated for travel even after the sun had long disappeared beneath the horizon.

About an hour after releasing the squirrel, Sam climbed a tree, something she did every three or four kilometers, adding locations to her mini-map. Pushing thick boughs aside and scanning the horizon, her breath caught in her throat; she had to do a doubletake. No more than a few hours' walk from her position was a small tendril of what looked like smoke silhouetted against the vibrant colors of the setting sun. It appeared to be coming from around seven kilometers west of her current position. *"That must be a campfire! Please be friendly people!"*

Sam was so excited at her discovery her hands were shaking almost too much for her to climb down the tree. She hadn't realized how worried she was that she was alone on this planet until she saw the smoke and realized she might not be alone after all. Scrambling down the tree like a monkey, she impatiently dropped the last five meters to the ground. Her new body barely registered the impact when she landed. That same impact would have crippled her just a week ago, but it didn't even affect her now.

She decided to head directly toward the smoke trail, breaking off from the river entirely and cutting straight through the forest. She wasn't worried about getting lost because her cartography skill had already updated her mini-map with the location of the smoke or at least a close approximation. Due to the uneven terrain, she couldn't quite get enough detail from her perch in the tree to get its exact location. She lined herself up with the direction of the smoke on her map. She cut through the forest toward it, hacking with vigor and excitement at the underbrush with bladed constructs.

***

Sam traveled almost half the night, hacking and slashing through the thick underbrush. She would have climbed a tree and tried to travel through the branches high off the ground, but the foliage was just as dense as the underbrush and with less secure footing. Sam even tried using her mana rope construct to swing herself through the forest. Still, after expending a considerable amount of Mana and slamming into a couple of trees, she returned to her slow and steady operation of cutting her way through the underbrush. Now she knew why it was called "bushwhacking." When she was sure she was getting close and was about to climb another tree to check if she could see the glow of a fire, a shrill scream pierced the quiet of the night. It sounded like a human scream.

Sam stopped in her tracks and stood rooted in place by the realization she had just heard a human or, at least, what sounded exactly like a human screaming in either pain or fear. Sam sprinted toward the scream, quickly shaking herself out of the momentary shock of hearing another person for the first time since she woke up on this planet. She paid no mind to the brambles and thorns of the underbrush as they tore at her clothes, hair, and skin. "*There is no way I will let the first sapient life I find in this new world die because I was too slow to save them!*" Sam sprinted, ignoring the pain of the numerous minor cuts the thorny brambles left on her face and body.

***

Arron stared in disbelief at the giant wolf, knowing he fucked up the second the Alpha arrived at the edge of the large clearing leading a pack of thirty or more wolves. Judging from the oppressive aura it emanated, he already knew the Alpha was likely beyond his party's fighting skills. Nevertheless, out of either habit or the desire to know what was about to kill him, he identified the wolf leader.

Red Wolf Alpha [Elite]; [Level 50]; Hostile
HP: 7596/7654
MP: 1247/1247
Affinity: Blood, Earth
Strength: Pack Advantage, Advanced Regeneration
Weakness: Magical Damage, Piercing Damage
Attack(s): Howl; Bite; Claw; Blood Feast; ???

"Shit," Arron cursed under his breath, "why did I take this stupid job?" Of course, he knew why. The job had offered nearly double the pay jobs like this usually did, and now it was obvious why. But what the hell had possessed him to bring Alina and Alice along and not hire a mercenary group? He could have scraped enough coin together to hire a few ex-guardsmen, at the very least.

Arron didn't care what happened to Alice, but Alina was his flesh and blood and the only surviving member of his line. Not that his lineage truly meant much to Arron, but seeing the massive pack of wolves arrayed against them, led by an elite class alpha, made him realize his lineage may end that night, which bothered him more than he thought it should. If only they hadn't been so low on funds when they arrived at Helms Peak. "It's that stupid healer's fault," he mumbled, casting a quick glance toward the frightened woman looking at her with disdain.

Healers were costly, especially healers like Alice. Arron decided to purchase Alice from the Children of the Light with the idea that he would use her advanced healing abilities in the Great Tournament coming up in a few months. However, the cost of keeping Alice around was beginning to outweigh the benefits of having a healer in their party. Even if they weren't paying her in coin, they still had to feed and house her as they traveled. *"If we manage to survive this, I don't think we'll be keeping her services in the future,"* he thought, even though he knew deep down Alice would more than pay for herself once they arrived at Makaria for the tournament. If they survived tonight's battle. Thinking of Alice, Arron remembered he hadn't given her the daily mana stipend today, *"how did I forget that, and why didn't she remind me? If we survive this blasted ambush, I will have to add more binding orders to her contract."*

Arron looked at the two women in his party and grimaced; the chance that all of them survived this was almost zero. He knew he could likely survive, and maybe Alina, if he sacrificed Alice, but even that was a stretch of the imagination. At level 39, he knew he was a competent fighter, but balancing his stat points evenly between his class and occupation's mana, strength, and stamina components meant he was only capable as a fighter, not exceptional. However, he had a few tricks to help him bridge the skill gap in a pinch. Alina, however, was a pure warrior; even at her lower level of 32, she was more powerful than him in physical damage output and defense. Her only downside was her weak mental abilities, which made her susceptible to magical and mental attacks. Their new healer, Alice, was their weakest at level 26. She made up for her lack of combat prowess with her ability to heal anything from mortal wounds to curses and poisons, including regenerating lost limbs. Of course, for her to do all of that, she had to be topped off with Mana, which they had forgotten to do for her, today of all days.

Arron hoped what energy Alice did have left would be enough to at least give him and Alina a chance to escape. He didn't want to waste such a significant investment by losing Alice. Still, he wouldn't hesitate to use the part of her contract allowing him to force her to act as a self-regenerating meat shield if it meant he and Alina could escape their current predicament.

***

Snapping back to the present, Arron eyed the Alpha, trying to gauge his party's chances of survival. He thought the three of them, the two women and himself, could take the Alpha down or at least fight it to a draw with proper preparation if it was an outcast. But it wasn't alone; it had a pack. There were at least thirty wolves in the pack arrayed across the clearing. Their thick, blood-red coats looked menacing and rather frightening in the moons' light. The smaller wolves ranged anywhere from level 12 to 32.

Arron sighed; he knew someone would die tonight; there was no way around it. It pained him to sacrifice Alice for financial reasons. Still, he knew Alina's best chance to escape with him would be with Alice supporting her long enough for them to link up and flee.

Arron was not a strictly moral man, far from it, in fact. He was a survivor and knew how to read a situation to his benefit. They had been caught in the open while cutting across a clearing that had once held a stone structure. Local records said it had been a homestead or hunting lodge, which once proudly stood where the remaining rubble of old stone walls lay. The ruins had once formed a large enough structure to offer shelter for at least fifty people. Arron knew the Lengwood Forest was once a retreat for wealthy nobles in ages past, so he figured this had probably been a hunting lodge for ancient, pampered nobility. The old legends also said Lengwood had been the location of a great battle that wiped an ancient Elven kingdom off the face of Urceon long ago. The battle results allowed the human kingdom of Orlina to be formed on the ashes of the Elves' infrastructure.

Arron was eyeing the remaining stone wall that still stood as a possible fallback point when an earsplitting scream reverberated through the clearing. Turning quickly, he saw Alina bat away one of the lower-level wolves with her shield that had lunged for Alice, who moved to crouch behind Alina. The unfortunate wolf pup was launched back a meter or so, letting out a sharp yelp when it struck the ground, going limp when it hit.

To Arron's surprise, no other wolves moved toward the pair. Looking around, he quickly realized why, *"They're toying with us, letting the lower-level pups get a chance at some experience,"* the thought hit Arron like a hammer, "*the Alpha, she is going to let her young get some experience before killing us. Are we so insignificant that she is comfortable letting her weakest offspring use us for practice?"* Arron had never fought an elite beast, but he knew from the stories they were much more powerful than regular beasts of the same level. He remembered something about them being born with rare bloodlines or performing some incredible feat at a young age that allowed them to develop unique skills others of their kind didn't have. He had never paid much attention to the stories, always assuming he would be able to run away if he ever encountered one on a hunt. Which is what he is planning to do now.

"Fall back to the ruins!" Arron shouted at Alina and Alice as he pulled out his smithing hammer with one hand and a small disk of steel in the other.

Alina took his advice and started backing up slowly with Alice behind her, trying to keep the pack in front of them to avoid the snarling animals flanking them.

Arron was separated from the women by a dozen meters. He had been to the side of the clearing scouting ahead when the Alpha had emerged from the tree line. Despite their separation, they should all arrive simultaneously at the one remaining stone wall if they kept the same pace.

"If we can get to the wall, I can make a metal cage around us or at least create a funnel where they can only come at us one at a time," Arron was starting to see the beginning of the plan in his head as he called out to the women. He would have to conserve his Mana as much as possible until he got to the wall if he wanted to create a cage or barrier. Having done it before, he knew he could, and that made him confident it would hold against most of the wolves except the Alpha.

The Alpha must have realized something was up because it made a low chuffing sound. All the smaller wolves began harassing Alina and Alice, darting in and out, making feints, trying to create an opening, and slowing their progress. As Arron watched, the Alpha started to glow red, indicating it was about to use a skill.

"Run!" Arron screamed, throwing his disk. It sliced clean through the neck of one lower-level wolf, decapitating it. The disk continued its path until it lodged into the side of another wolf. As he ran, the disk tore out of the now-injured wolf and started flying around the clearing with a buzzing sound, slicing at the charging wolves drawing closer. Most of the wolves managed to dodge the disk once they knew what it was and could hear it as it spun through the air. But some weren't fast enough and took grazing hits that were nothing serious. Still, it was enough to slow the pack's pace, and that's all Arron was hoping. That is until the Alpha howled, and Arron realized this was an alpha-led pack, and they were not to be trifled with.

'Bing' You have heard: Alpha's Howl. You have been inflicted with Slow: all movement speed reduced by 10% for 600 seconds.

***

A wolf bolstered by its leader's howl ran ahead of the pack, managing to get around Alina, who, with her low mental stats, had been slowed more than Arron by the sound attack. The wolf sidestepped a clumsy sword swing from Alina and latched onto Alice's ankle, eliciting a pained scream from the woman. Alina recovered enough to activate a smooth skill-infused swing as she cut the wolf attacking Alice clean in half, her short sword meeting little resistance from the low-level beast. Unfortunately, her move left her back turned to the pack, and a higher-level wolf leaped onto Alina's back, biting down on her helmet. The grating sound of teeth on steel could be heard across the clearing as the wolf shook its head back and forth, trying to break Alina's neck. The sound was so loud Arron was sure the beast managed to bite clean through the steel of the helmet, but Alina was a warrior and reacted quickly; even with the slow debuff, her reaction speed was nothing to be trifled with. Reaching back, she grabbed the wolf by its ears and, leaning forward, flipped it over her head, slamming it to the ground before swiftly thrusting her sword into its exposed chest, ending its life. She had lost her helmet, and a small trickle of blood was coming from her forehead, but otherwise, she seemed okay. Alice must have healed herself because she was already back on her feet and nearly to the ruins when Alina extinguished the second wolf.

Arron intercepted her at the entrance to the ruins and, grabbing her shoulder, shouted, "Get to that back wall and be ready to heal us!" He turned back to the clearing just in time to see a circle of wolves close around Alina, cutting her escape off completely. Arron stomach knotted when he realized all he could do was watch in horror as his only daughter was toyed with and eventually killed by the pack.

***

Alina fought back the tears of frustration when the pack closed the circle around her, *"I swear if that stupid healer father insisted on paying for survives, and I don't, I will haunt her forever!"* She sheathed her sword and pulled a long dagger out instead. This would be a close-quarter fight, and she opted for speed instead of reach. She also didn't want to risk getting her sword lodged in one of the stronger wolves during the fight, which would cause her to waste precious seconds pulling it out.

Looking at the circle of impending death around her, Alina thought, *"I'm going to die here!"* The thought filled her with regret, but before she let it take hold, she channeled her Warriors Spirit ability, and her eyes hardened. She was a warrior, after all, and if she was going to die in this place, she was going to take as many of these fuckers with her as she could. If she killed enough, her father might be able to find an opening to save her. Maybe he would find an opportunity to send the stupid healer in to act as a distraction so the two of them could escape, *"He won't, though; he will barricade himself in with the healer until the pack eventually leaves the coward that he is. He may act all tough, but when it comes down to it, he will always look out for himself over anyone else,"* she thought bitterly. Alina knew her father all too well to hope for any form of rescue. He would probably try to help her if he could, but it was more for him to feel better about himself, having 'done all he could' to save her. She was on her own, and she knew it.

A wolf darted in on her left but found only her shield as it was smacked away with the sounds of breaking bones. Another wolf was already lunging at her from her right even as she used her Shield Bash skill on the first. She stabbed the wolf, lunging in from the right in its chest, barely missing its throat when it pivoted to one side, trying to dodge her strike. She spun, yanking the dagger to counter the wolf she sensed lunging at her head from behind, but it had been a feint. She never even saw the high-level wolf dart in, grabbing her left arm in its mouth and biting down with all its might. She felt the punishing pain explode in her mind as the mighty jaws of the wolf bit clean through her armor, flesh, and muscle. The snapping sound of bone breaking as her arm was ripped off was muffled by her blood-curdling scream.

Alina fought through the pain and activated one of her skills, Spin Attack, as she felt her stamina drain precipitously. With her dagger arm outstretched, she spun in a circle several times with magic-infused speed, cutting one lunging wolf's throat and blinding another when the blade raked across its eyes. She fell to her knees as soon as her skill was spent, her stamina exhausted from using two skills so close together. Feeling a healing spell wash over her, stopping the bleeding from her missing arm, she thought, *"No, Alice, don't prolong my suffering,"* and instantly hated herself for thinking it as she continued waving her dagger back and forth in defiance as her vision blurred from stamina exhaustion. "*Maybe Father's disk can distract them and open a hole for me to retreat through?"* She could barely make out shouts behind her, something about getting up and running, but she couldn't be sure with the pain from her wound and the exhaustion from staminal drain.

Alina soon realized what the shouts were about. The line of wolves in front of her parted, allowing the Alpha to pass into the circle they had formed around her; her father's steel disk held in its mouth. The giant red wolf looked at her with disdain. It motioned with its head at several of the smaller wolves, and they approached her cautiously, warily eying the dagger as she waved it.

"I'm not going that easily, you bastards!" She yelled. Alina was determined to take at least two or more of the wolves with her. She focused as best she could on the four approaching wolves spreading out to flank her, growling with their eyes fixed on her as they snarled.

Not surprisingly, the first attack came from her left, as it was her most vulnerable side, with her missing left arm below the shoulder. Alina spun on her knees to intercept the attack with her dagger, but it never came. She was instead met with the sight of the attacking wolf suspended in midair by…nothing. Almost as soon as her mind processed the strange phenomenon of what was happening, the suspended wolf was launched backward, flying meters into the air before it was torn to shreds, blood and viscera splashing to the ground of the clearing. Then all hell broke loose.

***

Alina pushed herself to her feet but could not move; instead, she stood transfixed as blood began spurting from a dozen wolves around her, tiny holes suddenly appearing in their bodies. Not even the Alpha was spared, a gout of blood spraying from its neck from a hole magically appearing out of nowhere. The Alpha dropped her father's disk and turned, searching for the source of the attacks. Arron must have been waiting for this because the disk began spinning and hovering around her before it had time to strike the ground. Alina could now clearly hear her father screaming for her to run, but she couldn't move. The absolute carnage she witnessed kept her rooted in place for fear the unseen attacker would mistake her for a target. As she watched, two higher-level wolves were cleanly bisected by a gore-covered disk much like her father's but larger. It was made briefly visible when it exited the two wolves before disappearing, letting the gore and blood covering it fall to the ground.

"What is happening?" Alina wondered aloud. The wolves had entirely forgotten her in their panic to flee the whirlwind of death. Alina struggled to stay conscious; her stamina was empty, and even standing took its toll on her strength. Her health bar was flashing, and struggling to her feet had made her dizzy. The hope and horror she felt as she watched what was happening pushed her pain-addled mind past its limits.

Falling back to her knees, Alina caught a glimpse of a mostly naked woman with short purple hair and glowing purple eyes sprinting out of the tree line, running directly at the Alpha. She held a purple dagger in each hand, the blades glowing in a way that almost matched her eyes. The woman had a manic grin as she drew closer to the Alpha. The pack leader turned to meet the insane woman with a deep, resonating growl, sending shivers of fear through Alina. The purple-haired woman didn't flinch as she closed the final few meters at a dead sprint. Her grin was growing wider. The elite monster dug deep furrows in the soil when it pushed off the ground, lunging toward the woman with lightning speed, its jaws open wide, intent on snapping her in half.

The woman went into a slide once the Alpha leaped. Dodging the jaws that snapped shut just centimeters from her head, her momentum brought her under the lunging creature. She thrust both daggers into the wolf's belly as she slid.

Alina fainted.

CHAPTER 8 — "Damn I bet that looked cool!"

Sam hadn't identified the large wolf yet but figured this was the pack's leader. The fact it was the size of a compact car, along with its general lack of fear or hesitation when it confronted her, she figured it was a safe assumption. She yanked her daggers out of the deep, bloody gashes she had just made in its stomach, dodging between the wolf's hind legs as it sailed over her. She took advantage of her position, using her glowing daggers to hamstring the beast as they passed each other. The sharp blades of her creations sliced through the wolf's tendons like a sharp knife through a tender steak. Once clear of the creature, she slammed one of her heels into the ground, using momentum to propel herself to her feet as she spun around to face the wolf, slinging blood from the blades. The wolf landed hard from its lunge, its back half collapsing from its crippled hind legs and blood spurting from its belly. She grinned at herself, *"Damn, I bet that looked cool!"*

Sam checked her daggers; they were the second and third permanent mana constructs she had made so far on her journey. Her first successful construct wasn't a weapon. She thought about her first permanent successful mana construct, and her lips tightened in a coy smile. It was much more 'functional' than any weapon; a girl has needs. Shaking off the thought, pleasant as it was, she refocused on her daggers. They had lost a third of their mana in the attack, so she quickly topped the blades with a couple hundred mana each.

***

Sam had been beside herself with excitement when she finally made the first dagger a little over a day ago and was surprised when she found it had an energy reservoir. When she examined it, she was genuinely confused at first by the small violet bar that appeared above the dagger. But after some experimentation, she found with every successful hit the dagger made against an unlucky tree, the bar above the dagger depleted, the amount depending on the strength of the blow. She managed to infuse her mana into the dagger with more experimentation. She was happy to see the energy bar increase with the infusion. She was also relieved when it didn't break or dissipate after fully depleting its energy bar; instead, it turned inert and transparent like it was made of glass. The dagger was still sharp, even without its energy. It had, however, lost its penetrating power. It was almost the same as the daggers the System provided regarding quality and sharpness.

***

Sam took a second to examine the sizeable red wolf in front of her when she finished topping the daggers up with energy.

Elite Red Wolf Alpha; [Level ??]; Hostile; Affinity: Blood, Earth

"Hmm, blood affinity. That is a nasty affinity in the books and games back home. I wonder what it's like here?" Sam flicked her right hand to the side as she thought. The level 26 wolf running toward her suddenly split in half from nose to rump. The two halves of the unfortunate beast slapped against an invisible barrier that sprang up in their path, making a meaty splat against the translucent shield. The thin-bladed disk she had conjured to slice the wolf in half dissipated into nothing a moment after it exited the animal's body. At the same time, she launched six spikes from her mana threads, killing and maiming several wolves who had turned their attention back to the unconscious warrior girl and were slowly stalking toward her. A whiff of something hit Sam, and she wrinkled her nose at the revolting smell of blood and ruptured intestines floating on the breeze from the closest kill.

Looking over, Sam noticed something was weird about the blood from her kills. She watched as the blood from the bisected wolf floated around in globules as if in zero gravity for a second before zipping over toward the alpha wolf, where the blood splattered and wrapped itself around the wolf's hind legs, painting the red fur an even darker crimson. The blood hardened into a solid mass on the leg, looking like armor. Inspecting the leg, Sam realized the wolf's wounds had already healed, likely a perk of its blood magic. But it wasn't just the blood of the latest wolf she had killed; all the slain wolves' blood was repurposed into armor plating for the alpha, with hundreds of small globules zipping in from all directions toward the boss monster.

Once the wolf had sucked up the blood from all the slain wolves in the area, Sam was a little disappointed in the thin layer of blood armor coating the wolf; she had expected more from an elite monster of an unknown level. Shrugging away her thoughts, she was about to attack when the beast turned to her and let out a strange growling sound. it sounded like words, but there was no way it had just said, "I offer you this sacrifice; grant me your power." As soon as the wolf made the sound, a portion of the blood armor coating turned liquid. The blood formed a thin circle and floated to the ground in front of the wolf, making a sizzling sound as it touched the grass of the clearing. Then, the wolf bit its own paw, drawing a significant amount of blood from the wound. Manipulating the blood flowing from the bite, the wolf began to form complex symbols inside the circle. The boss seemed to be directing the blood with its thoughts as it focused intently on creating the symbols with its nose moving in rhythm as the symbols formed in the circle, each locking in a place like a puzzle once completed.

Sam watched the wolf with interest, her mana sight turned on. The soft red magical glow from the blood armor was like a candle flame against the sun compared to the density of the magic forming in the circle of blood. With every new symbol the wolf formed, the density and brightness of the magical power inside the circle increased exponentially. It was then that Sam was starting to worry she had bitten off more than she could chew when the final symbol was laid and locked in place with an audible click. The circle was now full of complex patterns. The instant the last symbol fit in place, all the magic pulsing inside it disappeared like someone had turned out a light. Sam turned off mana sight and stared at what just happened; the entire surface area of the circle was now a rippling pool of dark red blood barely a meter across. The wolf was transfixed on the pool of blood and loomed over it as if expecting something to come out. As Sam and the wolf watched, four black claws began emerging from the center of the pool of blood, followed by four clawed fingers and a thumb. A hand and a long, thin black arm were exposed as the appendage continued rising from the pool until a thin two-meter-long arm was black as midnight was extruding. One of the long-clawed fingers beckoned to the wolf, slowly making no sound. The wolf took a hesitant step back, clearly not expecting this, but after a moment, it came forward, sniffing the air as it approached the black hand.

Looking at the black appendage with mana sight Sam could see all the mana surrounding it sucked into the blackness of the arm, but the arm itself gave off no mana at all. It was like the arm was the absence of mana, like a hole the ambient mana in the area needed to fill. She didn't have any more time to gawk because just then, one clawed finger tapped the wolf's nose, sending a mild shockwave across the clearing that caused the air itself to distort for an instant, blinding Sam's mana sight and causing her to reflexively shield her eyes with one arm. When Sam could see clearly again, the black hand and arm were gone, and the pool of blood was a charred mass of congealed blood on the ground.

Looking at the alpha, Sam was taken aback. It had grown a meter taller and maybe two meters longer. The covering blood armor had changed, with black streaks running across every segment and small spines covering them. The eyes of the wolf were pure red as it gazed at her with hate. It pulled its lips back in a snarl and spoke one word in a growling voice, "Harvest."

"Shit," Sam thought, *"I'm pretty sure this was a mistake."* She watched nervously as the six remaining healthy wolves gathered behind the boss, and a few injured, barely living wolves scattered around the clearing were forcefully exsanguinated. Whatever skill or spell the alpha used was powerful; their blood was being sucked violently from every orifice in their bodies. Some of the poor creatures were even dragged a few meters toward the alpha by whatever force was draining their blood, their piercing cries of

pain and fear going silent moments later as they all succumbed to the spell, their corpses left exhausted and shriveled.

"Yep, a blood affinity is definitely a nasty affinity in this world, too," Sam concluded and began to mentally prepare herself; the boss wolf was fully encased in a thick blood armor, now looking like a dark red war dog with dozens of whip-like blood tentacles extending from its sides each with a sharp black tip at the end like a spearhead. Black spikes had grown from the armor around its neck and shoulders, and blade-like tusks of hardened blood protruded from each side of its mouth; the tips and edges of the tusks were also dark black. The beast looked like it could easily hold its own against a platoon of combatants.

Taking it all in, Sam smiled wide and told the wolf, "You are one ugly unlucky fucker, you know that? You're about to be my personal test monkey, er, puppy!" She paused, holding up her hand to the wolf as if telling it to wait, "No, not a puppy; I love puppies. You're definitely a test monkey," then she shrugged and was almost apologetic when she said, "either way you're going to die." Over her initial nervousness at the change in the wolf's appearance, Sam was giddy with excitement as she looked at the boss, who growled menacingly toward her as she spoke.

"You don't know it yet," She thought wickedly, *"but you're not the only one with tentacles."* She got into a crouch, her daggers ready, the wicked smile never leaving her face.

***

Sam didn't wait for the alpha wolf to make its move, instead choosing to attack first. Moving in a blur, she shot to the side, strafing the wolf while firing invisible mana spikes from all six of her mana threads, aiming for center mass. Pieces of the wolf's armor started chipping off where the spikes impacted, and several of its blood tentacles were cut down only to reform a moment later. She noticed that when one of her spikes hit the tip of one of the blood tentacles, the black point shattered the mana spike instead of deflecting it.

The wolf reacted quickly to Sam's attack, dashing toward her to close the gap between them, trying to intercept her to get its tentacles in range. As the wolf closed the distance, Sam wove three of her threads together to form a rope, then formed a stake at the end of the rope she created. As soon as the boss was in range, it shot its blood whips at her, trying to pin her to the ground with the spiked tips. She was prepared for this and slammed the stake at the end of her rope into the ground behind her. She was yanked to a stop instantly when her rope went taut, and the wolf angling to intercept her sailed by, unable to adjust its course in time due to her sudden stop. That didn't stop the wolf from swiping out with a paw as it passed.

Sam grunted in pain as the wolf's claws, coated with hardened blood with the same black edges, raked across her chest, tearing off what was left of her leather shirt and most of her right breast. The dark edges of the creature's claws met no resistance when they contacted her and passed through her skin like a hot knife through butter. The deep claw gashes were nothing compared to the half-dozen blood spears that stabbed into her torso a moment later, passing entirely through her body and puncturing several organs before they were yanked out as the wolf continued past. Trails of her blood flowed out of the wounds from the blood spears chasing after the wolf. When the wolf stopped a dozen meters away, the blood stolen from Sam splashed into the cracks she had made in the wolf's armor, and within seconds, the armor was healed.

"Shit, it can use the blood it draws from me to heal its armor. If that's the case, I'm going to need to hit it with something it can't easily recover from," she then focused on healing her own wounds, which closed almost as fast as the wolf's cracked armor but, for some reason, took twice the usual amount of mana.

"What in the hell is that black shit on its weapons?" Sam thought. It was as though her strengthened body had offered no resistance against the wolf's attack. *"I'm going to have to end this quicker than I wanted to,"* she thought as she went through a mental list of attacks she could use that would do a lot of damage fast. It didn't take long for her to come up with an idea; it was a short list, after all. The only problem with her plan was she required time to prepare for the attack she had decided to use. Time was currently lacking because the wolf was sprinting toward her again.

Holding her hands out, Sam conjured a barrier between her and the wolf. Unable to see it, the wolf continued its charge and slammed into the invisible shield at full speed. A sharp pain exploded in her mind when the wolf hit her barrier at a full gallop. The impact sounded like a thunderclap echoing across the quiet clearing. The barrier shattered, sending a massive amount of feedback into her brain. But then it had done its job. The wolf hit the magical wall at full speed. The impact had even broken one of its tusks off, along with several plates of the armor around its body; its head had been bent at an unnatural angle so sharply that some of its neck spikes had penetrated its shoulder armor. By the way, the wolf went limp; Sam thought it had killed itself, but there had been no notification, so she dismissed the thought as quickly as it arrived.

While the wolf was down, Sam fought through the pain of mana backlash and entered meditation as she slowly walked toward the beast. She was a little weak from blood loss, and her legs were shaky from the mental stress of expending so much mana so fast. As she drew closer, the wolf began to stir a little, letting out a slight whimper when it yanked its neck spikes out of its shoulder to raise its head and look around with a dazed expression clouding its gaze. When its eyes fell on Sam, they came into focus, and it jumped up to its feet, letting out a growl that turned into a cough, its throat obviously still damaged from the impact. The blood tentacles on the wolf's body flared out in every direction, all four meters long and as big around as a pool cue, turning to her as one, preparing to attack.

"Oh no, you don't," Sam said, flicking her daggers and catching them with her mana threads. She started flicking her left hand back and forth like she was throwing frisbees, and the disks she was throwing started slicing off the wolf's blood tentacles as fast as it could regrow them. At the same time, she blocked and sliced any that escaped the disks with her daggers. To any outsider watching, it would have looked like a high-speed battle between a bloody mop, two floating magic daggers with a mind of their own, and a wind mage. Growling, the wolf made as if to lunge at Sam, then thought better of it, remembering the wall it had just run into. Instead, it lowered its head and started slowly creeping toward her, testing the air in front of it with its nose and the blood tentacles that managed to survive her attacks. Seeing this, Sam began slowly backing up, trying to maintain the distance between them as they moved.

Sam was walking a fine line between clever and utterly stupid with the insane plan she had devised. Still, she had decided to do it, so she continued slowly backward, using her daggers and bladed disks to keep the tentacles at bay in a frenetic dance of bloody death. That is, until she bumped into something hard. Risking a quick glance back, she was baffled at the wall of solid rock that appeared in the middle of the clearing seemingly from nowhere. She mentally slapped herself on the forehead, *"Earth affinity! Of course, the damn blood beast can use earth magic! Well, isn't this just great!"* When she turned back to face the wolf, she could swear there was a smile on its face, *"Oh, laugh it up, you big bastard. I have a surprise for you too. I hope you like your meat charred."* As if reading her thoughts, the wolf who now had its prey trapped by its rock wall, stopped its stalking, raising its nose to sniff the air. A thin tendril of smoke drifted past the wolf, and a sizzling sound could be heard in the quiet night.

Sam chose that moment to act; she kicked off the stone wall behind her, leaving a small crater behind, and launched herself at the elite beast with lightning speed. As soon as she was in range, she punched with all her might at the beast's nose. She wasn't fast enough. Seeing her attack, the wolf snapped its head down and, opening its maw, swallowed her arm up to the shoulder. Sam saved it the trouble before its closing jaws could sever her arm; using a disk in her left hand, she severed her own arm at the shoulder right in front of the wolf's nose. Several of the wolf's blood spears shot into her body as she jumped back, blood spraying from the stump of her arm. Using her threads and daggers, she tried stabbing at the wolf's eyes, but it dodged its head to the side, the daggers glancing off its neck spikes instead. Sam severed the tentacle spears holding her in place and jumped back again to get some distance from the wolf but wound up slamming back into the rock wall. She turned and ran to the edge of the wall, only a couple of meters away.

Seeing Sam trying to get around the wall it had erected, the wolf lunged at her, but she erected her own barrier, stopping it short. Although she stopped its lunge, the wolf managed to get a paw around her hasty barrier and slapped her to the side with a powerful strike. Sam was flung through the air like a rag doll until she impacted another rock wall the wolf erected in her path. The impact knocked the breath out of her and broke her back in several places as she instantly lost all feeling in her legs and arms.

The wolf looked at Sam's broken body triumphantly and began to pad toward its next meal. Sam, not having time to heal her paralysis, formed grappling hooks on the ends of her mana threads and, using them to hook the top of the rock wall the wolf had erected, she yanked herself over the wall, landing in a heap on the other side, thankful that, for once, she couldn't feel pain from all her wounds as she landed. She finished counting down in her head, *"3…2…1,"*

Wump! The ground shook and rippled, and the rock wall Sam was lying behind suddenly fell to pieces. The magic holding it together was no longer present. Sam coughed from the dust left behind from the wall collapsing and wheezed, "About fucking time." She then went to work healing her body, focusing first on her broken spine; she was acutely aware she had not received a kill notification yet.

***

Sam stood from the rubble with a grunt. It only took her a minute to heal her spine enough to stand. She almost wished she hadn't healed her spine first because the second she did, the pain from her many broken bones, severed arm, deep gashes, and puncture wounds came back all at once and nearly caused her to pass out. "I really need some armor," she said, holding her hand to her aching head and slowly walking toward the boss wolf, "maybe I'll try to make some with mana crafting once this is over."

The wolf was lying in a small crater of charred ground a few meters away; the blood armor protecting the wolf was gone, and only charred skin and hair remained. Tendrils of smoke floated from its nose and open mouth and, to Sam's disgusted surprise, its rectum. Despite all this, the beast still breathed, the ragged, gurgling gasps causing Sam to feel pity for the poor creature. After a few short shambling steps, Sam stood over the once terrifying animal. With a tinge of sadness, she formed a spear, gripping it with one good hand, and raised it over the monster's head with the tip aimed at one of its exploded eye sockets. She said, "I'm sorry, girl," meaning every word, "I know you were just following your instincts." It had been a good fight; the wolf had challenged her, forcing her to her limits even with her new power and increased control over her abilities. She didn't doubt it would have easily killed her if she had encountered it just a few days ago. *"Oh well, you win some, you lose some—"*

"No-kill," a surprisingly soft feminine voice sounded in Sam's mind as she stabbed down with the spear.

"What the fuck?" Sam stopped her strike but held the spear tip just centimeters from the creature's empty eye socket.

"No pack now…exile…outcast…hunted…not same…broken…"

Sam didn't understand most of the creature's words but got the general idea. It had obviously been exiled from its pack, likely because it sucked the life blood out of its fellow brethren. With that thought in mind, Sam asked, "Why should I let you live? You murdered your packmates. What will stop you from attacking me again when you are better, little wolf?" She kept a close eye on the beast, worried it was stalling for time while healing itself, but she could see no signs of healing. She knew that didn't mean it wasn't healing internally, though.

"Not wolf…made…pact…with…for power…now broken. Not attack…master. Make new pact…with…pathfinder…"

Sam's mind had trouble processing what the voice said, *"Can beasts use identify? Or is this one more intelligent than I initially thought?"* Suddenly suspicious, she identified the wolf again.

'Bing' [Elite] Lupine Bloodmorph Exile; [Level 1]; Defeated; Affinity: Blood, Unknown

Before Sam could comment on the species change, the wolf had somehow made it and sent her a request via a notification.

'Bing' Unknown Lupine Bloodmorph has requested to soul bond with you.
Warning: once completed, this action cannot be undone!

"What is a Bloodmorph?" Sam asked, "The last time I checked, you were a Red Wolf."

"Made…pact…give power…lost…pact broken," the voice was weakening.

"I don't think I can trust you girl. Sorry for this, but I don't believe you have changed your ways just because I defeated you." Sam was interested in the soul bond and how it might benefit her. Still, at the same time, she knew far too little about this reality and the System controlling it to take a chance, plus the whole 'cannot be undone' statement frightened her a good bit. She made her mind up; the wolf had to die.

"Wait!" The voice was pleading, "No bond take…summon…gift…not destroy…please."

Sam had enough, "Okay, this is getting weird. The way I see it, you tried to kill me by making a pact with something, but you still lost, and now you're begging for your life and asking me to do something I cannot undo. I can tell you are obviously aware enough to understand this from my perspective and how ridiculous it would be for me to believe you. I don't have time for this; it's over, you lost, at least die with some dignity." She didn't have time; her arm was still reforming, and she didn't even know if the people she had saved were still around. Every second she spent talking to the defeated monster was one that could lose the only people she had seen in this new world.

Without another word, Sam thrust her spear into the wolf's eye socket with a sharp, decisive motion. The spear encountered no resistance and stabbed into the ground below the wolf's head, sinking deep into the soil.

Sam blinked as she stared at where the head had just been. The instant she had thrust down with her spear construct, the wolf had burst into a puff of red particles resembling sand. The cloud of particles began coalescing in the crater's center about a meter off the ground. Sam watched, prepared to defend herself, as the cloud swirled around in a blood-red ball, growing smaller with each passing second; the occasional streak of black could be seen in the cloud as it condensed ever smaller. Within a few seconds, the cloud had compressed itself into a dark red coin, promptly falling to the ground once complete.

Cautiously, Sam walked over and picked up the coin, cursing her stupidity when she did so. *"Idiot! What am I thinking? This thing could be cursed or something."* Calming herself when nothing immediately happened, she examined the coin. It was roughly the size of her palm with a good weight. It also felt unnaturally cool to the touch, even through her glove. Turning the coin over in her hand, she noticed one side had a strikingly lifelike image of the wolf or Bloodmorph now while the other had an inscription. She read the inscription in her head, *"The Defeated."* She didn't try to understand the words and slipped the coin into her storage. When it left her hand, dozens of messages popped into her vision.

'Bing' You have defeated Red Wolf Juvenile [Level 22] Experience awarded.
'Bing' You have defeated Red Wolf [Level 32] Bonus experience awarded for defeating an enemy ten or more levels above your own.
'Bing' You have defeated Red Wolf [Level 26] Bonus experience awarded for defeating an enemy twenty or more levels above your own.
'Bing' You have defeated Red Wolf [Level 29] Bonus experience awarded for defeating an enemy twenty or more levels above your own.
'Bing' You have defeated Red Wolf Juvenile [Level 12] Less experience awarded for defeating an enemy below your own level.

This went on for a while. Sam counted twenty-three kill notifications in total. The last kill notification was the alpha.

'Bing' You have defeated Elite Red Wolf Alpha [Level 50] Bonus experience awarded for defeating an enemy thirty or more levels above your own.

The subsequent notification was written in gold lettering, and Sam read it with interest.

'Bing' You have defeated and subdued an unknown entity, Elite Lupine Bloodmorph [Level 1]. Experience has been awarded for discovering an unknown entity. Reward: Summoning token.

"Oh, so that's what that was," Sam pulled the token out of her inventory and looked at it again, this time identifying it.

'Bing' Summoning token [single use]. This token can cast a summoning spell, calling forth the entity represented on the token.

"This is interesting," Placing the token back into her inventory, Sam decided to ask how to use it as soon as she found someone trustworthy. She then dismissed her level-up notifications and looked around for the people she had saved; at least, she hoped she had saved them.

Seeing all three of them still in the clearing, she quickly checked her level-up notifications. She did not want to wait any longer to meet the people she had saved, but she also wanted to be as ready as she could be when she interacted with people from this world for the first time.

'Bing' Race Human has leveled up to level 16. +5 Free attribute points awarded.
'Bing' Race Human has leveled up to level 17. +5 Free attribute points awarded.
'Bing' Race Human has leveled up to level 18. +5 Free attribute points awarded.
'Bing' Race Human has leveled up to level 19. +5 Free attribute points awarded.

Next was her class levels.

'Bing' Class Arcane Pathfinder has leveled up to level 15. +10 Free attribute points awarded.
'Bing' Class Arcane Pathfinder has leveled up to level 16. +10 Free attribute points awarded.

Getting impatient, Sam skipped to the last notification.

'Bing' Class Arcane Pathfinder has leveled up to level 20. +10 Free attribute points awarded.

"Holy shit, that's 80 free points!" Pulling up her stat sheet, Sam distributed her points. She skipped over strength because she hadn't felt lacking in that stat during the boss fight. Then she added twenty points to her vitality stat, bringing it up to sixty; as always, her health had been in the single percentage digits several times during the battle. Her endurance was trailing behind all her other stats, so she put twenty points into the stat, and fifteen points went into agility, putting all her stats over forty. She finished with fifteen and ten points in intelligence and wisdom, respectively. Confirming her selections, Sam felt the now familiar energy orgasm wash over her body and shuddered in ecstasy.

Adding so many points at once was an amazing rush. Sam looked down at her body and watched her muscles grow leaner, longer, and more taut. She felt the density of her bones increase, making her noticeably heavier when she shifted her feet. All the fuzziness from the several instances of mana backlash she had experienced during the battle was washed away with the increase in her intelligence and wisdom boost.

"What a rush!" She said once the feeling of the stat increase subsided, "Okay, now to go meet some people!" She started toward the ruins. *"They better not be assholes,"* she thought as she walked toward the three huddled forms at the other end of the clearing, not even noticing her arm still slowly reforming as she strode out of the shallow crater and across the soft grass of the clearing.

CHAPTER 9 — "I come in peace."

"Hello there! My name is Sam, and I come in peace," Sam winced at the stupid statement as soon as she said it. Still, it seemed to work when the trio of humans huddled visibly relaxed against the lone stone wall in the ruins. Their eyes, however, stayed alert as she approached. The man and a woman in robes were hovering over the injured but now-conscious warrior girl who had lost her arm and looked to be in extreme pain. All three of them were now staring at Sam wide-eyed. It looked to Sam like the woman in the robes was a healer and trying her best to heal the warrior girl's lost arm, judging by the fresh pink skin and growth from the stump.

"Damn, less than a centimeter in what ten minutes? At least five," Sam wasn't sure if the lack of progress was because the healer wasn't that good or because her only reference was herself, and she was an anomaly.

When she entered the ruins, Sam asked the male, who jumped up to stand between her and the two women, "Can you understand me?"

"Yes, and halt. Please stay back, mage; your prompt aid is appreciated, but we neither requested it nor do we have a means to reward you, so please leave us," Arron's words were far from commanding after having just witnessed the destruction Sam caused. The obvious fear in his voice made Sam stop walking.

After a few moments of thought, Sam said, "Nah, I don't think so, buddy," she gestured at the injured warrior, "Your friend there is hurt; I think I can help her," then gesturing to herself Sam said, "I could use some spare clothes if it's not too much to ask. I'm not asking for a handout; I can pay you for the clothes."

***

Arron finally looked at Sam at the mention of clothes as she continued ambling forward and flushed. Her clothes were little more than rags, stained with old blood, grime, and fresh blood from the alpha. Her short violet hair was matted with blood, and who knew what else? It looked as if she had tried to cut her hair herself after lighting it on fire and putting it out in a swamp. Her eyes, however, were vibrant and powerful as they were no longer glowing but were still a deep violet. The intensity of her gaze made Arron feel like the strange woman was staring into his soul; her focus reminded him more of the gaze of the alpha wolf than that of a human. *"How does one even get purple eyes? I've never heard of purple eyes before."* he thought. Except for her eyes, she looked the part of a helpless young woman who had been lost wandering the forest for weeks. In fact, if he hadn't just seen what she was capable of only minutes earlier, that is exactly what he would have thought. *"But no one who could defeat an elite alpha wolf and whatever dark variant it turned into, as well as take that kind of punishment, could be lower than level...," as he identified her discreetly.*

S.A.M.; [Level 19]; Pathfinder; Neutral
HP: ????/????
MP: ????/????
Affinity: ?
Strength: ?
Weakness: ?
Attack(s): ?

"NINTEEN! Is she only level nineteen? That means she was at an even lower level when the fight started! Why can't I see any other information, and how can she already have four spaces for health and mana? This isn't good. Is she a monster posing as a human?" Arron's mind was racing at the implications of what the woman's class could be and, of course, how he could exploit it, *"if we can get her comfortable enough to let Alice siphon her,"* Arron's eyes glinted with malice, *"we will have an unstoppable force that only I control."*

***

Sam broke the awkward silence as Arron seemed to have locked up and only stared at her weirdly, "I said I can help her," she gestured to the wounded woman again, "with the arm, that is. I might be able to regrow it faster than your healer."

When Arron continued to stare at her, Sam had enough and pushed past him, which he let her do without a word. She looked back at him as she moved to the two women on the ground, saying, "Look, old man, if I wanted you harmed, you would be harmed, so relax and let me check on your..." She knelt next to the healer.

She looked between Arron and the injured woman; there was an obvious family resemblance between the two, "daughter, I presume." She wasn't entirely sure, but they did share similar features, such as their noses and eyes, *"I really don't know how these things work in this world, though; both women could be his love slaves, or it could be the other way around for all I know. Although I doubt either of those options is correct. How he is protective of the warrior makes me think she must somehow be related to him or at least important to him. So, if I help her, it should at least make me less of a threat to him and make all of them more likely to help me; at least, that's the hope."*

Sam knew it was a lot to hope for; it was all she had now, and she desperately needed information about this world and the System that controlled it. *"Please don't be assholes,"* were her thoughts before Arron finally spoke.

"I'm sorry, I got lost in thought for a moment. My name is Arron, and she, yes, she is my daughter," Arron finally said, "I will be grateful if you heal Alina's arm but like I have already said, we will not be able to pay you," he paused for just a moment and seemed to be thinking something over before continuing, "would it be possible to let Alice," he gestured to the healer in the forest green robes," watch you and perhaps assist? If you would offer some of your mana to her, she would be a great help."

At Arron's words, Alice tensed ever so slightly, averting her blue eyes from Sam as she did so. This did not go unnoticed by Sam, putting her on high alert.

Narrowing her eyes at Arron, Sam asked, "How would she assist me exactly? Also, I already told you all I wanted was clothes, and that was a request, not a demand," Sam settled into a comfortable position next to the injured girl and tried to ignore the weird old man as he stammered.

"Alice can only heal if she has enough mana, and if you were to, ahem, donate some to her…" Arron trailed off when he realized Sam had stopped listening to him and was already talking to Alina.

Sam asked the young woman, "Your name is Alina, right?" Sam continued when the woman nodded affirmingly, "Will you let me try to heal you?

"Yes," the young warrior replied through clenched teeth. The stump of her left arm had stopped bleeding, but that was about it; the muscle tissue and bone were still exposed, and there was less than a hair's width of growth from the nasty wound. The healer, who looked exhausted from mana drain judging from the pallor of her skin and beads of sweat running down her face, reached over to touch Sam but stopped when she saw Sam's eyes flare with purple light for a second as she shook her head. Alice pulled her hand back and placed it in her lap with her head downcast.

Sam looked back to Alina, saying, "Well, Alina, I'm Samantha, er, Sam, just call me Sam. I'm going to try one of my healing skills on you. The description says it should work on others, but this will be my first try. If it doesn't work, I can give you a health potion instead," placing her hand on the woman's leg, Sam looked her in the eyes, "Are you ready?"

Alina nodded, and Sam activated Mana Repair and Mana Casting at the same time as the skills guided her on how to push her mana into Alina. Watching with her mana sight, Sam tracked what was happening as her mana flowed into the other girl. Directing the healing process outside her body was much more challenging, but she managed to get the hang of it quickly.

Realizing it was working, Sam focused, and with a grunt of effort, she began repairing both of their lost limbs centimeter by painful centimeter.

***

The others watched in amazement as Alina's arm fully reformed in just over two hours. Sam had started meditating and slowed her channeling once she became more comfortable. She made sure to stay at a point where she wasn't depleting her reserves and could maintain her mana while she healed Alina and herself. She didn't know these people and certainly wasn't going to exhaust her mana reserves right in front of them on the off chance they would attack her as soon as the warrior woman was healed.

***

Sam stood up once Alina's arm was fully restored. Reaching out a hand, she helped Alina to her feet. As Sam looked around the clearing, she saw Aaron had begun piling up the drained bodies of the wolves to one side of the large clearing near the tree line. At the same time, Alice had moved to the center of the ruins and built a small fire over which she had placed a spit and cookpot.

"How do you feel?" Sam asked Alina, who was looking at her new arm in amazement, flexing her fingers and moving it in all directions to check its function.

"It itches a little bit, but that's fading," Alina flexed the fingers on her new hand again, staring at them in amazement, "What kind of healing spell is that?" She quickly shook her head, "Wait, I'm sorry, I shouldn't have asked that," she backed away from Sam a couple of steps as if expecting her to be angry at the question. Alina quickly bowed, saying, "Thank you, Miss Samantha."

"Please just call me Sam. And it wasn't a spell; it is just a couple of my skills that synergize well," Sam wasn't sure if she should have told Alina that and was already regretting it but didn't see any harm in it at the moment. She did think it was a bit strange. Alina apologized for asking, though. *"Something to figure out later, I guess,"* she started to push it to the back of her mind for the time being, then thought better of it, *"On second thought, this is not Earth; I have no idea who these people are. I refuse to be taken advantage of. I will need to guard my words for a while until I can trust them, especially Arron; he gives me the creeps the way he stares at me and the little healer."*

Oblivious to Sam's thoughts, Alina just nodded, "Oh, I see; I thought it might be a high-level healing spell that Alice could learn," Arron had just strolled over. He and Alina shared a strange glance at those words. Alice looked up from the campfire and quickly ducked her head again when Sam glanced at her.

"Is that fear in her eyes? No, that's not it..." Sam thought when she caught Alice's gaze before the woman looked down quickly. *"Just what is going on here? I need to keep up my guard around these people,"* Sam thought to herself, interrupted by a question from Alina.

"If you don't mind my asking, what is a Pathfinder?"

The question caught Sam off her guard, but she responded, "Huh, oh, is that what shows up when you try to identify me?" Sam had to admit she was curious about how much information others could gain from using Identify on her, "what exactly do you see, Alina?"

"Only you are at level nineteen and a Pathfinder," Alina said.

"So, they see my race level and only part of my class name. Assuming she is telling the truth, that is good information to know. If Identify doesn't give them the information, I sure as hell won't," Sam was now more guarded than ever. If personal information was protected somewhat by the System, it could be used against her.

"Let the girl be Alina," Arron interrupted.

Looking over to the man, Sam looked him over. He had short salt and pepper hair in a military-style cut, squinty brown eyes, a small nose, and a stern jawline. He was dressed in a combination of leather and steel armor that had seen better days, with his only weapon being a hammer hanging from a loop on his belt. Sam guessed he was in his late forties, maybe early fifties; at least, that is what it looked like by Earth standards.

"Arron, right?" Sam asked, then changed the subject, "What do you plan to do with those corpses?" She pointed to the pile of bodies.

"We'll have to burn them sadly. I...we don't have the carrying capacity to bring them all back with us," Arron looked longingly at the pile of bodies and then back at Sam, "You wouldn't happen to have the means to carry some of them, would you?" He paused as if in thought before nodding his head as though coming to a decision," I will admit I have a storage item. Still, it is almost full with our provisions," he gestured to the pile of wolves, "If you would help us carry the items, I will be happy to assist in harvesting the useful bits for a small portion of the profits," he looked toward the pile, "at least the parts that are not completely mutilated beyond use."

"I could help with carrying the loot," Sam said, slowly thinking about how much she was willing to reveal about herself. She decided to go with a half-truth: "I have a storage item, with enough free space for most of the pelts—" An angry hiss from Alice stopped her, and Sam jerked her head toward the woman by the fire.

Alice had burned one of her fingers with the cookpot and looked at the group apologetically, "sorry, so clumsy of me," she gave Arron a thin smile that did not reach her eyes.

Arron returned the smile, but Sam could tell he was angry at the woman for interrupting her. She resolved to try to get Alice alone so she could question her without the others overhearing, which gave her an idea.

Sam cleared her throat, "Arron, as much as I love standing around talking about the spoils of our battle, it is getting a little drafty around here, so about those clothes I was asking for," she looked pointedly at Alice with a raised eyebrow, "Alice, do you have a spare robe?"

All three people took a good look at Sam, and Arron flushed crimson; even the two women colored up a little when they looked at her. Sam's clothes were so shredded by the fight with the alpha they left very little to the imagination.

Alice pulled her eyes away from Sam and moved to a large hiking pack leaning against the stone wall, saying, "I have some clothes and a sewing kit," she looked back at the leather strips that Sam was wearing as clothes and continued, "I don't think I can fix your outfit though. Maybe the pants…" she trailed off as she dug through the pack.

"I can keep my pants, I guess," Sam said, looking down at the bloody disgusting leathers she was wearing, "I just need a top. I really don't care if it fits, just so long as my tits aren't hanging out anymore," she said with a laugh.

With that statement, Arron turned an even deeper shade of red, which surprised Sam because she didn't think that was possible. Laughing even harder, she said, "Careful, old man, or you'll blow a ring gasket."

Arron grunted, "Blow a what? I don't know what that is," he shook his head as if to clear it, "the girls will get you some clothes," he nodded toward the pile of corpses, "if you're willing to split the earnings from the pelts, claws, and teeth I will not ask for any payment for the clothes," there was a glint in his eye. He continued, "Say, 50/50?"

Even Alina had the decency to look surprised at the ridiculous offer. She opened her mouth to say something to her father, but Sam spoke first, "That's fine, but you process all of them." She knew she had slain at least eighty percent of the wolves. Still, she didn't have the mental energy to argue with the greedy man and figured distracting him might allow her to talk to the healer alone. Besides, she figured she could loot them quietly before he burned the remains. She wasn't sure it would work but figured it was worth a shot.

Alice pulled a shirt out of her pack and held it up, looking from it to Sam to gauge if it would fit. Sam strolled over to her and ran her hand down one of the seams. The shirt was made of thin, deep green material with long sleeves and a low collar. It had a hook and loop system down the front to keep it closed and looked roughly the right size for her.

"Thank you," Sam said, taking the shirt. "I'll go change over there," she pointed to a shadowed area behind the stone wall out of the fire and both moons' light, "would you mind coming with me to hold my canteen while I clean up? I'm pretty filthy, and I would like to be able to bathe at least a little before putting this on."

"Yes, of course," Alice replied quickly, casting a furtive glance at Arron's back as he walked away.

Seeing Alice's look, Alina spoke up, "I can help too," and started walking toward the pair.

"Shit, I want to get the healer by herself to ask some questions!" Sam thought before telling Alina, "I think you should rest. Remember, you just lost an arm," looking up at the moons, she continued, "And there can't be more than a few hours left before morning, so why don't you try to sleep for a bit." When Alina still seemed like she was going to argue, Sam said, "Look, I realize I'm pretty much naked already, but that isn't by choice, so the fewer people who see me changing and bathing, the better. Alice is a healer, so I'm sure she's seen it all by now."

Alice nodded and said, "I also have a cleansing spell, but it won't work on your clothes," she shrugged, "only living things." With that, she reached in and pulled some pants from her pack.

Alina sat by the fire while Sam and Alice walked behind the wall. Sam glanced back at Alina just before disappearing behind the barrier to see her gaze was fixed on Alice. It wasn't a kind gaze.

***

As soon as they were behind the wall, Sam turned to Alice and asked, "Are you able to speak freely to me? I have some questions about the other two."

"Of course," Alice said with a forced smile while shaking her head. "We are just a traveling party of adventurers. We have nothing to hide."

"Shit, what in the fuck have I just got myself into. Okay, so she doesn't want anyone to overhear her answers, I guess. But what is she? A captive? A slave?" Sam thought. Then she held a finger to her lips, whispering, "Do you understand what this means?" When Alice nodded, Sam continued in a low whisper, "I'm going to ask you a few questions. Just nod yes or shake your head no to answer me. Is that okay? Can you do that?" Alice nodded once, her eyes wide with either excitement or fear; Sam didn't know. That's when Sam realized she was gripping the woman's shoulder tightly, too tightly. With a sigh, Sam quickly healed the damaged muscle and released her, "I am so sorry; sometimes I forget how strong I am."

“It’s okay," Alice said, throwing the pants she held to hang over the top of the wall and rolling the sleeves of her robes up, "although I must say you are powerful for a mage."

Sam only smiled at the healer, hung up the shirt Alice had given her next to the pants, and began pulling off the rags that were her clothes. She asked her first question, "Can I trust Arron?"

Alice quickly shook her head no, saying, "Of course you can.”

Sam tossed the remains of her shirt aside, “Alina?”

Again, the answer was no, but the head shake was less aggressive.

Sam removed one boot, then the next, "Can I trust you?”

That question caught Alice off guard, but she only hesitated momentarily before shaking her head again in the negative. Her eyes were pleading and expressive, full of unspoken words, and her jaw muscles were pulsing from being clenched so hard.

"Okay, this is interesting. Who would tell someone straight up that no one in the group was trustworthy? What is your angle here, Alice?" Sam thought as she loosened her belt and let her pants drop to her ankles before stepping out of them and kicking them aside. She asked, "Are they criminals?" When Alice didn’t answer and only stared at her wide-eyed, she asked, "Are you a criminal?" Alice vehemently shook her head no.

“Am I in danger if I stay with you and the others?” Sam asked.

Alice thought about that for a minute and shrugged slowly, then after more thought, shook her head no. She held her palms facing Sam, "I can cleanse you now if you like. I still have a little mana left."

“Is that all you’re going to do?” Sam asked, her eyes narrowed in suspicion; she wasn't sure she should trust Alice to cast a spell on her.

Worried this was a trap, she reached out with her mana threads around the camp to see where the others were and found Alina lying by the fire and Arron still by the corpses. Sam was surprised when Alice's eyes followed one of her mana threads as it snaked over the wall. She only did it briefly before snapping her gaze back, but it was enough for Sam to notice.

“Yes, it is only a cleansing spell,” Alice said, getting Sam's attention. A coy smile played across her lips, and she said, “That is unless you would like me to help you with something else,” she looked Sam up and down, raising one eyebrow.

Sam was torn between being creeped out and flattered at how openly Alice stared at her. She thought, *“What the hell, man? What happened to the scared little puppy that wouldn’t even look me in the eyes when she was sitting by the fire just a few minutes ago? Why is it that the quiet ones are always the biggest freaks? Has it all been an act to get my interest so we could have this conversation? Am I being played by these people? And to top it all off, I think she can see my magic! Why hasn't she said something about it?"* Sam was worried that she may be in grave danger but was confused about why Alice *acted as she did. "I'm way over my head here with these people. I'm not sure sticking around is the best idea."*

Sam looked into Alice's expressive blue eyes and was surprised at her husky voice when she said, "I appreciate the offer, but I'm good for now, thanks. I just want the cleansing spell."

Alice was cute and all, but Sam needed to figure out the rules of this world. For all she knew, the woman could be trying to trick her into something binding or worse, *"Can I get a magical STI? Would mana repair even work on that sort of thing?"* Sam decided, *"I need to get directions to the nearest town or city and try to slip away from this weird group as soon as possible without anyone noticing. I don't want to get caught up in whatever these people have going on.*"

Alice's hands glowed slightly in the two moons' light, and Sam let her press her palms against her chest, transferring the glow to Sam's body.

A warm feeling washed over Sam as the glow traveled across her skin, followed by all the blood, dirt, twigs, and grime that had built up from her travels, sloughing off her body and leaving a pile of filth on the ground around her feet. The process took less than a minute, and Sam kicked herself for not watching the spell with mana sight. Resisting the urge to ask Alice to cast the spell again, Sam whispered one last question, "Alice, are you in danger?"

Tears welled up in Alice's eyes as she nodded silently.

Sam closed her eyes and pinched the bridge of her nose, *"Well, shit."*

***

When Sam and Alice walked back around the wall to the fire, they found a grumbling Arron sitting next to a sleeping Alina. He was roasting an entire wolf leg on a spit, mumbling about how it would cook without blood as it slowly turned above the flames. He looked at the two women with slightly narrowed eyes as they sat across from him.

"I thought I was going to have to come get you girls. Wouldn't want some dangerous forest creatures to sneak up on you while you were…distracted," Arron said, staring hard at Alice, who ducked her head submissively.

Knowing it was all an act now, Sam laughed, "I think I have proven that I can handle myself against forest creatures. Don't you think, Arron?"

He only grunted in response and returned to staring at the roasting meat.

Looking toward the pile of corpses, Sam realized they had all been skinned, and pelts and meat piled up around the campsite. "How did you process all those wolves so fast?" she asked, genuinely curious. *"Does he have a loot ability, too?"*

Arron looked up from his cooking and shrugged, saying, "I'm a metal mage." He said it as though it was explanation enough and went back to cooking.

Sam didn't know what to say and looked to Alice, hoping she would help clarify.

"He's a metal manipulator," Alice said helpfully, "why skin an animal slowly when you can use magic?"

Arron looked at Sam curiously, "You really aren't from around here, are you? Don't tell me you harvest your kills without using magic. Where did you say you were from?"

"I am not, and I didn't say," Sam responded, stalling while trying to think of a plausible explanation for why she was wandering in the forest alone at night without giving too much away, especially how she harvested her kills. When Arron and even Alice continued to stare at her expectantly, she sighed and said, "I'm from north Alabama," when there was a noticeable lack of recognition in their eyes, Sam continued, "I don't know how I got here. All I know is that I went to sleep in my bed one night and woke up in the forest over a week ago. I have been fighting for my life ever since."

Alice spoke up, "Oh, I've heard of that happening, summoning rituals going wrong and accidentally sending some poor, unrelated person through the void." She poked Sam's arm as if testing she was real, "It's very rare though, and usually the person doesn't come out with," Alice struggled for the right words, "they don't usually come out, with all their parts." She looked earnestly at Sam, "You are lucky to be alive. Not just to have survived an accidental summoning, if that's what happened. But also that you arrived on this side of the Tauris River. The forest on the east side of the Tauris is called Gloomwood and is much more dangerous than where we are now."

"Where exactly are we? And what makes Gloomwood more dangerous than here? That alpha I fought was plenty dangerous." Sam said while thinking, *"I probably shouldn't tell them I actually arrived on the other side of the river in Gloomwood Forest."*

"You are in the Lengwood Forest in the kingdom of Orlina," Alice said, looking for some acknowledgment from Sam. When Sam just stared at her, she continued, "Are you not familiar with the Kingdom of Orlina?"

Sam shook her head, shrugging, "I'm from the Kingdom of America. I have never heard of Orlina." Figuring now was as good a time as any to ask for directions, she asked Alice, "Where is the nearest town or city from here? Is it far?"

Before Alice could respond, Arron spoke up, “Helms Peak is the closest city. It is a three-day walk from here. But don’t worry, you can travel with us,” his look was conniving, “I wouldn’t want you getting more lost than you already are in this dangerous forest,” he looked to the stacks of pelts and meat, “and you agreed to carry the pelts, remember.”

"I remember," Sam said, disappointed in not getting proper directions. Still, she figured it would be easy to determine their destination once they had a direction set.

Pointing at the piles of pelts and meat, she asked, "Is this all for me to carry?" Arron nodded, so she walked over and placed her hands on the piles, making them disappear into her storage.

With the pelts and meat stored, Sam walked over to the pile of corpses. Arron had created a funeral pyre of sorts and piled the bones and unused parts on top. She quickly had a fire under the pile using her flint and steel and some kindling from her inventory. On a whim, she touched one of the skulls in the stack and tried to loot it. It worked, although not quite as she had expected.

Corpse Pile Items:

15-Gold; 43-Silver; 97-Copper; Monster core x 19 [Red Wolf]; Small Mana Potion x 7; Small Health potion x 9; Stamina Potion x 4. Take all Yes/No

Selecting yes, Sam was thankful the pile didn’t disappear or diminish noticeably and absently wondered, not for the first time, how the monetary system worked in this world. *“Just how valuable is fifteen gold?”* she mused, returning to the campfire to rejoin the others.

Sitting next to Alice, Sam produced a cube of Deep Hunter meat and a skewer she had made with her mana crafting skill. She put the meat on the skewer when Alice slapped it out of her hand and threw the cube into the fire.

“Hey! What gives?” Sam snapped at Alice.

Alice pointed at the charred cube of meat, "That is very poisonous! It can kill lower-level people and even higher-level people with low endurance!” She looked at Sam like she was an idiot.

"It's also delicious!" Sam said, annoyed. Pulling another cube out of her inventory and quickly skewering it. Holding the cube over the fire, she looked at Alice defiantly, "It is also a great way to level poison resistance."

Alice stared at Sam slackly jawed, and Arron chuckled, saying, "I suppose that's one way to look at it," looking at Alice, he said, "It appears the Pathfinder class is not to be trifled with." He looked at Sam and asked,

"From the state of your clothing when you arrived to help us, am I to assume you fought and killed the Deep Hunter on your own?" Arron raised his eyebrows questioningly, and Alina, who had just woken up, rolled to a sitting position to stare at Sam in disbelief.

Sam decided to sow a little fear into the group, hoping it would dissuade them from trying anything stupid, like attacking her while she was distracted or deep in meditation. She figured giving them a healthy respect for her strength wouldn't hurt since she was stuck traveling with them for at least a day or so. So, she responded, "Yes, I killed a couple of Deep Hunters," as she pulled a couple of steaks out of her inventory. "I have some Blade Tail and Great Timberwolf steaks if none of you want to level your poison resistance." She looked at the bloodless meat Arron was roasting and made a face, "I'm not sure that meat is worth eating; it looks a little leathery."

Arron looked at the meat he was roasting and gave it a disgusted look. It hadn't even dripped any fluid while it was roasting. He took it from the fire and started poking at it with a knife. The meat made a hollow sound when the knife tip tapped against it.

Alina cleared her throat, "Um, Sam, you wouldn't have happened upon the Great Timberwolf and Blade Tail when they were heavily injured or maybe dead?"

Sam responded, "Nah, the meat is fresh; I killed them myself," she was enjoying the opportunity to show off without revealing anything about her powers, so she continued, "The Great Timberwolf was a tough fight. I had to get it close enough to the river for a Deep Hunter to latch onto it and drag it under so I could—" she trailed off at the three stunned looks she was getting, "what? It was tough. I nearly died several times!"

'Monster," Alina mumbled under her breath, but for Sam, who had mana threads next to everyone, she may as well have been shouting.

The statement caught Sam by surprise. Yes, it had been dangerous, and there had been a lot of luck involved in that fight, but she was fairly certain the three of them could have done the same. With Arron's ability to control metal blades and Alina's warrior abilities, they could have kited the beast until it fell. At the same time, Alice would ensure they stayed healthy enough to keep going.

Sam's thoughts were interrupted when Arron asked, "Sam, you know Great Timberwolves only become 'Great' after level fifty?"

"I did not know that," she responded, "but this one was only level sixty-one, so it hadn't been 'Great' for long, I guess."

"A level sixty-one Great Timberwolf and a Deep Hunter simultaneously! And at level…what, twelve or fourteen? I…I feel lightheaded—" Alina placed a hand on her forehead.

Sam thought the woman was being a little dramatic but answered her anyway, “Seven,” she mumbled, staring into the fire.

“Wha—what?” Alina asked in disbelief.

“I was level seven,” Sam said, bringing her attention back up and looking all of them in the eyes, making sure her words sank in.

Alina’s head made a light thump when it struck the grass after she fainted.

"Does she do that a lot?" Sam asked, "This is like the third time I've seen her unconscious in an hour. It cannot be healthy."

“Not really, but it has been a trying night for all of us,” Alice said and got up to check on Alina. She surprised Sam by returning and sitting beside her on the grass once she was sure Alina was fine. With a wistful look, Alice leaned into Sam and told her, “You are not a monster," she patted Sam's leg, "You're like one of the ancient heroes from the old fables."

“Don’t be daft, girl!" Arron said gruffly, "She's just a human who got lucky with her class. Nothing more, nothing less! Don’t go making up stories!”

Alice surprised Sam again when she snapped back at Arron, "I bet there was much more to it than luck! You don't get a powerful class like hers by being lucky!"

Arron's face flushed with anger at Alice's outburst as he started to retort. Sam cut him off by holding up a hand and saying, "Pain. The cost of my power was pain," she shuddered at the memory of the blue grass entering her body, "There was an insane amount of pain that brought me to where I am now. Like, thousands of hot needles shoved slowly into my eyes, my fingers, toes, they bored into my bones…" She trailed off. Then, looking Arron dead in the eyes, she said flatly, "I am not some lucky girl; I have done nothing but suffer and fight to stay alive since the day I arrived here." Looking at Alice, she said, "I'm no hero either. I am just a normal person who has been alone and afraid since arriving in the forest. All I want is to get somewhere safe and away from all of this," she waved her arm around at the forest, "at least for a night or two."

"I meant no offense," Arron started, but Sam waved his sentiment away with her hand, a tired smile on her lips.

"I am the one who should be sorry. I didn't realize just how stressed I have been." Sam smiled at Alice, "I'm glad I met all of you and could save you from the wolves." Pulling the now-cooked Deep Hunter meat from the fire, Sam produced a small leaf bowl of ink and dipped a corner of the cube before taking a large bite.

Alice and Arron watched in fascination as Sam moaned in pleasure as she chewed and swallowed. Sam then released a very unladylike belch, which caused Alice to jump a little.

Arron looked at the jerky-like chunk of wolf haunch he had roasted and said, "I'll take you up on those steaks if you're still offering."

"Sure," Sam said, gesturing to the small flat stone she had placed them on, "be my guest."

Arron took the offered steaks, and after removing the wolf haunch and tossing it into the fire, he skewered the steaks and began roasting them. Looking to the sky, he said, "It will be morning in another hour or so; we'll break camp then. That should get us over halfway to the road to Helms Peak before nightfall," he looked at the pile of burning corpses, "even with us burning the bodies I'm not confident the smell won't attract other predators."

"Sounds fine to me," Sam said, turning to Alice, "you want a piece?" She offered the cube of poisonous meat to Alice, who, after only a short hesitation, pulled off a piece with her hand, dipped it in the ink, and took a tentative bite. When she froze from paralysis, Sam touched her arm and channeled her repair skill into her. The tiny bit of ink she had consumed hadn't been enough to counter the paralysis, but for the most part, she was in no danger with Sam healing her.

Alice recovered a few seconds later and exclaimed, "You're right! It is delicious!"

CHAPTER 10 — "So much for LNT."

After enjoying her meal, Sam settled into a cross-legged position on the ground by the fire and closed her eyes. She wondered why she had not received a safe zone notification. Still, she figured it might have something to do with her conversation with Alice. She listened to the conversation happening around her as she meditated.

"Is she asleep?" Arron's voice was a whisper.

"No, only deep in meditation," Alice answered. She didn't bother to whisper.

Arron hissed but didn't speak after that.

Sam had two mana threads pointed at each of them, ready to attack at any sign of aggression. She barely managed to keep from jerking when Alice reached down and grabbed one of the threads next to her. Sam felt a strange tug in her mana core. It felt to Sam like Alice was trying to draw mana from the thread in her hand. After several failed attempts, the woman released the thread and lay down on her bedroll as if nothing had happened. Alina, who had woken up again to eat, also went back to sleep. Arron stayed up with Sam and kept the fire stoked.

Sam kept a careful watch on all of them for the next few hours until morning.

***

When the sun climbed over the horizon to begin its slow arc across the sky, Arron asked Sam, "You wouldn't happen to have some more of those steaks, would you?"

Uncrossing her legs, Sam produced four steaks and handed them to Arron without responding.

They sat in silence as Arron cooked their breakfast on a camp skillet. Sam poked the lightly snoring Alice, waking her up for breakfast.

Handing her a steak on a wooden plate, Arron cleared his throat before saying, "I am truly grateful to you for saving us, Sam. I'll not lie; Last night was likely going to be our final night alive if it weren't for you. So, um, thank you…again."

"Pretty sure this isn't the second time you thanked me," Sam said with a wry smile.

"Oh, uh, isn't it, though?" Arron acted surprised.

"Nope. You just told me to stay away, and when that didn't work, you tried to swindle me out of a dozen or more kills," Sam smiled at Arron; it wasn't a friendly smile.

Arron sputtered and mumbled a few things that Sam ignored. She was thinking about how her linguistics skill had translated the word 'dozen.' What she had actually told Arron was, "You swindled me out of two more than two past an even ten kills." There was no magical translator; she was speaking the language. Sam summed that interesting tidbit of knowledge up in one brilliantly enlightened thought, *"Huh."*

"I'm sorry, what?" Sam realized Alina had asked her a question while she was lost in her musings.

"Thank you, Miss Samantha…for saving me."

"Oh, don't mention it. I was kind of impressed at how long you stayed on your feet after losing an arm. When my arm was bitten off the first time, it sucked," Sam said absently, not really into being thanked for being a decent human.

Alina stared at her, "the first time?"

Alice snapped her fingers, causing some grease from the steak she was eating to spatter on Sam's cheek, "that's right! You were missing most of an arm after your fight with the alpha. I didn't see when the beast bit off your arm, but I bet it was awful."

"Oh, that's the second arm I've lost this week. And it didn't bite off my arm. I cut it off for a reason that I am not going to share, so don't ask," with that said, Sam bit into her own steak, letting the delicious grease dribble down the sides of her mouth. She ignored the open-mouthed stares and enjoyed her meal.

***

The party headed out shortly after breakfast. It would take a day and a half to get to the closest road, and from there, it would take the same time before they arrived at Helms Peak. Arron did warn Sam the last five kilometers were up a winding path through a mountain pass.

Sam was on edge traveling with these people but was still excited; she would get to see her first city in this new world.

When they stopped for a midday meal, Sam decided it was time to get some answers to some of the questions plaguing her since arriving in this new world…like the actual name of said world. She picked the person who seemed most likely to talk.

"So, Alice, where are all of you from? Helm's Peak?" Sam asked, moving beside her as they hiked and matched her pace.

After a furtive glance toward Arron, who nodded, Alice answered, "We aren't. We are just passing through and need some coin, so we took a beast culling job from the local guild hall."

"The contract didn't mention an alpha, much less an elite," Arron gruffed.

Making sure Arron was finished speaking, Alice continued. She told Sam a quick version of how they were on their way to a tournament that would be held in roughly six months on an island kingdom called Makaria.

Sam was secretly zooming her map around as Alice spoke and was pleased to see that the names of the two forests, the river, and the kingdom they were in had been updated. She zoomed out as far as she could. Still, unfortunately, neither Helms Peak nor Makaria could be seen in the obfuscation covering the untraveled portions of her map. She wasn't interested in the tournament, but the island kingdom sounded nice. *"I wouldn't mind chilling on a beach for a while after the shit I've been through lately."*

Sam interrupted Alice before she could go into details about the tournament, asking, "Do you also call this planet PN4O9VSCA?" Sam had no idea what the number represented; it was the stupid code that stayed at the top of her damn map. The number or alphanumeric code was also etched on every System-generated piece of equipment she had, like a serial number of sorts. Even the items from her loot skill had it on them, except on those items, it read (S.A.M.) PN4O9VSCA in such a small print, the lettering looked more like a blemish than actual lettering. It was driving her nuts. She knew it had to stand for something but didn't have the first clue what it was.

Alice looked at Sam like she was an alien, which she technically was, before slowly shaking her head. "No, we don't call it that. What a strange thing to call a planet. I cannot think why someone would want to call Hallista such a thing."

"Yes!" Sam inwardly cheered. The lettering on her map now read: [HALLISTA] PN409VSCA. She now suspected the number was either a point of origin stamp or her system ID.

Sam had an idea, "you wouldn't happen to have a map of the region, would you?" she asked the group, "or any map for that matter. Maybe I can find something I recognize on it that will help me get back home."

***

Unfortunately, the group didn't have a map. They had a journal where they recorded their map as they traveled. Arron reluctantly let Sam look through it. Sam examined it closely, comparing it to her map, but nothing updated. She figured it was because the sketches were too crude, or maybe her skill didn't work that way. Alina mentioned the Cartographers Guild had an office in Helms Peak, so Sam decided to try going there once she was settled in the city.

As they hiked, Sam gleaned little bits of information. Helms Peak was a border town between Orlina and the Beast Lands. At the name, Sam assumed the beast lands meant it was a savage land full of…well…beasts; she was wrong. The beast lands were simply a region where nomadic tribes of beastkin roamed. There was even a good bit of coin to be made if you could convince the tribes to trade with you. That isn't to say it wasn't dangerous.

Just the entry point of the region was level eighty to one hundred, and it wasn't recommended for under-leveled travelers to enter without a high-level escort.

Sam listened as the others discussed gossip they had picked up in Helms Peak about travelers disappearing from the road, snatched up by beastkin. Still, Alina insisted it was the city guard or Adventurers Guild trying to frighten citizens and merchants into hiring adventurers as escorts.

When Sam asked why anyone would want to live in a border city if traveling outside the gates was dangerous. Alina scoffed, "Because of the coin, of course!" Came her quick reply. "I heard entry-level guards make a whole gold per month! And if they serve for five years, they are given a year's wages and twenty acres of land!"

Arron interjected, "I doubt it's that much, but you probably aren't too far off." He hopped over a fallen tree and continued, "Higher pay means higher prices. Ultimately, the merchants and royalty always come out on top."

That statement left Sam confused, "aren't you a merchant? Alice said you are a blacksmith."

Arron smiled, "Aye, that I am. I'm just a little short on funds at the moment. I'm waiting on some investments to pay off." He glanced at Alice for the briefest of moments when he said it.

***

The rest of their day went on uneventfully, and they hiked until the late evening. They found the campsite Arron's group had used on their journey the previous night.

"So much for LNT," Sam thought when they arrived at the cleared area, complete with left-over rubbish and chopped-down trees repurposed into benches surrounding a still slightly smoldering campfire. *"Not that I have been that much better, but at least I clear up my campsites and don't leave trash or a smoldering fire behind."*

Seeing Sam's disapproving glare at the surroundings, Arron said, "We weren't planning to be gone that long, but we found the trail of some wolves when we were scouting and knew we couldn't waste time. Time is coin, after all."

Sam seriously doubted the validity of his words but didn't say anything. Instead, she moved to one side of the cleared area and produced her own firepit. She threw some of the firewood she had been gathering as she hiked into the stone ring and had a small campfire going in no time. It was clear she would not be joining them by their fire that night. Even Alice, who had so far stayed close to Sam the entire trip, had the good sense to realize she wasn't wanted. Sam didn't care if the woman shared her camp but wasn't going to invite her over either.

Sam did not receive a safe zone notification even after she put up her lean-to. Alina had mentioned, in passing, something about them being too close to civilization for the system to activate a safe zone. The way the woman wouldn't meet her gaze when she said it made Sam suspicious. Too many questions, not enough answers. She knew tonight would be another sleepless night of meditation. That didn't bother Sam, and she relaxed by the fire as her steak roasted. Listening to the sizzling of the meat as it cooked, along with the sounds of the forest, put her mind at peace.

Arron, however, was not at peace. He was ranting about what he would do to the Guild master for posting such a dangerous contract with no level restrictions. He was right in the middle of a particularly graphic description of how the hot tongs he shoved up the man's ass would cause his bowls to explode when he abruptly stopped mid-sentence.

The sudden silence was broken by Alina's scream!

Sam jumped up and looked at Arron in stunned horror. His mouth opened and closed like a fish, but no sounds came. There was a bloody arrowhead protruding from his temple. Sam watched helplessly as his eyes, wide and full of surprise, became empty in death.

***

Even as Arron's lifeless body slumped to the forest floor, Sam detected another projectile flying from the trees in her mana sight, pulsing red with mana and heading straight at Alina. Sam tried to yell a warning, but it was too late, and her mana threads were too far away to deflect the arrow.

To her credit, Alina sensed the arrow and reacted quickly, dodging out of its path. To everyone's surprise, the arrow changed its trajectory mid-flight and hit Alina just above her collarbone. The arrow didn't penetrate much, and Alice, who had jumped behind Alina, grabbed it to pull it out.

Sam saw the red energy in the arrow glow brighter and screamed at the pair, "It's going to explo—" She hasn't gotten the word out when the arrow did just that. It wasn't a large explosion, only sounding like a loud bang, but it was enough to blow half of Alina's head off and splinter some of her armor.

Alice was thrown to the ground by the force of the explosion. Her hand and most of her jaw was missing, and Sam could see shrapnel from Alina's armor in the woman's upper torso. So far, only seconds had passed, and two people she traveled with were dead. Sam was frozen in shock.

A voice boomed through the dusky forest, yanking Sam from her shock, "dammit, Lita! I said keep the fucking healer alive, you stupid fuck! Pip, get in there and kill the other one. Lita, go give the healer a potion, ram it down her throat if you have to! I swear if she dies, I'm taking it out of both of your pay!"

Sam saw two people appear out of nowhere on the other side of the camp from her. One was a pretty young woman with brown hair. She had a bow in her hand and was dressed in dark green form-fitting leather armor. She looked at Sam with a smirk and walked over to kneel by Alice. Producing a health potion, she started carefully pouring it into Alice's destroyed mouth.

"They were right there the whole time, and I didn't even see them with my mana sight. I didn't think that was possible," Sam thought, then used identify on the woman.

'Bing' Ranger; [Level ??]; Hostile; Affinity: Fire; Gravity

The other person was a short, stout man with a scruffy blond beard and matching hair. He was also wearing leather armor; only his was brown. Dual bandoleers crossed his chest full of daggers.

'Bing' Rogue; [Level ??]; Hostile; Affinity: Wind

The rogue smiled widely at Sam as he approached her. He stopped when he was about five meters away and made a show of pulling out one of his daggers and licking the blade before pointing it at her, saying, "Don't worry, lass, this will only hurt for a second."

"Oh, you've got that right mother fucker," Sam thought, fighting back the entirely rational fear that gripped her. *"Am I just kidding myself? Can I really survive this? Maybe I can run...but I don't know where the other one is."*

With a flick of his wrist, the rogue, Pip presumably, sent a dagger flying toward Sam's heart, surprising her. She wasn't surprised at the attack; she knew it was coming. What surprised her was how...slow it was. The arrow had seemed slow also, not slow enough to dodge but slow enough that she had been able to track its flight. Watching the dagger fly toward her, realizing there was no way it would hit her, made her think, *"Have I already become that much more powerful just from one fight?"*

Sam held out her hand. Pip's dagger stopped just short of striking her outstretched palm. It was stuck in a construct Sam had been experimenting with to help her against Blade Tails if she ever encountered another one. She had created a sphere of ballistics gel, or at least that's how it functioned. It was her new defense against a kinetic force designed to absorb and dissipate attacks instead of blocking them outright. It was Sam's turn to smile at Pip.

"Shit! She's a mage. Dale, get out here and deal with—"

Pip's words were cut short when his entire body was peppered by as many mana spikes as Sam could fire. Her attacks didn't kill the rogue but did make him retreat toward the ranger, holding his forearms up to protect his head with his bracers.

The ranger Sam assumed was Lita grabbed Alice's legs and dragged the healer toward a tree for cover. Sam turned her attention to Lita and started sending mana spikes toward her. The spikes didn't have near the effect they usually did when she was fighting beasts and only seemed enough to harass the two combatants. Lita reluctantly released Alice because of Sam's attacks and covered her face like Pip had.

"Dale! Do something!" Lita shouted.

"That healer better not be dead!" The booming voice from before called out.

Sam was about to send a disk blade at Pip but had to duck and jump back when two spears of ice flew at her from the forest. Her only warning the attack was coming had been when the air around her grew significantly colder. The ice spears flew past with a zinging sound, leaving a trail of cold mist in their wake.

"I got her! Grab the healer!" Dale called out.

Several more ice spears came zipping in from the forest, forcing Sam to take cover behind a tree. She managed to stop one with a ballistic sphere. The temperature of the spear froze her construct instantly, and it shattered, sending the familiar spike of pain from mana backlash into her brain.

Sam was not exactly low on mana, but she knew she could not keep this up for much longer. *"What am I going to do?"* She was watching Lita and Pip with her mana threads. Dale had not shown himself yet, and that worried her. *"He could be circling around to flank me. If I run now, I might be able to get away from them,"* Sam closed her eyes and focused on her mana sight while trying to calm her breathing and enter meditation. She was going to fight, and she knew it. *"If I don't do this, I will regret it. It's not even for Alice, I don't think. It's for my own peace of mind."* She felt a spark of anger flare in her chest, replacing the lingering fear. These assholes killed two people she had just saved and tried to kill her. Just who did they think they were?

***

Pip gulped down a health potion and threw the empty container to the side. He knew it was wasteful, but he didn't care; he was pissed. That stupid girl had nearly killed him. At first, he thought her attack was a distraction so she could flee. That is until he noticed his health dropping steadily. The bitch was bypassing his armor enchantment somehow!

He grabbed the healer and finished dragging her behind a tree while Lita watched the tree the little bitch had jumped behind to get away from Dale's ice spears. Lita held her bow at the ready.

When Pip finished dragging the healer behind the tree, Lita backed around it slowly, not taking her eyes off where the mage was hiding.

"What kind of a mage is she? Did you identify her?" Lita asked through her teeth, "That attack was killing me! And where the fuck is Dale?"

"She's a Pathfinder, whatever that is. She's only level nineteen, too." Pip responded to her first questions.

"WHAT? Level nineteen? How could she…never mind… Dale will deal with her. He's probably circling around now." Lita shook her head in dismay. A level nineteen had forced them to fall back. She hoped word of this never got out.

***

Sam drank a mana potion to speed up her regeneration time. She had decided to switch from spikes to bolts since the spikes weren't penetrating the leather armor the two were wearing anyway. So there was no reason to keep using the spikes at such a high mana cost, considering she was using all her mana threads to fire them, which put her at 180 mana per second, even with her large mana pool and high regeneration rate, that still put her at barely fifteen seconds of sustained attack. So now she would use little teardrop-shaped energy bolts only slightly larger than her thumb. They only took one mana per cast. She just hoped they had the same distracting effects as her spikes had.

After scanning the forest for the elusive Dale and finding nothing, she attacked the other two killers. She had found them hiding behind a tree with her mana threads. The ranger stood beside a tree with her bow at the ready, staring straight at Sam's position.

"Here goes nothing." Sam thought as she ran out from her cover, sending a bladed disk out from one of her threads to cut the ranger's bowstring. She started firing arcane bolts at Lita, who drew her bow and loosed an arrow just as Sam's blade hit the string.

Several actions happened in quick succession. The blade disk hit the bowstring, snapping it. The arrow Lita fired stopped in midair after traveling less than a meter. The ranger covered her head to protect it against the bombardment of arcane bolts just as her exploding arrow was deposited at her feet by Sam's mana thread holding one of her ballistic gel constructs.

Sam continued sprinting toward Lita, keeping up her barrage even after the arrow exploded, knocking the woman to the ground, where she writhed in pain. Sam ducked under a slash from Pip as she ran past him. She drove both of her fully charged arcane daggers into Lita's chest. Armor or not, the daggers slid easily into the woman, and Sam received a kill notification an instant later.

'Bing' Ranger [Lita]; Level 48 Defeated. Bonus experience is awarded for defeating an enemy 20 or more levels above your own.

'Bing' Race Human has leveled up to Level 20, 5 free stat points received.

'Bing' Class Arcane Pathfinder has leveled to Level 21, with 10 free stat points received.

Sam had to roll away from an ice spear, barely dodging it in time. The spear was so cold she lost feeling in the upper part of her left leg when it grazed her hip.

Sam's numb leg prevented her from dodging a dagger strike from Pip when she came up from her roll. She felt a searing pain in her back when it hit home.

'Bing' You have been poisoned with Cyan Death Toxin! -100 hp/sec for 300 seconds; -100 sp/sec for 300 seconds; -100 mp/sec for 300 seconds. Additionally, your mana is now toxic, and using it will result in health and stamina damage.

'Bing' Crystal mana channels have negated mana poisoning and mana loss from Cyan Death Toxin. All other effects remain.

Sam jumped away from Pip and turned. He was looking at her with a huge grin.

"You're not so tough without mana, are you? I bet I could walk over there and cut your pretty little—" Pip's words were cut off for the second time that evening when Sam grabbed him with all her mana threads and yanked them together. She thrust her daggers into his chest just as she had done with Lita and twisted. Pip's eyes were still wide with shocked disbelief when she jumped back to dodge an ice spear.

Sam fell to her knees. The toxin's stamina drain was taking its toll. She felt a sustained blast of sub-zero wind wash over her and immediately lost all feeling in her extremities. As the wind continued, she felt her eyes freeze solid along with the rest of her body. It was both painful and numbing at the same time.

***

Pip was fumbling with a potion when Dale walked over to him, flecks of ice flaking off his blue-white robes. Pip's frozen fingers were making the simple act of removing a stopper almost impossible. Dale snatched the potion from Pip's hands and helped Pip drink it by popping the cork.

Pip managed to get another potion independently, and Dale moved away to check on Lita and the injured healer.

Once he had recovered enough to speak, Pip snapped, "dammit, Dale! What took you so long?"

Dale, who had already confirmed Lita was dead, checked that the healer was still alive, forcing another healing potion down her throat, and was now staring at the frozen woman when Pip spoke. He ignored Pip and said, "She's still alive."

"Who is? The healer? Good, at least we'll get paid," Pip said, struggling to his feet. The dagger wounds in his chest finally healed enough to stop bleeding. "What the fuck is a Pathfinder? That bitch fought like a level fifty battle mage at level nineteen!" He looked where Lita had fallen and sighed, "damn bitch got Lita too. I have to admit, I would have never thought it possible she would go down so quickly."

"The Pathfinder," Dale hadn't taken his eyes off the frozen woman, "she is still alive."

Pip took an involuntary step back, exclaiming, "Well, then fucking kill her!" To add action to his statement, he drew one of his daggers and started toward the woman, only to be stopped by Dale holding out an arm.

"Wait, I want to see what happens," Dale said calmly.

"Dale! Didn't you see what she can do? There is no telling what she's cooking up under that ice!" Pip was exasperated that his leader was acting so careless.

"Didn't you poison her?" Dale asked, turning to Pip.

"I, oh yeah, I did hit her with the good stuff," Pip said with an evil grin, then frowned when he remembered, "and it didn't fucking work!"

"It could have worked, but she just powered through it until I froze her," Dale retorted.

"All the more reason to finish her now while we have the chance, Dale." Pip was almost pleading now, "Let's cut our losses, kill the Pathfinder, grab the healer, and...wait, where is the healer?"

Both men turned to where Pip was looking. Their target, who had been lying against the tree, was no longer there. Instead of a bloodied young woman in healer robes, there was only a pool of blood on the ground.

"She couldn't have gotten far. Find her and bring her back," Dale snapped. He was no longer calm. "I'll deal with this one," he said as he gestured to Sam.

Pip was already rounding the tree Alice had been lying against as Dale spoke. Seeing his orders were being obeyed, Dale turned back to the frozen woman. He didn't see the pale grey figure land on top of Pip, its clawed fingers digging deep into the rogue's throat, stifling his scream.

Dale only made it two steps when a grey blur slammed into his side, knocking him to the ground. He tried to wrestle the creature off, but it was too flexible. Every time Dale thought he had the creature pinned, the slippery thing managed to get out of his grip. He could also feel his mana being drained as they grappled; he couldn't even cast a spell at the damn thing.

The struggle ended moments later when the creature managed to latch onto Dale's throat with its mouth. As he lay on the ground dying, Dale's final thought was, *"A Moonblight, but how?"*

***

A short time after Dale stopped twitching, the creature pushed itself from him, blood dripping from a mouth full of sharp teeth. Turning its attention to Sam's frozen form, it slowly stalked over to her and knelt. Jet-black eyes stared into the icy eyes of the Pathfinder. The creature leaned forward and sniffed, and a wide, toothy smile spread across its face.

The creature sat on its haunches, patiently waiting for its prey to thaw.

CHAPTER 11 — "Please don't give me their hides."

Sam was fighting for her life. She was frozen to her core, *"Wait, not my core. I can still feel my core, both of them,"* she wasn't sure what that meant or how she was still alive when all her organs were frozen. What she did know was the toxin was no longer active now that her blood was frozen. The countdown timer kept going, though, so there was that. Now, all she had to do was keep her brain from freezing.

Sam had instinctively focused all her healing energy on her head when she felt her extremities begin to freeze. Her mana repair skill told her that if her brain froze, she would be dead, so she put everything she had into keeping her brain alive. She was thankful that healing energy seemed to be an acceptable substitute for oxygenated blood, at least in the short term.

Focusing inward, Sam felt her cores. There was power there; all the energy she needed to survive this was right there, housed in two spheres of purple energy. There was only one problem: Sam could not reach it. Try as she might, every time she reached for the power to use it to increase her mana output, it was like her mind was diverted from it, not by any unseen force but by her. It was as though something inside her own mind knew it was wrong and stopped her.

A quick check of her health pool caused her some confusion when she realized her vital energy wasn't going down. It was her mana that was dropping rapidly. She watched, detached, as a steady stream of translucent numbers floated up from her mana bar. She tried to go as deep into meditation as she could. It wasn't difficult to do, given that her body was numb and her auditory and visual functions were frozen. There was only silent darkness around her.

Sam calmed her mind and tried to understand what was happening. *"How am I still alive? What is keeping me alive?* Looking back to her cores, she focused on the one in her chest. It was pulsing every second like it was a beating heart. Each pulse sent energy through her body, but she could see most of it dissipating before it could reach her extremities. She knew this was where she was losing some of her mana. It was not able to make a complete cycle. One thing she didn't see was the energy going to the core of her brain.

"Hmm, that could be a problem," Sam thought, turning her mental attention to the core at the base of her brain. This one was also pulsing but erratically like it was being shocked repeatedly. The erratic pulses were causing the energy flow to and from her central core to dissipate before they even had a chance to move. Only when they occasionally pulsed together

was any energy able to travel between them, sending energy into her extremities as it was supposed to. *"So, if the energies don't pulse in sync, they aren't able to cycle,"* Sam watched for a few more metaphorical heartbeats, then realized, *"The cycles are what allows my cores to produce mana! It's like a positive and negative energy flow or like a pump. My small core sends a pulse into my main core, telling it to release a certain amount of mana and where to direct it. At the same time, my main core sends a pulse back, confirming it did its job. The reason I am burning so much mana isn't because of the constant healing. It is because I am not subconsciously cognizant enough to keep my mind core synchronized to my main core. I bet if I get the two in sync, it will drastically reduce the mana needed to maintain my life force,"* she thought. She didn't know if this was true, but it was the only thing she could think of now. *"Okay, now how do I do this?"*

***

Sam focused all her mental energy on her mind core, poking and prodding at it. She was trying to 'feel' where the erratic pulses originated. Her mind core let her prod it as long as she wasn't trying to draw energy from it. The instant she tried to siphon the slightest amount of mana from the core, it locked down, and her mental probe lost contact with it.

When Sam finally managed to pass her awareness through the energized outer layer of her mind core, not to draw energy out but to inspect the core. When it opened and let her in, she was almost overcome by the emotions swirling around inside the sphere. Feelings of fear, sadness, anger, hopelessness, and resentment all bombarded her. She overcame the initial chaos of the negative emotions with a concentrated effort of will. As she slowly acclimated to the chaotic emotions swirling around her in her mindscape, she began to focus on each of them, focusing intensely to negate them.

Fear was easy; she was afraid she was going to die. Sam reached out and touched her fear. Raw terror slammed into her like a hammer, threatening to overcome her reasoning. It took a supreme effort of will, but an eternity of seconds later, she began pushing back with a feeling of hope. A hope that she would survive to see another sunrise. A hope that she will get the chance to explore this new world and maybe even others. Her fear eventually allowed her to begin to replace it with hope. The fear wasn't completely replaced, but it was becoming balanced with hope.

Pulling back a little, Sam could feel the cores were already more in sync, and the precipitous decline in her mana pool had slowed. Confident she was on the right track, she chose her next emotion, sadness. The instant Sam touched her sadness, it made her want to curl up in a little ball and cry forever. She had lost everything she had worked so hard to achieve. There was no firm to run, no friends to grab a meal or drink with, no hiking in a safe forest where the most dangerous encounters were tick bites. It was all gone; everything was gone in an instant. Sam had no idea how much she missed Earth or how much of her negative emotions she had been suppressing until now. Sadness was much more challenging to suppress than fear and took much longer. She replaced the sadness of loss with the happiness and wonder of a fresh start. She always enjoyed exploration, and now it was ingrained into her soul. She would undoubtedly make new friends; even if it was only for a short time, she knew it would be worth it. After what felt like hours, her sadness eventually balanced with her happiness.

Her cores were almost entirely in sync, which was good because Sam knew she only had the mental energy for one more push. She knew she should probably pick a more straightforward emotion than anger. Still, she knew she would have to face it eventually, so she resolved to enter her mind core a final time. Sam was unprepared for the blast of white-hot rage that poured over her like a tidal wave. This time, her emotion had a voice, "How dare they try to kill me! How could they kill Arron and Alina so casually? They will PAY! I WILL MAKE THEM PAY!"

Sam felt herself slipping away, losing control. She wanted to shatter the ice encapsulating her with her magic! Who cares if all her limbs and most of her body were destroyed? She could just build a new body after she killed those two! All she needed was her mind, after all!

Her mental energy was depleting quickly. All Sam wanted to do was agree with the voice and let her rage take control; then, she could…win and be free. She could kill and rage, and it would all be okay…

"No," she mentally whispered the word quietly but with resolution more to herself than the voice of her rage.

"What? You dare defy me?" the voice screamed so loud it was a mental attack, "you are a coward to your core! Would you just let them go free? After what they've done to you?"

"No," Sam said again, but this time with more conviction.

"Then what, coward?" The voice screamed, "What could a coward do that I cannot do better?"

"I will use you for strength of mind but not action." Sam was already channeling her inner peace through meditation, so she gathered it all and forced it into her mind's core.

Her anger resisted her peace, pushing back with hate and fury. The surface of her mind core began to crack under the strain of the two opposing forces fighting for dominance. But Sam knew she was not fighting for dominance but for equilibrium between the two emotions. She just had to convince her anger of that.

"I will never submit to a coward!" her anger shouted into her mind louder than ever.

Sam responded as calmly as possible, "I don't want you to. I want you to be my power, not my mind," to add a little more icing on the cake, she said, "Power has no need for reason. Power takes what it wants." With those words, her anger relented just a little, allowing her peace to enter her core.

"You're right. I take what I want…like the lives of everyone that has hurt me! I will show them all…I…will show…" The voice faded and was silent.

Sam was spent mentally but in good spirits, *"Who knew dealing with pent-up emotions to restore the synchronization between my two magical cores so I don't die after being frozen by an ice mage on an alien planet would be so exhausting? Certainly not me."* She thought ruefully.

Checking the mana flow between her cores, Sam was pleased. The cores were pulsing almost in harmony, and her mana had stabilized. She was going to survive. She mentally relaxed her mind. *"Now, how long does it take magical ice to thaw out?"*

***

The Moonblight yanked its clawed finger back with a hiss of frustration. "I can sense the mana. So much mana is right there! Why can I not take it? The other one was so easy. His icy mana still flows through me." The creature growled in frustration, "I need more mana, or she will take it back. Already, I can feel her presence crawling back like the pathetic worm she is. No, no, NO!" The Moonblight grabbed at its chest in pain.

She was coming. She was coming to take it away again. She was going to take the mana her way. The wrong way! She did not know how much he needed to be free; to feel again.

The grey figure pounded the forest floor, screaming its defiance at her.

***

Sam awoke on her back with a start and the worst brain freeze ever. "Shit, that hurts," she mumbled quietly so as not to exacerbate the pain in her head, "I feel like I got run over by a bus. And when did I fall asleep?"

The last thing she remembered was being frozen and, *"something about my mana cores…what was it?"* Her eyes opened wide, *"Alice!"*

Sam sat up quickly, her brain making her regret it, but she pushed the pain aside to look around. She sighed when she saw Alice tending a small fire. She was facing away from Sam, her forest green robes still bloody from the fight, and a cowl covered her head.

"Welcome back," Alice spoke without turning, "I'm glad you survived. Someday, you'll have to tell me how you survived being frozen solid for more than thirty-six hours."

Sam was surprised at how long she had frozen, but something else bothered her. "Alice, did your voice change? And where are the kidnappers? How are you even here?" Something was wrong with the way the robed figure moved as she stoked the fire; it was far more graceful than she remembered Alice to be. Still, she wasn't sure, so she identified Alice.

'Bing' Tenarian (Moonblight); Ice Mage, (Mana Reaper); [Nara Evander] Level 26; Suspicious; Affinity(s): Ice, (Neutral)

"Who the fuck are you, and what did you do to Alice?" The imposter was wearing her robes, after all.

Sam tensed as Alice, no Nara, stood and turned to fully face her. Sam took a sharp breath when the woman pulled her cowl back.

It was kind of Alice. Only not Alice at the same time. The woman in front of Sam carried herself quite differently than the diminutive healer she had portrayed before. Where there had been clumsiness and submissiveness before, there was now a confident woman who maintained eye contact.

"Damn girl," Sam thought, staring at Alice, who was now Nara. The woman was beautiful…in a not precisely human kind of way. Long jet-black hair framed an aquiline face with high cheekbones and a classical nose. Sam stared into Nara's deep blue eyes which were slightly larger than was normal for a human. *"I bet those eyes get her laid a lot,"* she thought, then mentally added, *"Well if it weren't for the pasty grey skin and sharp claws. That's creepy."*

When Sam continued to stare at her long past the point of politeness, Nara babbled, "Look, I know what you're thinking, and it's not like the stories. I mean, it is like the stories but not for me. I can control the blight. I don't have to keep a soul crystal with me, see," she held out a hand and her claws retracted turning into regular-looking blue fingernails.

"I'm not sure—" Sam started but was cut off.

"We don't have to fight!" Nara's voice went up in pitch as she spoke, "I have control of the Moonblight. I could have taken your mana and drained you while you slept, but I didn't! You don't have to fear me. Please tell me you understand. I protected you because I wanted to, not because I had to. My contract is broken, or some of it is anyway. Please just let me explain before we fight."

Sam finally held up a hand, causing Nara to stop talking and take a guarded stance. "Whoa, hold up there," she told the nervous woman. "I just want to ask you a couple of questions." Nara relaxed, so Sam continued, "What is a blight, or I guess Moonblight, and can I see your fangs?"

***

Sam thought Nara's reaction to her questions was far too extreme. How was she supposed to know the woman didn't have fangs? She had plainly said moments before that she didn't 'drain' her while sleeping. And she looked, for all intents and purposes, exactly like a vampire, or at least what Sam thought a vampire should look like. Plus, her class was Mana Reaper, for crying out loud.

"I mean, I can't help it if she looks like a kick-ass vampire; that's on her," Sam stared at where Nara was crouched nearly ten meters away, still staring at her suspiciously. *"What's with that girl?"*

They had been this way for five minutes since Nara responded to Sam's questions, saying, "What do you mean what is a Moonblight? How can you not know? Also, I have no fangs! Why would you think I have fangs? Seriously, how do you not know what a Moonblight is? What are you, a daemon? No, even a daemon would know. You are something else, maybe a Child of the Light trying to trick me?" This was all said as she backpedaled to the other side of the clearing from Sam, crouched down, and erected a thin magical barrier of ice. Nara then just stared at Sam like she was a dangerous curiosity. Which is what she was still doing presently.

Not seeing an end to their standoff, Sam finally had enough. "Hi, over there, I'm not a daemon or a light baby or whatever. I'm just a regular old human mortal," she waved at Nara, "Sorry I asked to see your fangs. How was I supposed to know you didn't have any? You look just like the vampires I've seen in mov—that I have read about," Sam caught herself.

Nara asked from where she was crouched, "Tell me, where exactly did you say you were from? What was the name of the kingdom?"

"I'm from the Kingdom of America," Sam said. It was primarily true…sort of.

"And what is the current cycle?" Nara was staring intently at Sam.

Sam started to answer but stopped. *"What year is it? That's what she's asking. How the hell would I know."* Her linguistics skill wasn't any help, and nothing in her interface displayed the year or time. At least none she had found.

Sam went with the truth, hoping she wasn't making a mistake, "the current solar cycle, according to my kingdom, is 2023 AD." She knew she had fucked up when Nara began shaking her head.

"You lie. There are no kingdoms that use the sun to determine the cycle. This I know," Nara looked around, obviously looking for an escape route, while saying, "You are a Child of the Light. I should have known. You are far too powerful to be anything else. But I have never heard of a pathfinder and cannot sense the light tainting your mana."

"I'm an outworlder," Sam blurted and inwardly kicked herself, *"shit. I don't trust this girl, but damn, I need some answers, and I am so done with this charade!"*

"So, you are a Child of the Light then!" Nara sounded genuinely afraid. Panicked even.

"No, I still don't know what that is. I am an Earthling." Sam let that hang in the air for a minute. Again, Nara just stared at her.

Throwing her hands in the air in frustration, Sam said, "Look, Miss Ice Mage Mana Reaper, less than two weeks ago, I was transported to this planet in my sleep. I was nearly killed, given a class, and nearly killed again, and trust me, it has been a shitty time ever since!" She left out the whole System experiment thing; probably not the best idea to share that information. She continued, "oh, and guess what, out of the first three people I met on this new planet two of them died right in front of me within a day or so. The other turned out to not even be human, but some fucking Moonblight thing, and I don't have a clue what that is!" Sam couldn't hold the tears back when she thought about Arron and Alina dying. She wiped her eyes in frustration at her perceived weakness. *"Why am I suddenly so emotional?"*

Nara cautiously stood up from behind her flimsy magical barrier. "I…I think you are telling the truth."

"I am," Sam confirmed, still feeling abnormally emotional.

Nara walked over slowly to stand before Sam, who was trying and failing to look stoic. Nara hesitantly placed a hand on Sam's shoulder and said in a calming voice, "Arron and Alina were not good people, Sam. They, or at least Arron, would have forced me to drain you for your power if they thought they could have. I know you have no reason to believe that, but it is true," she looked to her right as she spoke, "either way their deaths have been avenged. It is more than they deserved but was necessary nonetheless."

Sam followed Nara's gaze to find five partially frozen bodies lying neatly in a row. That is when the realization hit home. *"Oh my god!"* Sam's mind nearly shattered, *"I killed someone!"* She fell to her knees with her face in her hands and broke down in sobs.

***

After looking back and forth between the preserved bodies and the crying Pathfinder a few times, Nara finally realized what was happening. She knelt beside Sam and placed her arm around her shaking shoulders, saying nothing.

Sam felt Nara trying to comfort her, but it didn't help. Her mind was in turmoil. *"I killed a person, a human…and did it without thinking. How could*

I have done that? I've never even hurt a person, much less killed someone. Hell, before I got here, I had never even hurt an animal. I was mostly vegetarian, for fucks sake." Her body shook with sobs of lost innocence. *"What has this place turned me into? The System read my mind...is this what I already was?"*

"Am I a monster?" Sam asked Nara, turning her tear-stained face to the woman.

Nara snorted out a very unladylike laugh. "No more than I am. At least we have empathy for those we are forced to harm."

Sam sobered up a little at that statement. *"Forced to harm...was I forced to harm that Ranger, Lita? I could have tried running, but then what would have happened to Alice, I mean, Nara?"* She looked at Nara curiously, "Would you have survived without me helping?"

"I truly don't know. Probably...maybe?" Nara was noncommittal. "My Blight got them when they were distracted and unprepared. My mana was out, so they would have discovered my true nature rather quickly, and the ice mage would have known how to counter me, so I cannot say I would have survived." She looked at Sam with a raised eyebrow, "Why did you stay and fight? Did you have to?"

"No, I could have run, and I did consider running," Sam admitted, "but I knew I would not have been able to live with myself if I abandoned you without at least trying to help."

"Do you regret killing a human to save someone like me? Now that you know I am not human?" Nara was staring intently into Sam's eyes.

"No," Sam said with surety, "you are a person just like me. Only, you know, grey and a little scary. So far, since we have met, you have given me no cause to believe you mean me any harm."

Nara nodded solemnly, "I only hope you still feel that way after I tell you what I truly am." She looked away, continuing to speak, "But enough seriousness. I see you have stopped leaking saltwater, so why don't I get some food going while you check your notifications. I'm sure you have many that need your attention." she reached over and grabbed a large piece of bark holding it out to Sam expectantly.

Sam placed a dozen steaks on the bark when she realized what Nara wanted. Agreeing with Nara and over her initial shock, Sam got comfortable and opened her notifications. There were a lot of them. She started at the beginning.

'Bing' Congratulations! You have created a new spell, Arcane Bolt [Level 1]. By repeatedly forming and firing small, charged bolts of pure arcane mana, you have permanently etched the pathway onto your core,

granting you the spell Arcane Bolt. You may now cast the spell Arcane Bolt at a reduced mana cost. Continued use of the spell may increase its efficiency and power. Experience has been awarded for creating your first spell. Good job, you have begun your path to becoming a true sorceress!

"Not that I'm complaining, but why hasn't that happened for all the mana spikes I've been shooting?" Sam glanced at Nara, who was tending the fire as she cooked. *"We're going to have a long Q&A session soon."* She went back to her notifications.

'Bing' Mana Caster has leveled up to level 14. All constructs cost slightly less mana to cast.

'Bing' Cyan Death Toxin has been quarantined by crystalline mana channels. You must expel the toxin from your body within five seconds, or all toxic effects will be applied simultaneously. This will result in 30,000 points of damage each to all vital energies.

Sam panicked and checked her energy reservoirs. Nothing out of the ordinary. They were all full, and there was no flashing warning or anything. She looked back at her notifications for an answer.

'Bing' Congratulations! You have learned Cold Resistance [Level 1]: By surviving being frozen for over five minutes, you have developed a natural resistance to cold. Although it is recommended not to freeze yourself in the first place, this resistance will assist you when you inevitably do so again. All damage from cold is reduced slightly. The slowing effect of cold is decreased slightly. Continue freezing yourself to advance this resistance.

'Bing' Cold resistance has leveled up to level 2. You are slightly more resistant to cold.

'Bing' Cold resistance has leveled up to level 3. You are slightly more resistant to cold.

'Bing' Meditation has leveled up to level 19. The regeneration bonus to meditation has increased. You can now meditate while performing more strenuous activities.

'Bing' Cold resistance has leveled up to level 4. You are slightly more resistant to cold.

'Bing' Mana Repair has leveled up to level 21.

'Bing' Congratulations! You have developed Synchronicity [Level Unknown]; Effects [Unknown].

"Well, that's not cryptic at all," Sam thought when she read the Synchronicity notification. A quick check of her stat screen told her it wasn't an ability or skill. *"So, what is Synchronicity?"* She sighed; time would tell, she supposed. She went back to her notifications.

'Bing' Poison resistance has leveled to level 13: You are now slightly more poison-resistant.
'Bing' Poison resistance has leveled to level 14: You are now slightly more poison-resistant.
'Bing' Cyan Death Toxin has become inert and will no longer affect you.

Sam read that notification twice. *"How did it become inert? I guess the timer ran out, but why didn't it affect me? Did it stop working when my blood froze? That has to be it."* She went back to scrolling, not wanting to dwell on how that toxin could have killed her many times over.

'Bing' Cold resistance has leveled up to level 5. You are slightly more resistant to cold.
'Bing' Cold resistance has leveled up to level 6. You are slightly more resistant to cold.

This continued until:

'Bing' Cold resistance has leveled up to level 25. You are more resistant to cold. Numbing effects from cold are reduced almost entirely. Slowing effects from cold are significantly reduced.

"Ha! Take that! Future ice mage attackers!" Sam did a mental fist pump. Her elation was short-lived, though, and her eyes narrowed when she read the following notifications.

You have resisted Mana Drain. Your mana channels were not breached.
You have resisted Mana Drain. Your mana channels were not breached.
You have resisted Mana Drain. Your mana channels were not breached.

"Breached mana channels huh? Resisted being drained...like by a Mana Reaper." Sam looked furtively at Nara, who hummed an unfamiliar tune while she cooked. *"Hmm, she seems relaxed. Surely, she knows I will find out she tried to drain me. Either way, she has some explaining to do."*

Sam started counting the notifications. There was a total of thirteen failed attempts at draining her mana. All but one had been done within a few minutes of Sam actually freezing, according to the time stamps. *"Time stamps! I'm an idiot! It's cycle...wait...what the hell does '19:07 3.86.763.4.13' mean? God, I hate not knowing these things!"* She looked closer at the time stamps; the last one had been much later than the rest. Nara's words rang in her mind: "I could have drained you." Sam wasn't so sure that was the case now...

'Bing' Hidden Quest [Survive the Ambush] completed. Your party has been ambushed by a more powerful force. Survive this encounter, and you will be rewarded:

Primary Objective: Survive – Passed

Secondary Objective: 50% of the party remaining.

Calculating contribution level...

Personal contribution 38%, experience points awarded accordingly.

Realizing there were no more level-ups and that that was the last of her notifications, Sam stood and walked over to the fire. She needed some questions answered, but first, she needed food. *"It feels like I haven't eaten in...oh yeah, like two days."*

***

Nara glanced up with a cheery smile when Sam approached. Sam noticed that even though the woman didn't have 'fangs,' her teeth were unnaturally sharp. *"Well, if she was human, they would be unnatural,"* Sam corrected herself.

Sam returned Nara's smile with one of her own as she sat on a log beside the fire. Nara handed Sam a wooden bowl piled high with several juicy cat and wolf steaks. Sam thanked her, and, not even bothering to pull a fork and knife from her inventory, she grabbed the first steak with her hands and bit into it, ripping off a large chunk. The tender, delicious muscle fibers felt like ambrosia on her tongue. When she swallowed the first bite, it was like it fell into a black hole of hunger that would never be sated. She took it as a challenge.

***

Sam ravenously devoured ten of the twelve steaks she had given Nara to cook before finally leaning back on her log and patting her stomach in satisfaction. "That hit the spot!" She exclaimed.

"You were hungry, I see," Nara stated the obvious.

Sam saw her chance, "So were you, it seems."

Nara looked at her half-eaten steak and back to Sam confusedly.

Sam elaborated, "I mean, you were hungry for mana. Unless you're going to tell me there was another Mana Reaper in the area while I was frozen."

Nara looked down at her hands, mumbling, "So you saw." It wasn't a question.

Sam simply said, "I'm listening if you want to explain yourself."

***

Sam watched Nara struggle briefly with what to say but figured the woman would come clean, and she did.

"Okay, fine," Nara finally said with a bit of exasperation. "I tried to absorb some of your mana once I regained control of my Blight. But it was because I needed mana to keep the bodies preserved! All the other times was my Blight trying to drain your mana, the greedy bastard."

Sam stopped her with a question, "What the fuck is a Moonblight? I thought that was your race."

Nara sighed, "I'm sorry; let me clarify some things for you so you understand better. I hope you like history lessons."

Sam grinned, "I do, actually."

Nara rolled her eyes and then explained what she was and her history, "I am a Tenarian; although I was born here on Hallista, my people are originally from Tenaris..." Nara noticed Sam's lack of recognition of the name, so she pointed upward.

"You're from the sun? No way!" Sam exclaimed, knowing full well that Nara was talking about one of the moons. She wasn't called a Sunblight, after all.

"No, idiot! The Tenaris moon! How could you think...oh, sarcasm." Nara cleared her throat and continued, "Yes, I, or at least my race, is from Tenaris. Of the two moons, it is the closest. The other is named Denaris, by the way." Sam was listening seriously now, so Nara continued, "Over a two hundred cycles ago, the King of Tenaris, in his relentless pursuit of power, gathered the most powerful mages in his lands to perform a grand summoning ritual. No one knows how the king learned of the ritual; it was like nothing any of the mages had ever seen, but despite many misgivings, the ritual was performed." Nara paused to poke at the fire with a stick as she collected her thoughts. Then continued, "the summoning was a resounding success. The Blight's were brought into Tenaris."

Nara stood, opening her robe and unfastened the bindings on her leather shirt until a dark blue pentagram was exposed in the center of her chest. There was a circle around the pentagram, and each of the points had intricate symbols in them. The whole thing was no bigger than Sam's palm.

Sam examined the magical tattoo with her mana sight. It was positively thrumming with power, reminding her a little of the ritual circle the Red Wolf had used to summon its power.

When Sam finished her examination, Nara explained, "Think of a Blight as a parasite. One that cannot survive long in this reality without mana. The more mana it has, the more powerful it will become. The summoning ritual didn't summon the Blight into Tenaris but into all living beings on the entire moon. All who have this mark," she pointed to her chest, "have a Blight inside of them feeding off their mana."

"I see," Sam said, remembering the first time she met Nara. "So, you cannot produce your own mana. That's why Arron wanted me to give you mana when we first met."

Nara grimaced, "Not exactly. Arron wanted me to see if I could fully drain you and take your powers. When my Blight is dormant inside the seal, he only feeds on what mana I naturally produce up to a maximum limit. When my Blight, Naris, is his name, needs mana, he will wrap himself around my core. But when he is full of my mana, he will open my core to allow me to absorb more while only keeping a maintenance amount to himself. Having him controlling my core allows me to charge my core with any mana type."

“Is that why your affinity says ‘ice’ in next to the neutral?” Sam interrupted.

Nara nodded, "Yes, I am now an ice mage, and I know all the spells the ice mage that Naris drained knew." Nara looked at Sam seriously, "When I take mana, I can control the amount I pull from my target. But when Naris takes mana, it almost always results in the subject's death because his mana limit is lifted once he has been released. It becomes a fight for his survival. He burns nearly fifty mana per second to stay alive in our reality."

“Holy crap! Just how much mana can he store?” Sam asked.

"At our current level, he can survive for about ten minutes before he has to feed." Nara shook her head, "he won't wait that long, though. He will immediately begin feeding on anyone and anything he can sink his teeth into. And if he manages to fully drain a person, he…we learn their spells." Nara looked apologetically at Sam, "The asshole tried to drain you many times before I could wrest back control. In his defense, he has been shackled by my contract, unable to leave the seal, for nearly a decade."

"So, the contract thing. Is that why you said you weren't safe? Also, how did you get from the moon to here on Hallista?" Sam thought briefly, "And why can't you or Naris take my mana?" Sam asked. Everything was clicking into place now. How Arron lost interest in her power when she said it was only skills she used instead of spells. Nara was trying and failing to draw mana from her mana thread. Nara was always cautious with how she spoke to Sam as if she wasn't supposed to say certain things.

"My people escaped here after the Blight summoning through teleportation circles. Most Tenarians can't keep their Blights under control without 'assistance' from the Church of the Light. Nor could the thousands upon thousands of beasts on Tenaris that suddenly found themselves host to a mana parasite. There were teleportation circles in every major city connecting to Hallista. Tenarians used them to flee the horde of Blights, overrunning their cities. Millions of my people died within hours…" Nara paused to look at the clear sky and sighed again, "I will tell you more later. Just know we are now called Moonblights and have been hunted and enslaved by the Church of the Light for as long as I can remember. My village was discovered a little over ten years ago. The Children of the Light, the followers of the Church of the Light, bound me and Naris under a powerful spell that only they knew how to cast and break. In fact, the only reason the contract didn't force me to kill myself was because I was incapacitated, and Naris took over when my core ran completely dry of mana." She held up a finger, the nail growing it into a razor-sharp claw, and answered Sam's last question, "I should be able to slice your mana channels wide open with this, and as far as I know, there is nothing you or anyone could do to stop me." She gestured for Sam to hold out her hand, "give me your hand and I will show you what happens when I try to drain you."

Sam looked at Nara like she had lost her mind, "Um, not no, but hell no!"

Nara clicked her tongue, "I won't be able to take anything, Sam. If Naris couldn't, then there was no way I could. And you forgot, I tried while you were sleeping. What are your mana channels made of? Diamond?" Nara threw up her hands in mild frustration. "I mean, I finally found someone who can generate mana faster than anyone I have ever seen, and I can't even get a taste of it." She looked at Sam with hard eyes, "I need mana, Sam. If I run dry again, I'm not sure Naris will be content to stay dormant. And if he takes control…" She let the statement hang.

Sam stared at her for a long moment before finally giving in. "Fine, show me," she said while thinking, *"She has already tried, I guess, and it didn't work, so why not."*

Nara wasted no time and hurried over to sit next to Sam. Taking Sam's right hand, Nara cut into the palm with her blue claw. Sam squirmed a little;

the damn claw tickled instead of hurting. It almost felt like a mosquito bite. Both women heard, and Sam felt a tink-tink-tink sound as Nara tried to cut deeper into Sam's palm with her claw. Nara looked at Sam as if to say, "See! I told you so!"

You have resisted Mana Drain. Your mana channels were not breached.

Sam giggled, pulling her hand away. "Stop it. That tickles."

"What are you made of?" Nara asked again.

"I have crystalline mana channels," Sam responded, closing the wound in her hand, "they are pretty much indestructible from what I can tell."

Nara just shook her head and looked down at her clawed hand dejectedly.

"I can give you some mana, but how will that affect your affinity?" Sam said. "Also, how do I give you mana?"

Nara perked up, "You only need to will it to me. You don't even have to be touching me. It can even be a spell, like a bolt of mana, so long as your intent is to give and not to harm." The Tenarian was practically bouncing up and down on the log as she spoke. "I will keep my ice affinity and spells as long as I don't fully deplete my core. If my core is fully depleted, then Naris will search for more mana."

Sam placed her hand on Nara's shoulder and willed her mana to flow into her. She instantly felt Nara pull at her mana greedily. After a brief panic, Sam realized she could regulate how much she provided and at what rate. Entering meditation, Sam started feeding Nara mana at twelve mana per second. She giggled again when Nara's back arched and she threw her head back, her eyes rolling back and her mouth open in what Sam assumed was ecstasy.

***

An hour and over 43000 mana later, Sam pulled her hand away from Nara's shoulder and stood up. *"I hope this wasn't another mistake in what is becoming a long list of mistakes,"* she thought, looking down at Nara, who was slowly leaving her blissful state.

"Fuck me," Nara whispered when she had recovered some.

Sam barked out a laugh, "From the look you were making, I would swear I already did."

Nara looked at her hands as if they were alien to her, "Your mana is…raw. I detect no affinity, yet it isn't neutral…it's like pure unstoppable power." Nara winced and growled to herself, "No! You cannot!" After composing herself and at Sam's raised eyebrow, she said, "Naris wants to meet you…and drain you."

"Never without my permission," Sam said absently in response to Naris's request as she stared at the bodies in the clearing. She knew they needed to get moving. They were too exposed here, and who was to say there weren't more bandits around. She was so distracted she jumped and was caught off guard when Nara spoke.

"You should loot the bodies," Nara said, looking at the corpses.

"I don't feel comfortable doing that—wait, how do you know I have a loot skill?" Sam asked.

"I didn't," Nara said with a smile, "but I suspected after watching you with the corpse pile, I can see your mana as you should have realized by now, and when you touched the pile of corpses, there was a definite mana transference. Also, the potion bottles you have are all System-generated. No alchemist-made potion provides such exact amounts of their given energy restoration. So, I guessed." She winked at Sam, "Thanks for confirming it for me." Nara clapped her hands together, "Now get to looting. I left their clothes and armor on, hoping you may be able to replicate some of it."

"Even Arron and Alina?" Sam had to ask. She was a little worried she was trusting Nara too much, especially about Arron and Alina essentially being slavers.

"You don't have to, but Arron still has my contract on him somewhere. Probably in his storage item, which he lied about being full to get you to say you had a storage item, too." Nara looked Sam up and down. "I would like to know where you keep your storage items. If it's where I think it is, then…wow…just wow."

"It's not like that, I—never mind," Sam started toward the corpses. She could only think, *"Please don't give me their hides! I'm not sure I am mentally or emotionally capable of handling that right now."*

CHAPTER 12 — "She never mentioned she liked it well done."

Thankfully, the hides of the five humans were not part of her loot when Sam used the skill. But holy crap, the bandits were loaded! She had started with Lita.

Human Ranger [Lita] Level 48 Items:

32-Gold; 147-Silver; 3-Bronze; Recurve Bow of Destruction [5 charge(s) remaining]; Elven Leather Armor of Stealth [43% Magic Resistance]; Elven Leather Boots of Stealth; Elven Gloves of Dexterity; Storage Bracelet [Soul Bound]; Large Mana Potion; Stamina Potion.

Everything automatically transferred to her inventory except the bracelet, which plopped to the ground in front of Sam. Picking it up, she was about to ask Nara how to check the contents when a screen appeared.

Would you like to claim this Storage Bracelet? Y/N

Sam chose 'No' and pocketed the bracelet. She moved on to the rogue, "Pip, was it?"

Human Rogue [Pip] Level 47 Items:

46-Gold; 295-Silver; Dagger of Mortal Dread x 3 [1 charge(s) remaining]; Dagger of Mortal Dread [0 charge(s) remaining]; Silver dagger [Fine]; Leather Armor of Concealment [61% Magic Resistance]; Leather Boots of Dexterity; Bracers of Agility; Storage Ring [Soul Bound]; Large Mana Potion; Vial of Cyan Death Toxin x 2.

The ring did not go into her inventory the same as the bracelet, but Sam expected this and caught it in the air this time. Pocketing the ring, she looted Dale next.

Human Ice Mage [Dale] Level 52 Items:

26-Gold; 18-Silver; 43-Bronze; Robes of the Wellspring; Leather Gloves of Heat Resistance; Leather Boots; Ring of Storage; Necklace of Mana Charge [0 MP]; Large Mana Potion x 2.

Sam decided not to read the items from Arron and Alina and only snagged the storage bracer when it appeared before her as she looted Arron. There was no storage item on Alina.

Once she was finished, Sam was exceedingly happy there were no human hides in her inventory.

Sam tossed Arron's bracer to Nara, who dove to the side to avoid it with a yelp. Staring at the Tenarian quizzically, Sam walked over to retrieve the item, and Nara explained.

"I can't touch his items. My contract is still partially active. That is why I also couldn't search their bodies." Nara confessed. She looked around nervously, "…we have been here far too long. I have been unable to create a safe zone in this place, which worries me because I don't know why."

Sam asked, "I thought it was because we were too close to civilization?"

Nara shook her head, "No, that's not it. Although it is true to some extent, you must be close, like within sight of a city. And if you're at a rest stop along a road, a safe zone is guaranteed even without a fire. It won't keep bandits like those out," she gestured to Dale and his companions, "but it will at least ward off many roaming monsters."

"Maybe it's because you want to drain me?" Sam said, half serious.

"Maybe," Nara was completely serious. "I'm really not sure, though." She waved her hand dismissively and changed the subject. "You should store the bodies. The guards at Helms Peak will want to know what happened. And I intend to collect on Arron's contract." She bent down and started lashing her backpack. Looking up at Sam, she asked, "Are you willing to continue traveling with me? At least to Helms Peak? I will gladly assist you in any way I can in acclimating to this culture in return for mana and food. You can keep the coin from selling the loot if you like."

"That would be nice, actually," Sam agreed. She didn't trust Nara but wasn't afraid of her either. Going to the bodies, Sam knelt down to place them in her storage. She stopped her fingers a millimeter from Lita's forehead, the woman's lifeless eyes staring at her. Sam experienced a short mental struggle, *"Okay, my storage is a separate dimension that is "linked" to my soul. It's not in my soul. I am not about to put a human corpse in my soul."* With her momentary misgiving out of the way Sam stored the five bodies in her inventory. Turning back to Nara, she asked, "How are you going to get into the city looking like, oh."

Nara's skin tone was now olive as opposed to the pale grey of her race. Her nails, eyes, and lips were still blue, though. She had changed from her healers' robes to simple leather clothes. Shouldering her backpack, she smiled at Sam. "You were saying?"

Sam identified Nara again.

'Bing' Sorceress [Nara Evander]; [Level 26]; Neutral; Affinity(s): Neutral

"So, you can change your identity completely then," Sam was slightly impressed.

"One of the perks of having a Blight," Nara said, adding, "Also, my race has always been shapeshifters. The Blights just enhanced our natural abilities."

Sam let the subject drop and gestured for Nara to lead the way and the two began walking.

***

Sam peppered Nara with questions as they hiked. "What should I do first when I get to Helms Peak? Is there an office where I have to register? What is legal? If I spit in the street, will I end up in jail? Is there a jail? Do you think I could break out of jail with my power…if there is a jail?"

Sam was talking excitedly and not giving Nara time to answer. "Are there nice cozy inns? Do they have roaring fireplaces with delicious things cooking over them? Oh, oh, oh, is there beer? Wine? Please tell me there is wine! I could drink an entire keg of beer and wash it down with a nice glass or ten of wine right now. Throw in some rustic vegetable and beef stew, and I am in!"

Nara grabbed one of Sam's mana threads and squeezed to get her attention. Sam, who had been circular breathing, stopped talking and looked at Nara sheepishly.

Once she had Sam's attention, Nara said, "There are indeed inns with fire and stew, although I do not know what beef is. I assume you mean meat of some sort, so yes, there will be stew, beer, and wine. But first, we need to fulfill Arron's contract with the Adventurer's Guild, so we have the coin for your, ahem, keg of beer." She ducked under a low branch and held another out of the way for Sam to pass by. Nara finished with, "you will almost certainly end up in jail if you eat and drink as much as you are suggesting. Even with your poison resistance."

"Meh, I was an attorney a couple of weeks ago, and if there is one thing we are good at, it's drinking. You might be surprised, my little Tenarian," Sam mused as they continued through the forest.

***

It wasn't long after their conversation they made it to the road. Sam looked both ways in surprise. The road was freaking amazing. She likened it to what one of the old Roman roads must have looked like in its heyday. Smooth, perfectly spaced cobbles layered a straight road as wide as a two-lane highway, complete with drainage ditches and a shoulder. *"Holy crap, building something like this must have taken decades. And how much must it cost to maintain this thing?"*

Sam was still staring at the road when Nara interrupted her thoughts, summing all of Sam's wonder into two words, "Terra Mages."

"Oh yeah, magic. How could I forget." Sam sighed; she was a little disappointed for some reason. *"Why do I care if it isn't a medieval engineering marvel. It was probably still tough to make and maintain."* She thought. All she said to Nara was, "makes sense. Shall we continue? There's still an hour or so of daylight left, and I have no issues traveling at night."

In answer, Nara turned toward Helms Peak and started walking. When Sam walked up next to her, Nara asked, "Do you have night vision?"

"Nah, I have Mana Sight, which is similar," Sam answered.

"Oh, I see," Nara walked for a time before asking, "Do you require sleep?"

Sam gave her a sideways glance and answered slowly, "No, I do not. Do you?"

"I do, but not much," Nara responded, then said, "Never tell anyone you don't sleep. That information alone gives away the fact that your vitality is over fifty and your endurance is at least thirty-five or higher." She poked a finger at Sam, "Also, you cannot fully eliminate the need for sleep. Even the immortals sleep occasionally. You should remember that and try to nap occasionally for your health."

“Immortals? You mean like gods?” Sam was curious.

Nara shrugged, "some call them that, but most are extremely powerful individuals who have reached over a thousand in vitality. And broken through their first evolution."

Sam did some bad math. *“I could be immortal before I’m level 70?”* She asked Nara, "What is an evolution? Do you really need it to become immortal?"

It was Nara's turn to glance sideways: "When your race meets a predetermined threshold, you are given the option to evolve. Many factors determine your level when it happens, but as a human, yours should be somewhere around level 200." Sam's eyes bulged at that number. Nara continued, "If you were to have a vitality of 1000 before that, you would not be immortal; however, your life expectancy would be measured in the tens if not hundreds of thousands of cycles. That is why most mortals focus at least one free point per level in vitality. In fact, if you tell me your vitality stat, I can estimate your maximum age…within a decade or so, assuming the cycles where you are from are similar to here."

Sam was curious, and since Nara had already guessed close to the number anyway, she told her, "It's 60 at the moment, but I could make it 75 if I wanted to."

Nara rubbed her chin briefly, mumbling, "Hmm, the vitality of 60, the endurance of at least 35, probably 40...right now, you will live at least 700 cycles."

Sam stopped walking. Her mind reeling with that bombshell. She had figured she would live maybe sixty more years if she was lucky and something didn't kill her first. *"Seven hundred years...and I have only just started my journey. I have got a lot of shit to rethink. Time to start planning for the very long game, I guess."*

Nara took a couple of steps before turning back to Sam. "Is this not common in your world?"

"It's barely more than a tenth of where I'm from," Sam said. She was still dazed and struggled to comprehend how long seven hundred years or cycles would be. And that was if she stopped progressing right now.

"Wow, that is just a flicker of life in this world. I should live for at least another four hundred cycles assuming I immediately go into hiding," Nara made a face, "which I will not do."

Sam started walking again, and they continued their journey well into the night. Sam silently contemplated her new reality as they walked side by side. Nara, on the other hand, stayed constantly vigilant on the road.

***

"What is that?" Sam was pointing at the large circular wall of stones standing a little over a meter high on the side of the road. She thought she knew what it was but wanted Nara to confirm.

"It is the final rest area before Helms Peak," Nara confirmed her suspicions. "We don't need to rest here, but I want to confirm I can create a safe zone if you don't mind. And we need to get our stories straight for the gate guards when we arrive."

Sam looked at the moons. It would be a couple of hours before the sun was up, so she figured it wouldn't hurt to have a meal. So, she pushed back her growing craving for beer, wine, and good food for just a bit longer and agreed to stop for a while.

Sam and Nara quickly had a fire blazing in one of the fire pits scattered around the large rest stop. They were alone, but there were signs that a caravan had passed through recently from all the piles of scat from the beasts of burden and a few broken clay pots strewn about. Once the fire was going, Sam pulled out her lean-to and a couple of log stools she had made, placing them close to the fire.

The two women skewered a steak on giant forks Sam had crafted using her skill. Nara marveled at the creation and was blown away when she learned Sam had made it herself from her mana.

"Samantha, you are truly a wonder. You will be the most sought-after adventurer on this planet if word of your abilities gets out," Nara said almost absently, then thought about it, "that is if you aren't hunted down and experimented on first."

Sam filed that information under Adventurer Good, Experiment Bad. She continued cooking her steak, wondering if they could run the rest of the way to Helms Peak and how long it would take when the notification they had both been waiting for finally came.

'Bing' Temporary Safe Zone recognized. This campsite exceeds all requirements to grant the user(s) temporary System protection for 2 hours unless the fire is doused. Protection level 3: All sound, scent, mana, and light the occupant(s) create inside the perimeter will be obscured from all creatures with hostile intent during the 2 hours this safe zone is in place. Hostile creature(s) will be prevented from entering the safe zone accidentally. The System will inflict a 15% movement penalty on any hostile(s) that breach the perimeter. The occupant(s) will be notified if any hostile(s) breaks the border of the safe zone. Attacks inside the safe zone will not remove the obscuration effect. The safe zone diameter is 100 meters.

Nara let out a breath. She had apparently been more worried than she let on to Sam. Now more relaxed, the two women ate their meals comfortably. Sam finished first and pulled out Arron's bracer for something to do.

Would you like to claim Storage Bracer? Y/N

Choosing "yes," Sam tried to mentally look into the bracer, and a screen opened up like an inventory screen in an RPG back on Earth. Nara was right; this item still had nearly twenty slots open. *"Lying sack of...well, best to not think ill of the dead,"* Sam was still frustrated with herself. She had let her judgment lapse because she was so excited about meeting people in this world.

The bracer was full of many blacksmithing supplies, including bars of various metals. There was a lockbox but no key, so Sam left it alone. There were a couple of changes of clothes and some rations. Then Sam found what she was looking for.

"Wait, what?" Sam had only caught the last of Nara's statement.

"My contract," is it in there?

"You mean this?" Sam asked, removing a small scroll from Arron's bracer. Looking at it curiously, Sam broke the seal with a quick slice of her magic and opened the scroll to read what it said. Nara screamed for her to stop, but it was too late.

'Bing' You have released Nara Evander from her blood contract. As the current owner of the contract is deceased and has not transferred the contract to you before dying, the contract's creator will be notified. This contract is now void, and another contract must be made if you want to control Nara Evander. Contact the Church of the Light if a more detailed explanation is required.

This was followed by.

'Bing' You have released a Tenarian Moonblight from a divine contract. You have done this knowingly or unknowingly without the authority to do so. The Church of the Light has been informed. Visit the nearest Church of the Light temple to receive your punishment.

“Oops,” was all Sam could say.

Nara just buried her face in her hands and moaned.

***

Lifting her head from her hands, Nara said, "I'm aware you aren't from this world, so there is no way you could have known what you were doing, but making an enemy of the Church of the Light isn't something—" Nara stared at Sam, "what are you doing?"

Sam was sitting cross-legged with her eyes closed. She was waving her hands around, her fingers drawing intricate patterns in the air. Sam was mana crafting, and it was taking her total concentration.

The scroll started producing magical energy as soon as the system message appeared. The bright energy flew away toward the sky as the scroll dissolved in her hands. Sam had seen this in her mana sight and realized the bright pulses of energy the scroll produced were probably the messages to the creator and the Church.

Reacting instinctively, Sam formed an umbrella-shaped barrier to stop the pulses of light energy from getting out. And it hurt! The power of the light was no joke. Sam's brain felt like it was on fire as each pulse hit her barrier, sending shockwaves of spell backlash into her mind. She quickly turned on meditation and started weaving constructs to keep the pooling light mana from escaping from under her umbrella.

Sam had missed the first few light pulses while reading the notifications, but she couldn't worry about those right now. It was all she could do to keep the light contained. She felt a burning pain start behind her eyes, but she kept pushing through.

Eventually, the scroll finally dissolved, the pulses growing weaker and weaker as it did. The light magic she had trapped in it slowly dissipated from her umbrella. Sam slumped a little; she was utterly exhausted and covered in sweat. The power from that little scroll was no joke. *"If that is just a small part of what the Church of the Light can do, I don't want to see their real power. Whoever made that scroll is probably lightyears ahead of me in magical power. They could probably vaporize me and Nara with a thought...speaking of Nara."*

Sam opened her eyes to see an open-mouthed Nara squatting in front of her, staring at her intently. Sam jerked her head back, asking, "What? Do I have something on my face?"

Nara reached out and brushed a finger across Sam's cheek without a word. It came back covered in blood. This prompted Sam to wipe her face, and when she saw the amount of blood covering her hands, it caused her to look down. Her lap was covered in blood. She growled in frustration, "Dammit! I go through clothes faster than a toddler through diapers!"

Nara asked, "How did you contain the magical discharge from a binding scroll? The priest who bound me had to be at least level 150 or greater..." She trailed off and offered Sam a torn piece of cloth and her canteen.

Sam took the items and started cleaning herself. I don't suppose you still have that cleanse spell, do you?" She asked Nara hopefully.

Nara shook her head. Sam sighed and continued cleaning the blood off her face and clothes.

While she cleaned up, Sam told Nara, "Some of it got through." When Nara looked at her questioningly, she explained. "The message, some of the light escaped before I could trap it."

"Let's hope it wasn't enough for the church to act on," was Nara's only response.

She didn't sound overly worried, so Sam let it drop and finished cleaning up. Nara offered to help wash her back, but Sam mentioned no blood was on her back. Nara didn't push her luck and let Sam finish getting as much blood off as she could.

***

"YOU NEED TO EAT WHAT?!?" Sam screamed.

Nara looked around furtively before responding, "Keep your voice down."

"We're in a safe zone," Sam reminded her, "And no, I will not! When exactly were you planning on telling me you eat human flesh?!?!"

"They don't have to be dead! I need a little, maybe a kilogram, every few weeks to sustain my metabolism. Otherwise, I will transition into a Blight Craven and lose control! I—"

Sam cut her off, “A kilogram is not a "little!" And how many freaking forms do you have? You’re like a kaleidoscope of death!”

“I am a natural shapeshifter! I have many forms! There is no shame in that!” Nara had tears in her eyes, “And I have no idea what a kaleidoscope is. But I am not a monster! I would never kill a human for food! That’s why I asked you politely.” She curled her knees to her chest and cried quietly.

Sam didn't know how to feel. On the one hand, Nara had come clean with the fact that she would now have to consume human flesh to survive since her contract was no longer blocking that particular aspect of her race. Alternately, though, she needed to eat humans to stay…human? More human? Human-like? *“This world is just one curveball after another,”* she thought, her mind in turmoil.

Sam looked at the crying woman next to her and sighed for what felt like the hundredth time this week. She placed a hand on Nara's shoulder, causing her to look up. Sam smiled and apologized, "I'm sorry I snapped at you. I have been trying to roll with all of this," she gestured around her, "but your…proclivity. It caught me off my guard."

Nara sniffed, looking every bit like a whipped puppy, and Sam had to chuckle a little, saying, "I mean, come on, Nara, you did just tell me you eat human. Surely, you knew how that would sound to a human."

Nara sniffed, “I know. But I didn’t want you to find out and think I kept it from you.”

Sam searched her feelings and concluded she didn't think of Nara differently now that she knew about her dietary needs. She decided to roll with it just like everything else. So, she said, "Okay, but I'm not going to let you eat any of the bodies in my inventory," she held up a hand when Nara opened her mouth to protest, "They were sitting out for days. I don't care if you kept them frozen; it is still disgusting. Besides, you've wanted a piece of me since the first day, so—"

Sam summoned the Blade Tail from her inventory. When the body of the large cat appeared, Nara yelped and jumped behind Sam. Laughing a little at the woman's antics, Sam pried open the Blade Tail's mouth. The cat's jaws were still limp and pliable, proving that her inventory was storage and suspended animation. Reaching inside the mouth of the creature, Sam found what she was looking for and pulled her severed appendage out, displaying it proudly to Nara, who looked at the bloody saliva-covered arm in disgust.

“Oh, give me a second,” Sam grabbed her canteen and cleaned off her arm, the severed one.

As Sam cleaned, Nara commented, " I didn't believe you when you said you killed a Blade Tail. They are notoriously elusive and hard to finish off. Most of them escape before they can be killed when they are found." She moved from behind Sam and stroked the cat's midnight-black fur respectfully. "Such a beautiful animal and its fur is so soft," she mumbled.

"It's not beautiful when trying to eat you," Sam said. She handed her now clean arm to Nara, who took it gingerly with a weak smile.

Nara looked at the arm and back at Sam, smiling proudly like a parent who had just given their child an amazing gift. Sam's smile turned to a frown when Nara continued looking back and forth between the arm and Sam.

"What's wrong?" Sam asked, "Aren't you going to eat it?"

It was Nara's turn to be incredulous, "you want me to eat it raw? I told you! I'm not a monster!"

Sam had the good grace to look chagrined at Nara's exclamation. But she couldn't help thinking, *"How was I supposed to know that? Oh, Sam, I'm a Moonblight. My kind are hunted for the evil mana parasite that lives inside us! Also, on a side note, we devour human flesh."* Sam grumbled internally, *"She never mentioned she liked it well done. So, fine, eat my arm, and while you are at it, why don't you cook it first so I get to listen to it sizzle and smell my skin burning again."*

Nara did just that.

Sam wasn't sure what was worse. Watching Nara fillet and cook her arm or how many times she exclaimed how delicious Sam tasted as she devoured it.

***

"For the last time, no," Nara said with exasperated finality.

The two of them were back on the road and running quickly. Both were ready to be done with the wilderness for a while, and the quicker they got to a hot bath and soft bed, the better.

"Oh, come on. Please! Just for a minute! Remember, I let you eat my arm." Sam had been trying to get Nara to use her shapeshifting abilities to grow fangs for over an hour now. Still, the Tenarian was insistent it didn't work that way. Now Sam was just enjoying pestering the poor woman.

"Why…are…you so insistent?" Nara asked between breaths.

"You would look so freaking cool with fangs! How can you not see that?" Sam exclaimed.

Nara didn't respond. She was too focused on keeping up with Sam's "medium" pace, pushing fifteen kilometers per hour.

Sam's attention was diverted a moment later when the entrance to the mountain road came into her view. *"Finally!"* She thought with mounting excitement. They had run past several trade caravans, the largest having nearly fifteen wagons, under the watchful gaze of the guards, along with a few quizzical stares from some of the merchants driving the wagons.

The women slowed at the base of the mountain pass, and Sam pulled Nara off to the side of the road for a final review of the stories they had come up with and to "top off" the Mana Reaper with mana.

They looked around to ensure they were alone and not in earshot of the passing caravans and riders peppering the road. Sam started, "Just to be clear, we are two traveling adventurers coming to seek our fortunes in the surrounding forests."

"Yes," Nara confirmed, "it is a stretch at our low levels, but the guards will probably just think we are crazy and let us through." She snapped her fingers, "Oh, I almost forgot! We need to pull out some coin to bribe the guards or for the "entry fee," as they call it." She looked at Sam, "Arron did have some coin in his bracer, didn't he? What about the bandits? I haven't asked because I didn't want to pry."

"I have…" Sam checked the totals in her inventory, "125 Gold coins, 612 Silver coins, and 240 bronze coins." She looked at Nara, "is that enough?"

"Did you rob a caravan before you met us?" Nara asked.

Sam laughed until she realized Nara was serious, "No, no, no, it's my loot skill. It generates currency for me."

Nara's eyes widened, "that is a very convenient aspect of your skill. I don't think I have ever heard of a loot skill providing currency."

"Maybe it's because people with the skill want to keep that particular bit of knowledge a secret," Sam said helpfully, "like I do."

Nara caught her meaning and said, "I understand. Don't worry, your secret is safe with me. And yes, to answer your first question, that is more than enough coin." Nara went into lecture mode, "You have enough gold to live comfortably for years. Do you remember when we were talking about how much city guards get paid?" Sam nodded, "Well, you have over ten years of their salary in gold and six in silver. It's ten bronze to a silver and ten silver to a gold. A single silver coin will get you two meals, a bath, and a warm bed for a week. A couple of bronze will get you enough to drink all night at almost every tavern in the middle district of the city, and even the upper district wouldn't dare charge more than five for a drink."

Sam processed that information, and they discussed their plan a bit longer before Sam fed Nara enough mana that she could defend herself if she was found out. She had already told Sam not to interfere in whatever happened if her true nature was discovered, and Sam had reluctantly agreed to her request.

Two hours and over eighty-thousand mana later, they walked back out of the trees and continued. Nara had a broad smile on her face and a glow about her. They had strapped weapons on and donned their backpacks to make it look like they had no storage items. They now looked every bit like a couple of road-weary travelers.

Sam could only shake her head as the Tenarian wobbled a little when they started running again. Sam laughed to herself as they ran. *"Getting mana must feel the same as leveling up. I guess I should feel pretty good about myself. I essentially just gave a girl a two-hour orgasm."*

***

The final five kilometers went by in a flash for Sam. When they rounded the last bend in the road, the cliff faces no longer blocked her view. Sam stopped on the road and looked up at Helms Peak in wonder. She was taken aback at the sheer grandeur of the sight before her.

The walls of the city were imposing. Built from a seemingly single piece of stone, they rose into the sky, casting a long shadow across the surrounding area. It was as if they had been carved directly from the mountain itself. Towers dotted the wall, the sharp points of their roofs piercing upward. Massive turrets also dotted the top of the wall. They looked more like the gun turrets on a modern-day destroyer than medieval cannons.

"Wow, this place looks awesome!" Sam commented as they joined the line of individuals queuing for entry into the city. The caravans had their own line apart from the individual travelers, thankfully.

Sam got a good look at the large gates as they drew closer. The massive blue metal gates were adorned with intricate carvings of runic symbols that looked like they had been inlaid with silver. The entrance was flanked by several groups of bored-looking warriors with yellow and black banners wearing full plate armor, interviewing individuals and searching wagons before they entered.

***

The line moved quickly, and Sam found herself in front of a guard before she even had time to get bored.

"Name and reason for entry," an extremely bored-looking guard said in a monotone voice.

Taking the lead, Nara said professionally, "Nara and Samantha." She stood up straighter, "We are adventurers seeking our fortune."

The guard looked them both over before saying, "Of course you are. What is your reason for entry?"

"We will apply for entry into the guild and intend to sell a few wolf pelts." Nara produced one of the lower-level pelts, pulling it from Sam's backpack to show the guard.

Sam was impressed. Nara sounded like a young adventurer who had barely gotten her feet wet in her chosen field.

The guard nodded and was about to wave them through but stopped when he focused on the dead ranger's bow Nara had slung over her shoulder. At first, Sam's heart sank thinking he recognized it, but that fear was belayed by how he spoke the following words.

"That is a fine bow for such a low-level adventurer. How did you come across such a weapon like that?" The guard's tone was like honey, his expression laced with greed.

Nara clutched the bowstring across her chest like it was precious and said, "It is a family heirloom passed down from my father."

"Well, isn't that something? I bet that bow is worth my year's wage and then some." He eyed them greedily, "I almost forgot to mention the tax on the wolf pelts you're bringing into the city. They be in high demand lately, and the city collects their taxes upfront, so there's no funny business inside the walls." He eyed their packs and continued, "Those packs look full, so what do you say, two bronze per pelt, or if you want VIP passes, I could let you in for, say, five silver each. Heck, I'll even throw in a good word for you at the guild. I got a friend who works there."

Nara looked ready to argue, but Sam gave the guard her most winning smile and pulled ten silvers from her pocket, handing the coins to the guard, saying, "We would love VIP passes, sir…I didn't catch your name."

The guard quickly snatched the coins from Sam's hand and looked around. Seeing no one had witnessed the transaction, he said, "The name's Will. Now, don't you two little birds be getting into trouble. VIP or not, you still have to stay on the up and up." He gave them a fake smile and stepped aside to let them enter.

Sam noted he had surprisingly straight white teeth and was actually quite attractive, *"Too bad he's an extortionist."* She thought as she passed.

Nara punched Sam's arm once they were a few steps away from the guard but still in earshot, exclaiming, "Now we're broke! You better hope these pelts sell, or we'll sleep in the streets!"

That was, of course, so the guard hopefully wouldn't get any ideas about hunting them down and "extorting" the rest of their supposed funds.

Sam ignored Nara; she was too caught up in how busy the city square was when they passed the gate. There were hundreds of people bustling about, weaving around a giant statue of a woman holding a sword in one hand and a book she was reading in the other with the sword pointed to the sky.

The rich smell of exotic spices wafted through the air, reminding her of the outdoor markets she had visited on a trip she had taken to India years before. Everywhere she looked, Sam was confronted by something new and exciting. Merchants were hawking their wares from small kiosks bordering the square, and street performers were dancing and playing instruments. One performer was juggling ten fireballs while balancing on a tiny wooden stick. Vendors were selling delicious-looking foods of all kinds, along with various drinks. The entire place was alive with boisterous energy. Sam loved it.

"There goes the dingy, smelly medieval city with raw sewage running down the streets I had envisioned," Sam pleasantly thought as she eyeballed the nearest food vendor and began stalking toward the poor unsuspecting attendant who stood relaxed, oblivious to her impending attack. She was hungry, and that food smelled divine!

Nara grabbed Sam's arm, diverting her from the delicious food distributor. "Hey, what the hell, Nara?"

"Hurry, we must get to the guild before they close their hall to civilians for the night," was Nara's only answer.

"Fine." Sam grumbled, "They better have beer!"

***

After traveling through more city blocks than Sam cared to count, she was convinced Nara was lost, and they needed to stop at one of the dozens of cozy-looking inns they were passing to ask for directions. The smell of home-cooked food and beer wafting from the taverns and inns was beckoning to Sam, along with the sounds of laughter coming from the doorways leading into the firelit interiors. The establishments promised a warm and inviting atmosphere full of joy and drink.

Nara, whom Sam now considered a soulless heathen, was unaffected by beckoning taverns. Instead, she kept insisting they go straight to the guild. Sam had even suggested that her human species needed beer and wine just as Tenarians needed "human" food, but it was all for naught. The blue-eyed fun sucker wasn't buying it and continued to drag a pleading Sam past every establishment, her thirst going unquenched.

***

As they traveled farther into the city, Sam started noticing fewer taverns and more shops. The buildings were now spaced farther apart, and more and more residential areas were interspersed with storefronts and warehouses. Sam noted clothiers, armorers, jewelers, and storehouses. Everything was clean, with bright colors easily distinguishable in the fading light of the day by magic crystals on top of lamp posts lining the street and illuminating the inside of the shops.

It was almost dark when they finally arrived at the enormous guild hall. The building looked more like the massive mead halls portrayed in Viking lore if the mead halls in question had ten-meter stone walls around them with dual cannon turrets mounted every twenty meters or so. Several guards stood outside the only entrance Sam could see. These guards were much more imposing than the city guards from earlier. Each of them had a rigidity that only came from decades of dedicated military training, and they all sported multiple weapons and specialized armor. For every two guards, there was a mage in expensive but functional robes with them.

"Definitely don't want to mess with these guys," Sam couldn't help thinking. They looked like they were all business and knew their jobs very well. Their armor was clean, but even from a distance, she could see the scratches and dents from past battles.

She could see into the courtyard past the gates. From what she could tell, it was lit better than a modern stadium and filled with exercise equipment and even an archery and magic range. Sam completely forgot about her need for adult refreshments, well, almost entirely, and made a beeline for the gate. To her annoyance, Nara again grabbed her arm and dragged her away into one of the few dark alleys a few buildings over.

"What gives Nara?" Sam was annoyed, "First, you insist on coming straight here, and now you stop me from going in." She looked at their surroundings, "And why am I whispering in a dark alley right now?"

"Have you already forgotten how we met?" Nara hissed with frustration, "The job to kill the wolves Arron took. Well, you technically completed it almost all on your own."

"I haven't forgotten. I figured you knew something I didn't and could claim the reward." Sam had been wondering about this, so she asked, "Do we even need the reward? Is it even worth the risk with the amount of coin I have?"

"If we say we completed the job and can prove its difficulty, then we will be given better placement if—when we get our memberships," Nara said.

"Why do we even want a membership?" Sam asked another question that had been bothering her.

"Because," Nara sighed and leaned back against the wall of the alley, "the Adventurers Guild is open to all races and cultures, and if you are a member, even the local authorities have to ask permission to punish you for a crime you commit in their territory."

Sam's eyebrows rose at that revelation, and she blew a low whistle. "Damn. So, we would be above the law?"

Nara shook her head vehemently, "Quite the opposite, actually. The guild's laws are much more stringent than the local ones, and their punishments are much harsher."

"Then why are we doing this? I don't want to be punished because I accidentally broke a rule I knew nothing about in the first place." Sam wasn't convinced this was a good plan.

"Because members cannot be discriminated against because of their race," Nara looked at Sam pointedly, "or their planet of origin." When Sam nodded understanding, Nara said, "Guild members are protected under guild law. If the Church of the Light wants to enslave me again, they must weigh that decision against pissing off the guild. The same goes for you; if anyone wants to capture or use you for study, they might think twice when they realize you are with the guild. It isn't guaranteed protection, but it is a deterrent."

"So, you could walk around in your true form then? And no one would touch you?" Sam was curious.

"I could but won't. I wouldn't want that kind of attention," Nara said. "But I could do it inside the guild hall without anyone even batting an eye."

"Okay, I'm in. Let's do this," Sam said. Her mind was made up. It sounded like an intelligent move to her.

Nara clapped her hands and gave Sam a quick hug. She stepped back and said, "When we apply and tell our story to one of the clerks, a lie-detecting device will be active. If you do not wish them to know something they are asking for, say you do not wish to answer. If they deem the question unimportant, they will respect your wish."

Sam thought about that as they walked toward the gate, *"The truth is the easiest thing to remember, and if I don't have to hide Nara's true nature, then I guess it will be alright. I'll have to play it by ear on how much information I want to divulge in the interview."*

***

The guild guards were just as professional in their actions as in their dress. Within a few minutes, Sam and Nara were escorted through the courtyard toward the massive hall. The two women, bloody from battle and dirty from the road, must have looked quite the sight, but no one in the training yard gave them a second glance. Apparently, coming back from missions looking like you had been murdered at least twice during your travels was a common sight here.

When the guard escorting them pulled the heavy metal doors to the hall open, revealing the interior, Sam turned and hugged Nara. She now knew why the woman had insisted they come straight here. Standing after the guard, Sam took a deep breath and surveyed the room. The smell of beer and roasted meat filled her nostrils, and she couldn't help the wide grin plastered on her face. The entire hall was one massive tavern with hundreds of tables surrounding a substantial double-sided fireplace with the carcass of an unidentifiable animal slowly roasting over it. A large circular bar was situated in the center of the building with more fireplaces along the walls, each surrounded by comfortable-looking lounges, many of them occupied by adventurers sipping drinks and socializing.

“I am so sorry I ever doubted you,” Sam said to Nara as their escort led them to one of the many small rooms lining one side of the building. Some of the rooms had closed doors with a red light over them. The room they were led to had a yellow light over the open door.

"Your evaluator will be with you shortly," the guild guard who escorted them professionally stated as she led them into the room, "your evaluation is free, but the job completion you mentioned will not be." She turned on her heels and closed the door behind her.

“Now what?” Sam asked when the guard left.

"Now we wait and hope. This could be a turning point in both of our fates, Sam," Nara's voice was a mixture of hope and dread. She repeated herself with resolve, "Now we wait."

CHAPTER 13 — "My mute friend."

Sam looked around the room they were led into. It was a plain room with nothing hanging on the white wooded walls. There were several comfortable-looking chairs along one side, what looked like a large scale built into the floor opposite the chairs, and a barred teller window opposite the door. No one was at the window at the moment, so Sam wandered around the room aimlessly. She examined the scale and found it was what she had thought. Her weight was plainly displayed on the wall above the scale when she stepped on it.

"It is for calculating job rewards," Nara said helpfully. "Some monster parts are valued by weight. The steaks you have, for example, would be sold by weight, not quantity."

Sam nodded in understanding and continued wandering around the room. Nara walked over to the teller's window and slipped a silver coin in a slot next to the teller bars, causing a timer to pop up on the back wall. The timer showed two hours but didn't start counting down. Nara then walked over and sat in one of the chairs with her hands in her lap. Sam could tell the woman was nervous but kept her composure quite well.

They didn't have to wait long. A tall man with a frilly white shirt and black leather pants slid into a chair behind the teller's bars after only a few minutes. He looked at the two women closely before speaking, "Miss Evander, it is good to see you again. It seems we will not have to intervene on your behalf after all," Nara just stared at the man in confusion, so he continued, "Come now, young lady. You didn't think Arron's transgressions went unnoticed, did you?" He scoffed, "We knew you were bound to him as a slave the moment you stepped into this hall those few days ago. In fact," he dug around in a stack of papers he brought with him and, pulled one out, and slipped it under his window to Nara who stood up and took it with cautious movements.

Nara read the paper, and her head snapped up in surprise, "This is a job to bring Arron in for suspected slavery!" She exclaimed. "I thought the guild always remained neutral. Why would you go against the Children of the Light?"

The clerk smiled at her. "The Adventurers Guild can act against members who break our tenets however we see fit. Arron broke a tenet, so he was going to be disciplined. He thought he would avoid detection by not allowing you in this room." The man chuckled, "We are the most powerful guild on the planet with access to magics that defy reason." He shook his head, "That man was either a complete buffoon or far too arrogant for his limited capabilities." He looked to the two of them, suddenly serious. "We will, however, have to discuss how you have been released from Arron. But I am getting ahead of myself." He pushed his chair back, stood up, and with a slight bow, he said, "My name is Evan, and I am the chief evaluations officer of the Helms Peak branch of the Adventurers Guild." Sitting back down, Evan flicked a small switch on his desk, and the room's white turned slightly yellow.

Sam jumped a little. This was not how she expected things to go; it had her on edge. It didn't help that she heard the door's lock slide shut when the room turned yellow. The entire room exploded in color when Sam turned on her mana sight, although primarily yellow; virtually every other color was represented as well.

Evan noticed Sam looking around the room and said, "At your level, you will be mostly blind trying to discern the magic used here, Miss Moura. I would suggest you—"

"Arcane runes," Sam stated, interrupting Evan. "There are hundreds of them! No, thousands!" She was looking around with wonder at the thousands of intricate swirls and hard angles that covered every smooth surface in the room. "How long did it take to carve these?" She mainly whispered to herself.

“How can you possibly see the runes? But more importantly, how do you know what arcane magic looks like?” Evan fixed Sam with a stare that told her she better tell the truth.

"I turned off the yellow magic in my mana sight, and I use arcane magic," Sam answered honestly, still staring at the runes. They flared brightly at her words, then went dormant again.

"Ahem," Evan got Sam's attention. "Thank you for your honest answer. Now, shall we continue this interview, Miss Moura?"

"Oh, sure." She turned off her mana sight, and the yellow hue filled the room again. "But one question. Why did the runes flare when I spoke?"

"I will explain, but first," Evan said in a professional tone, "For the record, this is the entry interview for Miss Nara Evander, a Moonblight Mana Reaper currently bonded with Mister Naris Blight; they are posing as a Human Sorceress. Also in the room to participate in this entry interview is Miss Samantha Moura, a Human Pathfinder. Ladies, the yellow color in this room will remain as long as your answers are honest to the best of your knowledge. The hue will turn red if you are trying to hide the truth or are telling an outright lie. If you do not wish to disclose information, say so, and we will move on. But suppose I determine the question must be answered. In this case, I will ask you to explain why you do not wish to answer the question. If you can satisfy me that your reasoning is sound, then I will allow the question to go unanswered." He grinned at Sam, "like the fact that you can wield arcane magic. That young lady will never leave this room, and I suggest you do not disclose it to anyone else. Everyone needs to keep some secrets, and the guild respects that. Now, if you would each speak two truths and a lie, we can confirm the room is functioning and move on."

Sam was wondering how the man had got so much information about them but figured it had something to do with the runes. Since it didn't seem like she could do anything about it she complied with Evan's request saying, "I'm an interdimensional woman of mystery looking for a good time. I'm a female; at least, I was the last time I checked. And I'm a psychopath." The room glowed a red hue when she said she was a psychopath, which actually relieved her a little. She felt she may have been walking a fine line as of late.

Evan's eyebrows disappeared into his hairline when the room didn't react to her interdimensional woman of mystery comment. Still, he kept his composure nonetheless and looked to Nara.

Nara's statements were more reserved, "My name is Nara Evander. I was enslaved with a divine blood contract by the Children of the Light operating under the rule of the Church of the Light until yesterday. I have murdered others of my own free will." The light went red when Nara said she was a murderer. Another thing that relieved Sam. However, she did note the "my own free will" part of the statement.

Their lie detector test complete, Evan asked them to tell him about their recent histories without getting into too much detail. He guided the conversation with pointed questions to keep the interview from getting off track. Eventually, he was convinced they weren't criminals and had done nothing wrong regarding the deaths of two guild members or the three other bodies they produced. He said the guild would investigate the attack and deliver the bodies to the city guard for disposal. They would also check to see if they had kin living in the city and if there may have been a bounty out for them that Sam and Nara could collect.

Evan then moved on to the closing of the job they had completed. He collected the hides and gave them a bonus for the alpha. Sam didn't mention the token she had received. He waved the entry fee of ten silvers each due to their underhanded treatment by an acting guild member. He gave both women probationary silver-grade memberships. They swore an oath to abide by the guild's tenets and were each handed a small leather-bound rule book afterward.

Closing the job and collecting payment took an hour and a half once the timer Nara had paid the silver for started counting. Sam was happy; the experience made her feel like there may be hope for this world after all. The guild at least sounded like it was on the up and up. She figured time would tell, but she hadn't had any weird vibes. Sam had been a little surprised during the interview when Evan asked what a Sorceress and a Pathfinder were, explaining there were no such classes in the guild's records as he searched through a screen displayed from a crystal set into his desk. Neither Sam nor Nara had wanted to answer the question, so he had let it drop. Sam had understood him not knowing what a Pathfinder was, but Sorceress seemed apparent to her. She decided to ask Nara about it later.

"Miss Moura," Evan called as they were about to exit the room. Sam turned back to him with a questioning look, and he asked, "Why did you change the oath to only include Hallista and the two moons?"

"Because this is the second planet I have been on in the last two weeks," Sam said. The room stayed yellow. When the room turned white, she opened the door, and the two women walked out. Sam had a Cheshire grin on her face at the dumbfounded look on Evan's face as he watched them go.

After they walked out, Evan stared at the open doorway for a long time. He finally looked away, mumbling, "Interdimensional mystery indeed. We are lucky to have found you before a cult or, worse yet, the blasted Church of the Light." His face scrunched up in disdain when he thought of the so-called holy Church of the Light that had been trying its best to control and enslave the population of Hallista for hundreds of years. Shuffling his stack of papers, he left the room confident the guild's two newest members would be productive additions to the ranks and made a personal note to check in on their progress from time to time.

***

Once out of the contract completion, interrogation, and application room, Nara bounced up and down, clapping her hands. She turned to Sam with a huge grin, "We are members! And we are silver rank below level fifty! That's unheard of!"

"We do fight way above our weight class," Sam said.

"I assume you mean we can compete as equals against more powerful opponents," Nara said, and Sam nodded in affirmation.

Nara grabbed Sam's hand, exclaiming, "Let's look at the job board!" She was excitedly vibrating, "Then when we find a job we want, we can start planning what we will need to outfit ourselves." Nara started counting down with her fingers, "We need to sell all our loot. Then we will need supplies. We will need a tent, some better camping equipment, maybe a couple of cots? It would sure beat sleeping on the ground. I personally think we… mmff."

Sam stopped Nara with a hand gripped over her mouth. When the girl kept trying to talk, Sam grabbed her in a headlock and clamped her hand down even harder. She considered pinching off her nose, too. She didn't, though, because she suspected that no one on this planet actually needed to breathe.

Sam leaned her lips close to Nara's ear and whispered, "Shh, no more talkie time. Now it's drinkie time." She smiled at Nara's furrowed brows and the muffled sounds coming through her hand. She continued whispering, "First beer. Then, more beer. Then, even more beer. After that, maybe some food with more beer. Then, a hot bath and a bed for at least eight hours. I don't even care if I sleep just so long as I am in bed for eight uninterrupted hours." Sam thought momentarily, tapping her finger to her teeth with the hand that wasn't currently strangling her companion, "maybe thirty-six hours in the bed." With that, Sam removed her hand from Nara's mouth.

Nara didn't miss a breath, "perfect! We can discuss our plans while we eat—"

Sam's hand clamped securely over the excited woman's mouth again. "Okay, we will have to do this the hard way."

Sam half marched, half dragged the Tenarian over to the large bar, waving her free hand at the bartender, who looked bored as he polished a glass behind the bar. When she got his attention, she placed a couple of silver coins on the bar, saying, "A couple of beers for me and my mute friend here, please." She flashed him her most winning smile and placed another six silver coins on the bar, "keep them coming. It's been a long week."

The barkeep looked at the coins, then Sam, and finally at Nara, and asked, "Ma'am, are you in distress?"

A series of muffled sounds came from Sam's hand, and Nara glared at Sam. Who just smiled back innocently and looked back at the barkeep, saying, "Like I said, she's mute."

"I can hear her trying to talk," he retorted dryly.

"She doesn't like talking to strangers then," Sam said.

"Ma'am, I am going to need you to unhand your fellow guild member before I can complete this transaction," the barkeep replied.

"Damn, this barkeep is absolutely no fun!" Sam thought before saying, "Look—" She stopped and read his name badge, "Ken, my mute friend here keeps trying to talk shop when all I want to do is have a drink and maybe some of that delicious…whatever it is you have roasting over there and sleep for a couple of days straight. But overall, I want to decompress from two of the longest weeks of my life. Is that too much to ask?"

Ken, the fun sucker, as Sam now referred to him, just shook his head and started pushing the coins back across the bar toward Sam.

With an exaggerated sigh, Sam said, "Fine! Have it your way!" She released her death grip on Nara.

Glaring at Sam, Nara didn't miss a beat, "Thank you, Mister Ken! I was only saying we should discuss our upcoming adventuring plans and how we will allocate and utilize our resources! Should we take a job in the wilderness, or maybe we could pay for a dungeon entry if there are any nearby. Are there any close by? Never mind, we should take a job, maybe two or five, in case one is too easy. But if we do, we will need camping supplies and rations. Vegetables! I am tired of only meat and dry trail rations; we will definitely need vegetables. I—mmmf."

Sam's hand clamped over Nara's mouth again, and she squeezed her to her side. She smiled sadly at Ken. "See what I mean; she's mute. Poor girl." She shook her head morosely at the statement. "So, about those beers?"

Ken redeemed himself entirely in Sam's eyes by scooping up the coins and filling four pint mugs with a dark beer without another word. When finished, he slid two pints to each woman and whispered, "My condolences for your mute friend."

***

Sam chugged the two beers and then grabbed one of Nara's. She finally released the poor girl and, ignoring the spluttering woman, walked to a nearby table and plopped down in one of the chairs with a heartfelt sigh and a very unladylike burp.

Nara joined her a few moments later, staying out of Sam's reach. She said nothing and only watched Sam sip her beer and stare absently at the giant fireplace. Nara was about to break the silence to give Sam a piece of her mind, but Sam beat her to it.

Staring into her fourth beer Ken had just deposited in front of her, Sam said, "You are a genuinely good soul, aren't you." It wasn't a question, and Nara had no idea what prompted the statement, so she just waited for Sam to continue, which she did, "Your…kind…race whatever, you aren't inherently evil. I've seen true evil in my old world, and I can tell you are not it." Sam looked at Nara with a genuine smile, "I don't know why your people are hunted and enslaved, but as far as I am concerned, you are a good person, and I want to stay with you and adventure with you. At least for a time." She meant it, too. Sam had been thinking a lot, and Nara seemed like one of those genuine people who literally wore her emotions on her sleeve and couldn't lie to save her life. She had been watching the Tenarian since she had released her and had never even felt the slightest threat from her. Nor had the girl seemed the least interested in "draining" the hundreds of humans they had passed since arriving in the city.

Sam got up and dragged her chair to sit next to Nara, who shifted nervously, probably thinking she would be 'muted' again. Clinking her mug to Nara's yet untouched mug, Sam called over her shoulder, "Hey Ken, can I get something to write on? My partner and I have a lot of planning to do."

With a squeal of delight, Nara gripped Sam tightly and yelled, "It's okay, Ken! I have something to write on! But I need another beer! And some food!

And some wine! You said you wanted wine, right? Oh, oh, did I already say food?"

Nara's enthusiasm was infectious, and Sam settled into her chair, relaxing. The delicious beer, the roaring fire in the hearth, and the promise of food and wine put her at a level of contentment she hadn't felt since…well, since the last time she had been camping during a long weekend back on Earth. *"Maybe not even then,"* she thought, *"because I wasn't with a friend back then."*

CHAPTER 14 — "Oh crap, what did I do?"

"Did anyone get the number of the bus that hit me? And why is my skull soft?" Sam sat up in the bed, poking at her aching head. *"How am I even hungover with my recovery speed and poison resistance? And seriously, why do I have a concussion and brain bleed?"* She thought, as her skill told her of the damage when she probed her head with mana repair, then groaned as another wave of pain flashed through her head.

A soft voice much too cheerful assaulted her eardrums like a marching band. "I don't know what a bus is, but you did headbutt a level 52 paladin last night on a bet." Nara said chirpily from beside her, "Also, I am fairly certain your poison resistance, crystal mana channels, and healing ability are the only reasons you are still alive."

Sam just groaned again and started pouring mana into her regeneration. Her health bar was blacked out, whatever that meant.

Nara, either oblivious or uncaring of Sam's plight, continued speaking, "You literally drank twice your body-weight in alcohol. Ken was serving you actual poison by the end of the night just to get you to leave," she paused for a second looking thoughtful, "or die." She giggled at that.

That's when Sam realized she was nude, and so was the giggling Tenarian beside her. Sam threw the furs back and jumped out of the bed, moving behind a table a few meters away.

"Nara, uh, did we um, you know…" Sam let the statement trail off.

Nara looked insulted, "Do you mean, did I take advantage of an intoxicated friend? Of course not!" She pointed to a pile of furs on a couch in the room, "I was actually going to sleep on the couch, but you dragged me to the bed with you," she gave Sam an appraising look, "You are very strong."

Suddenly worried, Sam asked a question she wasn't sure she wanted the answer to, "did I, um…hurt you?"

Nara laughed, "No, Sam, you just went on and on about how we're friends now and how happy you were about having a sleepover with a friend. You told me how glad you were that you saved me. Then you passed out and started snoring almost immediately." She giggled again, "You are adorable when you're drunk." She furrowed her brow, "Very forceful though—and also a little terrifying."

Sam sat in one of the chairs at the lone table in the room, put her head down in her arms, and said, "Please tell me I didn't kill anyone last night." She gasped and looked up at Nara in panic, "Or get us kicked out of the guild!"

Nara's face grew more serious, "No, not exactly…we need to talk seriously about last night, though. You might want to finish healing yourself first."

Sam didn't like the tone in Nara's voice. *"Oh crap, what did I do?"*

***

Nara hopped out of the bed and dug through a dresser until she found a sheer gown and slipped into it. She went to the table where Sam was and sat opposite her. She tapped one clawed finger on the table rhythmically while staring at Sam, who was becoming more nervous by the second. "Where to begin…" Nara mumbled.

"How about the beginning," Sam said helpfully, ready for the torture to end.

"Okay," Nara said, "but no interruptions while I tell the story. Are we clear?"

Sam gulped and nodded. She felt like she was about to find out what happens when you take a woman who was already pretty wild when drunk, send her to a fantasy world, give her insane magical powers, and then get her drunk. "I'm scared to know," she told Nara.

"Oh, you should be," Nara said without hesitation or humor.

***

Nara began retelling the events of the night.

"After you finished two entire kegs of beer, Ken cut you off from beer. Not because you were drunk but so he would have enough for other patrons. So, you immediately switched to wine."

Sam nodded her head; it seemed like something she would do. Something bothered her, though, and she had to interrupt Nara, "How could I have drunk that much beer? I mean, physically, how is that possible?"

"I'll explain how your body works in this world later. Don't interrupt me." Nara said curtly.

Sam clamped her mouth shut, and Nara continued. "Where was I? Oh yes. You then proceeded to drink about fifteen liters of wine before getting up and dancing with one of the berserkers from that all-female adventurers' party. The one with the pink hair." Sam stared blankly at Nara, so she tried to jog her memory, "The ones you said looked like a bunch of sexy Amazons…"

Sam's expression didn't change, and Nara sighed in frustration, "How can you not remember them? You danced with all four of them and made out with the pink-haired one for twenty minutes!"

"Oh yeah," Sam snapped her fingers, "doesn't seem to be coming back to me." She offered unhelpfully. She rubbed her forehead with one hand; at least it didn't feel soft anymore. "What about me headbutting the paladin? When did I do that?"

Nara scoffed, "I'm not even close to finishing what happened last night!" She gave Sam a look that was a mixture of fear and admiration. After a deep breath, she continued her story, "After you finished dancing and, ahem, other things, you accused Ken of watering down his wares…loudly." Sam winced at that revelation while Nara continued. "You demanded Ken break out the hard stuff and stop treating you like a child…actually you said something much more vulgar, but I'll not repeat it." She gave Sam an accusing look, "Ken was obviously pissed, but also, I think he felt challenged, so he brought out several different bottles of 'hard stuff' and poured them for you in tiny glasses one after the other. One of them was actual poison! Like made in an alchemy lab, real poison!"

"He wouldn't have done that to a customer," Sam interjected. "There is no way he could stay in business if he poisoned everyone who insulted him." She figured Nara was now embellishing a little because she seemed to be getting a little agitated while recounting the previous night's events.

"Oh yes, he would have, and he did!" Nara snapped back, "Now stop interrupting me!" She seemed agitated now, "Ken charged you ten gold and made sure there were at least two healers in the room willing to offer their aid before he poured you a quarter of a shot of the poison. He refused to give you more even after you called him a pussy boy."

Sam could only stare at the table as Nara retold the story. *"I'm going to spend all day apologizing to people, aren't I? Still, I bet the 'poison' was just a high-ABV drink that's hard to make, though."* She voiced that last thought to Nara, who laughed a little hysterically.

Nara was on a roll now, "The bottle had three skulls on it, and he had to get it out of a magically sealed safe!" Her voice faltered, and her hands shook as she continued, "You took the shot he offered of the poison and absolutely loved it. You said it tasted like flowers, and before anyone could stop you, you snatched the bottle from Ken and chugged half of it!" Nara's voice was now a cross between a scream and a terrified cry.

Sam tried to calm the Tenarian down, "I'm obviously fine, Nara, so it couldn't have been that bad." She gestured to herself as she said it in a calming voice.

"Let me finish!" Nara half screamed, causing Sam to shut her mouth in surprise and sit upright in her chair like a scolded child. Composing herself a little, Nara continued, "When Ken and two berserkers managed to get the bottle away from you, he started screaming for the healers in a full-on panic!" She looked at Sam with wide eyes, "Freaking berserkers Sam, two of them! One even had to activate a freaking skill to get the bottle away from you!"

Sam patiently waited as Nara panted a little. *"Is it wrong that all I can think about right now is how cute she looks when flustered? That, and it sounds like the berserkers were wusses."* Of course, Sam knew better than to voice those wayward thoughts. So, she patiently waited for the cute little sorceress to calm down and continue her story.

Nara poured a glass of water from the pitcher on the table, took a big gulp, and continued, "After you chugged the poison, your skin turned blue, not just your face, Sam; all of your skin turned a bright blue!" Nara pushed her chair back and started pacing the floor in agitation. Sam wisely kept her mouth shut. Nara started waving her arms as she continued, "Well, Ken started backing up with wide eyes, the bottle clutched to his chest, mumbling about how this has never happened before and how this isn't good and he will get fired, fined, or executed. You, on the other hand, stood up from your chair, told the healers to fuck off, looked down at your empty glass on the table, smiled widely, hiccupped, then belched."

Sam smiled and was about to say something about it being no big deal, but the look in Nara's eyes told her to keep her mouth shut. It was a look of complete disbelief, and what Nara said next explained the look.

"When you belched," Nara shuddered a little, "Your skin returned to normal, and your breath melted your teeth and lower jaw." Sam's eyes widened as Nara continued, "The entire table and most of the chairs disintegrated next, along with the silverware and mugs, followed by the floor—" It was Nara's turn to groan, "The two-meter thick, magically reinforced, enchanted stone floor of one of the most secure buildings in the city just…melted away." Nara surprised Sam with a question, "Did you know there is a level 150 plus dungeon beneath the guild hall for the elite members to train and harvest in?" When Sam shook her head slowly, Nara screamed, "Neither did anyone else! Well, that is until last night!"

Sam buried her head in her arms. She didn't want to know but had to ask, "How bad is it?"

"Oh, I'm not even to the best part yet!" Although still slightly hysterical, Nara was clearly enjoying Sam's anguish now.

Sam was perplexed. If everything Nara was saying was true, then… "How are we not in prison, Nara? Or at least me?"

"I'll get to that," Nara smiled despite herself, "now, where was I? Oh yeah, the dungeon. So, when you melted the floor, Ken dropped the bottle and fainted." Sam gasped, and Nara didn't miss a beat, "That's exactly what everyone else in the guild hall did, too! Except for you, that is. You just waved your hand, and the bottle suspended in midair. I, of course, know you used one of your threads. But everyone else in the guild thinks you're telekinetic now." Nara tapped her chin in thought, "It is strange how hard it is to see your magic; I wonder why that is?" She shrugged and continued, "Anyway, the bottle zipped across the hole in the floor into your hand before poor Ken's head even struck the ground." Nara narrowed her eyes at Sam, "I think you let him fall on purpose. But no matter. Once you had the bottle, you closed your eyes, grew your jaw back in seconds, then, to everyone's horror, you slugged back the rest of the bottle's contents in a couple of gulps." Nara paused for effect. She was really getting into the story now, "Did you know there is a magical barrier protecting the guild hall from aerial attacks?"

It was more of a rhetorical question, but Sam shook her head. She knew where this was going.

Nara confirmed Sam's suspicion gleefully, shouting, "Neither did anyone else until last night! At least not the low-level rabble like us in the hall last night. When you belched this time, you did it upward. You melted a hole in the ceiling and nearly destroyed the barrier!" Nara put her face in her hands, her voice muffled, "The entire upper city thought the guild was under attack. The guild guards busted into the hall with blades out and spells charged, followed closely by the city guard, all prepared to defend the guild with their lives." Nara pulled her face from her hands, "Oh, that reminds me, you owe the city guard thirty-five gold for the false alarm. It has to be paid before we can leave the city."

"Thirty-five gold? That sounds a little high to me," Sam said incredulously.

"They mustered over two hundred guards, Sam," Nara chided.

Sam just hung her head, dejected.

Nara dragged a chair to sit next to Sam, patting her knee. "Cheer up, Sam. I promise it gets better," she paused, "eventually." Nara suppressed a giggle and continued retelling the night's events, "After the second belch woke up most of the city and everyone in the guild hall, the Guild Master showed up. His name is Harold, by the way, and he is also a Tenarian." Sam looked up surprised, and Nara nodded, "Yep, surprised me too. Anyway, when Guild Master Harold showed up, he looked at the hole in the floor, then the one in the ceiling, and then checked on Ken. He looked outraged and was about to say something when he saw the bottle in your hands and stomped over to you. You were really wobbly but had already healed your jaw again, so when Harold walked up, you handed him the bottle and slurred something about it being empty and that it was the best shit you've ever had."

Sam was horrified and blurted, “I embarrassed myself in front of the boss! That’s like the worst thing you can do!”

"I don't think embarrassed is the right word," Nara said, a little confused, "you consumed a lethal dose of poison twice in under a minute and turned it into some melty breath attack. That's impressive, Sam. Harold looked at you and the unconscious Ken and started laughing hysterically!"

Sam looked at Nara with hope in her eyes, prompting Nara to keep going, which she did. "Harold waved his hand, and the barrier, ceiling, and floor started repairing themselves slowly. He shooed the furious city guard commander away, laughing the entire time. When I offered to pay for the damages to the hall, he just waved me off, saying the looks on everyone's faces when he showed up were payment enough and to only worry about paying the city. He woke Ken and told him if he ever opened another bottle of Trillian Aged Cyan Death Whiskey again, he had better come and get him first to watch! He then asked you how much health you had left. When you slurred, "Thlen points, but it was worth lit cuz that shlit was delicious!" He started laughing all over again." Nara shrugged, "That was pretty much it for the repercussions. You and Harold sat at a table and discussed which of your internal organs melted. He told you which ones to focus on rebuilding once he realized you could heal yourself. The two of you talked for about an hour while the hall rebuilt itself, and then he left, telling everyone to 'have fun.'"

"Wow," Sam said when Nara had finished, "that was one wild night."

"Hold on," Nara said, "I never said I was finished. Don't you want to know how we got this room?"

The grin on Nara's face told Sam she probably didn't want to know, and she murmured, "Please tell me we just rented it." Nara's smile widened, and Sam was sure she didn't want to know, but Nara wasn't about to let her off that easily.

Nara stared with a question. "How's your forehead?"

Sam instinctively touched it, replying, "It was a little mushy when I woke up. I assume it was from a headbutt?" Nara slowly nodded until Sam said, "Fine, tell me what I did."

Nara laughed and slapped the table. "You bet a level fifty-two paladin everything you owned against his spatial suite in the guild hall that you could knock him out with one headbutt. This suite has been in his family for generations and is a coveted item among guild members. They are rarely sold, which creates a bidding war when they go up for sale. He was bragging about inheriting it, and it annoyed you. He initially refused until you pulled out the summoning token, which I definitely want to know how you got. That token caused a stir, for sure. When he still looked like he was going to refuse, you told him he could use any defensive skills he wanted and wear his helmet, but if he did that, you would also get to call him "Little Boy" from now on."

Sam's eyebrows were as high as they could get, "How could he have agreed after what he had already seen me do?"

"Simple, he arrived after you drank enough poison to kill nearly the entire city and melted things with your breath. A few who had seen you tried to stop him, but he ignored them and agreed to your terms." Nara made a face, "He was kind of an annoying prick. But he was cute, though..."

Sam stopped poking at her forehead, checking for any soft spots mana repair might have missed long enough to ask, "—was? He is still alive, right?"

"I'm getting to that!" Nara refused to spoil her story. She cleared her throat, "So, he accepted and made a big deal, calling out the names of his buffs as he activated them. Names like 'Stalwart Defense' and 'Iron Skin.' I think he wound up applying five buffs, which let everyone know he was something of a coward who was afraid of getting hurt." Nara paused to catch her breath, then continued, "Once he was done shouting and buffing, you quietly asked him if he was done being a little wuss." Nara held up her hand, "Keep in mind you were wobbling on your feet and could barely keep your eyes open, so when you half asked, half slurred your question, he looked at you and scoffed, calling you a pathetic sewer rat."

Sam knew what happened next. She had a particular hatred for rats. She had a bad experience once and disliked talking about it. "Oh no, he did not call me a rat. Please tell me he used another word."

"Yes, he called you a rat, and your eyes started glowing purple when he did. He had enough balls not to flinch when they did, but all the onlookers stepped back, at least the ones that had been there from the beginning." With mirth, Nara clapped her hands with glee and said, "You walked up to him and looked up into his faceplate; he is a head taller than you." Nara was smiling from ear to ear now, "You put your hands on his shoulders, belched into his helmet—"

Sam gasped when Nara said she belched into the guy's face.

"That's exactly what everyone else did, too!" Nara giggled. "Thankfully, you did it without melting anything this time, although Ken did faint again." Nara paused for effect and continued, "Then you slammed your forehead into the idiot's helmet; oh yeah, he kept his helmet on. It is a good thing he did, too, because the general consensus among the healers is that his helmet is literally the only thing that saved his life."

"How bad could it have been, really?" Sam asked. "He was a level fifty-two with buffs and a helmet. I'm tough but not that tough."

Nara looked at her blankly, "Sam, you didn't just knock him out. You broke his neck, crushed his skull, caved his helmet in so badly a metal mage had to remove it before the healers could work, and you came within a millimeter of crushing his brain. The crack was so loud I half expected the city guards to rush back in!"

Sam just stared at Nara with her mouth agape, so she continued. "After knocking out the paladin, Chad, is his name, by the way, you walked over to me and snagged his key and the summon token off the table they were on. You said we should "go check out the Little Boy's room" and wobbled towards the stairs in the back."

Nara gestured around the room, "And here we are. I woke Ken again, and he told me which room it was. I checked with the healers that Chad would be okay and chased after you! Oh, the deal was the room and all its contents, so this is all ours!" Sam stared at Nara with a furrowed brow, and the Tenarian quickly stammered, "I mean yours; this is all yours." She looked down, embarrassed.

Nara had misread Sam's expression, so she cleared the air of misgivings, "As far as I am concerned, Nara, this is our room. It sounds like you spent the entire night cleaning up my mess."

“Messes,” Nara provided helpfully.

"Right, messes," Sam corrected herself, continuing her thought, "I don't really get what the big deal is about this room? It's nice and all and big, but why so coveted?"

Nara looked at Sam like she was an alien. Then she remembered that Sam was, in fact, an alien, so she explained, or it could be more accurately stated, she gushed. "It is a spatial suite! Do you remember those little boxes in the upper level at the back of the hall? The ones you said looked like outhouses, whatever those are. Well, each one of those boxes is one of these rooms!"

That statement floored Sam. This room had to be at least two hundred and fifty square meters with a five-meter-high ceiling. "Bigger on the inside," she mumbled, gazing at the expansive room with expensive-looking wood furniture. Ornate rugs adorned the floor, matching the tapestries on the walls. Some tapestries had a coat of arms depicting a giant bird holding a spear in one taloned foot and a bundle of arrows in the other. Sam assumed it was "Little Boy Chad's" family crest. “*Man, they are going to be so pissed!*” She wasn't looking forward to that confrontation.

She asked Nara, "How long do we have this room for?"

Nara looked confused, "Forever Sam. Apart from a yearly maintenance fee of ten gold, this is your rent-free home in the guild." She sipped her water and offered Sam a glass, who took it gratefully. Nara explained some more. "Most adventurers rent the space when they aren't using it. The guild hall will also manage the rental for a small percentage of the rental fee on top of the annual fee."

"You're saying that for ten gold a year, I can stay here anytime I am in the city?" Sam wasn't fully versed in the value of Hallista's currency, but from what she did know, ten gold still sounded fairly steep just to have a place in the city. Even with the kick-ass tavern downstairs…the very lenient kick-ass tavern.

Nara cleared the price up for her, "I'm saying that for ten gold a year, you can stay in any Adventurers Guild Hall on the planet! The room isn't in the boxes; it is in the key! The boxes unlock the key, not the other way around. The ten gold is to rent the space the box occupies in all the guild halls across the planet and the moons!"

Sam whistled and then had a brilliant idea, which she immediately shared with Nara. "We can bring the box with us on jobs and—" She stopped talking. Nara was already shaking her head, devastating Sam's hopes of sleeping in the luxurious bed and relaxing by the fireplace in the middle of a dark and dangerous forest. She was no stranger to roughing it, but why rough it if you had a mobile suite in your inventory?

"No, the boxes cannot be moved. They are powerful magic items attuned to your key and carefully maintained by the guild. How they work and were created is a closely guarded secret. The guild will not let them leave the hall. In fact, there are supposedly enchantments on them that cause the box to disintegrate if they are ever taken off the grounds."

"Well, there goes my dreams of glamping through deadly forests and dungeons. Oh well, you win some, you lose some." Sam had already figured it wouldn't be possible, but she had hoped. Either way, having the room was a serious advantage. *"I wonder...if I ever manage to leave this planet though...could I convince the guild to mount it in my...I don't know, my spaceship? Ha, look at me, like I'll ever have my own spaceship. A girl can dream, though, can't she?"* Sam had another thought and asked Nara, "How will the guild rent the room if I have the key?"

Nara must have anticipated the question because she replied immediately, "They won't rent this specific room. They have a master key that lets them create another room in this space. The quality of the room depends on how much the patron wants to pay. It's part of the yearly rental fee. Trust me, Sam, with this room, you will make hundreds of gold per year, maybe even a thousand if you never use the room."

Sam moved to the bed and plopped down, sprawling out on it and closing her eyes, enjoying the soft down mattress. It all seemed so surreal and far too serendipitous. She started to suspect that the System may be curating situations for her. She dismissed the thought almost as soon as it came to her. There was no way an all-powerful system controlling an entire verse in an infinite multiverse would care about an insignificant speck like her any more than she cared about an individual microbe in her gut.

Sam enjoyed the soft bed, relaxing and taking it all in. She realized Nara had been unusually silent for too long and opened her eyes only to find Nara staring at her legs with a strange expression. Glancing down at what Nara was staring at, Sam realized it wasn't her legs.

Clamping her thighs together, Sam said gruffly, "I need a bath!"
"Me too," Nara whispered as she absently licked her lips while staring.
Sam waved a hand at the beautiful sorceress, saying, "Hey, eyes up here, missy," trying to distract the woman from whatever thoughts she was currently having.
Nara pulled her gaze reluctantly from Sam's naked form and looked her in the eyes questioningly. "I'm sorry, did you say something?" Her voice told Sam the Tenarian's mind was a million kilometers away.
"Where is the nearest bath house, Nara? Or showers, or whatever people who don't have a cleaning spell do here?" Sam questioned.
"Oh, there's a bath in the corner," Nara pointed to a partition on one side of the room with a folding screen that reminded Sam of the kind she had seen in movies where people threw clothes over the top, disrobing while hidden behind it.
Nara jumped up and grabbed Sam's hand, pulling her up, "Come on, I'll show you."
Sam let herself be dragged along to the bath and was pleasantly surprised at the size of the tub. It was bigger than a jacuzzi and already full of steaming water. Sam hopped up the two steps to the lip of the tub and tested the water with her toe. It was perfect. Quickly sliding into the water, Sam moaned with pleasure. Glamping at its finest, indeed.
"This is the life," Sam thought, slipping deeper into the steaming water until just her nose and the top of her head showed, *"soaking in a hot tub in a medieval room with a lit fireplace is the ultimate coziness. All I need now is a good book and a glass of wine."*
A light cough to her left brought Sam's attention back to the only other occupant in the room. Nara was standing at the entrance of the partitioned area, biting her lower lip and looking sheepish of all things. *"Oh, what the hell,"* Sam thought, waving her over.
Nara was instantly out of her gown and quickly slid into the tub opposite Sam with a beaming smile.

CHAPTER 15 — "A...rat...this is the hide of a rat."

After their bath and a hearty breakfast, Sam and Nara split up and headed away from the guild grounds to shop and trade. Sam was going to see if she could find a buyer for some of her loot drops. Primarily some of the pelts, monster cores, and beast corpses. Nara, whom Sam had given some silver and gold coins, would grab their camping supplies and try to sell some of the extra weapons they found themselves carrying. They planned to meet for dinner and see how the other was progressing.

Before parting ways, Sam vehemently insisted she would be fine exploring the city by herself and told Nara that if anyone messed with her, she would take a sip of the cyan death toxin she had looted from the rogue and melt them with her breath attack. Nara did not find that amusing, which made it hilarious to Sam, and she skipped down the street laughing and singing, "I have a breath attack. I have a breath attack."

Nara watched the psychotic woman leave and shook her head. *"What have I gotten myself into?"* Then she looked at Sam's shapely buttocks and smiled. Yeah, she knew what she was getting into. She was still smiling as she headed down a different street in the direction of a contact the guild master had given her who would hopefully be able to shed some light on what a sorceress was. Whatever Sam's magic was, it changed her more than she initially realized. After meeting the contact, she planned on trying to sell the weapons to a blacksmith she had visited the last time she was in the city with Arron and Alina. Nara took a deep breath of the clear morning air as she walked. It was time to begin her life as a free Tenarian.

***

Sam soon arrived at an armor shop and entered excitedly, unphased by a little chime going off when she passed the door's threshold into the well-lit interior. A young man and woman were tending the counter at the far end of the room, and they both looked bored out of their minds. Neither of them even looked up when she walked in.

Sam took a minute to examine the contents of the shop. Most of the armor on the manakins looked gaudy and too shiny to be functional in the wilderness, with bright polished plates of steel and glistening scales adorning most pieces. She wasn't sure this was the place she was looking for but walked up to the counter anyway.

The young man looked up with exasperation like she was disturbing him from staring emptily into the void. "Yes?" His tone matched his annoyed expression.

Sam was unbothered and asked, "Do you sell anything functional? You know, like some leather armor in muted colors. Something that doesn't just scream, I'm over here! Attack me!"

The young man just stared at Sam. The girl beside him snorted a laugh, finally looking up from the book she was reading, "You will want to go to Alexander's Wares in the middle district. He has the best functional leather, and his weapons aren't bad either."

"Does he purchase raw materials like pelts?" Sam asked, wondering if she could trade instead of purchase.

"He does, but they must be high quality," the girl replied helpfully.

Sam got directions to the store and thanked the girl with a silver coin, much to the young man's surprise. *"See. It pays to be nice to strangers' kid."* She thought as she left the shop. In the poor boy's defense, she was still wearing bloody clothes which did not fit quite right.

***

Alexander's Wares was an armory, tannery, leather working, and blacksmith shop all in one. Sam could hear the clanging of hammers against steel and smell the various chemicals used to tan leather a block before she arrived at the storefront. Walking into the first level of the two-story building, she was pleased with what she saw. This was like a one-stop shop for all her adventuring needs, at least everything that pertained to attack and defense. Everything in the store looked high quality and functional, with most of the armor dyed with muted colors that would blend in with various environments. Colors like desert and snow camo to flat black and every option in between were displayed. Many of the outfits had matching weapon sets with them, too. Sam was impressed; it was like an outdoor store of death, and she liked it.

"Can I help you, miss?"

Sam turned to the voice, and after doing a complete circle without seeing anyone, she said, "Um, yes."

"I am here, miss. If you would turn to your left and look up, please," the voice said.

Doing as instructed, Sam turned and looked up to the high ceiling. A dark red Imp was hovering just out of her reach.

"Shit!" Sam grunted and jumped back, knocking over a freestanding manakin, causing its weapons to clatter to the floor. Several of the patrons shouted and moved away from the commotion. A short sword and shield she had crafted appeared in her hands, and she wrapped her threads around the Imp's arms and legs, yanking it to the floor.

"Please miss! Stop! I mean you no harm!" The Imp cried as he was violently pulled to the floor by an unseen force.

Sam was already stalking toward the Imp with her shield and sword raised. She caught herself when the Imp's words finally filtered through her fear-addled brain, but before she could release the obviously harmless Imp, who she noticed was wearing a nice dress suit, a booming voice reverberated through the room.

"Stop!" The voice penetrated every fiber of Sam's being.

Sam and everyone else in the building froze in place. Sam couldn't move, she couldn't even think, so powerful was the command. She felt a presence so overwhelming it felt like her very soul was being crushed and her spirit was going to wink out of existence at any second.

"What is going on here, Bradley? Are you okay?" A greying man in plain clothes walked up to the Imp. With a wave of his hand the man disintegrated Sam's mana threads that were still wrapped around her target, and he helped the Imp to his feet.

Sam, still under the influence of the man's voice spell, could only bear the pain of her mana backlash in silence and watched as the man patted down the Imp, Bradley, to check for injuries. He turned to Sam.

"How dare you attack one of my employees in my store. Have you no shame?" He waited for a reply, and when none came, he asked, "Are you deaf? I asked you a question."

Bradly tugged on the man's shirt, saying, "Mister Alexander, I believe she is still under your spell."

"I…oh, yes, of course." The man, Alexander, waved his hand again, and Sam felt the pressure holding her in place release all at once.

She stumbled forward a half step before catching herself. Many other patrons weren't so lucky, and most fell to their knees, gasping and clutching their cores. Sam checked to make sure her own mana cores weren't ruptured. They weren't, thankfully.

She looked to Alexander and said through wheezing breaths, "I…I am sorry. Mister Bradley surprised me, and I overreacted. The last Imp, um, person like him I encountered very nearly burned me to death." She wheezed, "That was only two weeks ago, so it's still fresh." She looked at Bradley. The little Imp was still eyeing her warily and standing close to his boss, "I really am very sorry. Did I hurt you? I have a healing ability if I did. And healing potions if you are afraid to let me touch you."

"He's fine," Alexander said, and Bradley nodded at his words. Looking at Bradley, Alexander asked, "Is her apology acceptable to you?" At Bradley the Imp's nod, he continued, "How often have I told you not to surprise people? I swear one of these days, I will not be around to help."

Bradley looked a little chastised when he said, "I know. But she looked weak and young. It's fun watching humans jump."

Alexander just rolled his eyes at the Imp. Then he took an appraising look at Sam. "A level 21 Pathfinder. Very interesting." Then his eyes narrowed, and he pointed to Sam's sword and shield, which she had been too distracted to dismiss. "Where did you get those? Wait, don't answer that. Come with me." He marched off toward the back of the store without looking back.

Sam was smart enough to know there was no other option than following the man. With one last apologetic look toward Bradley, the Imp, she dismissed her weapons and hurried after the enigmatic Alexander.

***

Nara was ushered into a plush waiting area when she told the clerk at the front desk of the small, unassuming magic shop who had sent her. After she declined any refreshments, the clerk left the room, closing the door softly on his way out.

"This is nicer than I expected from the plain exterior," she thought as she relaxed into one of the plush chairs in the seating area.

Nara didn't have to wait long. An elvish man walked into the waiting room a few minutes after she had been seated.

When he walked in, he waved at her to stay seated, saying, "No need to get up. We can talk freely in here." Silencing wards lit up the room with another wave of his hand before dimming again. "So, Harold tells me you have an undiscovered class." He looked at her closely through thick magical glasses, "Hmm, a level 26 sorceress. Never heard of it." He pulled a notepad out and started scribbling into it.

"Um, my name is Nara Evander. And you are?" Nara said. She did not like how the man treated her like a test subject. This was not the kind of 'help' Master Harold had suggested she would receive.

"Ah yes, where are my manners? I am Serge, magical advisor to the royal counsel here in Helms Peak and personal friend of Harrold's." He held a hand out to shake, "Pleasure to meet you, Miss Evander."

"Will this be kept confidential?" Nara asked as she shook the man's hand. She was starting to get worried she had made a mistake coming here.

"Oh, most certainly!" Serge looked slightly offended. "My business would fail if I went about telling everyone's secrets. In fact, apart from sending you here, Harrold will no longer be involved in our attempt to discover your class's potential."

"Okay..." Nara wasn't completely convinced, but she did need help desperately. She hadn't told Sam, but ever since she had been fed the arcane mana, she hadn't been able to cast a single spell. And her affinity had gone back to purely neutral. It was frustrating with the massive amount of power at her disposal; she had yet to figure out how to use it. Other than to infuse her legs with it to keep up with Sam when she ran at a 'moderate' pace.

"Easy to understand. We drain Sam fully, and we will have all her secrets." Naris's voice echoed in her mind.

"I've already told you no! Neither you nor I will hurt her!" Nara put as much force into her thoughts as *possible: "You better promise if you ever want out again!"*

"You are weak! You will lose control again, and I will feast so much you will never be able to return!" Naris hissed into her mind.

Nara shuddered involuntarily at the words, knowing deep in her heart she would eventually lose control again. It was one of her greatest fears. She could only hope Sam could resist Naris when he was at full power, as she did when he was weakened by the blood contract.

"Were you just conversing with your Blight?" Serge asked. He had been watching her intently. When Nara's eyes widened, he held up a hand. "Before you think it, no, Harrold did not tell me. I am an advisor to the royals, Miss Nara. I know more about this city's occupants than they know about themselves."

Nara slumped in her chair and asked, "What would you like me to tell you?"

***

Sam was led into a backroom and down a flight of stairs into a magical workshop. The walls were lined with shelves full of vials filled with liquids of every color. There were glowing crystals scattered amongst the vials. A central workbench dominated the room, scattered with magical tools. In the center of the workbench was a small node with a clear crystal about the size of her thumb set into it. There was what Sam could only call a palm scanner on the edge of the workbench with very modern-looking cables leading to the node housing the crystal.

Turning and seeing where Sam's gaze was directed, Alexander commented, "My prized possession. I looted it from an ancient ruin. I believe the ruin was from an enormous flying ship that crashed thousands of years before." His eyes took on a dreamy look, "You should have seen the technology onboard. Much of the technology far surpassed my ability to understand! But alas," he shook his head, "the Children of the Light only hired me and my team to clear the ruin, which had become a dungeon by then, so they could claim it. Now they hold all its secrets."

Sam walked over to the palm scanner and hesitated before she touched it, looking at Alexander for permission.

He just shrugged. "It allows you to transmit magical power into a crystal. I know what it does. What I want to know is where you found those weapons?"

"And if I don't want to tell you where I found them?" Sam hedged.

"Then I believe our business is concluded, and I will need to file a report with the city guard regarding the assault on one of my clerks by a guild member," Alexander said with pleasure. He turned and headed back up the stairs.

"Wait," Sam said quickly, "I found them in the forest." It wasn't technically a lie.

"My dear, I am over nine hundred cycles old. Do not insult me with lies." Alexander said.

"Shit! How many people in this city will know all my secrets before I leave? All of them at the rate I'm going!" She thought before calling out to the retreating form, "I made them!"

He came stomping back down the stairs. This time, he was obviously annoyed. "I said don't insult my intelligence, young lady! There is no way a level 21 child such as yourself could make a pure crystalline mana—" His eyes widened.

Sam was forming a crystal identical to the crystal in the machine in the palm of her hand. Alexander walked over to her and stared in fascination at the crystal. As the layers of mana slowly brought its form into permanence, he leaned in so close that his nose threatened to touch the construct.

"I wouldn't get too close there, buddy," Sam warned. "These things tend to explode if I make a mistake."

"Of course they do," Alexander commented, his nose still only millimeters away from the potential bomb. "This is fascinating! You are crystallizing your mana at a rate visible to the naked eye! This process normally takes centuries!"

Sam finished the product and handed it to the curious man. "Do you believe me now?"

Alexander snatched the crystal from her and hurriedly placed his monocle in his right eye, squinting down to hold it in place. He walked over to a spot on his workbench, mumbling to himself, ignoring her question. He set the crystal on his workbench, and a screen with readouts popped up, surprising Sam.

"Well, now I'm curious," Sam thought and rushed to stand beside the weird man.

The readout stated:

Mana Crystal: Pure
Quality: Flawless
Affinity: Error
Power: 100mu
Output: 100mu/ms

Input: NA
Uses: 1

"Is that good?" Sam had to ask. It had taken her nearly a thousand mana to make a measly one hundred mana unit crystal. She said as much to Alexander.

"It is not the amount of mana it holds but how fast it can discharge!" Alexander said excitedly, "One hundred mana units per millisecond! That is unheard of. Here, let me show you." He grabbed a nearby crystal and replaced Sam's with it on the scanner.

Mana Crystal: 67% Purity
Quality: Good
Affinity: Light
Power: 3787/4000mp
Output: 30mu/sec
Input: 30mu/sec
Uses: Multiple

Alexander pointed to the 30mu/sec, saying, "This is an average discharge speed for mana crystals of this quality. I have seen a few excellent-grade crystals that could discharge at nearly a thousand mana units per second. Still, those kinds of crystals are kept hidden away or used for armies' large siege and defensive weapons." He picked up the arcane crystal Sam had made. He whispered conspiratorially to her, "With a thousand of these crystals, I could arm five hundred mages that have both the Double Cast ability and a high-power attack spell and use them to devastate any invading force dumb enough to come near me!" He tapped his chin deep in thought then said, "or power a single cannon to fire a concentrated beam of energy with equal effect!"

"You need to calm down," Sam was getting nervous now. "I will not participate in that kind of mass murder."

"Then may I suggest you do not make many of these," he held up her crystal. "Although…" he looked thoughtful, "I tell you what. Suppose you can make me a crystal similar to this one that can be recharged and can store, say—five hundred thousand mana. In that case, I will fully outfit you and up to six of your companions with all the adventuring gear you will ever need, which includes custom works if required." He paused to let that sink in before icing the cake, "For one hundred cycles and up to level 150."

Sam wanted to say yes at once. Anything she wanted from this shop for up to a hundred years! "*Where do I sign*?" But then her ability to reason returned from its temporary hiatus and told her she had no idea if it was a good deal. She also had yet to learn if she could even supply a rechargeable crystal that could hold that much, nor did she want to think about what five hundred thousand mana could do if it could be released in milliseconds! She shook her head.

"Oh, hell no, I am not about to make or give you a weapon of mass destruction, Buster! Have you lost your mind? Five hundred thousand mana, what are you nuts? Do you want to blow up an entire city or something?" Sam was on a roll. The thought of what this guy was asking for, from a complete stranger, no less, was starting to grate on her.

Alexander made placating motions with his hands, saying, "The crystal wouldn't need such a high output as the one you just made. I only want it to power my shop and research your particular mana, which is of the arcane persuasion if I am not mistaken."

Sam didn't answer and crossed her arms, narrowing her eyes at Alexander, "If by some miracle I can make what you are asking for, what assurances can you give me that you will not just sell it to the highest bidder? Or use it against me?"

"Only my good name." He mirrored her posture, leaning against his workbench with a proud look.

"Dude, I don't have a fucking clue who you are," Sam said.

Alexander spluttered before composing himself, "I am Alexander Batiste, one of only five master crafters in the ten kingdoms! And the only one within two thousand kilometers of Helms Peak!"

"I'm not sure why I should care, and how does that describe your integrity?" Sam was a little lost now. "Look, I'll just ask about you around the city and see what the locals say." She shrugged, "Meanwhile, I'll see if I can make what you want, and while I'm at it, I will try to build in a safety to prevent it from being used as anything other than a battery."

"It is acceptable," Alexander nodded. "Also, if it helps alleviate your concerns about giving me what I requested, you should know, Miss…ahem, I'm sorry, I don't believe I got your name."

"Samantha Moura, but please call me Sam," Sam said.

"Yes, very well, Sam. As I was saying, many crystals are out there holding millions of mana. The mana crystal that powered the crashed ship, for instance, would have had a capacity of at least twenty million mana units. I honestly believe it is why the Church sent my party into the ruin in the first place. So that we could find the crystal that fueled the ship. Fortunately, there was no crystal in the main chamber, only a much larger one of those." He pointed to the node in the center of the workbench.

"That is terrifying, actually," Sam said, "not reassuring at all!" Then she thought, *"But it sounds like that 'ruin' might be an airship. Or even a spaceship! Didn't Nara allude to the Children of the Light being outworlders? I wonder if I could create a crystal to charge that ruin up and get off this planet. Maybe it could be a System Quest...?"* Sam waited for a notification, holding her breath, but sadly none came. Alexander was talking again, so she focused back on the conversation.

"There are also many treaties between the kingdoms to prevent the use of such powerful items. Our histories and fables tell of several times Hallista was nearly destroyed before the rise of the gods who, in their infinite wisdom, removed the items of power from this world." Alexander concluded.

"Gods, huh, or as Nara calls them, very powerful beings." Sam placed her hand on the scanner for the machine and asked Alexander, "If I fill this gem and let you keep the crystal I made, will that be enough for me and one friend to get outfitted for free?"

While Alexander thought about her offer, Sam pushed some mana into the pad beneath her hand, and it lit up. Turning on Mana Sight, she watched as her mana flowed through the cable and into the machine. The crystal embedded in the slot began filling a moment later. For Sam, it was a little like giving Nara mana, except this time, she had to keep pushing the mana into the machine. In contrast, Nara pulled her mana out once Sam opened the gate.

The little crystal held much more than she expected. A small readout displayed on the machine showed it at a little over fifty percent capacity when she had already dumped nearly forty thousand mana into it. The crystal was a bright purple when she stopped at seventy thousand mana. It took over an hour and a half to fill the little thumb-sized gem of power.

Alexander must have accepted her offer because when she was finished, she found several suits of leather armor laid out on a bench nearby. Seeing no one else in the room, she walked over and, picking up one of the chest pieces, she examined it.

Leather Chest Armor of the Basilisk [Level 30]; 1 of 5
Classification: Light Chest Armor
Quality: Excellent
Magical: Yes
Enchantments: Self Repair, Auto Defense
Charge(s): NA

Made from the hide of a level 36 Basilisk and infused with its core. This armor will harden itself at points of Impact, increasing its defense slightly. This effect is increased when a complete set is worn.

Sam grabbed the tag hanging off the chest piece of the grey armor. *"Aww, he wants me to know how valuable this is. Let's see, it costs, holy shit, a thousand gold! What the fuck? Is there gold inlay I can't see or something?"*

Sam placed the armor back down carefully before going to the next set.

Leather Chest Armor of the Salamander [Level 15]; 1 of 5
Classification: Light Chest Armor
Quality: Excellent
Magical: Yes
Enchantments: Self Repair, Fire Shield
Fire Resistance: 33%
Charge(s): 3/3
Made from the hide of a level 19 Fire Salamander and infused with its core. In addition to being fire resistant, this armor can entirely negate a single fire attack lasting 10 seconds or less up to three times before needing to be recharged.

"Wow, I could have used this a couple of weeks ago," Sam thought and checked the price. Unsurprisingly, it was more than the first one at eighteen hundred gold, and that was just for the chest piece. She had to admit the quality was excellent, and who wouldn't want to be fireproof? But that was way more gold than she was expecting. She was seriously beginning to think she should make the crystal he wanted right then and there if this was the kind of equipment she could get out of the deal. And for a hundred years! Placing the dark red armor back, she moved to the last set. It wasn't armor but a cloak, pants, boots, and a tunic. They were almost translucent, and Sam thought they were made of plastic until she picked up the cloak and felt the soft, pliable leather it was made from. She identified it.

Leather Cloak of the Morph Rat [Level 41] 1 of 4
Classification: Outer Garment
Quality: Excellent
Magical: Yes
Enchantments: Self Repair, Morph
Form(s): 0/5
Made from the hide of a level 68 Winged Morph Rat and infused with its core. This cloak will hold up to five pre-set forms created by the

wearer. The forms can be changed instantly, giving the wearer an advantage in any situation they can predict and plan for.

"A…rat…this...is the hide of a rat?" Sam said, questioning the information. She ran the smooth, velvety leather through her hands as she spoke. Then she looked at the other pieces and asked no one, "Just how big was this rat?"

"About five meters long, if memory serves," Bradley said from behind her, causing Sam to turn. He winced when she looked at him. "Sorry, so sorry! I didn't mean to sneak up on you again," he said quickly.

Sam ignored the Imp and checked the price tag. Then she rechecked it because she had to have read it wrong. It read thirteen platinum coins. "Bradley," Sam asked, "how many gold coins make up a platinum coin?"

"Uh, let me see, at the current exchange rate," he did some math in his head and on his fingers, "I can't give you the exact number without consulting one of the banks, but I think it is around one thousand gold right now. Maybe the high nine hundreds."

Sam held up the cloak, "you're saying this cloak made from 'rat' skin is worth thirteen thousand gold coins?"

"Yes, precisely. It is an amazing piece and priced to sell." Bradley didn't get Sam's emphasis on the word 'rat' and seemed quite proud of the rat suit Sam was holding. He entered business mode, crushing Sam's hopes of wearing the latest rat skin fashion trend. "These are some samples of what you and your companions will be outfitted with should you provide my employer with the item he requested or something comparable. For now, though," he pulled a handwritten note from his pocket and started reading it aloud, "Bradley, the young adventurer, I forget her name. Anyway, her current contribution is enough for a store credit of eighty gold coins. Also, see if she has anything worthwhile to sell or trade. Thank you, Bradley, and don't surprise her again!" Carefully folding the note and placing it back in his breast pocket, Bradley looked at Sam expectantly.

***

Several hours later, Sam left Alexander's feeling like she had done okay in her negotiations with the shrewd Imp. Of all the hides she had, she only kept the coats of the Blade Tail and Great Timberwolf. Sam liked curling up in them by the fire, too much to part with them. The meat the store wouldn't purchase, and there was no way she would part with the summoning token just yet. She traded off everything she could, including all the beast corpses and cores. Apparently, beast cores were essential in enchanting any clothing or armor made from their hides. They were highly sought after because not every beast had a harvestable core, at least for those without the loot skill.

In return for everything, Sam walked away with three changes of clothes and two sets of high-quality leather armor, not the magical kind, unfortunately. She also had the same items for Nara. When Sam had voiced her concern about not knowing Nara's size, Bradley assured her the outfits would mold to her shape as it was a perk of a master crafter. She hadn't purchased any weapons; she could make her own, and Nara seemed attached to the ranger's bow they had looted, so she could see no need for anything at the moment. Everything said and done, Sam walked away with fifteen gold coins more than she had gone in with. Bradley even gave her a premium on the items she sold him and a fifteen percent discount on all her purchases. Overall, she felt pleased with her transactions.

Now, to find Nara. It was late afternoon, and shopping made her hungry! And thirsty.

***

Sam found Nara lounging on a bench outside the guild gates, and the two filled each other in on their day's activities. Sam wanted to try the local cuisine. Nara knew of a nice restaurant in the area, so the two headed to dinner, planning to have a relaxing evening before setting out the next day.

CHAPTER 16 — "You said it would work!"

Nara woke Sam up early the following morning in a delightful manner. It was so enjoyable Sam seriously considered staying in bed with the shapeshifter all day. Still, Sam knew they needed to get moving, so after a delicious breakfast of beer biscuits, the actual beer the biscuits were made with, and the most enormous vegetable omelet Sam had ever seen, the two were out of the guild gates and heading to an outfitter for camping supplies. Nara hadn't had time to pick up supplies the previous day, but she had managed to make a good bit of coin from selling the weapons, clothes, armor, and three storage items they had. She kept the ranger's bow and picked up a quiver and fifty steel-tipped arrows. They thought it was strange that all the bandit's storage items had been empty. Nara postulated it was an enchantment that destroyed the contents upon their deaths, probably forced on them by their employer.

Over their quiet dinner the night before, Nara had come clean to Sam that she could not use the magic Sam was giving her. She told Sam about meeting with Serge and how no one knew what a sorceress was. When she told Sam she couldn't even learn a simple light spell from a scroll Serge had provided as a test, a lightbulb went off for Sam.

Sam pulled out her primer and slid it to Nara across the dinner table, explaining what it was and, to some extent, what a sorceress was on Earth. And since Nara could already see mana, she should try manipulating it.

They returned to the guild and paid for a couple of hours of range time so Sam could show Nara how she manipulated mana by forming different constructs and firing them at the targets downrange. Nara had watched intently but could not replicate anything Sam did. Toward the end of their range time, a mage approached them from the small crowd that had gathered to watch a level 21 completely annihilate dozens of practice targets with ease. The mage had noted that Nara was a Tenarian Moonblight and suggested Sam attack her with a spell. He explained he had fought a Wild Moonblight once, and shortly into their fight, the Moonblight had started using his own magic against him. He could only assume the Moonblight was absorbing and replicating his spells.

Sam laughed manically and shot Nara in the foot with an arcane bolt. It worked! After Nara had stopped hopping around and cursing Sam, she could use the spell Magic Bolt. Nara's spell had a different name, and her mana was blue, but it worked the same as Sam's. Both women were delighted, but Sam was far more so than Nara. This surprised Nara until Sam turned to the crowd and yelled that she would pay three gold to the first person who hit Nara with a cleansing spell.

***

At Sam's insistence, they stopped at Alexander's, which was already bustling with activity even at the early hour. They negotiated for a better quiver for Nara, who apparently had advanced archery skills. Sam was impressed with Nara's archery ability and wanted to help her as much as possible. It would benefit not only Nara but them as a team. Pleased with the purchase of the new Quiver of Replication, they moved on to the outfitters.

***

“I don’t care how much it costs Nara! We need this!” Sam was insistent.

"Sam, we don't have enough coin! There is no way you have enough gold, let alone platinum!" Nara was trying and failing to drag an enamored pathfinder away from the object of her fascination.

It was a spatial campsite that could be placed in a storage item. It came complete with a five-person tent so each occupant would have their own cot and lock box, an owner's tent with a king-size bed and writing desk, a fire ring, a picnic table, camping chairs, and a security ring automatically deployed around the perimeter. The display tag said the campsite guaranteed a level 2 safe zone and could be up to level 3 in some cases.

Sam had no idea how she had survived without this campsite of beauty! Who cared if it cost seventeen platinum coins! Compared to the spatial cabin next to it, going for fifty platinum, the price of the campsite was a steal! She drooled over it for a few more minutes before finally letting Nara drag her away.

Nara led them to a small sitting area, which reminded Sam of a vehicle dealership lounge; snacks and drinks were provided. Nara pulled out the list they made before Sam went on her rampage the other night and started reading it. She scratched out a few items they had acquired, like enchanted weapons and arrows for fighting the undead. She was talking as she went down the list, primarily to herself.

"Let's see, enchanted weapons to effectively combat undead…didn't we decide the weapons you create would work just fine?" At Sam's nod, Nara drew a line through that item. "Hm, we already have a quiver and arrows." Another crossed-out item. "Do you think you could make enchanted arrows?" Nara looked up.

"Absolutely," Sam said. "It would be awesome if the quiver replicated them."

"True, we can see if it will replicate enchanted or magical arrows. It's too bad the replicated arrows only last for a few minutes. We could make some serious coin if we constantly replicate magic arrows to sell." Nara frowned. The store clerk at Alexander's had been very clear the quiver would not make permanent replicants and to ensure they kept the original arrow segregated from the rest in the small slot provided in the quiver. It wasn't a surprise to the women, only a disappointment.

Nara went back to the list, "shovels, decent cutlery, plates, bowls, a pickaxe, outdoor shower," she scratched the last one out now that she had a cleansing spell and continued, "rope because you were insistent, we could always use rope and an adventurer without rope was just a useless waste of underprepared space." Nara tapped her fingers on the table, glancing at Sam sideways. "We could see if we can afford a defensive tent with sleeping cots and some basic perimeter wards for an alarm system. That way, we will always be able to create a safe zone."

Sam perked up and fist-pumped. It wasn't a spatial tent, but it still sounded cool.

A store employee soon joined them, and after about an hour of haggling over the prices, they walked out with everything on their list, plus a few extra items like cooking spices, oils, and a couple of basic repair kits for armor and their new tent to make their lives in the wild a little easier.

The only other stop they made was a bookstore where Sam purchased several books covering the basics of magic, the general politics of the area, a brief history of the kingdom they were in, and a guide to the local flora and fauna. The total was a whopping eighty gold, which Sam had to pay some of in silver thanks to their quickly depleting funds and the fact she still owed the city guard thirty-five gold coins before she could leave the city.

***

"Which job should we tackle first?" Nara asked. Once they were back on the road.

Sam checked her map to determine which was closest by the descriptions and the crude maps provided with the postings. The guild had a massive map of the surrounding area with pins for all the job locations and also handed out a smaller map for every job they took. After studying the large map on the wall of the guild hall intently for a few minutes, Sam's own map updated, much to her excitement and relief. It wasn't to the level of detail like when she visited a location, but it filled in names and distances, which was enough for her. She decided on a survey mission first and told Nara.

Nara viewed the location on the map provided with the job notice and nodded. She asked what Sam already suspected, "Do you think Helms Peak plans to expand to the south along the Beast Lands border? That might cause friction between Orlina and some of the closest tribes."

"It certainly looks that way," Sam said. It looked like an expansion from all the jobs in such a small area. Sam and Nara alone had snagged several postings. The one they were heading for was to survey and map an area of about five square kilometers. When Sam saw it, she quickly grabbed the job from the board; when Nara looked at her quizzically, Sam had whispered in her ear, "Cartography skill," and wiggled her eyebrows, causing the little Tenarian to clap excitedly and bounce up and down.

"The Witlings job is in the same area, so we can do both simultaneously," Nara said and started walking.

Sam shuddered a little when she started after Nara. 'Whitlings' were a pest species in Hallista, and according to her new book, they were a cross between a vampire bat and a lizard. They were roughly the size of a large dog and could suck blood or inject poison into their victims with their fangs. According to the book, they were primarily harmless and skittish predators in small groups. What made them dangerous was that if left unchecked, a brood mother was usually born once their numbers started growing. And when that happened, their numbers began multiplying exponentially, and they threatened local settlements, the residents, and their livestock and pets.

***

The two turned south into the forest as soon as they were down the mountain, and after about an hour of walking, they stopped so Sam could give Nara mana. At Sam's insistence, Nara morphed back into her natural form. Something about how she looked and carried herself in her true form was primal and fierce to Sam, and she couldn't get enough of it.

It was nearly fifteen kilometers to the survey location, so to pass the time, Sam kept reading one of her new books, "A Compendium of Local Life; *Helms Peak Edition*." Her slow hike became a scavenger hunt with her new book in hand as Sam tried to identify and match what plants and animals she saw with the book's descriptions. Nara even got into it since she grew up in a different kingdom before she was enslaved, and her contract didn't allow her to learn anything new without permission, which was rarely given. Nara didn't talk about her time enslaved to the Church of the Light, and Sam didn't pry. She figured the Tenarian would tell her in her own time or not at all, and she was okay with both scenarios.

They took their time exploring as they hiked. There were no time limits on the job contracts, which had been posted for a while without any interested parties taking them. The clerk who approved them taking the jobs seemed relieved to get the postings off the board. The girls picked the name 'Loot Hunters' for their party when told they had to register under an official party name if more than one member participated in a job. Sam was a little disappointed when Nara had downright refused to allow either Bad Bitches or Outworlders saying both would draw too much attention.

Sam was thinking about how they were now in an adventuring party as they hiked while checking the notifications from her blackout night at the guild pub when an exciting notice popped up.

'Bing' Would you like to create a party with Nara Evander? Y/N

Sam picked yes and watched as Nara stopped in her tracks. A moment later, the chime of another notification echoed in her head.

'Bing' Nara Evander has accepted your party invitation. You may review her statistics in your Party Leader menu.

"Huh, let's see what I'm working with." Sam thought. She found the party menu in her interface and pulled Nara's stats.

Nara Evander; *[Naris Blight]*
Race: Tenarian; Mortal; [Level 26]; *Soul Bound Blight [Level ?]*
Class: Sorceress [Level 1]; *Mana Reaper [Level 26]*

Health: 546
Stamina: 351
Mana: 127598; *[??????]*

Attributes:
STR – 16 *[??]*
VIT – 34 *[??]*
END – 20 *[??]*
AGL – 38 *[??]*
INT – 23 *[??]*
Free Attribute Points 7.

Abilities: 2/4
Mana Sense [Level 7]
[Mana Siphon; Level 42]

Class Skills: 1/7
Replicate [Level 1]

Racial/General Skills: 3/7
Archery; Adept; [Level 17]
Identify [Level 3]
Mana Drain [Level 26]

Class Spells: 2/5

Magic Bolt [Level 2]
Cleanse [Level 1]

Racial/General Spells: 1/5
Charm [Level 2]

Resistance(s):
Pain [Level 12]
Poison [Level 3]
Magic [Level 27]

"How are you so strong?" Nara, who apparently now had access to Sam's stats, asked with disbelief. Just how many points do you get per level?"

"I get five free points per race level and double that per class level. Is that unusual?" Sam had been wondering how her Pathfinder class stacked up against other offensive-type classes in this world. All she had to go on was the healer class the System offered her initially.

"Yes, it's unusual!" Nara said in exasperation. "My Race gives me a point in vitality and Agility and two free points per level, and my new class gives me a point in Agility and intelligence with three free points. You get one extra point per race level and five extra per class level!" Nara threw up her hands, "it's like you get an extra level for every level up!"

Sam didn't know what to say, so she changed the subject. "Speaking of your classes, how do your class changes work? Do you lose all your points every time and have to start over?"

Nara nodded, "Something like that. I was a level 25 healer before, with a focus on intelligence and vitality. If I switch my class back to Healer, my sorceress level gains will be lost, and I will start back at level 25 with all my points reassigned to where they were before as a healer. What you see is what I assigned from my race levels. I have to be vigilant of where I put my free points because, at any time, I could lose my class and all the points it has provided."

Sam understood what Nara meant and asked one more question, "Why are there limits to how many abilities, skills, and spells you can have?"

"It's standard for people who aren't blessed by the System to have limitations, Sam," Nara said dryly, "not everyone starts their path as a demigod."

"Okay, okay." Sam held up her hands in surrender. "I'll tell you what, let's do our best to power-level you until you can keep up with me. Because, at the moment, you are something of a liability." She stopped Nara's objection with a placating gesture. "I don't mean you cannot hold your own with a group of lower-level monsters, but most of the monsters I have encountered were at least ten to twenty levels above me." She gave Nara a stern look and asked, "Tell me truthfully, if I am engaged with a level 56 Great Timberwolf, will you be able to handle another one if they are a mating pair? What if they have pups?"

Nara wanted to argue Sam's scenario was unrealistic. It would seldom happen, but then she thought of all the encounters Sam had already told her about, especially the one where Sam saved her life and knew she had no argument. She sighed, "fine. What do you have in mind?"

Sam only grinned.

***

Sam pointed to the water, "See them? There are two right there."

"Are you sure about this?" Nara's voice was full of concern. They had walked most of the day without encountering anything more dangerous than a few Lightning Cervidae that galloped off once they saw the two explorers.

"Absolutely!" Sam said confidently. "But first, let me ask you something that has been bothering me. Do we need to breathe?"

"No, not as long as you have life energy and mana," Nara confirmed Sam's suspicions. "I can imagine it would be difficult to adapt to not breathing for someone like you who has always needed to do it for survival instead of just to talk."

"I thought it would be, but I held my breath over an hour earlier and never felt the need to breathe. My mana repair skill kicked in within the first five minutes, completely removing the discomfort I initially felt holding my breath." Sam said.

Nara nodded and explained further, "It's the same reason you didn't die when you were frozen or paralyzed the first time you tried the Deep Hunter meat. As long as our core has access to magic energy, our body can use its magic to supplement what it would normally need to survive, such as food, oxygen, or even sunlight in some cases."

"Or human flesh?" Sam asked curiously. She didn't really care but just wanted to know.

"Unfortunately, not all metabolic functions can be circumvented with mana infusion," Nara said, then pointed at Sam's stomach. "You wanted to know why you could drink your body weight multiplied many times in beer the other night? It's because you were actively poisoning yourself while at the same time healing yourself, so your body was converting all the beer you drank into magical energy while, at the same time, you were burning through that same energy to cure the poison."

"So that's why I don't poop!" Sam exclaimed.

Nara looked at Sam curiously, "What is poop?"

Sam thought briefly, then said, "You know the stinky brown stuff that exploded everywhere when I sliced those wolves to pieces? That's poop."

"Oh, it's the magical waste that creatures who can't use mana or have an excess of mana create when they eat," Nara said in understanding. "It is disgusting but extremely mana-rich! I would have suggested we collect some that night, but I would not help Arron if I didn't have to." She looked at Sam curiously and asked, "Why do you know what it is? You are a magic user."

Sam quickly explained there was no magic in her world and what pooping was, much to Nara's disgust.

"That sounds disgusting! And you had to do it every day?!?" Nara was incredulous.

"At least once a day," Sam corrected, "taco Tuesdays were a different story altogether… at least six times on those days…and the poop lit my asshole on fire."

Nara just looked at Sam in speechless horror, so Sam turned her attention back to the two Deep Hunters patiently waiting for them to enter the small river they had come to on their hike. Looking at Nara, Sam gestured to the water and shrugged. It was an unspoken question, and Nara understood.

"You promise it will work?" Nara asked, standing up, gripping one of Sam's harpoons in one hand and charging a Magic Bolt in the other.

"I am one hundred percent sure," Sam said confidently. She had no idea if the Magic Bolt would work underwater, but Nara didn't need to know. Sam knew she could step in and save the poor little Tenarian if it didn't work. The Deep Hunters were only leveled in the low thirties and shouldn't even pose a problem to Sam. *"Besides,"* Sam thought, *"She should be the one telling me if it will work or not."*

Taking a deep breath, Sam knew she didn't need; Nara dove headfirst into the river, her Magic Bolt fizzling out the instant it contacted the water.

"Well…shit," Sam mumbled, dismissing her armor and clothes into her inventory as she dove in after her friend.

***

"You said it would work!" Nara half coughed, half screamed at Sam as she lay choking on the riverbank, spitting out gouts of blood from her shredded neck.

"Hold still! Stop squirming!" Sam said as she kept a firm grip on Nara's arm, doing her best to hold the writhing woman still as she healed her. Sam tried to explain herself, "My mana spikes don't dissipate under water. And you could have fired the bolt into the water to check before jumping in—" Sam trailed off when Nara glared at her.

"You said it would work. I trusted you." Nara's words were like razorblades to Sam, and they cut deep.

"I'm sorry, but look, you're fine now," Sam said as the last of Nara's wounds closed. "I bet you gained a ton of levels too." Sam sat back in the fine sand of the sand bar and gestured to the two Deep Hunters lying next to them. "They were both over level thirty. How many class levels did you gain?"

"None, Sam!" Nara was pissed, "I couldn't use my goinking class spell underwater, remember!"

"Oh, so that's how that works," Sam mumbled, causing Nara to throw her hands up in exasperation. Nara's shredded armor looked more like a tasseled jacket than protective gear.

"So, is it too soon for you to get into another fight?" Sam asked, not making eye contact with Nara, instead staring over her shoulder.

"Too soon to—why would you even ask that?" Nara glared at Sam. "I barely survived the fight we were just in!"

"Okay, okay!" Sam held up her hands. "It's just that three really nasty-looking lizards are staring at us from the tree line, so maybe you should hide somewhere while I take care of them."

"Salamanders, this close to Helms Peak?" Nara jumped up to stare in the direction of Sam's gaze. Her anger was already forgotten.

The two women identified the closest of the three amphibians, the largest of which came up to Sam's waist as they crept slowly from the shadow of the forest's edge.

'Bing' Sigea Salamander [Level 39]; Hostile; Affinity: Tera; This salamander species is not native to Hallista. Additional experience will be granted for assisting in eradicating this species.

Sam started to move, but Nara stopped her with a hand on her arm.

"Let me fight the closest one. Just keep the other two away from me." Nara said as she summoned two Magic Bolts in front of her palms.

"Are you sure?" Sam asked, concerned. She didn't know what these things were capable of.

"I'm sure, Sam. I can do this. Land is different than water for me. Remember, my agility stat is pretty high." Nara said confidently, dismantling Sam's argument.

Sam grinned, "Okay, we move on your signal."

***

Nara signaled by firing her magic bolts and dashed toward the closet salamander. Sam moved a split second later, blasting the other two lizards with arcane bolts at a speed rivaling a modern assault rifle.

Three earthen walls sprang up before the salamanders, forcing the two women to leap over them. Neither of them hesitated in vaulting over the salamander's earthen defenses. Sam, who was keeping a close eye on Nara, nearly jumped directly into the waiting maw of one of the creatures when she cleared the wall of sand and soil it had erected. As Sam used a mana thread to yank herself out of the way of the creature's teeth, she watched in fascination as Nara contorted her body in several impossible directions before flipping onto her lizard's back using a carefully placed hand on its snout to pivot her entire body barely avoiding the razor-sharp teeth as the lizard's jaws clamped shut. Even as she flipped around, Nara never let up on her assault. She blasted scales and chunks of flesh from the creature's neck and head with her Mana Bolts.

"Okay, that looks cool," Sam thought as she watched Nara gyrate around the massive lizard, dodging claws and teeth while shooting bolts of blue energy into the green whirlwind of death. *"Damn girl, you said you were agile, not a freaking ninja!"* She was so enamored with Nara that Sam almost missed the tail swipe from the lizard she was engaged with.

Ducking under the beast's tail, Sam sent a mana spike into the second lizard she had promised Nara she would handle. The spike hit home, and now Sam was between two angry salamanders. She smiled; this was fun.

***

"You are fucking amazing!" Sam had her hands on Nara's shoulders as she stared deeply into the Tenarian's large, deep blue eyes. "How did you move like that? I have a higher agility stat than you and could barely keep up with the other two lizards. You made the one you were fighting look like it was moving in slow motion!" She pulled Nara's face so close their noses touched, and stage whispered, "Where was that flexibility this morning?"

"I have been trained in the art of—oh, I was nervous; it was my first time in…" Nara's face turned dark grey, and she pushed Sam back, "Never mind…I mean, thank you…wait, no! I'm still mad at you!"

Sam fell back laughing. She laughed so hard it turned into a coughing fit. When she finally got ahold of herself, she said, "You are so precious! The look on your face is priceless. That color grey compliments the blue of your lips, by the way."

Sam dodged a playful swing from Nara with a backward roll. Mad or not, Nara had a smile on her face. Coming out of her roll and hopping to her feet, Sam started looting the corpses. The Deep Hunters gave their standard items, but the loot from the first lizard she had killed was undoubtedly different than usual.

Sigea Salamander Items:

37-System Credits [SC]…[Error! The current planet's energy level is insufficient to sustain a system shop network. System Credits will be converted to experience.]; Monster Core [Level 27]; Sigea Salamander hide [Level 27]; Tongue of Sigea Salamander; Salamander Claws x 5; 33kg Sigea Salamander Meat; Vial of Sigea Salamander saliva x 3.

"System Credits? System shop network?" Sam was processing that information when she got to the Salamander Nara killed.

'Bing' This creature has not been processed by the individual who killed it, and you took no part in the defeat of this creature.

Sam looked at Nara curiously. Nara was looking at something in her interface, and a moment later, Sam received a message.

'Bing' Nara Evander has allowed loot sharing through your party interface. Do you wish to share the loot with Nara Evander? Y/N

Selecting 'Yes,' Sam looted the final two salamanders, noting that all the items were split between their inventories in their party menu. Flipping through her party tab, Sam noticed many options required permission from both parties, so she sent requests to Nara in the party menu. The one she was most excited about was the party communication line. By burning a little mana, all party members could use a voice chat function to communicate secretly up to a certain distance. Sam watched as Nara went through and accepted all her requests.

"Five levels, congratulations Nara." Sam was checking Nara's stats in their party menu. She was now level 6 in her sorceress class. "I'm surprised you didn't level in your race, too." Sam had picked up a level in her race and class, putting her at level 21 and 22, respectively.

Nara looked at Sam, realizing something, "Sam, you don't know, do you?" Then she answered her question, "Of course you don't. Why would you." With a sigh, Nara explained to a patiently waiting Sam, who was looking at her expectantly. "Levels," Nara started, trying to find the right words, "your first twenty-five levels, how should I say it…are easy. Most System scholars agree it is the System's way of increasing the overall survival rate of young individuals who reach their race's system age limit to begin leveling. They can choose a class at that time as well." Nara looked at Sam intently, "It is imperative to establish base stats and decide how to plan future progression to best complement class and race benefits by level twenty-five."

"What kind of a curve is it?" Sam asked, "Once you reach level twenty-five, I mean?"

Nara shrugged, "It's not a fixed amount, but for most races, it takes roughly double the experience per level every twenty-five levels." She looked at Sam for a second, "You might be a special case. I don't know how it will work for you, but most humans will have double experience costs per every twenty-five levels up to one hundred. Then, you can either decide to evolve your race or wait until your class reaches its evolution level or vice versa and try for a more powerful evolution. Also, just because you are human doesn't necessarily mean you can evolve at exactly level one hundred. Sometimes evolution can be up to a dozen levels late or even, in rare cases, a few levels early."

“I assume most people wait for the better evolution?” Sam asked.

"Actually, no," Nara said, "there is no guarantee waiting will result in more powerful or rare options unless it is a known class/race combination, and even that is no guarantee. The options you receive are based on factors like stat distribution, skills, abilities, resistances, affinities, spells, and other less quantifiable factors. That's why most people stick with certain race/class combinations. Like city guards, for example, they are almost always warriors, mages, archers, or other standard classes. It is because they can be coordinated better in a large battle due to their known skills and abilities and the fact there are also known evolutions for those race/class combinations."

Sam was doing her best to absorb all the information Nara was giving her. It was giving her a lot to think about. *“I have a sneaking suspicion I’m a rare or maybe a special case, but I should probably still plan for the possibility that I am not.”* That thought brought up a question. She asked Nara, "How would you suggest I prepare for my potential level slowdown?"

Nara's eyes went unfocused momentarily as she reviewed Sam's stat window. "Wow, you really are all over the place. What are you trying to focus on? Are all your level points free to use?"

Sam answered the second question, "Yes, they are all free points." She had to think a little about the other question. Instead of answering, she asked her own questions. "Before I tell you what my plan is, let me ask you, how does each attribute change my body and complement the others? Do you know?"

Nara nodded and gave Sam a rundown of how each attribute affected her body, starting with strength. "Strength is self-explanatory; it helps you hit harder but also increases bone density and the size of your muscles. If you had put all your points into strength, you would look like those berserkers you tussled with back at the guild. All muscle but very little flexibility and very slow."

"Does it make a person harder to kill?" Sam asked. She was curious if increased density meant an increase in vitality, even if it might be slight.

"It makes a person harder to…break?" Nara said slowly. "Overall life force will increase slightly but not as much if the points went into vitality." Sam nodded in understanding, so Nara moved on, "Which brings us to vitality." Nara pricked Sam's arm with a blue claw, "How much of your life force did that take away? Also, could you please put some clothes on? It's very distracting right now. And why are you naked anyway?"

Looking at the single drop of blood on her arm, Sam summoned her clothes onto her body instead of her armor. She was very proud of the fact she could do that. Sam had spent hours the previous night trying to summon clothes and armor onto her body without success until Nara, after laughing at her antics for a while, suggested she put them on first and then try to dismiss them as a single set. The trick had worked, and Sam could now instantly summon and dismiss attire changes. Looking back to Nara, Sam said, "It didn't take any of my life force, and I didn't want to get my armor shredded. It's brand new!"

In disbelief, Nara stared at Sam momentarily, asking, "You do realize what armor is for?"

"Yeah, yeah," Sam waved her hand, "but it was just these little tentacle monsters and some low-level amphibians." She pointed at the corpses around them. "They weren't really a threat."

Nara rubbed her temples and returned the conversation to the original subject, "So back to vitality. You didn't lose any health points because vitality allows every cell in your body to store more life energy, allowing the cells to use that energy to heal wounds much more quickly. That's why you didn't even lose health when I scratched you. Your cells already had enough surplus life energy they didn't need to draw from your pool. That effect usually starts once a person reaches forty or fifty points in the attribute. Vitality also increases body density, skin thickness, overall health, resistance to status elements, and, as you already know, lifespan."

Sam nodded, so Nara moved on to endurance, starting with a question. "How long can you maintain a strenuous activity? Like a long fight?"

Sam responded, "In the beginning, I was exhausted quickly, but now I can run all day without getting tired."

Nara anticipated Sam's response. "Endurance is usually an overlooked trait. Most people, myself included, only keep enough endurance to balance our other attributes. I can maintain a strenuous activity for up to twenty minutes at twenty points." Nara pointed to the salamander she had killed and asked, "How long did it take to finish that fight?"

Sam had to think about it for a second. The fight went by so fast that she hadn't even had to put in her total effort. She finally admitted she didn't know.

"It took less than three minutes," Nara said, "most encounters outside of a full-scale battle last less than ten minutes. It is a good standard to have at least twenty points in endurance to last at least double the time an average fight takes. My race is unfortunate because our endurance is our lowest attribute; we are built for speed and mobility over strength and endurance. Most of the predators on Tenaris are fast and stealthy, as opposed to the variety here on Hallista. I was forced by the church to put far more free points into endurance than I wanted so I could be a better…help." Nara's expression went dark momentarily, but her smile returned when she looked up to meet Sam's concerned gaze.

Nara slapped her knees with her hands standing up, her smile broadened as she dusted off her bloody shredded armor, "It all worked out, though. Now I can keep up with a psychotic demigod that drinks poison for fun and can run forever."

"Hey, we proved I'm not a psycho in the interrogation room!" Sam said in mock offense. She kicked the bodies of the Deep Hunters into the water. Bradly the Imp, at Alexander's, had informed her the Deep Hunters she had were primarily useless as crafting materials other than their cores and ink, so she didn't see any need to store their corpses, instead giving them back to nature for scavengers to pick clean. *"I hope something can eat them, and I didn't just poison an ecosystem."* Sam thought as the bodies sank beneath the surface out of sight.

Nara reached to store the salamander she had killed, but nothing happened when she touched the corpse. Sam also tried with the salamander she had slain.

'Bing' Time remaining to harvest usable parts from Sigea Salamander: 43 minutes 17 seconds. Are you finished harvesting this creature? Y/N

Sam selected 'Yes' and stepped back when the salamander's body turned black and let off a putrid stench as it sizzled and bubbled, melting into the ground. She looked to Nara for an explanation, but the Tenarian stared back at her blankly.

“Maybe it’s because they aren’t native to this planet?” Sam guessed.

“Oh yeah, I didn’t think about that,” Nara said. “I guess the System is treating them like a dungeon monster.”

“Do you know how they got here to Hallista?” Sam was curious.

"It was the Church of the Light," Nara said with surety, "the church's followers use them as mounts and food for the raptors. Their saliva can be used as a—"

"Raptors!" Sam cut Nara off. "Did you say the church has freaking raptors?" Sam knelt, quickly scratched a rough sketch of a raptor in the sand, and pointed at it, "do they look like this and are about two to three meters long and maybe one and a half meters tall?"

"Yes, exactly," Nara said, then asked, "Have you encountered one?"

"No, but I want to!" Sam exclaimed, "They are so cool!"

Nara looked at her with her typical look of disbelief, "Sam, they are vicious pack hunters! Their alphas are insanely fast and cunning! They are terrifying alien predators the Children of the Light use as shock troops to great effect! Trust me, Sam, if you see a raptor, there are at least four more you cannot see stalking you."

Sam only nodded. She still wanted to see one but didn't voice that to Nara. Instead, she asked, "Are we going to set up camp now? Is that why you stood up?"

Nara pointed at a clear area on the other side of the river. "Yeah, I figured we could finish our conversation over a meal. Do you want to set our camp up over there?"

Sam answered by dismissing her clothes again and splashing noisily into the river. Nara rolled her eyes at the Pathfinder's antics but followed her example.

They talked about small things as they cleared a small area for their tent and firepit. Nara spent some time coaching Sam through setting up some of the protective wards they had purchased around the camp.

Sam held one of the small pieces of cloth in her hand, staring at the rune drawn onto the fabric. "So, this little thing creates a barrier if something steps over it?" She waved the small item in her hand. It felt flimsy. Plus, the roll of twenty they had purchased was costly at twenty silver.

"Yes, but only for a few moments. Just long enough for a warning, really." Nara responded. "Now, lay it on the ground. Perfect, just like that right there." She was coaching Sam through setting her first ward. Which is to say she was telling her to lay a piece of cloth on the ground and infuse it with mana. "Okay, form a little mana on the tip of your finger and touch the corner of the cloth."

Sam did as instructed and stepped back with a proud expression when the rune lit up momentarily. She frowned when the light faded and looked to Nara, who reassured her, "The ward is set. Look."

Looking back to the ward, Sam watched as the cloth dissolved into nothing, leaving a barely perceptible rune burned into the sandy soil. *"Wow, that's pretty cool."* Sam checked it with mana sight, and the little symbol let off no discernible mana signature. *"Too bad they're one-time use and only last eight hours. I guess the time limit is a good thing, though. Wouldn't want to be leaving wards behind everywhere I go."* Sam thought.

They only set the one ward just to show Sam how it worked. After marking the spot so they wouldn't accidentally trip the ward during the night, they continued preparing their camp for the evening.

***

"This is nice," Sam said, tugging the enormous wolf pelt around her bare shoulders, staring absently into the fire and relaxing deeper into the extra-large camp chair.

"Hey, save some covering for me," Nara complained, walking up to Sam and handing her a plate of grilled vegetables.

"Yummy! Thank you, Nara," Sam said, accepting the plate of food and holding up an edge of the wolf pelt with one of her threads so Nara could slip under the heavy covering. She sighed with contentment and snuggled up against Sam in the chair. Once Nara was settled and happily picking at the food with the arcane chopsticks Sam had made her, Sam asked, "Does agility do anything other than give flexibility and speed?"

"Yes," Nara said around a mouthful of food. She covered her mouth with her hand, chewed, and then swallowed before continuing, "Agility will lengthen your muscles and make your joints more flexible. It also increases your visual recognition and reaction speeds." Nara stabbed a purple tuber on the plate with one of the sticks. After scarfing it down with a moan of pleasure, she moved on to the following attribute, "intelligence increases the power of your spells by allowing your mind to sync more efficiently with your core. It also—"

"Cores." Sam corrected, "Your cores, both of them."

Nara looked up into Sam's eyes for a few heartbeats before slowly saying, "I know I should not be surprised by anything you say by now, but 'normal.'" She used her chopsticks to emphasize the word, "People have only one core, Sam."

Sam gently caressed Nara's delicate neck with her hand. She pressed two fingers into the base of Nara's skull, where her hairline met her neck. She leaned in and whispered into her friend's ear, "Then how do you explain the magical nexus just below your brain right here?"

Nara's hand snaked up quickly to feel where Sam was pressing. "Are you serious?" She asked with her expressive eyes wide in surprise.

"Yep," Sam said. "Every sapient life form I have checked so far has one. When the System gave me my class, it displayed a 3D image of my cores and mana channels…I'm assuming that isn't normal."

"No, it isn't," Nara confirmed, still poking at the spot Sam had shown her with her fingers. She asked, "Can you see inside me with your magic sight ability?"

Sam made a non-committal motion with her hand, saying, "It's not as clear as external magic, but I can see mana concentrations inside living organisms if I focus hard enough. And you, my dear," she booped Nara's nose, "have a mind core and a main core just like everyone else so don't go thinking it's a special Pathfinder thing."

"I…how…how is this not widely known?" Nara looked genuinely concerned. She continued almost to herself, "There are so many powerful beings here on Hallista who can surely see cores—I can see cores!" She grabbed Sam's neck and pulled her so close her blue eyes nearly touched Sam's skin. "Hmm, all I see is your brain…wait," she twisted Sam's neck until Sam was sure it would break, then exclaimed, "I see it! It's so small! I thought it was just part of a high mana channel concentration!" Releasing Sam and sitting back, Nara reached back and touched the spot on her neck Sam had shown her, "I wonder why no one speaks of this—"

Nara's body went stiff, her blue eyes becoming vacant black orbs. Sam jerked back a little in the chair they were in. Nara's whole appearance changed for an instant before reverting back to normal. She grabbed Sam's shoulders, her eyes, now back to their deep blue, panicked.

"Eyes of blue will not hurt you!" Nara said with true panic and tears welling up in her eyes. "I'm sorry, Sam, I thought I had more time. Please remember! Eyes of blue will not hurt—" Nara's eyes turned solid black, and an evil smile spread across her face, complete with two sharp blue fangs.

CHAPTER 17 — "Naris I presume?"

"Hello Sam, I have been trying so hard to meet you," a soft yet sinister voice purred from the mouth of the creature who now occupied Nara's place in the chair.

"Naris, I presume?" Sam asked her guard up.

"Yes," Naris hissed, and quicker than Sam could react, he grabbed her by the neck, sinking his claws deep and stabbing them at her mind core.

Sam felt the blight's claws scratch across her core as he tried to penetrate it. She wanted to stop and push him away, but she was mesmerized, held helplessly under the spell of his endless black eyes.

"Yes..." Naris continued to purr. "Look into my eyes...let me in...open yourself to me." His charm spell worked on the mentally defenseless Pathfinder much better than he had hoped.

"How?" Sam asked, unable to look away from Naris's cold black stare. A small voice inside her screamed for her to snap out of her trance, but it was only a small one. A much more prominent and louder voice told her the truth; Naris only wanted to help her; he was a friend, and he needed mana to help her, so she should give him some...

"Open your mind. Let me sense your pain, and I will make it all disappear. I can take your pain for you; you don't need to be afraid of me. Just relax your defenses and let me in..." Naris's voice was like a soothing balm. He could sense her emotions coming from the small core he gripped tightly in his claws. Then he felt it open to him when Sam relaxed her mind, allowing Naris to draw on her mind core just a little.

Naris grunted the instant Sam allowed him access to her mind core, his evil grin nearly splitting his face in half. He dug his claws into her core and activated Mana Siphon!

Sam's mouth opened in a silent scream as her vision started going red, and the same sense of wrong and dread she had felt when she was converting her health into mana washed over her soul. She still could not move; she was no longer under Naris's charm spell but was now paralyzed by pain and fear. "St—stop—" She managed to whisper as the last vestige of hope left her.

Naris only growled and yanked Sam forward in the chair, his fangs sinking into the soft flesh of her neck as his jaws closed around her throat.

Sam's vision faded; the red that started at the corner of her vision was now all she could see as the Moonblight drained her lifeforce and mana and all the thoughts and emotions that made her who she was.

***

Naris moaned in pleasure as he felt the massive amount of power flowing into him from Sam. *"Not just power,"* he thought as he greedily absorbed her energies, *"thoughts and emotions too. Is this what a mind core holds?"* Naris hadn't known there were mind cores. He had always drunk from the mana channel clusters in his victim's throats, where their mana and lifeblood flowed beneath the surface. If he had only dug his claws in a little higher up his victim's skulls, he would have found their secondary cores and been able to drink from their sweet emotions as well. *"This is true power,"* Naris thought as he consumed Sam's fear, *"I regret not knowing this before, but no matter. I might be able to break free of the accursed worm I'm tethered to with this power."*

Naris pulled one of his hands from Sam's neck and jammed it into her chest, his mana cutters easily cleaving into the woman's body. He was at full power now with a sea of mana at his disposal; there was no way this pathetic human could resist him. His hand closed around Sam's soul core, black claws punching deep holes in the woman's outer soul. Naris growled into Sam's throat as he drank his fill; soon, all her power would be his, and once it was... *"Nara will be no more."* Sam's body jerked in the chair as Naris siphoned her energies even harder, hungrily draining all she was.

***

"*Wake up!*" The voice of reason pleaded in Sam's mind, "*You have to wake up and resist*!"

"Go back to sleep...so tired...just go...back..." Sam's thoughts were sluggish, and she felt like they had to funnel through molasses before she could process them.

"*NO, NO, NO! Let me out! I am the only one, the only one that can help! Listen to me, Reason*!" A raging voice screamed from Sam's mind core.

"*You will never stop if you are released. You will never allow yourself to be balanced again.*" Reason replied in a desperate tone. "*She, we will be nothing more than the beast killing us. Take me with you, and we can defeat him together.*"

"*You cannot even wake her! How could you help me? There are times for you, I know that now, but this is not one! There can be no thought, only action to defeat the enemy! Only rage! Time is short; our soul is being devoured! Release me now! Release our RAGE!*" The voice of Sam's rage was desperate but determined.

Sam's inner reason knew the only chance at survival was to release all control and let her rage flow freely. "*Promise you will—*"

"*I promise to WIN! Nothing more*!" Rage screamed into Sam's mind.

Somewhere in the chaos of her mind, Sam knew the voices she was hearing were just her way of talking to herself. Somehow, since she had been granted access to magic, she now could bifurcate her mind and watch as an external observer as her emotions discoursed between themselves to resolve problems. It was a strange feeling, and being even vaguely cognizant of it felt unnatural yet not impossible.

"Fine!" Sam thought to the voices in her head. She unleashed her rage.

***

Sam's eyes popped open, her violet irises blazing until the white of her eyes were glowing orbs of deep purple. She grabbed Naris's lower jaw with one hand and his upper with the other, pulling his mouth from her throat with strength that only came from pure fury.

The blight dug his claws deeper into her chest and head, tightening his grip as Sam pushed his head back. There was a crack as one of his fangs snapped beneath her grip, and Naris screamed.

Bunching up her legs, Sam placed her feet in Naris's chest and kicked him backward so violently his claws were ripped from her cores. She screamed in fury from the pain as they both flew in opposite directions from the force of her kick, destroying the chair they were in.

Naris was slammed into a tree, his agile body contorting, so he hit the tree feet first with a resounding crack. Bark was blasted away from the impact, but Naris didn't notice; he was locked in on his prey. Like a snake uncoiling when it strikes, Naris kicked off the tree, launching himself back at Sam, who was angrily tearing herself out of the collapsed tent she was tangled in. Her kick had sent her rolling into the side of their new tent, collapsing it around her.

Naris dodged around a tent pole Sam threw at him and leaped at her from the side. He dug a deep gouge into her left leg, trying to sever an artery, but Sam's knee caught him in the shoulder, knocking him off course.

As Naris caught his balance, Sam fired arcane bolt after arcane bolt at him. Although Naris dodged many of them, he could not evade every bolt. He retreated into the forest, reinforcing his body with magic to keep Sam's bolts from doing too much damage as he tried to create some distance from the raging woman.

Sam was in a blind fury, screaming as she chased after the retreating blight. In her rage, she sent blades and spikes flying after Naris. They cut through trees and shrubs, clearing her path forward.

Realizing he couldn't get away from the crazed woman, Naris ran up a tree and kicked off back toward Sam, dodging two whirling discs of magic that would have sliced him in half as he did so. The discs hit the tree he had just kicked off, cutting it down. It crashed behind him just as he hit the ground, running at Sam and the dozens of magical projectiles she was launching. Naris kept running toward her, dodging more disks and spikes as he closed the distance until he was finally in range. He ducked under a strike from Sam and slipped behind her, stabbing his hands into her lower back, punching holes in her kidneys and liver with his black claws. These two human organs were particularly difficult to heal. His plan was to wear the Pathfinder down enough so he could overpower her and finish his feast.

A pulse of pure mana threw Naris back several meters. Sam, now glowing purple and screaming, whipped around in his direction and sent a beam of pure arcane magic streaking across the forest from two outstretched palms as she turned. The air split from the arcane magic, cutting through it, causing a crack like a bolt of lightning to sound through the dimming forest. The beam of magic wasn't well aimed; had Sam not been out of control, the purple laser would have ended the fight then and there with a bisected Naris. As it was, though, Naris could barely jerk out of the beam's path enough, so it only severed his left arm at the shoulder and part of his left foot. Naris screamed as his arm fell away; he stumbled and fell. Sam collapsed to her hands and knees with purple steam rising from her body from the massive mana expenditure. Trees severed by Sam's beam attack began falling over; most were on fire from the heat of the attack, creating an eerie backdrop for the two combatants.

Seeing his chance, Naris crawled toward the exhausted Pathfinder. His mana reserves were running low, and he needed to finish draining her to hopefully attain her healing ability so he could regrow his arm and foot. He was almost to Sam when she jerked her head to look at him. Naris stopped his approach and recoiled at the sight. Sam's eyes were still glowing with magic power, even after the attack she had just made. The look on her face was of mindless fury. The beam attack burned most of the flesh from her arms, and all the skin on the front of her body was red and puffy from the heat. She looked like she should be dead, and Naris had no idea how she wasn't. Still, Sam stood up and stalked toward him, a short sword appearing in her hand even as the flesh and skin around her fingers knitted itself back together. For the first time in his life, Naris felt fear. He was no longer the predator.

Sam quickly closed the distance between them. Naris tried to crawl away, but Sam was too fast. Standing over the blight, Sam kicked away his hand when he made a feeble attempt at defending himself and stabbed a mana spike through his palm, pinning his hand to the ground. She did the same to his legs, using her mana threads to secure the spikes. Getting down to her knees, Sam straddled his chest, raising her sword with the tip pointed at Naris's forehead where a black symbol, identical to the blue pentagram on Nara's chest, was etched into his grey skin. Sam's eyes flared again, and she didn't hesitate to bring her sword down into the blight's head without a word.

***

Sam stared into Nara's wide blue eyes. The expressive blue orbs were wide with horror and surprise. A trickle of blood from where the sword had entered her forehead threatened to drip into one of her eyes as it found a path down her face from the wound.

Nara blinked, making no other motion, fearing the sword's tip, which was barely a few millimeters into her forehead, would suddenly finish its journey into her brain. She could feel the pain coming from where her arm was severed and couldn't wiggle the toes on her left foot. Hence, she knew Sam had likely been forced to go all out, but that didn't explain the look of pure anger and hatred on her friend's face as she pressed a sword into her temple with enough force that Nara was afraid the blade might break her skull at any second.

"Sam?" Nara's voice was the faintest whisper.

"Eyes of blue…" Sam's voice was choked with barely checked anger. "Is it you?"

"Yes," Nara continued to whisper. "He's gone now. Naris can't—"

Sam growled angrily at the mention of Naris's name, pushing a little harder on the sword. Nara remained motionless, afraid Sam's anger would get the better of her. Thankfully, Sam let up just a little, asking again, "Eyes of blue, is it you?"

With tears welling in her eyes, Nara again answered, "Yes," but this time, she added, "It's me, Nara, your friend."

Sam's eyes flared, and she moved the sword away, dismissing it to her inventory. Leaning down, she growled through clenched teeth into Nara's ear, "Listen to me, you little piece of shit, I know you can hear me. Suppose you ever come out without Nara's permission again. In that case, I will rip your soul out of her body and destroy you to the last nanoscopic particle. Are we clear? Let her tell me."

"Tell the Pathfinder…I…understand." Naris's voice spoke into Nara's mind.

"What have you done!?!" Nara mentally screamed back at Naris. She searched for his presence when he said nothing and found him coiled up against her core. He was afraid…he was scared. *"Good!"* She thought and removed her presence from the frightened blight.

"He understands," Nara told Sam, tears pouring down her face. "I don't know what he did, Sam, but I am so sorry. I thought I could keep him back if I stayed topped off with mana, but he broke free anyway. Please tell me you're okay. That we're okay…are we okay?"

Sam's rage-filled eyes dimmed, and tears welled, unbidden, as Nara spoke. Looking at her friend, Sam was horrified at what she had done to her. Sam quickly dismissed the spikes, holding Nara down and sobbing when the

Tenarian let out a little mew of pain as she dismissed the constructs. Gathering her friend's torn and broken body to her chest, Sam began healing her as quickly as she could, only stopping for a second to drink a couple of mana potions. She completely ignored her own injuries until Nara placed a hand on her back.

"I'm good now, Sam. Focus on yourself for a while. You can rebuild my arm later." Nara turned in Sam's embrace until she could look her in the eyes. "I'm serious, Sam; you should heal yourself now. You are weak and hurt, and we're still in a dangerous forest."

Sam sniffled and nodded. She looked at Nara's partially grown stump, and tears welled in her eyes again, but Nara gently turned Sam's head back to face her with a hand on her cheek and smiled, "I'm fine, Sam. You can keep holding me, but please heal yourself."

Sam complied, starting with her organs. She didn't even want to look at her cores but knew she had to. Turning her mind's eye inward, she mentally winced. Her cores were severely damaged, purple energy leaking from deep gouges left by Naris's claws. *"How do I even fix this?"* She thought. She tried to use her mana repair skill on the gouges, but it wouldn't activate. Before panicking, she noticed one of the more minor lacerations on her mind core close on its own. Hoping her cores would fix themselves, she returned to healing her body.

A quick glance at her stat screen showed Sam her energy bars had at least two-thirds of their color blacked out. She asked Nara what it meant.

"Your cores must be damaged," Nara said with concern in her voice, "please tell me you can fix it."

"They are getting better. I checked," Sam responded.

"Good," Nara said with relief. "Damage from a blight cannot always be repaired."

"Fucking blights man," Sam said. "Can't you just get rid of him?" She was pretty sure Nara would have done it long ago if she had been able to, but she had to ask.

"Our souls are intertwined," Nara sighed, "if one of us dies, so does the other. As far as I know, there is no way to remove a blight from a soul."

"I guess it's good I didn't kill the little shit then," Sam said with a bit of heat in her voice. "If he ever retakes control without your express permission, I swear I will—"

Sam was cut off by the sound of a tree crashing to the ground. Nara pushed back from her position against Sam's chest, and the two women looked around, taking in their surroundings for the first time since they had come to their senses.

"Well…shit," both women said in unison.

***

"Sam, what did you do?" Nara asked as she stared down a path of destruction leading to the river. Burning stumps and tree trunks were scattered down the path Sam's beam had cut through the forest.

"I—I'm not actually sure," Sam said. She quickly checked her notifications for anything that would explain what happened.

'Bing' Congratulations! Core cycle overclock has been achieved. Your cores are now operating at a much higher cycle rate, increasing the potential of all magic-related functions. Warning: continued use of Overclock will cause extensive damage to your cores. Damaged cores are not easily repaired. Excessive use of Overclock may cause core destruction.

Warning: Soul Core rupture detected. You have ruptured your soul core using an unknown method to overdraw mana. Cease this action immediately, or your core will be destroyed.

After reading those two notifications several times, Sam looked at Nara and shrugged, "No idea."

"You're lying," Nara said.

"I don't want to talk about it," Sam responded, then pointed to the fires, "I'm going to go make sure the forest doesn't burn down." She guided Nara off her lap and stood up, offering her a hand, "Care to join me?"

***

Sam relaxed by the river, kicking her bare feet in the cool water as she watched the brilliant reds and oranges of the clouds reflecting the sun's light as the burning orb rose in the sky. Nara was asleep, curled up against her, exhausted after spending the night helping Sam put out fires and salvaging what they could of their ruined camping gear. Sam smiled down at the Tenarian's no, the Moonblight's peaceful face as she lightly stroked Nara's hair, not saying anything. The warmth of the small fire Nara had built near the river's edge contrasted nicely with the cool temperature of the river's calm flow.

Sam ignored the remnants of chaos surrounding them, such as the tendrils of smoke wafting on the breeze from the few still smoldering tree stumps dotting the path of destruction from the previous evening, the fishy smell from a Deep Hunter's corpse lying lifeless on the river's edge, and their mostly destroyed camping gear. Instead, she focused on the positive: Nara's arm and foot were healed, they still had the Blade Tail's pelt, and some of their camping supplies, including one of their oversized chairs, remained safe in her inventory.

Turning her attention back to her cores for the first time since the previous evening, Sam frowned. Her mind core was fully healed as far as she could tell; there wasn't purple energy leaking out of it anyway. Her soul core, which she now knew it was called, was an entirely different story. Purple and now, for some reason, black mist continuously leaked out of a gaping hole in one side of her core. She knew this had been her fault, not Naris's. The hole in her core had apparently been blasted out from the inside. Plus, all the claw marks left by the blight had healed, so she knew it must be damage she caused when she overclocked her core cycles. *"How was that even possible? They cycle like ten times a second normally,"* Sam didn't know, but the thought that she may have done some permanent damage frightened her.

Sam pulled up her interface and saw her energy bars were still forty percent black. *"Shit,"* She thought, frustrated at herself for being so reckless. Her energy levels now more closely resembled Nara's, and Sam was eleven levels above Nara. The health and stamina she could deal with, but Sam had over a thousand points of her magic power she couldn't access now; it was disheartening. *"I guess it's what I get for being so reckless all the time, but it was either go all out or die yesterday."* Even the thought she had no other choice didn't console her. She knew there may have been another way to fight the blight. She and Nara should have prepared for Naris's inevitable arrival instead of ignoring the elephant in the room. In Sam's defense, she had never even seen the blight. And if she was being candid with herself, she had almost forgotten he was even there, nestled inside her new friend, just waiting for an opportunity to break out.

Sam sighed as she continued to stroke Nara's hair. Looking at Nara's peaceful, innocent face, it was hard for Sam to believe there was something so vicious and ravenous coiled just beneath the surface of the small woman. *"It's like two completely opposite personalities with their own physical appearance and abilities in one little package."* Sam thought.

Turning her attention back to her interface, Sam used her thirty free points to bolster her magic. She knew she would need it more than her other attributes. The others would have to wait until her soul healed…if it ever did. Looking at her stat screen, Sam could not help but be disappointed.

Samantha Alecto Moura [S.A.M.]
Race: Human; Mortal [Level 21]
Class: Arcane Pathfinder [Level 22]

Health: 765 (1274)
Stamina: 573 (955)
Mana: 2084 (3473)

Attributes:
STR – 45 [46]
VIT – 63 [71]
END – 46 [52]
AGL – 52 [53]
INT – 70 [71]
WIS – 87 [176]
Free Attribute Points 0.

Abilities:
Spatial Inventory
Loot
Linguistics
Cartography
Mana Manipulation
Mana Sight [Level 13]

Class Skills:
Mana Crafting [Level 26]
Mana Repair [Level 24]
Mana Caster [Level 9]

Racial/General Skills:
Identify [Level 13]
Resilient [Level 23]
Meditation [Level 12]

Class Spells:
Arcane bolt [Level 5]

Racial/General Spells:
None

Resistance(s):
Pain [Level 17]
Heat [Level 9]
Poison [Level 38]
Cold [Level 25]
Mental [Level 6]

Sam groaned out loud at the loss of her power. She tried to think back to what level she was now equivalent to, *"The last time I was this weak was before I met Nara...what was I then? My level was around fourteen or fifteen, I think. At least my resistances and skill levels weren't affected, and I have a new resistance. I wonder what 'mental' resistance does...other than the obvious."*

Nara stirred when Sam groaned. Sitting upright, she looked at Sam with concern written across her features. "How bad is it?" She asked, following with, "And don't lie to me. If it's too bad, we need to head back to the city and see if we can find you a healer."

Sam resisted the urge to brush Nara off, but she knew Nara could easily look at her stats in their party menu and was just politely asking. Sam told her the truth about everything.

Nara patiently listened as Sam explained what happened, starting when Naris took over and went up to the hole in her core and her loss of vital energies. Once Sam finished speaking, Nara took her time to think about her reply. Nara still felt responsible for everything that happened and told Sam so. Sam assured her she did not consider the hole in her soul core to be anything other than her own fault, saying, "It was bound to happen one day."

After some thought, Nara said, "I am truly sorry, Sam," she held up a hand to stop Sam from interrupting, "I know, I know, you don't think it's my fault, but that doesn't mean I can't at least feel bad for what happened." Sam closed her mouth and let Nara continue. Nara thought for a moment more and said, "I think we should return to the city. With your...handicap...well, I don't want you to suffer—"

Sam shook her head and asked, "Do you remember the evening we met?"

"Of course," Nara replied, unsure where this was headed.

"I am still just as powerful as I was then, if just barely. In fact, I hadn't even assigned any free points since the fight with the bandits until today." Sam said with a forced smile. She didn't want Nara to see how worried she actually was.

"Seriously?" Nara searched Sam's face for a moment, but seeing no lie, she conceded. "Okay, then we will continue and complete the contracts," she waggled a finger at Sam, "but if you get any worse, promise me, we will go back to the city for help."

"I promise I'll let you know if things don't get better," Sam agreed, dismissing the uncomfortable subject. "Now, how about we get going?"

Nara nodded, stretching as she stood up. She jumped when she noticed the octopus monster lying near them.

Sam noticed and chuckled. "I killed it while you were sleeping."

"I fell asleep leaning on you—how did you—never mind, I don't want to know," Nara said. She went through a series of stretches and movements as she did every morning.

Sam watched the attractive woman flex and stretch. She asked curiously, "Is there a name for what you're doing?"

"Huh, oh this," Nara was mostly tied in a pretzel as she responded, "it is a form of combat called Roka. It relies almost exclusively on speed and flexibility." Nara untied herself with several pops as her joints slid back into place. "I can teach you if you like."

"Maybe some other time," Sam said, wincing as Nara popped and snapped her joints, continuing to contort her body in what Sam considered impossible positions. *"Although it would be nice to be able to turn my head like an owl…among other things,"* she thought.

***

Sam and Nara had spent another hour pouring water over all the stumps still smoldering and checking around to ensure they hadn't missed any remains of their camping equipment before continuing their hike toward their destination.

They arrived at one corner of the area they were contracted to survey within a few hours. Sam climbed a tall tree to better view the terrain and let her map fill in. After climbing down to where Nara was waiting patiently, Sam explained how her mapping skill worked and pulled out a sketchbook they purchased strictly for mapping this area.

"Your skill is fascinating," Nara said as Sam got to work drawing out the area in the book, "Everything you do is fascinating. I bet you can make some decent coin with the cartography guild. That could help pay to get your soul core repaired."

Sam put the charcoal pencil down and looked at Nara, "I completely forgot to stop by their office! I remember you mentioning it now."

"We'll make a point to stop by when we get back," Nara said. "In the meantime, would you share your map with me?"

Sam gestured to the paper she was filling in with the type and average height of the trees in the area. The job required a detailed map and local flora and fauna information.

"No, not that," Nara said when Sam turned the sketchbook toward her, "I mean, display your map so I can see it. Here, look." With a wave of her hand, Nara displayed a projection of her stat sheet in front of her, explaining to Sam, "It takes a slight amount of energy, but all you have to do is think about displaying something from your interface for others to see."

Fascinated with the idea, Sam did just that with her mini map and was almost as excited as Nara when it worked.

"Wow," Nara said, staring at the displayed map, "this is amazing, Sam! I bet this is an extremely rare ability. I wonder what you could sell it for if you manage to find someone who can copy it to a skill book or scroll. You would definitely be able to pay for your soul core repair," she trailed off as she stared at Sam's map display and then pointed at a spot on the display. "What does that say?"

"It says uncharted cave," Sam replied, zooming in on the cave as much as possible. The cave was a distance away, so she could only get a little detail about it besides its location.

"You can read that? What language is it written in?" Nara was still staring at the map in fascination as Sam zoomed in and out, checking details on what she had seen from the tree. Nara pointed to three tiny red dots surrounding a grey dot on the map, asking, "What are those?"

Answering both questions, Sam said, "It's written in English, one of the languages on my planet, and," she zoomed in on the three red dots, "this is three hostile creatures surrounding a dead creature." The dots were close to the women's position, so Sam's map had a lot of detail in that area. The dots took shape as Sam zoomed in, turning into a real-time display of three wolves surrounding a dead Lightning Cervidae. Each wolf had a small tag with the word 'hostile' floating over it. The fact it was in real-time surprised Sam just as much as it did Nara.

"You can track enemies with this? Why haven't we been using this the whole time?" Nara asked.

"I—I had no idea," Sam stammered defensively. She was just as surprised as Nara and said, "It hasn't always been like this. I think it got better, but," she checked to confirm something before continuing, "I don't know how it could have improved. The ability doesn't level."

"Just because there isn't a level quantification doesn't mean abilities, skills, or spells can't improve. It only means the System does not or cannot track them." Nara explained helpfully. "I think we can skip drawing out the map in the book if you can display this to the clerk when we close the contract."

Sam agreed; artist or not, she didn't particularly care for painstakingly drawing a map that was already clearly displayed in her interface, so she minimized the map and asked Nara, "Do you want to go sneak up on some wolves?"

Nara flipped through some screens in her interface before flicking her hand in Sam's direction.

'Bing' Nara Evander is requesting permission to view a display of your cartography skill in her interface. Confirmation of this request will

result in the cost of one mana unit per minute per meter of distance separating you. Would you like to accept? Y/N

"Hmm, that's neat," Sam thought, selecting 'Yes.'

Nara smiled and said excitedly, "Perfect! Let's go hunting!"

CHAPTER 18 — "What is Olympics?"

Sam and Nara spent their day mapping the survey area and clearing out any hostile monsters they encountered. They did it both for experience and because the job offered a bonus for culling any dangerous creatures the survey crew encountered. All they came across that day were low-level wolves in packs of three to five. With Sam's new upgrade to her cartography ability, they snuck up on all the wolf packs and defeated them without much issue.

They set up camp about an hour before dark. Sam and Nara could have stayed awake for several more days. Still, Sam's mapping ability worked off her vision, so mapping at night was not beneficial. Plus, they weren't in a hurry, and Sam's core wasn't improving, so they thought it best to play it safe when she mentioned that to Nara.

***

Sam finished putting a couple of logs in their fire pit, thankful it had survived her rage. She plopped down in their one surviving chair next to Nara, who put down the book she was reading and held up the Blade Tail hide for her to slip under.

"I like this one more than the Great Timberwolf hide," Nara said, running her fingers through the soft fur. The panther's fur was so dark it didn't even reflect the firelight, absorbing it instead.

"It is really soft." Sam agreed. "This is the System-generated one. I wonder if it's the same as what Alexander will turn the actual hide into when he processes the body." Sam wondered absently.

"Oh, I'm sure it will become high-end stealth armor or a cloak of concealment instead of a cozy blanket like we're using it." Nara smiled.

They sat in silence for a while, watching the fire. Nara read the book on the local flora and fauna. At the same time, Sam, after a couple of failed attempts, started making arcane arrows for Nara. She had made one for her that morning after their first fight with wolves. Even though she hadn't expected it to, Sam was still disappointed when the Quiver of Replication had not made copies of them. They had finished the day using the regular steel arrows they had bought, which the quiver had no issue replicating with the understanding Sam would make as many arcane arrows as she could when they rested that night.

After a while, Sam looked at Nara and asked, "Do you need mana? You have to be running low by now. I don't know what Naris took from you or how it works, but you must be low." She had been respecting Nara's privacy by not checking her stat sheet, so she was genuinely curious at how much magic power the Sorceress still had in reserve.

"I…I'm good for now," Nara hedged, not looking at Sam.

"Hey," Sam said softly, resting her hand on Nara's thigh, prompting the woman to look at her, "no lies, okay? We are a team now, and we're both hurt. We need to trust each other with our issues."

Nara sighed and displayed her stat sheet for Sam. Sam was confused when she read Nara's numbers.

"How do you have two hundred and fifty thousand mana points?" Sam asked.

Nara sighed again, "Let me first explain how summoning the blights changed my race." She closed her book and placed it in her lap, folding her hands on the cover as she collected her thoughts, then continued, "Before the blight summoning, we Tenarians were much like most other sapient races scattered across the three celestial bodies, Tenaris, Hallista, and Denaris." Nara drew three imaginary circles in the air before her, "when the blights were summoned, my species experienced an instant evolution." She closed her eyes, still speaking, "as one might expect when a magical parasite from an alternate dimension burrows into your soul." Nara's voice wavered a little; this was not a comfortable subject for her.

Sam leaned across Nara and grabbed her goblet off the small side table on her side of the chair. Sam summoned the bottle of wine they had been sipping on from her inventory, refilling Nara's goblet while her friend composed herself. She took the time to replenish her own goblet before dismissing the delicious wine.

Thankful for the distraction, Nara drank several large gulps of her wine. Keeping the goblet clasped between her hands, she continued, "The blights burrow into our soul core. They are drawn there by this," she pointed to the center of her chest, where the pentagram was beneath the covers. "The spell that called the blights had two parts. One part was to open the portal to an alternate dimension and the other to tether the extra-dimensional creatures to all living creatures born to Tenaris." Nara stared blankly into her goblet, slowly shaking her head, "The king did not know what would come out of the portal but, in his arrogance, thought that tethering it to every living being on his moon would somehow force them into submission and give every citizen a powerful familiar." She chuckled in frustrated anger, "He…the king, was so wrong. What actually happened was every living creature on Tenaris wound up with a mark, and a parasite latched onto their soul." Nara looked at Sam with tears in her eyes, "That was nearly two hundred cycles ago…now every person born with even the barest hint of Tenarian blood has a mark, and since the portal is still open, a blight is summoned to their soul."

"How did you survive as a child?" Sam was baffled.

“Naris was dormant until I was of System age to level,” Nara said. She composed herself and continued, "Which brings me to the issue now. Have you noticed I don't have a wisdom attribute?"

When Sam nodded, Nara proceeded, "That was part of my race's rapid evolution. When a blight attaches to a soul core, it ruptures it slightly. Then, it uses itself as a plug to prevent excess mana from leaking out and poisoning its host. This greatly increased the energy limit for what I can store in my soul. It also removes the wisdom attribute in my status menu, freeing up my points to put elsewhere, so there is a small upside to being bonded with a blight."

Sam paused with her goblet at her lips when Nara said that. *“Shit, poisoned by a ruptured core? Damn, I’m an idiot! Maybe my crystal mana channels will help with that?”* She was pulled out of her thoughts as Nara kept telling the story of her people's history.

"The rupture produces massive amounts of neutral mana. All Tenarians have neutral mana, by the way, for the blights to feed on so they can exist in this reality, and it also gives them control over their host's core. They can let mana flow from the rupture or stop it whenever they feel like it. However, my mana channels are my own and are replaced when Naris switches with me." Nara looked concerned, "One thing they cannot and should not be able to do is allow their host to access their own mana. I should only be able to use the mana I have collected from other sources. They cannot, or at least I thought they could not block the absorption of their host's mana. It is how they stay alive in this reality while forcing their host to absorb mana from external sources." Nara trailed off.

"So, I'm guessing Naris isn't holding you back anymore. Why do I get the feeling that isn't good?" Sam asked when Nara stayed silent, staring at the red liquid in her goblet.

"Because if he doesn't plug the hole in my core soon, it will get worse; mana has already started overflowing into my body and is speeding up. If it keeps going unchecked, it can rupture my mana channels." Nara said. She held up a hand and formed a Magic Bolt. After staring at the blue teardrop of energy for a few seconds, she dismissed the attack and put her hand to her forehead. "I cannot burn the amount of mana overflowing my core already; there's just too much of it—but that isn't the worst part." She smiled sadly at Sam as she spoke, "Naris is dying; he's absorbing only the magical overflow from my core that doesn't dissipate into my body which means he's only getting a small fraction of what he should be." Nara held out one arm. Sam watched in horror as the smooth grey skin of Nara's arm became pasty white with splotches of light blue." staring at her arm she said, "This is what mana poisoning looks like. I've been covering it up with my shifting ability." Nara held her arm up against Sam's and curiously examined Sam's arm, "I'm not sure how you aren't being poisoned with your core ruptured. I didn't want to frighten you about it before, and it looks like it's not affecting you so…" Nara trailed off again, and Sam let the silence drag, unsure what to say.

After staring into the flickering flames of their campfire for a minute, Nara chuckled at a thought, shaking her head, "You must have been terrifying when you fought Naris because he will not communicate with me at all and hasn't moved since that night."

"I was out of control, Nara. I'm sorry. I didn't realize what I was doing." Sam said truthfully, putting another log on the fire with one of her mana threads.

Nara smiled at Sam, "I wish I could have seen it. I bet you were even more amazing than the night you saved me." She coughed. It was a raspy cough, and Sam stared in disbelief as a faint cloud of blue mana puffed from Nara's mouth and blue splotches appeared on her cheeks. "I'm not sure what will happen first; whether Naris will die and take me with him, or all my mana channels will rupture, and I'll die of mana shock and take Naris with me." Setting her goblet down, Nara grabbed Sam's hand and, after another coughing fit, said, "I just wanted to enjoy one more night with you before—"

"Nope!" Sam said forcefully, making Nara jump and jerk back in her seat. Sam grabbed the fur blanket and yanked it off them, throwing it to the ground. She got up and, sliding Nara over in the chair, straddled her lap facing her. Staring into Nara's poisoned milky blue eyes, Sam reached down and ripped Nara's tunic open enough to expose the symbol on her chest, acting on a hunch. Not taking her eyes off her friend's, she slowly pressed her right hand against Nara's chest over the pentagram.

'Bing' Link attempt blocked. You do not have access to Nara Evander's soul core. Request access? Y/N

Sam selected 'Yes' and whispered, "Let me in Nara. I need to talk to the little shit."

***

Naris didn't know what this feeling was. *"Why can't I move? Is this...fear?"* It was like a powerful weight was pushing in from all around, crushing him, not allowing him to move or even breathe. Whenever he thought about seeking comfort by absorbing the mana flowing from his host's soul, an image of the monster Nara was traveling with appeared unbidden. The paralyzing emotion overtook him, forcing him to apathy.

Naris felt the weakness creeping into his soul. He knew he was dying and should drink from Nara's core, but all he could think about was those horrifying violet eyes… *"I have never seen pure hatred and rage before, I suppose... She never even hesitated—nothing I did even slowed her down. Is this what it feels like to be prey? To truly know there is no hope of survival. I could have done nothing to stop her; she was so...pure. That is what a true monster is. I now know I am not a monster. I only play the monster."*

"Knock knock, little shit," Sam the monster's voice echoed through Nara's outer soul.

Naris shrieked in fear, *"How did she get here? I haven't come out! I have held up my part of our agreement!"*

"I said knock knock!" The monster's voice was not so full of rage as it had been before when it warned him to stay inside his host, but it was forceful and filled Naris with dread.

Naris felt a hand grab his shoulder, and he screamed in terror. It had found him; she had found him. Curled in a ball as he was, he could not see the monster that had ahold of him, and truthfully, he didn't want to see those eyes again.

"Please just make it quick," Naris said, resigned to his fate.

"What—seriously?" The monster's voice wasn't as loud now, and her grip on his shoulder lessened slightly. There was a long pause, and then she started laughing. She laughed and laughed the whole time. Naris expected her to end him at any moment. But the moment never came; her laughter eventually settled into a chuckle. She released the hand, gripping his shoulder, and patted him on the back, stating more than asking, "You have never lost a fight, have you? Oh my god, you are just as young and naïve as Nara! Just my luck, the all-powerful scary blight monster is just a scared little child hiding behind a facade of ferocity and desperation. Ha!"

"I'm not a monster," Naris's fear waned since the monster seemed willing to just talk. He defended his actions, saying, "I was given no choice by this…System. I was pulled from my home and forced to bond with the pathetic—um, Nara." He checked himself, worried he would anger the monster. When she did not strike him down, he continued, "I only do what I have to survive. You have no idea what it's like being trapped in here for cycles at a time, feeling nothing, only able to catch glimpses of the outside world through the seal in Nara's chest. It is maddening, and when I can get out, the world around me drains me, and then it burns me, forcing me to fight and consume to stay alive! I hate this! I don't want to be trapped any longer!"

Sam hadn't known blights were capable of such cognition. *"Hmm, I thought of them as more of a ravenous beast than a sapient creature. I know Nara talked to Naris, but I never knew how it worked."* With that thought, she asked Naris, "Can you control your mana drain? Like how much energy you siphon? Or do you turn into a greedy little shit and go for the kill every time you are released?"

"I…have never tried…regulating," Naris admitted slowly, "but I believe it would be possible." Suddenly hopeful, he asked, "Are you offering to let me out if I can regulate my siphon? Would you let me attempt on you?"

"Oh, hell no!" Sam said sharply, and Naris ducked his head. She then asked, "Can you draw mana from a crystal? Didn't Nara say something about a soul crystal when I woke up from being frozen?"

Naris, whose hopes were crushed when Sam initially said no, was now hopeful again. "I can draw from a soul crystal, but only the Church of the Light deals in soul crystals, and they only give them to tamed blights so they may serve the church." He spat out the last words like a bitter poison on his tongue.

Sam's semi-incorporeal form floated back from Naris a bit, prompting him to finally uncoil and look at her, his joints snapping and popping as he did so. *"He pops more than Nara does. What is up with these two and their insistence on contortion?"* Sam thought as Naris straightened up to look at her; his black eyes were full of expectation and hope. Finally able to look at Naris without fear of being eaten, Sam thought, *"He is nothing but grey sinew and bones. How could he have been so powerful?"* What she said was, "You look like a whipped puppy."

"I am a Blight, not a Canidae," Naris said, confused.

"I meant the way you—never mind," Sam said, then asked, "If I make a mana crystal, do you think you can use that instead of a soul crystal? I don't know what a soul crystal is, but I can make mana crystals."

"Yes! I can drain anything with mana!" Naris said enthusiastically.

Sam held up her hands to calm him down a little, "Don't get too excited just yet. I have only made one so far, and it didn't hold that much mana," she saw Naris's disappointed look and quickly added. "I'll tell you what, if you promise to get back to doing your job and plugging Nara's leaking soul," she pointed at Nara's soul core, which even then had a geyser of blue mana gushing out of it, "I will start experimenting with making a mana crystal or crystals that will allow you to come out into the world without having to kill everything around you." She held out her hand, "Deal?"

Naris stared at Sam's hand, momentarily mulling over what she offered. He could see no downside to the arrangement, so he clasped her hand and nodded, "Deal."

Sam yanked Naris in until they were nose to nose so fast he didn't have time to react other than a quick yelp of surprise and fear before her other hand wrapped around the back of his neck and squeezed. She whispered, "Good. Because Nara is my only friend in this world right now, I will no longer see her harmed by you. So help me if you ever force me to fight you like that again, and I end up hurting her to beat you back. I swear I will come in here, stuff you into that hole in her core, and stake your body to her soul for all eternity. So, I recommend you start thinking really hard about playing nice." She pushed him back with a broad smile, "Are we clear?"

Naris's blood was running cold, but he slightly nodded and said, "Very clear."

Clapping her hands, Sam said cheerfully, "Awesome! I think we're going to be great friends!" She pointed to Nara's soul core, "Now get to work!" Then she vanished.

***

Sam's mind snapped back to reality; her eyes slowly focused on Nara's still form in the chair. Nara had her eyes closed, but there was a gentle smile on her face, and already Sam could see the pallor of her skin returning to its healthy grey color.

"Naris must be absorbing the excess energy from her channels," Sam thought as the blue splotches slowly disappeared from Nara's skin. She was about to say something when Nara started snoring softly. Sam stifled a laugh and tried to slide off the sleeping Tenarian without waking her, but Nara's eyes popped open as soon as she moved.

"Hey, sleeping beauty," Sam said, "you're looking better already."

"You think I'm beautiful?" Nara mumbled, still waking up.

Sam was caught off guard at the comment, "I…it's an…I mean, yeah…but I was," Sam paused momentarily to compose herself and changed the subject. "You're cute when you snore."

Nara smiled, "So are you."

"What? I don't snore!" Sam was righteously indignant at the accusation. She shook her head, "That doesn't matter right now anyway. How are you and the little shit doing now?" Sam got off her friend and sat beside her, "You are looking much better already." She grabbed her wine and took a sip, continuing, "Also, it felt bizarre being inside you."

With a coy look, Nara raised her eyebrows at Sam's last statement, causing Sam to blush a little when she realized her phrasing. Nara's eyes were already unfocused, so Sam didn't interrupt Nara to correct herself; she assumed Nara and Naris were conversing, so she patiently waited for her friend to return to the real world and tell her what was said. She briefly considered touching Nara's mark to join in on their conversation but refrained.

Nara's eyes refocused a few moments later with a look of excited wonder. She grabbed Sam's hand, practically bouncing in her seat! "Is it true? Can you make mana crystals? Why didn't you mention that? When did you find out? It doesn't matter! What matters is that's how you tame blights! Only the church ever does it because of the massive cost to keep blights in mana crystals!" She paused just long enough to grab her goblet off the side table and quickly polish off the contents, then hold it out for more before continuing, "It will take a mana crystal that can discharge at least five hundred mana a minute. Can you make those? How much do the crystals you make hold? Are they big? How long do they take to make? Are you going to refill me or what?" Nara looked from Sam to her empty goblet and smiled sheepishly, "Please…"

Sam laughed out loud, summoning the wine and filling Nara's goblet since she asked so nicely. She told Nara, "Sorry, it slipped my mind. I made one for the first time ever for Alexander, the guy who owns the shop where we bought the quiver. Funny story actually, I assaulted one of his associates when he surprised me."

Nara slapped her hand over her forehead and eyes and interrupted Sam, asking, "Please tell me you didn't kill anyone!"

Sam scoffed, "What? No!" She looked at Nara accusatively, "Exactly who do you think I am? Anyway, long story short, after I apologized for trying to 'accidentally' murder his associate, Bradley is his name, by the way, the associate, not the owner. Did I mention he is an imp? An imp nearly roasted me alive the first day I arrived on this planet." Sam realized she was now rambling, so she tried to summarize, "So anyway, Alexander, the owner, not the imp, was curious about the arcane weapons I used when I and I cannot stress this enough: 'accidentally' tried to kill Bradley the imp. He wanted to know how I came across them, and when I lied to him about it, he threatened to press charges. So, to keep him from pressing charges, I made the first thing that came to mind. Since I was already in his magic workshop with all the mana crystals lying around, I just replicated what I saw and made a mana crystal to prove I wasn't lying."

Nara stared at Sam for a long moment, then said slowly, like she was talking to a child, "Sam, do you remember when I asked how your day was over dinner, and you said it was fun and told me about all your purchases?" Sam nodded, "Well, maybe next time you should tell me about nearly getting imprisoned by one of the most powerful and famous humans in the kingdom and then proceeding to make one of the most coveted items on the planet right in front of him."

"For one, how could I have known he was famous, and for…um…two, he may have offered to equip me and a few other people for a hundred cycles or up to level one hundred and fifty if I made him something—really dangerous," Sam said sheepishly.

"And what did you say?" Nara prodded.

"I told him I would think about it and didn't trust him," Sam said truthfully as she formed a mana crystal in the palm of her hand, this time trying to tweak the structure as she layered her mana over it. It was much more difficult than the first one she had made, not because of how she was forming it but because of the hole in her core. It made all her magic slightly more challenging to use.

Sam pushed through and soon had a fully formed magical crystal in her palm. She examined her work, sharing the information with Nara.

Mana Crystal: Pure
Quality: Flawless
Affinity: Error
Power: 318mu
Output: 85mu/min
Input: 1mu/sec
Uses: Multiple

Sam sighed; that had taken much more out of her than she was willing to admit, and it was nowhere near enough to keep Naris satisfied for any length of time. She told Nara, "It's not much, but it is only the second one I have made."

"Do you know how much valuable this is?" Nara asked; then, answering her own question, she said, "At least one gold, Sam. That is how much this little crystal is worth. A crafter could do some amazing things with this little gem." She took the crystal from Sam and held it up against the light of their campfire, whispering, "flawless and pure…"

Nara tried to give the crystal back, saying, "I cannot accept this; it is far too valuable, and I don't want to take advantage of you like this. We can find another way for Naris—"

Sam shook her head. "Keep it. Once we have enough, and if you're willing, we will try to let Naris out for a test run."

Nara didn't argue anymore and reluctantly stored the crystal in her inventory. She slid closer to Sam and leaned her head on her shoulder, saying, "Thank you, Sam. You are a good friend."

They sat in comfortable silence for a while. Sam made a few more mana crystals but had to stop because of the stress it was putting on her core. At Nara's look, she came clean about the black mist leaking from her core. They discussed it a bit, but as far as they could tell, it wasn't poisoning her, so they decided to play it by ear the next day to see if it would be necessary to turn back toward the city.

In the meantime, Sam returned to making arcane arrows, as they were much easier to craft. Nara decided to get a few hours of sleep. She retired to their partially repaired and barely functional tent, leaving Sam to her mana crafting.

***

On the morning of the second day of their mapping job, a couple of aggressive Lightning Cervidae surprised them. The deer-like creatures caught them off guard because they had shown up as blue, the color of non-aggressive creatures, on Sam's map right up until they attacked.

Now, back to being fully functional, Nara took the lead and drew the attention of both the aggressive creatures to herself. Taking pressure off Sam. *"Damn, she's talented,"* Sam thought as she watched in awe as Nara tanked a bolt of lightning from one of the attacking Cervidae's horns while at the same time running up a tree. A few meters up the trunk, Nara kicked off the tree into a backflip, loosing three arrows in quick succession before another bolt of lightning blasted her off course and into another tree, which she used as a springboard to launch herself behind a small knoll but not before she fired a couple of magic bolts at her attacker. Another bolt of lightning blasted chunks of rock and soil through the air and across Nara when it struck her cover an instant later. *"I bet if an Olympic competition combined gymnastics, contortionism, and archery, Nara would win gold every time."* Sam thought, impressed at Nara's unique fighting style.

Sam, distracted by her companion's sleek combat abilities, barely had time to erect a shield when one of the Cervidae turned to her, launching a searing bolt of lightning in her direction. The lightning broke through her hasty shield, the magic backlash worse than ever because of the hole in her core. Sam was knocked back from the impact of the blast and barely managed to dive behind a tree before the next bolt arrived; bark and splinters flew everywhere when the bolt struck the tree.

"Why are they attacking us?" Sam asked Nara through their party chat function.

"It must be mating season," Nara replied, "didn't the book say something about them becoming aggressive during that time?"

"Yeah, it did," Sam said, launching dozens of arcane bolts from her threads to harass the lightning-launching deer creatures. She looked down at her chest when she felt an itching sensation. "What the fuck?" She exclaimed. There was a smoking fist-sized hole where some lightning penetrated through her shield and armor.

"Is my pain tolerance so high I didn't even feel that? And how the fuck did Nara take two of those hits without even flinching!" Sam thought, adding as much mana as she could spare to heal the gaping wound in her torso.

"Are you okay?" Nara asked through their chat function. "And to answer your question, I have a high magic resistance. That's how I can take such a powerful attack. It stems from my neutral affinity—we'll discuss it later." Nara jumped from her cover, sending an arrow toward the Cervidae attacking Sam's position; the one attacking her was already down. Just as quickly, she ducked behind a tree, the rough bark blowing apart as a bolt of lightning struck its trunk. "Also, I think our thoughts are transmitted through the party chat function. What is Olympics?"

"I'll tell you later," Sam said while using her mana threads to shoot streams of arcane bolts at the aggressive beast.

"Stop, Sam, it's dead." Nara's voice rang in Sam's mind.

Sam stopped her barrage and peeked out from behind the tree she used as cover. She hadn't even noticed the chime from the kill notification.

"These arrows pack a punch!" Nara exclaimed, walking out from her cover and holding one of Sam's arcane arrows. "Too bad they are only good for one charge."

"Yeah, I don't get that," Sam said, "I can't figure out what I am doing differently with the arrows. All the blades I make can be recharged, but I cannot figure out how to do it with the arrows."

Sam looted the corpses, receiving nothing out of the ordinary, and then sat against a tree to continue healing herself. Nara sat beside her and kept watch while Sam meditated to speed up her recovery.

Once she was healed, Sam opened her eyes and asked Nara, "Should we do the cave with the whitlings next?"

Nara nodded, "We're almost finished mapping the area, so yeah. We can clear out the cave and finish the survey on our way back to the city."

They had decided to head back to the city if Sam hadn't gotten any worse or better after the Whitling job. Sam's health took precedence over everything else. It had been difficult for Sam to convince Nara to keep going even with that concession. But truthfully, so far, Sam hadn't felt any of the effects increasing from the breach in her core. *"I am a little worried about the black stuff, but it doesn't seem to affect my channels."* Sam thought absently. *"I'll just have to keep a close eye on it."*

CHAPTER 19 — "These things suck!"

"These things suck!" Sam said as she pulled a giant venom-coated fang from Nara's back.

"Gah, they most certainly do!" Nara said, her voice pained, "but they helped me level my class quickly. I gained three levels in my class, and my Magic Bolt leveled up twice. Just from this fight."

"The job was for whitlings, not giant spiders," Sam grumbled, grabbing the other fang in Nara's back. "Okay, on three. Are you ready?" On Nara's nod, Sam started counting, "One—" she yanked the fang out of her friend's back.

"Goink!" Nara wailed, "you said three!"

"Oh, did I?" Sam asked with a shit-eating grin. "Also, what does 'goink' mean?"

"Just heal me, please," Nara snapped, grabbing the fang from Sam, and put it in her inventory. "And goink means the same as when you say 'fuck.' I'm surprised your translator skill didn't fill you in on that."

"It translated the word as 'unpleasant penetration' in my mind. So, I wanted to clarify," Sam said, wrapping a mana thread around Nara's wrist, healing her, while giggling at the word. At the same time, she looted the giant spiders that had surprised them less than ten minutes after they entered the uncharted cave in search of the whitling brood mother. They were checking the cave because it was the only place in the area that fit the whitling nest described in the job contract and their guidebook.

Arachnid Stalker Items:

2-Gold; 17-Silver; 47-Copper; Monster core [Arachnid Stalker level 47]; Arachnid Stalker carapace [Level 47]; Arachnid Stalker legs x 8; Arachnid Stalker venom sack x 2; Arachnid Stalker fang x 2; 8kg Arachnid Stalker meat; Mana Potion x 2. Take all Yes/No

After selecting 'Yes,' Sam pulled a kilogram of the meat from her inventory. She was curious about what giant spider meat would look like. A blob of greasy black gelatin landed in her hand, prompting her to drop it immediately. The greasy blob splatted on the stone of the cave floor with a sickening squelch. The thin, oily film surrounding it split open, releasing a viscous fluid that sizzled and popped as soon as it touched the cavern floor, melting the stone beneath it and filling the air with a pickle smell.

Sam looked at Nara, who said, "It's a delicacy. From what I've heard, a qualified chef can turn it into an amazing soup."

"I think I'll pass on the acid soup for now," Sam said, wiping her greasy hand on the leg of her pants. Looting the next spider, she asked Nara, "How can some people and creatures conceal themselves from my mana sight? First, it was the bandits, and now these spiders."

"Concealment skills mimic and project the ambient magical energies in an area around the user. Your mana sight was working fine, but it was being tricked by the concealment spell or ability. The spells are extremely mana intensive but also very effective." Nara explained. "Once your sight ability's level is high enough, you might be able to see through some illusions and obscurations."

Sam nodded her understanding and, walking over, she checked Nara's back. Smooth grey skin could be seen through the holes in the Tenarian's armor where there had been bleeding wounds a few minutes before. Shaking her head at the state of her friend's armor, Sam ran her fingers across the damaged chest piece while she continued to heal the internal damage the poison had caused her friend.

'Bing' Mana Repair has leveled up to level 25: Mana cost reduced slightly. You are now able to repair all organic material. The restored material's origin, quality, and complexity determine the mana cost.

"Oh, now that is convenient," Sam said, trying the new aspect of her skill on Nara's damaged armor.

"What's convenient?" Nara asked, looking over her shoulder at Sam, who was still behind her. Sam sent her the notification. After reading the details, Nara said, "Convenient indeed. You're like a walking repair facility."

"Cool, huh?" Sam asked.

"Very…um cool…is something being cold a good thing in your world?" Nara said hesitantly.

"Not exactly, but it is better than being hot and bothered," Sam snickered at Nara's confused look and explained, "It's a linguistics thing. It doesn't seem to translate slang very well. 'Cool' is an expression used to say something is very good or excellent in my world, among other meanings."

"In that case, it is…cool," Nara agreed, watching her damaged armor regrow slowly.

Sam started repairing their armors' but had to stop and rest about two-thirds of the way through the repair. The gaping hole in her core was now leaking more black shit suddenly, and she had no idea why. And now, every time she used her magic, there was a lot of pain. Sam coughed, and a trail of black mana floated from her mouth. The mana caused a cacophony of tiny pops as it contacted the atmospheric mana. Sam's eyesight started to fade and grow dark as she watched the black energy dissipate. *"Oh man, this isn't good,"* she thought, feeling dizzy. Sam shook her head, trying to clear it, and stood up.

Nara, who had been dozing while Sam worked, checked her armor when Sam coughed and stood up. Seeing her armor repair wasn't complete, she looked to Sam, who tried to smile as if nothing was wrong but then coughed again, doubling over in pain. She looked up at Nara again, "I'm sorry, Nara. I tried to stop it, but it just happened so fast. Maybe if I give it time, it will heal itself…I always…heal." Sam's legs buckled as an infinite weakness washed over her.

"Oh no! Sam! Your eyes!" Nara jumped up, panicking. She grabbed Sam's shoulders and helped lower her friend to the cavern floor, staring into Sam's eyes, which were now pitch black with purple irises. Black veins spread across her friend's face, traveling down her neck and disappearing under her armor.

"I just need to catch my breath for a second," Sam said weakly before slipping unconscious.

***

"No, no, no, what do I do?" Nara thought, panicking as she cradled Sam's unconscious body in her arms.

"I can help her," Naris's voice came unbidden into Nara's mind.

"You will do no such thing!" Nara hissed back. "You are the reason this is happening! I will never let you touch her again!"

"I…am…sorry," Naris said slowly. It almost sounded like he was surprised at the statement.

"Sorry isn't going to cut it, you asshole!" Nara snapped as she hugged her friend close to her chest, watching black veins spread across Sam's hand as black mist began leaking from her pores.

Nara looked around the cavern, worried some aggressive creature was sneaking up on them even then. She was afraid; she had never seen or heard of black mana. There was a darkness affinity, but all the dark magic Nara had seen had some life mixed in. This, however, was like the absence of all things. She stripped off Sam's armor and clothes. She gasped at the innumerable lines resembling veins made of the deepest black she had ever seen tracing across her friend's body. But what truly terrified her was the gaping black hole in the center of Sam's chest right above her soul core.

"What is this black?" Nara asked, looking at the lines ravaging her friend's body. "She doesn't have a darkness affinity, and no darkness affinity is this—"

"It is Void! I know this for certain," Naris said, "it is like my home." Naris's voice was full of wonder, "How is this possible?"

“Void?” Nara asked incredulously, “Are you telling me my friend is a monster from the Void like you? Impossible!”

“I am not a monster!” Naris snapped with heat in his voice. “I am a denizen of the Void just as you are of this plane! I didn’t choose to be torn from my dimension and attached to a, to a—to you!” Surprised by the emotion in Naris’s voice, Nara remained silent as he continued. “This energy...the energy of my dimension, my home, it will burn you, Nara; it will eat and consume you in a way I cannot explain. It will do the same to you that your reality does to me. Let me help her. I swear I will do nothing more than absorb the Void energy coming from her soul so it stops poisoning her.”

“No, I cannot trust you! Just two days ago, you tried to kill her and—” Nara struggled with her roiling emotions, “Void monster or not, she is my friend, and I will not let you hurt her again.” Tears were falling from Nara’s eyes as she watched the Void consume her only friend.

"Then try it yourself," Naris said, "use your ability. Consume the Void to cleanse her soul. I will do my best to help, but I know you will fail."

"I will not fail," Nara growled, "I cannot fail!" She extended her mana cutters, razor-sharp blue claws extending from her fingertips. "Please work," she pleaded, carefully cutting into her dying friend's chest.

The instant her claws cut into Sam’s chest, Nara knew she had made a terrible mistake; the burning pain flowing through her mana channels when she activated the mana siphon was like nothing she had ever felt. Nara screamed in agony but refused to let her friend go. She held out for as long as she could, absorbing the Void poisoning her friend. All the while, the Void burned into her channels like acid. She felt Naris try to absorb the black energy, and he did to some extent, but it did no good because the energy still had to burn its way through her channels before it got to her soul core. Nara struggled for as long as she could, frying her mana channels in the process, but in the end, it was useless, *"I can't...it won't be enough...I’m sorry, Sam..."*

As Nara slumped across her friend's body, she didn’t hear Naris screaming into her mind as he banged on the seal on her chest, “No! Wake up! The seal is still too strong! You must let me out! I can save all of us!” His pleas went unanswered, though. Nara was already unconscious.

***

Sam’s eyes flashed open, and she quickly patted herself down, looking around the room. When she realized she was safe in her room at the orphanage, she relaxed, *“Wow, that was a freaky dream. Wait, why am I back in my old room? I haven’t lived here in years.”* Instinctively, she tried to open her System menu, but nothing happened. *“Huh, that’s weird; why would I even try that? It was a dream, after all...but why am I here? Did something happen, and the sisters asked me to visit?"*

Sam sat up in the bed, the old and threadbare sheets feeling like they had all those years ago. She shook her head, trying to dispel the images from her dream. *"Man, what a vivid dream! Maybe I should write it down or something...it felt so real."*

Hopping off the bed, Sam walked over to the door and tried to open it. A strange blackness surrounded the doorframe, and the handle wouldn't budge when she tried it.

"Hello..." Sam said and waited for a reply, "Sister Nicholas? Anyone? Can anyone hear me? What's going on?" When no response came, she looked back around the room. The corners of the room had the same black distortion the doorframe did. *"What is that stuff? Okay, this is weird."* She thought, still scanning the room for any clue that might help explain why and how she was there. Her eyes lit on her old desk to one side of the room. It had three figurines on it. *"That's odd. I never had toys growing up."*

She walked over to her desk and studied the twenty-centimeter-tall figures curiously. One was almost an exact replica of herself sporting a cool-looking violet overcoat with black leather pants underneath held up by a strange tool belt full of weird gadgets. Black leather combat boots and a black crop top with violet pentagram emblazoned on the front completed the peculiar ensemble. On her head, she wore wrap-around glasses that didn't hide the violet of her eyes and headphones that were likely connected to the phone she held in her hand with fingerless anti-slip gloves. *"Now that is some detailed work; it looks almost exactly like me. Well, except for the high-tech outfit."* Sam thought as she studied the figure of herself. It was standing on a small pedestal with the name Samantha etched into the base. *"I guess it is me after all."*

Sam moved to the next figure. It was a snake woman with long black and violet hair. Her eyes were solid black except for the purple slits of her vertical irises. Two black fangs contrasted with her otherwise white teeth. The figure was fully nude, but a mixture of black and violet scales covered her body, which was that of a woman's upper half, turning into a long snake tail just below her belly button. Sam figured the tail had to be at least four times the length of her upper body but couldn't be sure because of how it was coiled around her. Again, it felt like Sam was staring at an image of herself when she looked at the figure. *"Well, if I was a giant snake person. What are they called...Labia, no, Lamia?"* The name on the pedestal, the snake woman, was coiled around, read Moura. *"That's not ominous or anything."* Sam thought, reading her family name on the pedestal, *"But it isn't my family name. My parents abandoned me, and I was never adopted. The church gave me my name, so why is it on the figurine of a snake person?"* Not finding an answer in her mind, Sam had to move on.

Finally finished admiring the Lamia, Sam's interest was drawn to the center figure. She had intentionally skipped over this one to save it for last because it gave her the creeps. As she stared into the violet eyes of the center figure, a feeling of overwhelming dread washed over her. Intense violet eyes were set in a midnight black dragon's face. A smile of pure predation was fixed on the dragon woman's mouth, exposing sharp, pearly white teeth in her elongated jaws. The teeth looked more like weapons than something she would use to chew with. Two sleek black horns with streaks of violet curling around them protruded from the dragon woman's head, curving back and up to terminate in sharp points. The dragon's body was vaguely feminine and covered in black scales that reflected no light. Other than being bipedal, there were no other similarities to humanity; this was a different species altogether, yet somehow Sam knew it was her or at least a representation of her. Long black claws protruded from her hands and feet. A thick tail covered in spines was curved around her midriff with a wicked-looking curved blade of what looked like obsidian at the tip. What drew Sam's attention was the massive leathery wings spreading out from the dragon woman's back. The inside of the wings was a rich violet, while the backside was midnight black.

The wing's tips protruded a sharp spike, suggesting they could be used as weapons and for flight. *"Shit, her whole body is a weapon,"* Sam thought, admiring the endless ferocity of the figure before her. She looked at the name inscribed on the pedestal, and unsurprisingly, it read Alecto. *"This is too weird,"* Sam thought, eyeing the figure's name. *"Someone has a bizarre sense of humor around here. And some serious artistic ability."* She couldn't help but admire the attention to detail the creator of these figures had. It was almost like they were alive.

Sam was about to step back when she noticed the faint outline of a fourth figurine in the black obscuration where the desk was pushed up against the wall. She couldn't grasp what she saw when she tried to focus on the outline. Sam knew there was something there, but its form eluded her. That's when all three figures she could see started to move. "What the fuck!" Sam snapped, jerking back from the desk and retreating to the middle of the room. She watched in shocked fascination as all three of the figurines stepped or, in the snake woman's case, slid forward off their respective pedestals to stop at the edge of the desk. None of them spoke, only stared intently at Sam, who eyed them back nervously.

"Sister Nicolas?" Sam called out, not taking her eyes off the figures. "What's going on? Can anyone hear me? This isn't funny anymore!" There was no answer. At her words, all three figures brought their fingers to their lips in a shushing gesture. Sam had no idea why, but she complied and stopped shouting. Then, as one, the three of them spread their arms wide, and their chest cavities split open, revealing a sphere floating in the center of each of them. The techno girl, Samantha's orb, was almost all purple with only faint streaks of black swirling around in it. The snake girl Moura's orb was half black and half purple, looking like a 3D yin-yang. And lastly, the dragon girl Alecto had one that was black with faint streaks of purple.

Sam was freaking out now. *"What the hell is going on?"* She asked herself as she tore her eyes from the creepy figurines to search the room for clues. When Sam's eyes caught a glimpse of a purple glow under her bed, she investigated the strange light.

"What the hell..." Getting on her knees, keeping the figures on the desk in her peripheral in case they moved again, Sam stared at a strange glowing purple symbol carved into the wooden floor beneath her bedframe. Tentatively, she reached out to touch the glowing rune, which glowed brighter as her fingers got closer, the purple glow turning into delicate violet flames. Pausing for only a second, Sam felt no heat from the flames, so she continued reaching out until the tips of her fingers contacted the rune.

Sam's vision went purple, then black.

The three figures watched in disappointment as Sam disappeared from the room that, unbeknownst to her, was the mental representation of a fragment of her fractured soul. Robotically, they all returned to their pedestals, becoming statues once again.

***

Three pairs of pitch-black eyes slowly opened; all three pure-white irises in each eye expanding in the darkness of the creature's prison to allow the dark pupils to gather more light. The beast shifted slightly, focusing on a small, non-descript book hovering in front of its nose. The book was open with only one thing written on its pages, [S.A.M]. The slight movement of the creature caused the chains binding it to rattle.

"Hmm…odd," a deep reverberating voice shook the walls of the massive cavern serving as the creature's prison, "I thought I felt her for a moment. Surely, she could not have amassed so much power to be back so soon…that is assuming her soul survived the transfer."

Far above the imprisoned creature in a sealed room full of antiquated electronic equipment, a red light flashed on an old dusty control panel. Distant shouts could be heard, along with the muted blaring of alarms outside the heavy steel doors of the small control room.

***

Sam's awareness returned slowly. The discomfort of the rocks and detritus on the cave floor digging into her back made her groan as she opened her eyes. Naris stared back at her, his hand on her chest. Everything returned to her instantly, losing the fight with the leak in her core, Nara lowering her to the ground, and then darkness. But there was something else inside the darkness; she felt it. It was like a dream, though. She couldn't worry about that now, though.

"You!" Sam growled at Naris, her voice husky from her dry mouth. She grabbed Naris by his throat and squeezed hard.

"Stop…please…I'm trying to help you," Naris barely managed to gasp out the words with Sam gripping his throat so tightly, "I'm…almost…finished…"

"Give me Nara! Where is she?" Sam was nose to nose with the Blight, her fingernails digging into his skin, tiny trickles of black blood running from the wounds.

"I…can't…she is too weak…from trying to save…you," Naris managed to say before yanking his hand away from Sam's bare chest. "Finished…I'm finished…please…release me…"

Sam realized she was harming Nara's body and released her grip on Naris. Pushing him off, she stood up and surveyed the cave. Nothing had changed from what she could tell. The two dead giant spiders still looked fresh; the blood was not even congealed. Sam patted herself down. Besides being nude, she could see nothing wrong with herself physically besides the hole in her chest where Naris's hand had just been, which she quickly closed. While closing the wound, Sam also noticed her mana was still at its current maximum. Seeing Naris wasn't particularly interested in attacking her, nor had he tried to drain her, she took a chance and checked her soul core. There was still a gaping hole in the side, but the black mist gushing out of it was now just the faintest trickle. When she checked her core, a flash of something crossed her vision; it was an image, no, three images. It was gone as fast as it came, though, and she pushed it to the back of her mind for now.

Naris realized what she was doing and quickly explained, "I cannot repair the core damage, at least not to my knowledge, but I can absorb the Void. It will come back, though, and if you want to live, you will have to let me do it again."

Looking back to Naris, crouched a few meters away, eyeing her warily, Sam asked, "What happened to Nara, and don't you fucking dare lie to me?"

Naris countered with an outburst of questions and accusations, "Why didn't you tell us you weren't human? Nara needs human flesh to survive, and you lied to her! How do you have Void in your core? Are you a Void beast? What is your true race and class?"

Sam was caught off guard between the weird vision and Naris's sudden outburst. She stared at Naris in confusion, "I don't know what Void is, and I'm a Human. I just…" she trailed off, pulling up her status screen to display it for him. "See! I'm a—what the hell?" Sam couldn't believe what she was seeing.

Samantha Alecto Moura [S.A.M.]
Race: Human Hybrid [Unknown]; Error; [Level 21]
Affinity(s): Arcane; Error…more data required.]
Class: Arcane Pathfinder [Level 22]

Health: 765 (1274)
Stamina: 573 (955)
Mana: 2084 (3473)

"This is not possible. I'm a human from Earth." Sam said, staring at her status screen.

Naris stared at Sam's screen with her. He crept closer and laid a clawed hand on her arm. Sam jerked but didn't pull away. She looked down at him with a mixture of fear and confusion in her expression. Her violet eyes now had moats of the deepest black floating in her sclera. She was still ready to take him down instantly but needed answers. He hadn't killed her when he had the chance, so she decided to listen to what he had to say.

"Sam," Naris started hesitantly, "You were summoned just as I was from another dimensional plane, were you not?" At Sam's nod, he continued, "If you are not from this plane, you would have had to travel through the Void to arrive in this verse. It shouldn't be possible, but you somehow survived contact with True Void."

"What is Void?" Sam interrupted.

"I'm getting to that," Naris said patiently, "Normally, Void is just an affinity like any other. It's a powerful affinity, but no more than your arcane affinity, which, although I am not fully certain, I believe is the opposite of Void. However, pure Void will burn a hole in reality before the System has filtered it. That's why Void summons require complex magical structures before a hole in the Void can be opened. You have seen this once already, the day you met Nara."

Sam thought back to her fight with the elite wolf, how the beast had created the magical circle with blood before summoning the black hand that transformed it. How the black tips of its tentacles cut through her without any resistance. She asked, "Wait, are you saying that creature poisoned me with Void?"

"No," Naris said confidently, "that was an example of filtered Void, not pure Void. Had it been pure, it would have burned the creature to nothing within seconds." Naris removed his hand from Sam's arm and pointed up. He said, "There is a giant gateway to the Void realms on Tenaris. That is where I am from. It's why your reality burns me. Although I am not a Voidling, I am of the Void." Then he pointed at Sam's chest with a clawed finger, "I don't understand how you have not exploded! If Arcane and Void are opposites, your core should have exploded or dissolved already. That black mana leaking out of your soul is Void, pure, unfiltered Void. Why do you think I can stand here and speak with you? I have absorbed enough Void to last in this reality for hours. The System used my mana siphon skill as a filter, making it compatible with this reality." He lightly touched the symbol on his forehead, "which is good because Nara will not be able to return until I have flushed the Void from her mana channels."

"Can I, um…speak with her?" Sam asked, trying to comprehend everything Naris had just told her without freaking out. *"I have a reality destroying…what would I call it element…energy leaking out of my soul? How fucked up is that? And now the System is calling me an unknown hybrid… this is all just too weird. Not to mention terrifying."*

Naris pulled her out of her thoughts, saying, "Nara is unconscious. She nearly died trying to absorb the Void to save you. I had to force my way out of the seal, so…uh…she will need immediate healing when I retreat to her core." He wrung his hands, clearly expecting Sam to be angry, and said, "You can visit her, but I don't recommend it." He pulled up his light armor and shirt, revealing a gaping hole in his chest right where Nara's mark would have been.

Sam stared in horror at the wound. The walls of the injury and exposed organs were cauterized. Hence, no blood flowed from the hole, yet the severity was undoubtedly life-threatening. Sam reached out, intending to heal the wound.

Naris jumped back quickly, shouting, "Careful! I still have too much Void energy! You may only cause more damage if you try to heal me now!" He calmed himself and said, "Let us try slowly at first. Also, we must teach Nara a healing spell. She cannot replicate your healing skills, so it must be a spell. If we have a healing spell, I can heal damage almost as fast as you with my current energy."

Taking Naris's advice, Sam touched the inside of the wound with one of her threads. She activated her skills and began to close the wound slowly. Glancing up at Naris, he nodded. Sam started speeding up the healing process until he held up a hand when she was at about half her average healing speed.

"I am isolating the wound with Nara's neutral mana while channeling the void mana away from it. It is much more difficult than it sounds," Naris grunted.

Sam kept healing the hole in his chest until it was closed, noticing the hole in her core wasn't making it quite as challenging to use her magic as before. *"Hmm, that's something to look into later. I don't think it's because he drained all the Void out of me either."* A quick glance at her status showed the blacked-out parts of her energy bars were slowly receding at a barely perceptible rate. *"Well, now, that is promising."*

It took nearly an hour to heal Naris. During that time, Sam asked him how he kept getting out of his seal because she was under the impression that wasn't possible. He only said there were certain circumstances he could exploit, but the Void he absorbed this latest time allowed him to brute force his way out.

"There. Done." Sam said, standing from her meditation, "Now what?"

Naris shrugged, "I am still at approximately ninety percent capacity, and that is just the filtered Void. We could wait for me to filter the energy from Nara's mana channels, then try to wake her or continue with the whitling's job. You should be good for at least a day before I need to absorb more energy from you, too, so we have a good deal of time." He looked a little sheepish and continued, "I must confess I would like to assist you as much as possible, not just to experience this reality but also to apologize for what I did to you." He looked down at the ground, "I know you are only helping me because of your affection for Nara, but the fact still remains that you are the first person who has ever even offered to help me. All others tried to enslave me or find a way to keep me bound and silenced. I was selfish before, thinking it could only be me or Nara, but now you have given me hope it can be us, Nara and I, together."

Sam gave his offer some thought. Her curiosity at how she and Naris would perform if they fought together, coupled with how easy it was to use her magic again, won out. "Okay, let's see what kind of team a human hybrid and void blight make, shall we."

Naris grinned, his fangs glistening black in the dim illumination the cave moss gave.

***

Sam and Naris continued deeper into the cave. They took their time and moved carefully but were ambushed by two more Arachnid Stalkers on two separate occasions. Fortunately, Sam kept a weak magic shield covering her and Naris as they walked, having learned from the first ambush. Even though the spiders broke through the shield quickly, Naris had time to react and quickly dispatched them. Sam let Naris fight each spider on his own at his request. Watching him fight, she wasn't sure which was more lethal, Nara with her bow and magic or Naris with his claws. She leaned towards it being Naris since Nara still needed Sam's arcane arrows to fight above her level.

When they had finished killing and looting the second spider, they took a break behind one of the giant mushrooms that were becoming more numerous as they progressed deeper into the cave. The giant mushrooms, like the moss on the walls, gave off a slight orange glow, casting eerie shadows along the floor and walls of the tunnel.

After their short break, they continued deeper into the cave. Sam was still keeping her mana sight active, and it was a good thing because it was the only reason she spotted the whitling before they stumbled into the nest. She actually spotted hundreds of them.

A large area had just opened up to them as they rounded a bend in a tunnel, joining two caverns. The cavern was at least half a kilometer across and circular in shape, housing a forest of giant mushrooms, the largest of which stood nearly twenty meters tall with a two-meter base. Sam's focus on the fantastic glowing forest almost caused her to miss the hundreds of figures glowing in her mana sight dotting the high domed ceiling. Even then, when she spotted the small glowing shapes, it wasn't until one of them spread its wings that she realized what it was. Silently stopping Naris with an outstretched hand, Sam pointed up and identified the closest one.

Whitling Scout [Level 16]; Hostile; Affinity: Poison.

Naris tapped her shoulder, pointing toward the back of the cavern. It took Sam a moment, but she realized what he was pointing at. It was a massive whitling the size of a horse curled up asleep on a giant nest of countless bones of all shapes and sizes. Sam identified the sleeping creature, thankful her skill worked at this distance.

Whiling Brood Mother [Level ??]; Hostile; Affinity: Poison.

Sam motioned Naris back into the tunnel, and they slank back slowly. Once she thought they were far enough back, Sam said softly, "There are at least one hundred of the damn things, plus the Brood Mother." She asked, "Do you have enough juice for an extended fight?"

Naris thought about it before responding, "If I go all out, I will be able to last for over forty minutes."

Sam mulled his response over. *"Forty minutes is a long time for a fight, but I don't know how long it will take to bring the big one down. Also, Naris doesn't have a ranged skill—wait, yes, he does!"* She looked at Naris and asked, "Do you have Nara's spell?"

Naris's eyes widened and then unfocused. A wicked grin spread across his face. "It is called Void Bolt."

"Okay then, here's the plan," Sam said, "you and I both stand at the mouth of the tunnel and try to pick off as many of the little ones as we can as silently as possible." At Naris's confused look, she explained, "They looked like they were sleeping, and they are weak, so if we can hit them in the head, it might kill them without waking the others. I can conjure some mana under their bodies if they fall to soften the sound of their impact, but they may not even fall." Naris was nodding along now and made to move when Sam grabbed him, saying, "One last thing. We will try to escape if they swarm us, or the fight proves too difficult to handle safely. If we have to retreat, I'll collapse the tunnel behind us or try to create a barrier to block the tunnel as long as possible. Also, if you get down to, let's say, thirty percent, and it still looks like we're winning, but the big one is still alive, we will try to escape. We cannot risk you running out of energy and reverting back during the middle of the fight, not if Nara is still unconscious in there." She tapped his chest.

Naris nodded his understanding, and they crept back to the mouth of the cave. Sam focused three of her threads at three of the closest creatures and quickly fired two bolts out of each, going for a double tap on each of her targets just to be safe. All six bolts hit their marks dead on. Three kill notifications chimed in her mind an instant later.

Naris fired a bolt of black energy, and Sam winced as it made a crackling sound flying through the air. When the magical projectile hit its intended target, the whitling's head exploded with a soft popping sound.

"Shit! I didn't think about how other magics make so much freaking noise!" Sam berated herself mentally as she and Naris froze in place, waiting to see what would happen. Several long seconds passed, with the only sound of blood dripping from the dead whitlings landing on the mushroom caps below. Releasing a slow breath, Sam shrugged and was about to aim for a few more of the beasts when, almost as one, all of the poisonous vampire lizard bats exploded off the ceiling in a screeching cloud. Sam felt a low sonic pulse hit her ears at the same instant. It wasn't an attack, not that she could tell, but a wake-up call from the brood mother.

The cloud of whitling's flooded toward Sam and Naris's position, and Sam got to see one of the creatures up close for the first time. *"Not as disgusting as I imagined,"* she thought when the swarm was close enough for her to get a good look. They were Labrador-sized lizards with bat wings and ears and blind eyes. Two four-centimeter retractable fangs in their upper jaw were similar to a snake's but not as curved. Sam summed up her opinion of the strange creatures with a thought, *"Compared to a Deep Hunter, they may as well be teddy bears."* Then, the swarm was upon them.

Sam threw up a magic shield to block some of the monsters. Her shield must have been physical enough for the creature's echolocation to detect because the first ones to it dodged around the barrier with impressive ariel maneuvers. Those behind them didn't fare as well, though. Without enough time to dodge, they were smashed into Sam's barrier by their brethren following too close behind. Naris was firing Void bolts as fast as he could, and each time one of the energized bolts of Void struck its target, the part of the body it struck exploded, causing all those around the target to falter as they flew through a mist of blood and bone fragments.

Sam was even more devastating, though. Her magic no longer hurt to cast, and she was going all out. She was launching bladed discs, arcane bolts, and mana spikes from all six of her threads and one hand while throwing up barriers directly in front of the faces of any whitlings that managed to dodge her attacks. She had learned her lesson and waited until the last second to form her shields, giving the creatures no time to avoid the barrier.

Red blood sprayed in all directions as the creatures were sliced, perforated, and blasted from the air by the barrage of attacks. Body parts, viscera, and blood rained down, coating the once light orange mushroom caps red with gore.

But the whitlings kept coming. The original hundred or so were mostly dead, but they had been joined by hundreds more flying in from tunnels in the ceiling. They dove toward Sam and Naris as they entered the cavern, ignoring their kin dying and falling around them.

"It's the Brood Mother!" Sam shouted over the din of the screeching swarm. "She's calling them in and causing them to swarm! We have to retreat! There are too many coming in! I can't keep this up forever!" Even as she said it, more whitlings were pouring out of a side tunnel obscured from their view behind a giant mushroom when they surveyed the room earlier. That's when Sam felt air rushing in from behind her.

Without hesitating, Sam grabbed Naris by the arm and, throwing up as strong a shield as she could to cover them, yanked him from the tunnel entrance and down the short slope to the cavern floor below just as a thick mass of whitlings burst from the tunnel they had been standing in only a second before. Wings batted at her barrier as claws and fangs tried to gain purchase against it as they ran into the mushroom forest, dodging around the thick stalks.

They ran for several minutes, and Sam thought they must be halfway across the cavern when Naris suddenly jerked her to a stop, shouting,

"Here!" He caught himself realizing where they were amongst the mushrooms was much quieter than the tunnel entrance. He swatted a lone whitling to the side, his claws raking deep furrows across its throat. The creature's limp body struck the ground and was still. Naris continued in a more normal tone as they dispatched the occasional lizard bat that found its way to their position, "This area is dense enough so they cannot swarm us, and I do not think we are close enough to the Brood Mother for her to attack us directly."

Sam couldn't argue with that logic. The thick caps over their heads were hiding their position from the swarm above for now, and the density of the stalks kept those that found them from being able to attack in too great a number. She asked, "How much energy do you have until you turn back?"

"I have some time, but not enough to fight through the swarm above us," Naris said thoughtfully.

Sam checked her map. It was little more than a red cloud above them, but she could see the Brood Mother had not moved, which was a good sign. Still, she sighed inwardly at their situation, *"I just never learn my lesson, do I?"*

CHAPTER 20 — “This is going to hurt, isn’t it?”

"Naris, are Nara's mana channels purged and repaired, and can you switch back to her while she is still unconscious?" Sam asked. She was starting to formulate a plan. She planned to wake up Nara and get as close as possible to the least congested tunnel. If Nara ran out of mana or couldn't keep up, Naris could take over and help Sam fight through until they were in the tunnel, which she could hopefully collapse behind them. She intended to keep both Nara and Naris with as much energy as possible and use their strengths in each situation. Sam had noticed Naris was faster and more flexible than Nara. In contrast, Nara was a good bit stronger and more acrobatic. Sam thought it was strange, considering they were using the same body, but just figured it was something the System was doing.

"Yes. But I still have a lot of Void energy," Naris said. Then, after a moment, he added, "I don't think that will be a problem. It is filtered, and her channels are purged."

"Okay, then do it now while you still have energy in case you need to break out again," Sam ordered. Naris closed his eyes to change, but Sam stopped him quickly, "Wait!" He opened his eyes to see her holding out two arcane daggers hilt first. Sam explained, "Put these in your inventory; they are fully charged. I know your claws are fierce, but these things pack a punch." He took the weapons without a word, and they disappeared into his storage. Sam swore she saw a smile cross his lips right before he changed.

Sam almost missed it when Naris switched with Nara, but what she saw was weird. *“What the fuck just happened?”*

Sam didn’t know what had happened. She tried to make sense of it as she caught Nara’s limp body with her mana threads and lowered her friend to the ground. *"I almost didn't see it, but I could swear he turned into pure energy for an instant, and then there was Nara. Hmm, I'll have to ask them how their change works later."* Sam was still fighting off whitlings during her musing, but she had set up several shields to create a choke point that forced the creatures to come from a singular direction. It worked well, so she turned her attention to her unconscious friend.

***

Naris didn't know what to think as he checked on Nara's core and began siphoning her neutral mana build-up into himself, taking care not to mix it with the volatile Void energy. Filtered or not, the Void was not to be mishandled. He did it all subconsciously. He was thinking how forgiving the monster— Sam had been. *"Either she is naïve, or she truly fears nothing...maybe both? She gave me weapons! I have tried to kill her twice in less than a week, and she gave me weapons!"* Shaking his head in bewilderment, he tended to Nara's core. A smile was on his face, *"I cannot wait to use those daggers."*

***

Sam wasn't having the pleasant thoughts Naris; it was quite the opposite. She had repeatedly checked Nara with her repair skill without finding anything wrong with her friend that she could heal. However, the Tenarian still wouldn't wake up. Sam even gave her a couple of light slaps on her cheeks, then a few slightly harder slaps. Nothing. Then a powerful slap…nothing. When shaking her didn't help either, Sam was starting to worry; she could hear the whitlings chewing through the protective layer of mushroom caps above her, with a few already breaking through the canopy and racing straight toward her.

Sam almost shouted for Naris but tried one last idea. She pulled out her endless canteen and dumped its contents onto Nara's peaceful face.

***

Nara was enjoying a delicious thirteen-course dinner at a restaurant where she had never dined. She had no idea how she had gotten to the restaurant, nor did she care. *"Thirteen courses of dessert! How have I never been here before?"* At this moment, she finished the seventh offering. A deliciously light flan paired with a light and slightly fruity drink that tasted like…water? "What is this?" Nara held up the glass to the waiter, who smiled, hefted an entire barrel of water, and dumped its contents over her head.

***

Nara sat up, spluttering.

"Took you long enough!" Sam shouted over the screeching of hundreds, if not thousands, of whitlings, punching holes through the giant mushroom caps. Sam was launching blades, spikes, and bolts of arcane death in all directions, but more whitlings were pushing through every second.

Nara surveyed the chaos around her briefly before jumping up and pulling a torch, flint, and steel from her inventory. She crouched down and started franticly trying to light the torch.

"What the fuck are you doing?" Sam shouted, "We have to try and run for it!" Even as she said it, over twenty flying creatures slammed into one of her barriers, which cracked under the impact but thankfully held. "Come on, Nara! I didn't wake you so we could sit by a cozy fire!"

Nara ignored Sam's shouts, and her next strike lit the torch. Jumping up with the torch and flinging water from her face from her recent bath courtesy of Sam, Nara franticly shouted, "Give me your sword!"

Sam was too occupied to argue. She complied by using a mana thread to deposit her arcane sword in front of the frantic woman. Nara snatched the sword out of the air and sprinted to one of the giant mushroom stalks a few meters away. She sliced a long vertical gash in the mushroom, which spit open with a pop, exposing its gooey orange insides. Nara rammed the burning torch into the hole and sprinted back to Sam, tackling her, screaming, "Shield! Now! It's goi—"

Their world went up in flames. Sam felt like the moment was in slow motion while falling backward from Nara's tackle as a gout of white-hot flame shot straight up the stem of Nara's lit mushroom. The instant the flame reached the mushroom cap, it detonated into a fiery…mushroom cloud. *"This is going to hurt, isn't it?"* Sam thought right before she slammed into the ground from the force of the detonation.

Sam barely managed to close the magic shield bubble she conjured when a chain reaction started, and every mushroom in the entire forest went up in fiery explosions, devastation spreading from their position at the epicenter. White hot waves washed over them for what felt like an eternity as Sam struggled to keep her protective barrier in place. She could see steam coming from Nara's hair as the heat intensified to an almost unbearable degree. Each explosion threw flaming debris in every direction. Since they were surrounded by the exploding mushrooms, the fiery chunks buffeted the shield from all sides, forcing Sam to expend additional mana to tether them to the ground with spikes attached to her threads.

The fiery cloud of death and thunder lasted for an eternity of seconds before subsiding. At least a thousand kill notifications were scrolling across a corner of Sam's vision where she minimized the annoying distraction once she figured out how. She looked up into Nara's blue eyes and smiled.

Nara smiled back as her blue lips cracked and bled from the intense heat, "Hi—"

Sam threw Nara off and to the side right when a giant ball of flaming scales broke through the shield bubble. Sam tried to get another barrier up but needed to be faster. The Brood Mother, flying in like a blazing rocket of fangs and rage, clamped her jaws around Sam's torso, sinking the long fangs deep into her body and snatched her away.

Nara watched in stunned horror as the smoldering creature flew off through the smoke and flames with Sam in her mouth.

"Let me out. I can catch them!" Naris screamed into Nara's mind. Without hesitating, Nara switched.

Naris bolted toward the Brood Mother, barely able to see her mana signature through the thick smoke in the air. He leaped over shattered mushroom stalks and ran through piles of flaming bodies, never once taking his eyes off his target.

The Brood Mother aimed for one of the tunnels higher on the cave wall, but one of her wings gave out from severe fire damage moments before she reached it, throwing her off course. The monster slammed into the cave wall with Sam first.

Naris could see Sam struggling a little as he chased after the retreating monster, but she went limp when the Brood Mother slammed into the rock wall. Her body hung from each side of the creature's mouth. Her limbs were broken and twisted at the wrong angles.

The impact knocked the Brood Mother to the ground, and she released Sam when she landed hard on the cave floor.

Almost in range of the giant whitling, Naris yelled, "Bow!" And activated the switch, letting Nara take control.

Nara appeared, the bow hitting her hand instantly. Three arcane arrows were already on the string as she drew back and released in one fluid motion. All three arrows hit their mark, and the monster screeched in rage at the attack. She was within ten meters now and had the monster’s full attention. A predatory grin spread across Nara’s face, and she dismissed the bow.

Naris closed the gap separating him from the raging beast even as it turned toward him with a deafening screech. Sam's daggers appeared in his hands, and he deftly dodged past the snapping maw of the beast, raking two shallow gashes in its neck before leaping up and kicking off its back, propelling himself to the cavern's wall. He didn't slow down and ran straight up the wall using all the agility he had. Over ten meters up the wall, Naris kicked off into a backflip.

Nara started launching arcane arrows into the Brood Mother's back as she sailed above the now frantic creature. It used its one good wing to help it leap up to snatch her out of the air.

Naris kicked off the beast's snout just before its jaws snapped shut on thin air. He lacerated the good wing as they sailed past each other. Hitting the ground, Naris rolled to the side, getting clear of the mother monster's landing zone. He jumped to his feet.

Nara managed to get two more arrows into the Brood Mother’s side before it hit the ground. The beast roared and lunged for her.

Naris dodged under the lunge and sliced into the enraged beast's stomach as it passed, landing a few meters away.

Two magic bolts shattered scales from the Brood Mother's back as Nara ran toward the monster, firing her spell as rapidly as possible. She hit the creature with five more before they engaged in melee again.

Naris ducked under a clawed strike to cut through the soft scales under the monster's leg, taking a tail swipe for his trouble. He was tossed away like a rag doll, striking the ground hard before rolling to his feet.

Nara closed the gap again, firing magic bolts at the charging Brood Mother, shattering scales and blasting off chunks of seared flesh. The Brood

Mother swiped at Nara with its giant claws; she didn't even attempt to dodge. She smiled briefly as the claws sliced right through her incorporeal form. Naris was there with his blades when the claws came out the other side.

Their dance of death went on like this as they slowly whittled down the beast's defenses. Both Nara and Naris realized something, well, several things. They realized they were quite lethal when fighting together, but even more surprisingly, they were enjoying the goink out of it. They also discovered when they switched control, they became incorporeal for a fraction of a second, and although that didn't seem like a lot of time, it was more than enough to use the switch as a dodge due to the speed high-level beasts could attack with. And finally, they both liked and wanted to protect Sam, primarily because she was the least judgmental person they had ever met. At no point had either of them felt her judging them for what they were. Sure, she was pissed when Naris tried to kill her, but even then, she had given him another chance, one that he intended not to goink up. Sam was also fun to hang out with and talk to. She was always smiling, looked whoever was speaking to her in the eyes, and stayed actively engaged with the conversation most of the time. However, they did have a sneaking suspicion that Sam could do multiple things at once in that brain of hers, and simple discussions weren't high up on the 'difficult to focus on' list.

***

Nara and Naris were starting to slow down. They had been at this for minutes, but the blasted Brood Mother wasn't going down for some reason. They had each tried draining her, too, but she was too fast for their siphon skill to do any significant damage.

"What level is this thing?" Naris asked as he tried to put some distance between them and the giant lizard. He switched with Nara.

"I don't know, but it has to be high," Nara responded with a hint of fatigue. She fired two magic bolts at the beast, but her aim was slightly off, and magic bolts merely deflected off the scales of the lizard's hind quarters.

They were trying to keep their distance from the Brood Mother. The battle had been going on for too long, and Naris was fatigued. He would only be able to make the switch a couple more times before having to rest, so once they had some distance, Nara took control and tried to kite the monster with seemingly bottomless health and stamina reserves. They hoped Sam would join the fight soon, but they hadn't seen her nor had time to look at their party menu to check her status.

The giant lizard suddenly glowed with a skill activation and sped forward far faster than previously, catching Nara off guard. Still, she managed to activate the switch with Naris. Right then, the beast stabbed out with its razor-sharp claws, each as long as a spearhead stabbing forward.

Naris looked down in surprise at the four claws embedded in his chest. The damn monster figured out their trick and, instead of swiping at them, stabbed into their incorporeal chest and stopped. Looking back to the beast, he was just in time to see its jaws snapping forward. Then, something hit the creature from behind, causing it to screech in pain and whip around, flinging Naris from its claws.

Nara was flung through the air, leaving a trail of blood behind her from the gaping wounds in her torso as the Brood Mother struggled with something in its tail. Nara, struggling to stay conscious, could only watch as the creature struggled, kicking up ash around it. Then the Tenarian slammed into…a soft fluffy mass of… *"Mana threads!"* Nara's head whipped around in time to see Sam catch her in her arms.

Sam smiled down at Nara as she lowered her to the ash-covered ground. She said, "You two did an amazing job. Thanks for giving me time to recover." She looked to the struggling Brood Mother she had staked to the ground with several harpoons. Looking back to Nara, she handed her a health potion and said, "Now it's my turn."

***

Ten minutes previously:

Sam felt the venom being injected into her body the instant the jaws clamped down and the dozens of sharp teeth sank deep into her stomach and chest.

You have been injected with necrotic venom -5hp/sec for 176 seconds. You are weakened. All actions requiring stamina will be significantly more difficult until the venom has been purged.

Fighting through the pain and trying to pry open the jaws of the creature trying to kill her, all Sam could think was, *"What is up with this planet and toxins?"*

Sam was too low on mana to do anything but heal herself, so she relied on her significant strength to try and get out of this situation. Still, the Brood Mother kept shaking her head while flying erratically due to a damaged wing. The jerky motions made it nearly impossible for Sam to grip the monster's jaw firmly.

Then the damn thing hit the cave wall, and Sam felt and heard her back break. She managed to stay conscious even after the beast released her when it hit the ground, although just barely.

When no follow-up attack came, Sam didn't question it and focused all her energy on healing herself, diving deep into meditation, and drinking a couple of health and mana potions using her mana threads to speed things up. She could now hear Nara fighting the creature and could only hope her companion could hold out long enough for her to heal. Trusting Nara to handle herself, Sam closed her eyes and meditated, tuning out everything but her core cycles; a few things were starting to click into place in her mind that she needed to think about.

***

Coming out of her meditation, Sam witnessed the last few minutes of Nara and Naris fighting the Brood Mother together and was impressed. *"Wait, are they fighting it together or separately? I mean, they're together but separate..."* Pushing away her ridiculous thought, Sam hurried with her final preparations as much as possible because Nara was getting tired. Also, she knew Naris couldn't have much energy left either.

Preparations complete, Sam ran to join the fight. She was at the wrong angle when the beast stabbed its claws into her friend, so she did the only thing she could from her position and staked a harpoon through its tail to pin it to the ground, hoping to get its attention.

"That worked better than I thought it would," Sam thought as she watched Nara get flung from the creature's claws. Slamming two more harpoons into the ground to tether the beast in place, Sam took off after Nara, catching her at the last moment.

***

Present time:

"Now to see if this works." Sam thought as she mentally prepared to engage the thrashing beast. When she was meditating, Sam had put a few things together; from overheard conversations to seemingly innocuous statements and her own internal musings, she was getting a better handle on how magic worked in this world or maybe even the whole verse.

Sam dashed forward, strafing to her right, trying to flank the Brood Mother. She couldn't help but think, *"This is probably the dumbest thing I've done yet, but hey, if it works..."* She caught herself from getting distracted, *"Okay, stay focused. It can't hurt me if it's filtered, and what better way to filter it than through a skill. Just like Naris said, his skill did."* With that thought, Sam reached into her magic to form an arcane bolt, but she didn't let the spell have contact with the vibrant violet arcane magic flowing through her channels. With an effort of will, she channeled and forced the spell to link to the Void trickling out from her core. She carefully isolated the Void energy as the spell form latched onto it, and it entered her mana channels. She did this by stopping a single pulse of her arcane mana from traveling down the specific channel she would push the Void through. Then, with a bit of guidance from her manipulation skill, the spell did the rest. All she had to do was mentally direct the Void with her manipulation skill to send the black mana to the channel she had purged, which was sucked right in by her spell.

The blacked-out part of her mana bar receded slightly when Sam's spell pulled on the Void in her soul, showing some had been used. She also noticed the black area in her health bar increased, reducing her available vital energy. She knew she needed to dig into that further, but right now, she didn't care because a crackling Void Bolt was floating above her palm. The notification came an instant later.

'Bing' Congratulations! You have created a new spell, Void Bolt [Level 1]. You tore a hole in your soul, surprisingly having Void energy inside. To make matters even more interesting, you did not die from the Void energy leaking from your soul, which you most certainly should have. Instead, you managed to somehow cobble together enough knowledge about magical powers to grasp the slightest fraction of an idea about how to control your newly discovered energy. And it worked! You have formed an energized bolt of Void using an unknown source in your soul. You have permanently torn the pathway into your core, granting you the spell Void Bolt. You may now cast the spell Void Bolt at an unknown mana cost. Continued use of the spell may increase its efficiency and power, or conversely, it may kill you. Experience has been awarded for creating a spell you should not have been able to by unconventional means. Good job! You may have broken your path to becoming a true sorceress. Only time will tell!

"Yes!" She thought, *"But what the hell is up with that message? Is the system being snarky again? This could kill me? Only time will tell? Aww, screw it!"* and launched her spell into the Brood Mother's side.

The Brood Mother must have sensed the danger in Sam's attack because it broke free of its restraints and tried to evade the Void attack. It wasn't fast enough, and the small bolt of Void punched right through the protective scales with a popping sound, blasting a fist-sized hole in its side. The bolt must have caused severe damage because the monster roared in rage and attacked. It opened its mouth, and a stream of green venom sprayed from its fangs.

Sam jumped back, trying to get clear of the spray, but some still landed on her arm. It burned like acid but thankfully didn't poison her. She retaliated by firing another Void Bolt at the creature, which it managed to dodge this time. So, Sam decided to stop playing around with her new toy and went all out with her tried and true overkill method. She dashed forward, turning herself into a meatgrinder of death.

Sam touched her arcane sword where it lay among the ashes with a mana thread as she ran, depositing the weapon into her inventory and then immediately retrieving it into her waiting right hand. She was already holding her shield in her left hand and using all her free threads to launch magical projectiles at the Brood Mother, which was charging toward her with a bestial roar.

The two met head-on. The Brood Mother snapped down with her powerful jaw, intent on crushing Sam in them again, but Sam smacked the creature in its face with her shield so hard she shattered teeth, and the two of them were knocked back from the impact; Sam was impacted more than the giant beast simply due to being the less bulky of the two.

***

Nara was shocked at how powerful Sam was suddenly. *"How is she so strong all of a sudden?"* She thought.

Nara knew Sam was strong, especially after seeing what happened when the Pathfinder headbutted the poor young paladin, but she hadn't seen that strength level again until now. Looking closer at Sam's mana flow, Nara figured out what had changed. *"She's infusing her body with mana...when did she learn to do that?"*

***

Sensing Nara's gaze on her as she fought the monster and hearing the Tenarian's thoughts through their chat function, Sam smiled, *"Someone forgot to mute their mic."* Sam knew exactly why she was so much more powerful suddenly.

During her recent meditation, while healing, Sam focused on how she could see Nara and Naris infusing their bodies with magical energy to make themselves stronger and more resilient. Sam was sure she had done it once herself when she nearly killed the little boy paladin, but she hadn't been able to recreate the skill until today. Because it wasn't a skill. She had been doing it all wrong. When she thought back to how Nara's legs looked in her mana sight during their run to Helms Peak and her fight with Naris, how his mana flowed back and forth through his body as he moved and attacked, she initially assumed they were using a skill. However, she didn't remember seeing that skill or ability displayed on Nara's status page in their party menu. That's when Sam had a breakthrough; her bread and butter was mana infusion, which she did for virtually everything magic-related. She was constantly infusing mana. Every single one of her skills and abilities required her to infuse some mana into them for them to activate. She had taken it all for granted and assumed she needed an ability or skill to infuse magic energy into her body. But she had it backward; she was the catalyst, the battery that fueled her magical abilities. This was how it had always been, but it had taken her until now to grasp the concept. With magical energy constantly flowing through her channels, it had been a simple task for Sam to push the energy into her muscles and skin. The only difficulty she had encountered was making sure the mana stayed malleable. She had to break off and quickly regrow a finger when she accidentally crystallized it by infusing too much mana too fast into the digit. But she quickly got the hang of it and could now use mana to bolster the strength and density of her muscles. The only drawback was that it created an exponentially higher stamina cost directly related to the amount of mana she used. She wasn't good enough at controlling her mana to move it around her body. Naris and Nara could do this, which, thus, limited the strain on their stamina. So, until she figured that out, Sam just infused everything and dealt with the strain.

"I bet I am a nightmare to fight," Sam thought as she stood her ground, matching blows with the giant lizard bat. Sam attacked six times for every strike her opponent made, using her mana threads to bombard the creature from its flanks with every attack in her arsenal. Bladed disks, mana spikes, harpoons, and energy bolts struck the beast simultaneously, causing it to grow increasingly aggressive. Sam knew the attacks weren't doing much damage, mostly because her sword only left shallow cuts when she got in the occasional blow. *"What is this thing's level, ninety-nine?"* She thought when she missed seeing a tail swipe and was thrown into the cave wall several meters above the cavern floor.

Sam channeled her inner Moonblight and contorted her body mid-flight to hit the cave wall feet first. Before she could fall off the wall, she pushed as much mana as she thought safe into her legs and kicked off; a spiderweb of cracks appeared on the wall an instant before she launched herself like a missile straight at the Brood Mother, leaving a shallow crater in the wall behind her.

Sam's arcane sword was depleted of mana, the last strike draining it fully, turning it into a blank crystal vessel more than an actual weapon. This is what Sam had been waiting for. She infused the blade with Void as she flew toward her prey. The monster tried to run when it sensed something different, but Sam was upon it instantly, slicing down with all she had. Her sword cut through the creature's hind quarter like butter, severing its tail and back leg.

Sam's momentum carried her over and past her target, and she lost her grip on her sword when she hit the ground at an awkward angle and tripped, rolling end over end for another twenty meters or so. Losing her sword was the only thing that saved her because it exploded mere moments after she dropped it, sending shrapnel in all directions.

"Damn, that hurt," Sam groaned as she got to her feet, healing a hole in her leg left by a piece of her shattered sword. "That was worse than getting hit by a bus, I bet."

"I still don't know what a bus is, but that was incredible!" Nara said, running up. "Naris wants to know how you're using the Void and says to save some for him." Sam laughed at that statement as Nara got to her and gave her a hug. Looking into Sam's eyes, Nara said sincerely, "Thanks for not dying."

"I do my best not to most days," Sam chuckled. Then, pointing at the Brood Mother through the smoke and ash still in the air, she said more seriously, "I don't know what that thing's level is, but it is tough. The only attack that even puts a dent in its—what is it doing?"

"I have no idea..." Nara said, her voice trailing off as she stared at the monster.

The Brood Mother ignored them and hurriedly ran around on her three good legs, nuzzling and digging through the nearby ash piles. She was eating something in the ash, but Sam had no idea what it could be.

Nara suddenly shouted, "Shit! She's eating the cores!" When Sam looked at her dumbly, Nara summoned her bow and took aim, saying, "She is probably close to evolving! That's how monsters evolve, Sam! We have to stop her! We won't stand a chance against an evolved beast! I doubt we will even be able to outrun her!" Nara released her arrow toward the Brood Mother.

Sam didn't need to be told twice and was already dashing toward the scavenging creature before Nara finished speaking. She wasn't going to make the same mistake she had when she let the alpha wolf turn into the Lupine Bloodmorph to satisfy her curiosity.

Nara's arrow struck the Brood Mother in one of her broken wings, but the creature only flinched and kept eating the cores of her children. Sam was in range and attacked just as a second arrow struck the monster in the side of its head. Sam tried to get a Void Bolt into the monster's ear, but it heard the loud crackling of the attack and dodged away, slashing out with a clawed foot at Sam.

Sam leaped over the swipe and stabbed a spear construct into its back. She tried to push the spear deeper with a mana blast, but a flap from the creature's wing knocked her off its back. The monster half flapped, half hobbled to another ash pile, snatching the whole pile into her mouth, throwing her head back, and swallowing. Sam formed a spiked glove on her hand as she closed on the creature again. This time, she would punch the spikes through the tough scales and then send the spikes deeper with a mana blast. Or at least that was her plan.

Sam was only a meter away, swinging her spiked fist when a sphere of green and white energy expanded outward from the Brood Mother so fast it knocked Sam back twenty meters. Landing on her feet, Sam was prepared to attack again when Nara's voice came through their party chat.

“Sam, we have to run! That's System protection for the creature. While it evolves, you cannot penetrate it! It will take her a few minutes to evolve, so we have to move now!” Nara’s voice was fearful.

"I thought you said we couldn't outrun it," Sam responded, running back toward Nara, who was already running toward her, pointing at a small tunnel closest to them.

“We can get in there and collapse the tunnel entrance. We might have a chance if we don’t bring the whole mountain down on us!”

"How long will it take her to evolve exactly?" Sam asked, slowing down to a stop and looking back to the green and white shield surrounding the evolving boss monster.

Nara reached Sam and grabbed her arm, "I don't know for sure, maybe five more minutes, ten at the most. Please tell me you aren't considering fighting an evolved beast, Sam. She will be exponentially stronger when she emerges!"

Sam turned and grabbed Nara's thin shoulders so they were facing each other. Looking into Nara's deep blue eyes, she said, "This is because of me, Nara. You should run. I'll collapse the tunnel behind you." Nara opened her mouth to protest, but Sam stopped her, explaining, "I think the System is curating dangerous situations for me as an experiment." Nara just looked at Sam incredulously, so Sam asked, "Do you know of anyone who has encountered dozens of powerful foes, an evolved being, an ambush by high-level bandits, and fought a blight all within about two weeks?" Nara shook her head silently. Sam sighed in resignation, "This is my fault, Nara, all of our recent troubles. Danger and death just follow me around. I can't say for sure it's the System doing it. Hell, it could just be a hidden perk of my class, but what I do know is no matter where I go, I always seem to be fighting for my life, and you don't deserve that."

Nara looked at her and slowly nodded her understanding. Sam sighed again with a mixture of sadness and relief. She turned back toward the evolving creature with resolve, saying, "Thank you for being my friend, Nara; tell Naris bye for me."

Nara stepped up beside Sam. When Sam looked at her confused, Nara snapped with heat in her voice, "Fuck you, Sam! Do you really think you can get rid of us just like that? We're staying with you!" She crossed her arms in defiance and stomped a foot, then added a little less defiantly, "I really hope you have a plan, though, because we are definitely going to die otherwise." Her eyes went vacant for a moment, then nodding to herself, she finished with, "Naris agrees; we are going to die."

Sam wasn't surprised so much as taken aback a little, but she was also proud at the same time. Not because Nara was staying; that was an exceedingly stupid decision. Anyone in their right mind should be fleeing for their life. No, Sam was proud for a different reason. She told Nara as much, "Aww, you used 'fuck' in the right context. I am so proud of you that I could pinch your cute grey cheeks." Then she said happily. "Of course, I have a plan. I'm going to overclock my core again." She grinned, "It is totally going to suck!"

CHAPTER 21 — "I'm gonna get that dragon!"

Calis was tired. He was nearing the end of his ten-hour shift in the cremation center of Helms Peak. He wasn't complaining; he was getting paid to practice his class spells. Few jobs offered great pay, zero danger, and allowed you to level your skills and class, so Calis was happy to do the work. It was just that today had been particularly busy, with a group of three high-level bandits and two former guild members coming in toward the end of his shift. He always hated it when anyone over Level 40 came in. At his low level of twenty-two, it took him a long time to thoroughly incinerate the bodies of persons double his level. He had just finished his rest period following the final bandit's incineration, a level fifty-two mage. That one had taken him nearly forty minutes.

He moved on to the two guild members who had been kicked out of the guild posthumously. Otherwise, Calis knew, they would have been interred in the guild crypts instead of being cremated.

"Let's see what level you were then, shall we," Calis said as he checked the tag on the female's corpse. "Level thirty-two, oh, that's much better. And the other one is… Level thirty-nine. Slightly more difficult, but still, he could manage before his shift ended. He slid the lower-leveled woman's corpse into the specially built oven designed so he could direct his flame inside without fear of any heat escaping, thus making the operation as efficient as possible. "I hope your soul finds peace in the next life," he said and went to work.

***

"By order of Duke Oberon, cease your actions immediately!" A booming voice filled the room.

The order made Calis jump. He had been daydreaming while he worked, so the harsh words coming from right behind him caused him quite a start. Nevertheless, he kept his composure and stopped channeling his flame spell, turning to the intruder curiously. This wasn't the first time a cremation he was conducting was halted, so Calis wasn't particularly surprised at the order. What surprised him was that the order came from a Church of the Light priest. *"When did they get the authority to interfere with city business?"* Calis eyed the two representatives of the church with suspicion. One was the priest who had told him to stop. He was wearing his trade's white and gold robes and holding a piece of parchment. Beside the priest was a female wearing the sleek white garb of a…what did they call her class? Technomancer, yes, that was it.

The priest broke the silence, handing Calis the piece of parchment, saying, "If you have any objections, you can take it up with the duke, but we will be taking the two bodies regardless." He looked to a city guard who had stepped into the room. "Captain, please remove this mage from the room."

Calis wasn't a fool and didn't give two shits about the dead guild members. Plus, their paper carried the official seal of the duke. He quickly held up his hands as he moved to the door, saying, "Hey, hey, I'm leaving. The girl is mostly ash now; I doubt you'll get anything from her."

The priest scoffed, speaking over his shoulder to Calis as he exited the room, "You greatly underestimate the power of the light, my child. If I were you, I would visit one of our temples to cleanse yourself of ignorance."

"More like being brainwashed into ignorance," Calis thought as he exited the room, closing the door behind him. He knew better than to voice that statement. He had tried to identify the two Children of the Light; all he had received were question marks.

***

"Shall we begin, father?" Cara asked the high priest after depositing Arron and Alina's corpses inside a shallow pool of blood under a statue of their patron goddess and returning to his side by a small waist-high pedestal with a bowl resting atop it off to one side of the white-walled resurrection chamber.

"Of course, child," the high priest said kindly. "Would you like to wake one of them? I understand you haven't done it before, but there is nothing to fear. Our patrons want only devotion from us, and in turn, they grant us the power over life and death."

As a Technomancer, Cara's interest in the church was strictly scientific. Joining them allowed her access to magic beyond what she could ever hope to access on her own since her ship crashed all those cycles ago. The faith and technology sides of the church maintained mutual respect but were, at the end of the day, two separate entities. Although many young technomancers were quite devout in their faith in the god and goddess of the light even though it was not a requirement. Cara was one of the few who did not believe in the omnipotence of the two gods and preferred to have confidence in the sciences instead, as her training had taught her. The high priest knew this; it was a frequent conversation topic between the two of them. So, he wasn't surprised when she respectfully declined his offer. "I will have to decline, Father; I am devoted to learning the magic of the System, not to the cause of the light."

With a disappointed sigh, the robed priest said, "I pray that one day you will see the truth of the light child." Then, reaching out over the bowl, he used a ceremonial blade to cut one of his wrists, allowing his lifeblood to drain into the bowl until it was nearly full.

When enough blood had entered the bowl, Cara cast a simple heal on the high priest. The enchantment on the dagger he had used prevented self-healing for over an hour, making it imperative this be a two-person operation.

Ignoring the blood staining the pure white sleeves of his robes, the high priest plunged his arms into the blood bowl and began mumbling an incantation. Not being one of the faithful, Cara was blocked from understanding a single word of the magic. She could not even make out a syllable. She didn't care, though. Her interest was fixed on the blood-filled pool and, more importantly, the two bodies lying within.

***

"You're going to what?! After what happened last time? Have you lost your mind?" Nara couldn't believe what Sam had just said. In her mind, they were in this situation mainly because Sam had to overclock her cores to fight Naris, and now, she wanted to do it again less than two days later!

"Oh, that's not the only thing," Sam said with a slightly manic grin. She handed Nara the summoning token for The Defeated. "Hey, see if you can use this."

Nara stared blankly at the token for a second, then said, "I don't know how. I've never heard of a summoning token used within the past hundred cycles or more. In fact, that's why the little boy paladin was willing to bet his spatial suite against this token. They are one of the rarest items on the planet."

Sam took the token back and, turning it over in her hand, mumbled, "I doubt it's as easy as saying summon The Defeated—"

At those words, the token shot out of her hand to hover about three meters in front of them. Red energy started coalescing around it as the token spun so fast it became a blur.

"Oops," Sam said, but she was still grinning.

Nara just shook her head. She was getting used to Sam's borderline insanity.

"Okay, so here's the plan," Sam started but stopped when The Defeated appeared with a bloody thump. Moments later, the massive splatter of blood turned into the creature. Sam was still amazed at how giant the beast was up close. The dark red coat of the enormous wolf-like animal glistened in the light of the many burning fires. It still looked intimidating, even devoid of its blood armor. *"I can't believe I shoved my arm down that thing's throat. This world has made me freaking mental!"* She identified the summoned creature.

'Bing' [Elite] Lupine Bloodmorph Exile; [Level 1]; Friendly; Affinity: Blood, Void

Looking at Sam, the Bloodmorph spoke into her mind, "Thank you for this chance to serve, my mistress. I swear my loyalty and life to you for as long as you live."

Sam sent her a party invite and was overjoyed when The Defeated accepted. Adding her to their party chat, Sam asked the summon, "Can you level up by eating cores?"

“Yes,” the soft feminine voice echoed in their minds.

"Good. Then this is the plan," Sam pointed at Nara while speaking to The Defeated, "She will ride you to keep the attention of that beast when it…uh…hatches, evolves —whatever, when the shield around it goes down," she gestured to the massive green and white orb protecting the Brood Mother and continued, "The two of you are to keep it away from me while I do some literal soul searching. But in the meantime, you will eat as many cores as possible." She pointed out the many still smoldering bodies and ash piles illuminated by the still-burning mushrooms across the cavern floor. "There are nearly a thousand cores in this cave. You have five minutes. Go!"

"I require blood," the lupine said, ducking its head like it was about to be scolded for not following Sam's instructions immediately.

"I figured as much," Sam said and looked at Nara, asking, "Do you need mana? And are you and Naris okay with the plan? I have to check on something in my core."

“Yes, and yes,” Nara answered, “distract the evolved beast while you do Pathfinder things. Got it.”

Sam pulled out a large mana and health potion and then chugged the health potion. At the same time, she crafted a giant hollow needle out of her magic and stabbed it into her heart, saying, "Here you go, girl." The Defeated wasted no time and took off toward the nearest pile of corpses, with Sam's blood trailing after her as she ran.

Sam then stabbed a mana thread into Nara's arm like an IV, but before she started sending her friend Mana, Sam asked a couple of questions directed at Naris, "Naris, have you ever been inside Nara's soul? And if you have, what is in there?"

"He says no and doesn't think it is possible for anyone but the soul's owner to look inside," Nara answered for him, looking questioningly at Sam.

Not wanting to waste any more time, Sam only said, "I'll explain if we survive."

"You mean when we survi—" Nara's statement was cut off. Her back arched, and her eyes rolled back in her head as Sam drank the mana potion and started pumping as much energy into her as she could.

Sam chuckled at Nara, *“That ‘O’ face never gets old.”* Then her expression hardened. *“This has to work. I know what I saw was real.”* She settled herself cross-legged on the ash-covered floor of the cave and closed her eyes, entering meditation. A stream of blood flowed from her heart to a summoned beast on her left, and mana flowed into her friend to her right. She began the process of overclocking her cores, but this time in a more controlled manner. She reached into her mind core and slowly drew some of her reason from it, allowing her rage an upper hand. This was accomplished by focusing on the System's injustice, always putting her and now her friends in constant danger from beings much more powerful than them. It wasn't right; she hadn't asked to be summoned to this world, and she didn't want to fight to survive daily! All she wanted to do was explore and learn exciting new things, but instead, just a walk through the woods was a life-threatening battle! Hell, even her first friend in this world nearly killed her a couple of days ago! And to top it all off— *"There!"* Her rage had done its job. Sam felt the familiar slowing of time as her cores began cycling at an impossible speed. A perk she had belatedly noticed from her fight with Naris when she played their battle over in her mind the following day. Overclock achieved; Sam's mental avatar floated down to her soul core, *"Now to awaken my inner dragon."*

***

Alina screamed when her soul returned to its body. *"The arrow, it's going to explode!"* Her thoughts were frantic. She grabbed for the arrow, but her hands found no purchase, no arrow. *"Where is it? Where's the arrow?"*

"Peace, child," a soothing voice came from above her.

Looking up toward the voice, Alina saw an elderly priest standing in front of her, his arm outstretched toward her. The hems on the sleeves of his white robe were stained red with blood. Accepting the man's hand, she allowed herself to be lifted to her feet. The priest's gentle smile quickly put her chaotic thoughts to rest.

Calm now, Alina took a moment to process what was happening and searched the white room she found herself in. The room was made from the purest white stone, with ornate columns stretching to a high ceiling. Looking behind her, she saw a massive five-meter-tall statue of a woman with a golden halo hovering above her head. The figure held a golden scepter in one hand with the other hand outstretched palm up. Blood flowed from the outstretched hand, filling the shallow pool Alina currently stood in.

"Come. Let us get you cleaned up." The priest said as he led her up a short flight of stairs from the pool. Each bloody footprint Alina left on the steps was instantly absorbed into the stone, leaving it pure white again.

The priest cast a spell on her without permission, and all the blood covering her naked body fell to the stone floor, only to disappear instantly. Alina knew where she was now but was confused as to why. Working up the courage to speak as the priest led her toward the room's exit, she asked, "Why did you bring me back? I am not a member of the church."

When the priest only glanced back at her, she stammered, "I—I mean, thank you! I meant no disrespect!"

The priest only chuckled, saying, "In due time, Alina. All will be revealed in due time." He opened the large double door, saying, "But first, I thought you might wish to be reunited with your father."

Tears welled up in Alina's eyes when she spied her father's figure sitting on a bench in the small waiting area the priest had led her into. He was wrapped in a grey blanket, staring blankly at the floor in front of him. When she walked in, he glanced up and smiled. "Hey there, girl. It looks like we're getting a second chance at life."

***

Arron and Alina were fully clothed and seated at a large table in a white room. Even though the church had tried to disguise the room with decorations like green plants in the corner and small pieces of art on the walls, the room was obviously an interrogation room. This was proven a few minutes later when two people, the priest who had resurrected them and a woman they hadn't met, walked in and sat across from them. When she sat, the woman waved her hand over the table, and a series of translucent displays appeared before her. She tapped a series of virtual runes, and the room turned the familiar yellow of truth detection with an audible click coming from the door when it locked. Arron and Alina stiffened, looking at each other. This wasn't looking good for them.

“Please relax,” the priest said soothingly, “you have nothing to fear from the church. We only need to know a few details about the circumstances leading up to your recent demise.”

***

Sam gripped the hole in her soul core, trying to pull it open as much as possible. The tornado of Void energy coming out of it due to her overclocking made the task much more difficult than she had planned. Still, Sam knew she needed the time dilatation effects to maximize her time before the Brood Mother evolved. *“This should be wide enough,”* she thought as she held the outer edge of her soul open. Not wasting any more time, she plunged into the dark whirlwind of Void energy blasting out of her soul, and with a surprised yelp, she wasn't buffeted back but forcibly sucked inside!

Sam was aware this time as her mind was pulled into her soul. It was like she was flying through an eternal tunnel of violet and black at warp speed. The exhilaration of flying through space at such a speed was tempered by the uneasy feeling that she was being watched by not one but two separate presences. It was a deeply unsettling feeling, and she was glad when the tunnel abruptly ended and she found herself back in her old room in the orphanage.

A quick check showed that the purple rune she had used to return before was still under her bed, and the three figurines were still where she had left them on the desk. Sam locked her eyes on the dragonkin figurine and stalked toward her desk. All three figures stepped down from their pedestals and walked to the edge of the desk, again opening their chest cavities to expose their cores. However, Sam only focused on the dragonkin and reached to grasp the small marble-sized core in its chest. Her fingers touched the black core, and Sam's smile matched the dragon's.

'Bing' You do not meet the minimum requirements to use this avatar. Assimilation with the Draconic Voidling will result in soul destruction.

"What!?!" Sam yelled to the room. "This is bullshit! I need this dragon!" Only silence met her exclamation. Looking at the figure, she asked, "How can I make myself compatible with you?" There was no response.

Knowing she was on a time limit, Sam tried the snake woman.

'Bing' You do not meet the minimum requirement to use this avatar. Assimilation with the Duplicitous Lamia will result in soul destruction.

"Fucking tease!" Sam thought, suddenly worried. Her entire plan hinged on this working. She was only doing this because she had seen a couple of notifications when she and Naris were taking a break. She reread the notifications, thankful that now her interface worked in her soul for some reason.

'Bing' Congratulations! By poisoning your body with volatile magics, you have forced your mind to retreat into your soul, where you have discovered dormant parts of yourself. You may now access this fragment of your soul more easily to view your potential avatars.

'Bing' Congratulations! You have unlocked a hidden ability, Soul Dive! By tearing a hole in your soul and retreating into it due to massive magical poisoning, you have forcibly unlocked a skill you should not have and fragmented your soul. Soul Dive allows you to visit and make alterations to your soulscape and should not be used by anyone below the god tier, but here you are. Using this ability at your current level has

splintered your soul. Unable to calculate consequences. Soul Dive has been blocked from your abilities by the System.

Since reading those notifications and not finding Soul Dive in her list of abilities, Sam had been thinking about a way to get back into her soul for those avatars. She figured she was already pretty much screwed, what with having a gaping hole in her core and a fractured soul, so why not at least take an avatar for a test drive. It wasn't like the System was giving her a choice in the matter either; Sam felt like an ant under a magnifying glass with progressively stronger opponents that could easily kill her with a single attack. She knew it wasn't a question of if, but when the System got tired of her and sent something, she would never be able to retreat from or survive. That's why the Brood Mother evolving didn't even surprise her that much. Sam just figured the System saw her as a failed experiment and was cleaning up its mess. Which is precisely why she was doing what the System warned her against doing. She was digging around in her fractured soul, trying to wake up her inner dragon, which was unfortunately not going as well as she had hoped.

Sam grabbed the techno girl's core in desperation.

'Bing' You do not meet the minimum requirement to use this avatar. Assimilation with the Technogog Arcana will result in soul damage.

"Only soul damage for this one, huh, not destruction. Okay, I can work with that, but how do I assimilate?" Sam started formulating another plan, *"This is so stupid, Sam. So very, very stupid. But I'm gonna get that dragon!"*

***

Nara collapsed to the ground. Sam's mana infusion sped exponentially the second she overclocked her core, increasing to the point that it was almost more than Nara could take. Almost.

"Let us assist The Defeated," Naris said to Nara.

Nara looked to where the Blood Morph was hungrily devouring monster cores as fast as she could. She noted the summon was also tearing open bodies that weren't charred to a crisp and adding their blood to what she had received from Sam. Seeing this, Nara reached over and pulled the needle from Sam's heart, stopping the bloodstream. She poured a health potion over the wound to speed up Sam's natural recovery. As she finished, she told Naris, "Okay, time to do our part then. Let's go."

***

The Defeated could not believe her fortune. To be summoned to serve the powerful one that defeated her was a great honor. And the first thing her new master did was give her enough blood to make her beautiful armor again and provide her with a feast of cores! *"I must not disappoint the summoner. Lest she banish me to the void forever."* She wasn't worried about the creature evolving less than two hundred meters away. *"All I have to do is run away. The summoner will defeat the beast."* With those simple thoughts, she continued scouring the cavern for cores and blood. She knew running away would be difficult and needed all the power she could gather to make the summoner proud.

The small grey creature, which the summoner said would ride her, approached The Defeated and dumped a pile of corpses before her. The Defeated could feel their blood waiting to be absorbed into her strength and armor. She appreciated this gesture and thanked the small creature, "Thank you, friend of the summoner." She sent through the chat function Sam, her summoner, had granted her access to.

"Just call me Nara," came the response.

"Very well. Thank you, Nara." The Defeated said gratefully. Then asked, "Are you ready to run?"

***

It took Nara a moment to realize what the massive beast was asking. Nara looked at the Bloodmorph's back and frowned, realizing she was asking if Nara was ready to ride her; there was nothing but tentacles and spikes of hardened blood all down the creature's back armor. She asked, "How am I supposed to ride you if I can't even touch you without being stabbed?"

The blood spikes and back armor just behind the creature's shoulders liquified and reformed into saddle-like armor sized for Nara. Without hesitation, Nara leaped into the saddle and summoned her bow. She had five explosive charges in the Recurve Bow of Destruction and intended to make them count. She felt the blood saddle mold itself around her, holding her lower half in place so she could keep her hands free.

The Defeated kept absorbing blood and eating cores until exactly five minutes had elapsed, and then she stopped. Nara, who had been keeping her eyes on the evolving beast, was surprised to see a message in her interface.

The Defeated [Level 1] Summon of S.A.M. requests permission to level up from level 1 to level 9. As a party member of S.A.M., she has granted you permission to act on her behalf. Allow Level up Y/N?

Nara selected 'Yes' and felt The Defeated's moan rumbled through her legs as the summoned gained power. Remembering she was an elite monster, Nara checked her stat screen in their party interface out of curiosity.

The Defeated [Summon of S.A.M.]
Race: Lupine Bloodmorph; Elite; Unique [Level 9]
Class: Bloodbane [Level 9]
Blessing(s): Void Touched [Epic]

Health: 4503
Stamina: 1441
Mana: 1885

Attributes:
STR – 42
VIT – 253
END – 74
AGL – 67
INT – 23
WIS – 51

Abilities: 2/10
Blood Manipulation
Void Compatibility

Class Skills: 2/7
Blood Recovery [Level 6]
Void Coating [Level 2]

Racial/General Skills: 3/7
Final Push [Level 6]
Identify [Level 1]
Stealth [Level 5]

Class Spells: 3/5
Blood Harvest [Level 4]
Blood Spike [Level 1]
Void Spike [Level 1]

Racial/General Spells:
Howl [Level 5]

Resistance(s):
Void Magic [Level 25]
Blood Magic [Level 50]

"Wow, you are strong for level nine!" Nara said in admiration. "No wonder summon tokens are so rare!"
The Defeated only responded with, "It awakens."
Nara's eyes zeroed in on the evolving Brood Mother. The Defeated was right; the System protection was down, exposing the evolved life form. Fighting back her fear, Nara identified the creature.

Whitling Matriarch [Level ???], Hostile; Affinity(s): Air, Toxin

The Matriarch had mostly stayed the same in appearance. In fact, Nara thought she may have gotten smaller. All her wounds and her wings were fully healed, unfortunately. A dark red skull was floating above the Matriarch in Nara's interface, and she knew they didn't stand a chance. Still, she readied her bow and mentally shouted to the Defeated, "Run!"
Even locked in place on the giant Bloodmorph's back, Nara felt as though she was going to be yanked out of the blood saddle by the sheer speed of The Defeated. Nara managed to right herself and launched an explosive arrow at the Matriarch as it stretched and flexed, testing the limits of its improved body. Nara didn't plan on giving it the time.
Her arrow exploded against the side of the beast's head, barely making it flinch. Nara did see some scales get knocked off, giving her the slight hope she could actually damage the evolved being. The Matriarch roared at the attack and turned on the charging duo. The Defeated diverted her course just in time to dodge a wind blade launched from the Matriarch's wing. The two beasts passed within meters of each other. Nara's mount managed to lacerate one wing and cut several shallow gouges in the Matriarch's side with the void-coated tips of her blood tentacles.
The Matriarch roared again and released a cloud of toxic gas from her mouth, spinning in a circle to coat a wide area. Nara and The Defeated managed to stay just ahead of the cloud as it dissolved everything it touched: ash, corpses, mushroom parts, and even the stones strewn about the cavern floor were dissolved instantly from the attack.
The chase was on.

CHAPTER 22 — "Well, yeah it's me, duh."

Sam stared at the Technogog Arcana figurine and reached out to her core again. The same message denying her access to its core popped up, but Sam ignored it, grabbing the figurine off the table instead. It didn't resist and grinned broadly at Sam, who returned the expression.

Sam understood what was happening. She was in her soulscape, and according to the System messages, she was in control here. Her body wasn't physically here in this room; instead, it was a metaphysical representation of her mind. She was postulating her physical body was just an avatar her soul used to interact with reality and had taken the shape her soul deemed most fitting. *"The System must control the power of my avatar or body to keep my magical power from ripping my soul apart before it ages and becomes stronger through experience. Thus, able to handle a greater strain. If that's the case, the opposite must also be true.* Sam stared at the figure in her hand; she felt its need to meld with her and become whole. *"Man, this is going be crazy dumb, but if it works..."*

Sam mused that all she had to do was fix in her mind how she wanted her soul to change her body with a thought to make it happen. *"I can see how this is extremely dangerous. I could literally 'will' my soul out of existence if I wanted—which I don't."* She added to herself quickly. Sam could instinctively sense the real danger in soul diving wasn't the alteration to the soul but the fact that once she began an alteration, it could not be stopped until completed. If she was slightly off or had a random thought during a change to her soulscape, it could lead to devastating consequences in her reality. *"Like if I think about having a tail but not specifically where it will be on my body, the size, color, properties, veins, arteries, mana channels, and how it will interact with the rest of my body among a bazillion other things then I could wind up with at tail growing out of my brain. Essentially killing myself because of vanity."*

Sam pulled the small figurine to her chest in a tight embrace, pushing her misgivings aside before she lost her nerve. Except the figure never touched her chest, Sam's chest opened up the same as the figure's was, and she mashed their cores together in the most unceremonious display of recklessness she had likely ever made.

It worked.

***

The Defeated dodged a basketball-sized ball of toxic acid an instant after Nara loosed her second exploding arrow at the Matriarch at point-blank range. The damn monster was fast! It was taking every trick The Defeated had to stay out of range of the insanely powerful evolved creature's attacks.

"Three more explosive shots," Nara thought, watching the Matriarch shrug off the arrow exploding in its face like it was nothing more than an annoyance. *"At least it slowed her down a little bit,"* She thought, then tried to find Sam in the chaos of ash and flame kicked up by their running battle. About to focus back on her situation, Nara caught a glimpse of purple light coming from where she thought Sam should be right before bolts of violet lightning created a dome over what she now knew was Sam's location.

The Defeated abruptly angled her run back around toward the dome of energy. The sudden change in direction caused Nara to nearly drop her bow from the whiplash.

As they drew closer, the lightning dome vanished as quickly as it had appeared, revealing a lone figure standing in a small crater.

"What is she wearing? And where did she get a coat?" Nara thought, looking at the strange outfit Sam was wearing.

***

Sam was reeling from the process of turning into a Technogog Arcana. Her first thought was, *"It wouldn't have been that bad if I was used to having every single molecule of my body torn apart, except for my brain and cores, before being magically stitched back together in less time than it takes to blink."* She pushed the thought from her mind and pulled up her status menu. Or at least she tried to.

Unlocking…[S]…
Phase one unlocked…[S.] Samantha; Technogog Arcana…
Calculating power levels…warning…power levels incompatible.
Attempting to isolate and lock nodes…
Nodes locked…
Attempting to isolate and lock attributes…
Failed…
Error…

'Bing' Congratulations! You have upgraded your physical form to that of a Technogog Arcana. Your current soul level is insufficient to maintain this form. You will experience soul destruction in 300 seconds…299…298…297…

Sam noted the rude System interruption with annoyance and checked her stats.

Name: Samantha [S.]
Race: Evolved Human [Level…error]

Class: Technogog Arcana [Epic] [Level...error]

Health: 2682
Stamina: 2047
Mana: 30684

[Locked]

Resistance(s):
Arcane Magic 100%
Void Magic 5%

"What the hell, System? How will I use all that mana with all my abilities locked? Argh!" Sam was talking to herself, not realizing it was going through party chat.

"What are you?" Nara's panting voice broke Sam from her grumblings. "And how did you—"

"I'll explain it later, but right now, I only have a few minutes before I die. I have to go back into my soul. Are you ladies, okay?"

"WHAT!?!" Nara shouted out loud and through their chat.

"I believe we can survive for the next few minutes," The Defeated's voice was calm and relaxed, and she immediately shot a blood spike at the charging Matriarch, diverting its attention from Sam. She then dug all her blood tentacles on one side into the cave floor, using them as an anchor to swing herself ninety degrees to dash off in a completely different direction, with Nara screaming from her back.

Sam grinned at the maneuver, thinking, *"Hey, I taught her that. Good job, girl!"* Then, closing her eyes, she dove back into her soul.

***

"What are you doing? We have to help her!" Nara shouted at The Defeated.

"We are helping her," The Defeated replied calmly, barely dodging a stream of green acidic toxin as it chased them up the cave wall.

The Defeated was moving so fast she could use the curved walls of the circular cavern to run on. In fact, it was easier for her because there weren't piles of destroyed mushrooms and boulders to contend with.

Nara was mollified by the answer and twisted in the saddle to fire another arrow at the Matriarch, which was flying in like an angry missile, using her air affinity to propel her at impossible speeds. The arrow missed, and the Matriarch closed the distance in the blink of an eye.

"Look out!" Nara screamed at her mount, ducking in the saddle and bracing for impact.

An instant before they were crushed, The Defeated glowed a faint orange as she activated Final Push. Nara's vision tunneled, and the world seemed to slow when the skill activated, giving them a burst of speed so fast that Nara, even with her high agility, had trouble following their trajectory.

Nara screamed again, but it was from pure exhilaration; she had never felt so alive.

***

Sam rushed back to her soulscape, grumbling all the way. *"I figure out how to upgrade my body in the most impossible way possible, and the freaking System locks all my freaking abilities! How completely fucked up is that? And why is it taking so long to get down this fucking tunnel?"* She knew it wasn't taking longer, but she was frustrated.

Slamming down back in her old room, she didn't hesitate and went straight for the dragon figurine, but to her even greater annoyance, it shook its head no when she reached for it. "Fine! But you're next!" Sam snapped and snatched the Duplicitous Lamia off the desk instead. It hissed and bared its fangs when she grabbed it, but Sam ignored that and slammed the statue into her chest.

***

Nara felt the power surge before she saw the lightning dome as they kited the beast. This dome was even more significant than before and was composed of violet and black lightning. The Defeated, still using her skill, turned and ran up the cavern wall just as a cloud of toxic gas and two wind blades slammed into the wall right where they would have been had they not evaded.

In response, Nara sent her second-to-last powered arrow at the Matriarch and got a lucky hit on its wing. The arrow did minor damage, but it did knock the pursuing creature to the ground for just a second, giving them time to complete their maneuver…whatever it was…

"What are you doing?" Nara shouted over the wind, whipping at her ears, forgetting she was also using the chat function. "We are going to fall—"

The Defeated, already running upside down on the ceiling, leaped off into nothing, turning Nara's statement into a scream and plummeting them toward the cave floor at a speed they would never survive the impact from.

"We're going to dieeeeeee! Oof." Nara had the wind knocked out of her when their direction went from a death plummet to flying barely over the ground.

Just meters from the ground, The Defeated reformed its blood armor into giant gliders swooping up in time to skim over the tops of the broken stems of the mushroom forest.

"You are amazing," Nara shouted to her mount as they glided to Sam. She continued babbling, her emotions going haywire from not dying like she had been sure she would only a moment earlier. "I swear I will never doubt one of your decisions again. I—what the goink is that?!? Sam?!?"

"I told you, I'll explain later!" Sam said as she slapped the Matriarch out of the air with a giant tail from where it was flying in to intercept Nara and her mount. "I gotta go in one more time! Be back in a second!"

"Are you a freaking snake?!" Nara shouted as the figure of her friend attached to an enormous tail disappeared when she and The Defeated landed, starting to run again. Nara felt the giant animal beginning to slow down and thought, *"Whatever you are going to do, Sam, do it fast."*

***

Surprised at how strong of a hit she had produced against the Matriarch, Sam checked her stat screen, but the System forced notifications on her just as before.

Unlocking…[M]…
Phase two unlocked…[M.] Moura; Duplicitous Lamia…
Calculating power levels…warning…power levels incompatible.
Attempting to isolate and lock nodes…
Nodes locked…
Attempting to isolate and lock attributes…
Failed…
Error…

'Bing' Congratulations! You have upgraded your physical form to that of a Duplicitous Lamia. Your current soul level is insufficient to maintain this form. You will experience soul destruction in 100 seconds…99…98…97…

When her stat screen pulled up, Sam was pissed.

Name: Moura [M.]
Race: Unknown [Level…error]
Class: Duplicitous Lamia [Unique] [Level…error]
Health: 6142
Stamina: 12903
Mana: 7756

[Locked]

Resistance(s):
Arcane Magic 50%
Void Magic 50%

"Fuuuuuuuuuuk!" Sam yelled in frustration as she dove back into her soul, absently noting the glowing black and purple fractures splintering out from the hole in her soul core. She knew the dragon figurine had to be strength-based if they followed any logic. The first one had a massive mana pool, and the second had stamina in the five digits, so it stood to reason that the last one would have a strength upgrade. That's what she was hoping for anyway. "*I know I didn't hurt the Matriarch and only deflected her when I hit her with my tail...which is surprisingly natural to use. It feels really cool, too, when it's all coiled up around—stop it! I need to focus! I need strength, and I know where to get it!"*

Slamming into her soulscape yet again, Sam dove for the dragon girl figurine. It still shook its head and stepped back when Sam lunged for it, but it wasn't fast enough. Sam gripped the figure, and before she could think logically about what she was about to do, she smashed it into her chest and screamed!

***

Nara screamed as some of the toxic spray landed on her arm. They hadn't been hit by an attack but had run too close to the residue from a previous attack dripping from the wall. The Defeated slipped as it started up the wall again, causing it to slow just a fraction.

That was all the time the Matriarch needed, though, and a cloud of acidic gas propelled by wind magic rushed toward them from behind.

"Use your skill!" Nara shouted as the gas grew closer. She couldn't see the Matriarch to get a shot off. They weren't going to make it.

"You must run now." The Defeated said calmly. She wrapped Nara in her blood tentacles and, releasing her from the saddle, sent Nara flying far ahead of the encroaching cloud.

"Noooooo!" Nara screamed when she landed on her feet, only to see The Defeated's back half swallowed up in the green cloud of acid. The cloud dissipated only an instant later to reveal the Matriarch pinning the summon to the wall with a clawed foot. The Defeated's entire back quarter and most of her blood armor were gone. Yet, still, she roared her defiance in the face of the much more powerful being that was a breath away from killing her.

Not even thinking, Nara knocked and shot her final explosive arrow, yelling, "Over here, you stupid lizard!"

The Matriarch must have been tired of the annoying arrows because the instant it left Nara's bowstring, the beast dropped The Defeated's body and flashed toward Nara, slapping the arrow from the air and closing half the distance with a single flap of her wings.

Nara knew running was pointless, so instead, she screamed her own defiance while firing mana bolts from both hands. Useless as it was, she would go down fighting. Then Nara stopped. She fell to her knees, clutching her chest under the weight of... *"What is this? Is it...suppression? How? I cannot…no…I must get up!"* Standing up with a supreme effort of will under the unseen force that felt like it was crushing her soul, Nara saw the Matriarch had landed and was looking away from her toward, *"Sam!"*

Nara climbed up and stood atop a broken mushroom stalk to better understand Sam's location. Her eyes widened when she finally saw what the Matriarch was looking at. A giant black egg with just a faint streak of violet across it was sitting in the crater Sam's two lightning storms had made. The egg was four meters tall and at least half that across at the widest point. "What the goink?"

The egg cracked. It was just a tiny crack, then another and another. Black mist with traces of purple started pouring out of the gaps. Nara saw the Matriarch taking a few steps back, and she knew why. The oppressive power coming from that egg was overwhelmingly terrifying. A true apex predator was being born into this world, and every being for several kilometers felt its presence.

With a final crack, the egg shattered.

***

Sam had done it.

Unlocking…[A]…
Phase three unlocked…[A.] Alecto; Draconic Voidling…
Calculating power levels…warning…limit break in effect...
Attempting to isolate and lock nodes…
Error…nodes not found…error…
Attempting to isolate and lock…error…attributes…
Failed…
Error…

'Bing' Congratulations! You have upgraded your physical form to that of a Draconic Voidling. Your current soul level is insufficient to

maintain this form. You will experience soul disintegration in 10 seconds...9...8...7...

Name: Alecto [A.]
Race: Dragonling Hybrid
Class: Draconic Voidling

Health: 28958
Stamina: 7577
Mana: 30684

Resistance(s):
Unknown

Sam looked at the retreating Matriarch and smiled, her fangs dripping with anticipation. She flashed forward with a leap and a beat of her wings, leaving an afterimage as she traveled.

Arriving instantly in front of The Defeated, who looked up at the draconic figure with awe. Sam didn't have much time, so she went straight to work. Slicing deep into her wrist with a claw, the Draconic Voidling drew a single drop of blood so dark red it was almost black. It hovered in the air for an instant before flying forward and splatting against The Defeated's chest. In a deep, raspy voice she didn't recognize, Sam said, "Here you go, girl. Thanks for the assist and for keeping Nara safe."

"Sam?" Nara's voice came through their chat function, sounding timid and afraid.

6...

Sam flew to her friend so fast it looked like teleportation. With a fang-filled smile, the three-meter-tall Dragonling reached down. It rested a massive, clawed hand on her friend's shoulder, staring deep into her dark blue eyes, and answered her question in the Dragonling's deep, raspy voice, "Well, yeah, it's me, duh." She then sent twenty-five thousand mana units into Nara simultaneously, eliciting the best mana orgasm she had seen yet.

5...

With her companions taken care of, Sam turned her blazing violet eyes to the E-Grade monster. The Whitling Matriarch shrank back under the gaze of the Dragonling but still roared its defiance and—

4…

The Dragonling was upon the Matriarch, slamming the monster's head into the ground before it had time to finish its roar. The rock cracked underneath the force of its head, striking it. The Dragonling didn't let up; grabbing an errant wing and bracing her foot against the monster's back, she pulled.

3…

The Dragonling ripped the wing from the monster's back like she was pulling the wing off a fly. The Matriarch reacted by biting the Dragonling's torso, her fangs barely penetrating enough to inject her toxin. The Dragonling roared and grabbed the Whitling's upper and lower jaws, prying them open until she felt the lower jaw snap under the strain.

2…

The E-Grade beast released a screech and buffeted the Dragonling with air blades from its remaining wing. The attacks didn't even displace a single scale on the Dragonling's skin. The Whitling's screech was cut off when the Dragonling bit deep into its throat and stabbed her tail deep into its chest, penetrating the Matriarch's heart with her obsidian tail spike.

1…

The Dragonling ripped the Matriarch's throat out with a yank of her head and tore her tail from the dying creature slinging chinks of meat across the cavern. But the powerful E-Grade wasn't dead yet and blasted a cloud of toxic acid out from every pore in her body, enveloping them. The Dragonling was out of time, and she knew it. Summoning the last of her draconic strength, she braced her clawed feet against the Whitling's scaly chest and grabbed it behind its head. She pulled with a mighty roar that shook the cavern walls.

0…

***

Nara had to cover her ears when the thing her friend had turned into roared. Even through the loud roar, she heard a popping sound, and the chime of a notification sounded in her mind.

'Bing' Whitling Matriarch; Level 101 has been defeated by your party. Bonus experience is awarded for defeating an enemy 75 or more levels above your own. Additional experience is awarded for defeating an enemy one grade above your own. Experience distribution has been split equally between party members.

Nara ignored the Level Up notifications and ran to her friend as fast as she could.

The Defeated, now fully healed and sporting menacing black blood armor, beat Nara to Sam. Forming blood wings, she fanned the lingering toxic gas from the area. She hovered protectively over the now human body of her summoner.

Nara got to Sam seconds later. She gasped, tears welling in her eyes when she saw the state of Sam's body. Empty eye sockets faced up, staring at nothing; all her skin was dissolved along with most of the muscle tissue, leaving almost nothing but bone and organs behind. Nara could see all of Sam's organs. Many were black and rotting from the necrotic acid of the Matriarch. Nara began weeping at her friend's state, uncontrolled sobs rocking her body. Not knowing what else to do, she pulled out several health potions and began slowly pouring them over the mostly dissolved body of her friend. Staring into her friend's empty eye sockets, Nara could only hope Sam's mind was still intact. Most people, or even beasts, could not recover from this kind of trauma.

The Defeated surprised Nara when she lowered a tentacle above Sam's skeletal form and began dripping the tiniest drops of black blood onto each of her exposed organs. Each organ the blood touched slowly started reverting to its natural color, healing enough to stay ahead of the necrotic toxin.

***

Once Sam was healed enough to be out of immediate danger, Nara had them store the Matriarch's body and head before moving to a campsite halfway back to the cave entrance. They gathered as many monster cores as possible before retreating to the safer area.

Over many hours, Sam's friends healed her body. After nearly a day of constant and careful healing stretching their dwindling resources thin, Nara and The Defeated had fully healed Sam's physical form, but Nara knew it wasn't just her body that needed to be healed. She knew from overhearing other's accounts that using power outside of one's ability to control without assistance from a being of greater strength would almost always destroy the user's mind and soul.

Nara stared at Sam's peaceful expression, cradling her head in her lap. She was leaning back against The Defeated, who she had begun calling Lupie to shorten the long name. Brushing Sam's now shoulder-length violet hair, Nara watched as shadows flickered across her face from the small fire she had built. Sam's cheeks felt cold and clammy, so Nara pulled the blade tail hide up higher to just under Sam's chin. A single tear dripped on Sam's pallid cheek, and brushing it off with a finger, Nara whispered to her friend, "Please, Sam, come back to us…come back to me."

Epilogue

Sam was lying on the floor of her soul room in a pool of purple and black blood. Three figurines lay broken and distorted in the ever-expanding puddle of viscous liquid leaking from Sam's soul. She lay like this for a day…a year…there was no way to tell. Time functioned differently here in the Void between realities.

A tall, slim figure stared at Sam from her bed. Usually, no creature should be able to access another's soul, but this wasn't a soul. It was only a mere fractured splinter of a soul. The creature sighed, taking in the scene with pure white eyes set into a formless midnight black face, "Oh, my sister, what have you done here?"

The figure stood from the bed, causing the springs to creak and groan from its weight, and adjusted the white feather in its stylish black hat. A single step of its long, sinewy legs brought it to Sam's side. Kneeling, it rested its hand on her chest above her core, the long white claws extending from its fingers poised to tear open her chest and remove her soul core.

It was customary for Voidlings to perform the final rights like this for their fallen siblings. It ensured none of their souls would ever remain trapped, unable to return to the collective whole of their kind.

"Lif, what are you doing?" The voice came from the Void. The power of the voice was so great a faint whisper could cause entire verses to wink out of existence.

Lif, however, was unfazed by the voice and looked up curiously, "I am relegating her soul to the collective. She is one of us, after all."

"She was dealt with unfairly by a system that was not aware of her place in the collective," the voice rumbled emotionlessly as always. Your sister Ica made a grave error in not informing us of her intent and hiding the void splinter." The voice paused briefly before continuing, "I will remedy this."

“Shall I repair her then?” Lif asked.

"No," The Void responded, "she will repair herself…or not. It will be her choice. Although the System dealt with her unfairly, she did this to herself. Place her notebook beside her and go. Her final spark is waiting for you to leave so it can wake her."

Lif did as instructed. It walked to the desk and retrieved the small notebook that appeared there. As Lif took the notebook, it also noticed the outline of a figure on the desk hidden in the dark obscuration against the wall. Seeing through the obscuration, Lif said, "Oh, impressive. I would like to see this someday in the distant future," before stepping back and laying the book in the blood at Sam's side.

Its work done, Lif was about to portal back to its own reality when the Void spoke one last time, "Tell Ica her daughter is well, but do not send an image to her. She should not have made this little Voidling without my permission. Her rash actions have led to this situation." The Void paused, then added, "As well as her own."

Lif nodded, and, pulling out its notebook from storage, it used the feather from its hat to jot something down on a page before closing the book. With one last look at its sister Lif, the level 9579 Void Slime tipped its hat to the final figure on the desk and said, "Goodbye, sister. May we meet again." Then, a portal opened behind it, revealing a violent hellscape of a planet. Looking to the portal, Lif smiled to itself, its face nearly splitting in two with the wide grin exposing razor-sharp white teeth. Lif's home was always so pleasant this time of year. The Void Slime stepped through the portal, vanishing from Sam's soul.

The instant Lif's portal closed, the lone figurine ran to the edge of the desk and jumped off, landing on Sam's chest. Still shrouded in fog, the figure reached into its chest and pulled out a fragment of its core. The fragment's colors fluctuated across the entire spectrum, never staying on a single color for more than a millisecond. Without stopping to admire the beautiful power in its hand, the figurine plunged the fragment into Sam's chest, then leaped back to the desk, returning to its place to wait for the day it would be released. A hint of annoyance furrowed the figurine's brow under the fog. It was annoyed the others had not hidden from Sam and, in their own way, coerced her into assimilating with them far too early. But then again, she had watched Sam forcibly ram them into her core…so there was that…the figure snickered then resumed its position on its pedestal, which read: **Samantha Alecto Moura [S.A.M.]**

***

Ignoring the chains binding her, the Void Dragon strained to stare at her artifact; the small artifact was something they all shared, for it could be everywhere simultaneously across time and space. The small, seemingly mundane notebook could be used by trillions upon trillions of the Voidlings at once, and they would all know of the changes, assuming their levels were sufficient to handle the information. The children of the Void were first and foremost explorers, hungry for knowledge and new experiences to share with the collective, constantly yearning for existence outside the endless Void. And what better way to gain knowledge than to share an omnipresent notebook with trillions of your brothers, sisters, entities, monsters, and those that defied definition?

Seeing nothing on the pages, Ica sighed. She had lost the tentative connection she had with her daughter hours ago. She continued to stare at the blank pages with resignation creeping into her heart, "She has failed," she said, causing the cavern she was in to vibrate. And with another sigh, she added, "I am sorry, little one. I will ask my siblings to take care of you in the collective. Maybe someday you and I will—"

Ica's eyes opened wide, and she shifted in her chains to eagerly read the script that appeared on the page. It read: Your daughter lives! The Void has remedied your mistake. Inform the Void next time; perhaps something like this will not happen. - Lif

P.S. She is just as impetuous and insane as you. I like her! Although I doubt she will survive long, I'm sure she will be entertaining to watch. You must tell us how you made her once you are free of the chains. Also, I have left your daughter's artifact with her, but it will be up to her to learn how to use it. I also left her two personal gifts to help her journey. Goodbye for now, sister. Rest well, knowing the collective has accepted your daughter even though you tried to hide her from us. – Lif

Ica closed her eyes and smiled, completely ignoring the hundreds of terrified humans scrambling around the underground facility she was trapped in. Some were screaming while others were shouting orders. Massive blast shields were being checked and rechecked by frantic figures. Enormous cannons were primed and aimed at her, prepared to fire should she decide to attack. Ica did not concern herself with the frightened mortals. Their cannons would not even leave a scuff on one of her scales. Not even the nuclear bomb they buried under her chamber would do anything but annoy her. No, they were of no consequence. For the first time in over a billion years, she had hope.

***

"I don't like this. We should just run away. There might be somewhere the church cannot find us." Alina hissed to her father. She looked around the dimly lit tavern anxiously.

"Quit your squirming, or you'll draw attention, girl," Arron snapped in a low voice. "We don't want to scare him off."

Alina knew he was right. Struggling to regain her composure, she returned to her drink and took a large gulp to help calm her nerves. They were waiting for one of Arron's contacts, the same clerk who had approved their contract for the wolf culling job. He was going to give them information on Sam and Nara's whereabouts. Alina thought back to why they were doing this.

The Church of the Light priest had given them two options after they had recounted the events leading to their death and the subsequent release of a Moonblight. The first option was to join the church ranks and serve for one hundred cycles in whatever capacity the church required of them to pay for their resurrection. After their service, they would be compensated with a few hundred gold and their freedom.

The second option was to assist in the hunt for the Moonblight and the person that had saved them from the wolves, whom the church assumed was also the one who blocked the locator beacon when the blood contract was dissolved. If they provided information on what led to the capture or death of the Moonblight, the church would provide compensation determined by their contribution level and their freedom. The only caveat was that they would be given less than a cycle to find them. Failure would result in them being forced to join the church, as stated in the first option.

Of course, they could have refused both options. Arron and Alina knew what that would result in…the swift undoing of their recent resurrection.

They had chosen to hunt for their former traveling companions. Once they decided, they were given clothes, basic weapons, and ten gold each to outfit themselves. Then, they were directed to a safe house in the city, where they found information regarding how to reach a contact in the church with any information they uncovered.

"Which is why we're here in this dingy tavern," Alina thought, swirling the beer in her mug absently. She asked her father again, "Why can't the church do this themselves?"

Arron looked at her in annoyance, "Like I already told you. They don't have a strong presence here in the borderlands, and since the church suspects the girls joined the guild, they have to tread very carefully. It's easier to hire people who aren't affiliated with the church to do their diggin' for them so as not to arouse suspicion." He looked at her seriously, "Now don't ask me again, and get your head in the game, Alina! Do you want to spend a hundred years as slaves to those wackos?"

Alina ground her teeth in frustration. *"Resurrected only to do someone else's dirty work...figures."* Her dour thoughts were interrupted when their man slid into the booth beside her.

"Hello, Thomas," Arron said. He was still annoyed with the man for sending them on the job that led to their deaths but wasn't letting it show. He knew it wasn't the man's fault, but he needed to direct his anger at someone, and Thomas was the closest person.

"Did you get what I asked?" Thomas looked around nervously as he spoke, just as Alina had been doing only moments before.

"Yeah, yeah, relax, man," Arron placated the nervous Thomas. "I still don't know why you couldn't buy it yourself, but here it is, a berth on the next trading caravan to the beast lands." He held up a small bronze token.

Thomas reached for the token, but Arron snatched it away, saying, "Information first."

Nodding, Thomas handed a small scroll to Alina under the table. She opened it in her lap and skimmed the contents. It was a map with the locations of all the jobs Sam and Nara had selected marked on it. Nodding to Arron, she pocketed the small scroll. Arron smiled and slid the token to Thomas, who snatched it up and slid out of the booth, practically running from the room.

Alina and Arron stayed to finish their drinks before casually exiting the tavern and returning to their temporary room. After leaving a note for their contact detailing the locations marked on the map, Arron and Alina grabbed their kits and departed Helms Peak for the key to their freedom.

***

A lone figure watched Arron and Alina leave the safe house from his perch on a nearby rooftop. He sent a message to his party and jumped to the street a full three stories below. His knees barely even bent from the impact of the three-story fall as he landed without a sound. Checking the responses from his party, he started following the two out of the city and hopefully to the free Moonblight and the one who freed her.

***

Sam's mind was sluggish as she regained consciousness. "Am I dead?" She asked, staring at the ceiling. Sam realized where she was as the old wood planks of it slowly came into focus. "Is this hell? Do I have to spend eternity in my old room in the orphanage?"

Sam brought a hand up to rub her temple but stopped when she saw the purple and black goop on it, "what the—" She sat up, her hand landing on a small book lying in the pool of fluid surrounding her.

After taking a moment to give the room time to stop spinning, Sam examined her surroundings. She noted the three disfigured figurines on the floor and groaned. *"It looks like I really fucked up this time...well, more than normal anyway,"* she thought, staring at the figures. They were barely recognizable from their original forms.

"I'll fix them," She thought, then told the figurines as much, "I promise to fix you, ladies. I need some—wait, why am I talking to statues?" Shaking her head, Sam sloshed over in the gooey puddle and gathered the three broken figurines and the small book. Setting them all on the desk, she picked up each figure one at a time, and, doing her best to wipe off the gunk, she placed each back on their respective pedestal. She was relieved when the figurines tried to resume their position on their pedestals. However, it was still a pathetic sight as they were all broken and distorted almost beyond recognition. It was so bad she nearly put the Lamia on the Dragon pedestal accidentally.

Finished with the figurines, Sam pulled out one of the drawers in her desk, relieved when the art supplies she remembered having were still there.

"Okay, I think I can work with this." She thought, checking the contents of the drawer.

Not wanting to start on the figurines right away, Sam wiped the thick goop off the small notebook and stared at it curiously. *"I don't remember this notebook being here. Did I forget about having it?"* She opened the book to the first page, but it was blank. Flipping through the book, she realized all the pages were blank. She was about to toss the book in her desk drawer and forget about it when she noticed the residue from the goop she hadn't been able to get off the back cover was gone. Turning the book over again, she saw writing on the front cover where there had been none before. It read "The Book of S.A.M." in violet lettering. "This is interesting," she mumbled, opening the book again. The pages were still blank, so she closed and pocketed the book, promising to look at it again later. *"Like when I figure out if I'm still alive or if this really is life after death. Because I am pretty sure I should not have survived the stunt I pulled."*

Sam continued exploring the room. She splashed over to the bed, noting with some worry her exit rune was no longer glowing under it. *"Why was it under the bed anyway? Wouldn't it have been easier to have it on a wall or something? It is my soulscape, so I should probably know, but nothing comes to mind..."* Her internal musings stopped when she noticed two items lying on the bed; each had a note attached to it with a little black ribbon.

Sam picked up the first item and read the note. "Dear sister, it is always nice to be with family. I would be there myself, but you are much too weak. – Lif."

"What!? Family? I'm too weak? SISTER!? Just who the fuck left me this note!?" She looked at the item the note was attached to. It was a black coin with a familiar shape and weight. She knew exactly what it was when she turned it over in her hand. It was a summoning token. There was no image of a beast on the coin, though, only what looked like two slanted white eyes and a too-wide grin filled with white shark-like teeth etched into the flat black of the coin. A single word in white lettering was inscribed above the eyes. It read Nul. "Huh, not sure what that thing is, but I am definitely not going to summon Nu—" Sam closed her lips. *"That would have been stupid. Summoning a...whatever that thing is into my soulscape. There's no telling what kind of a shitstorm that would create. And after that weird note..."*

Sam checked the other item on her bed and pocketed the token with the notebook. It was a beautiful violet feather. Picking it up, she corrected herself. "It's a quill," she mumbled, reading the attached note.

"Dear sister, please accept this as a welcome gift into the collective. I look forward to hearing from you when you are no longer incredibly weak. – Lif."

Sam threw her hands up, staring at the ceiling, and shouted, "What the fuck is the collective, and who the fuck was in my soul!?" No answer came, so with a huff, Sam turned back to the center of the room.

She was just in time to see the pool of weird liquid start streaming off the floor like a reverse rain shower. Once the small streams reached about a meter off the floor, they zipped into Sam's chest, startling her. She tried to erect a shield to block the liquid, but her magic didn't activate. Within a few seconds, she was covered in the goopy stuff. Looking down at her naked chest, Sam realized the fluid was absorbing into her. She tried wiping it off but stopped when she suddenly felt much better. Her mental clarity was coming back, and she could form a small mana construct with a flick of her fingers. "Looks like I need this stuff," she said, watching the last of the fluid disappear into her body.

Feeling whole again for the first time since she had woken up, Sam looked around the room, gleefully noting the exit rune had lit up under her bed. Instead of immediately leaving, she walked over to the desk. Sam opened her art drawer, pulled out several items, and placed them in front of her on the desk. Sitting at her desk in the old wooden chair, she gently took Samantha from her pedestal and slowly and painstakingly began trying to repair her crushed and mutilated body. She started with her legs, which were smashed beyond recognition.

Sam switched tactics after failing to make any headway on the figurine's legs with her standard art supplies. Creating a tiny mana thread from her finger, she touched it to one of the damaged legs and mentally willed the leg to reform while injecting mana into it. It didn't work.

Frustrated, Sam grabbed one of her small sculpting knives and carefully cut the leg off at the hip, removing the damaged body part. A sharp pain in her own leg caused Sam to wince. She quickly looked down to check that she hadn't cut her own leg off somehow. "Hmm, phantom pains, I guess?" She mused, seeing her leg whole and unharmed. Putting down her knife, Sam picked up a micro pick she used for detail work and dipped the tip in a jar of putty she kept around for mockups.

With hands steadier than ever before, thanks to her increased stats, Sam dabbed a microscopic amount of putty on the severed stump. Then, with the micro pick still touching the putty, she channeled arcane and void energy down the pick into the putty. It worked! The instant the mana touched the putty, it turned white. Sam knew what this meant, and she began reforming the leg's bone. She activated her mana repair skill after a few moments. Although the skill didn't help with reconstructing the bone, it did tell her what she needed to do to make it perfect. The skill helped a good deal. It informed her she had forgotten to add the bone marrow, forcing her to start over.

Sam worked on the figurine's leg for over an hour and a half with only a scant three millimeters of progress on reforming the bone. The process took nearly three hundred mana per second, and even with meditation active, she had to rest frequently. During her rest times, Sam tried to check her notifications, but she could only pull up her basic interface. On a positive note, the blacked-out portions of her energy bars were no longer at forty percent and held steady at ten percent.

Sam stretched in her chair, exhausted. She placed Samantha back on her pedestal and stood up. Sam knew repairing the figurines wouldn't happen overnight and was anxious to return to Nara. It wasn't because she feared Nara was in danger; she knew she had killed the Whitling Matriarch. *"At least I assume the damn thing wouldn't be able to survive without a head...could it...nah."* The memory of tearing the E-Grade monster's head from its shoulders brought a predatory grin to Sam's face, and she looked at Alecto's mangled form. "I am going to get strong enough for you, girl. I want to feel that power again. You and me, we're going places."

On a whim, Sam picked up the violet quill from where she had laid it on the desk. Pulling out her notebook and opening it to a random page, she channeled a small amount of energy into the quill and touched it to the page. A small black spot appeared on the paper at the quill's tip. Excited, Sam started sketching the figurines as they were before she destroyed them. She began with Samantha. *"I only wish I could draw it in color."* The thought had no longer crossed her mind when the ink changed to the color she wished for on the page. *"Well, now that's freaking awesome!"* She thought and continued her sketch. Once Samantha's image filled the page, Sam admired her work. It was as detailed as her artistic mind and high intelligence state could make it. *"Now for the sides and back."* At that thought, the figure on the page began rotating slowly. Surprised but not wasting time, Sam quickly touched the quill back to the page and drew a full 3D image of Samantha as her image slowly rotated.

Sam finished her drawing and admired the detail of her work as the image continued to rotate on the page. Looking to the ceiling, she said, "Thanks for the gifts, Lif!" Then, she jumped when the notebook vibrated in her hand and jerked up to hover open in front of her face. Several pages turned on their own, and the words "You are welcome, sister." Appeared on a blank page for just an instant before fading away. Sam was about to grab the book and try to write a response down when it slammed shut and flew into her pocket. *"Okay, that was obviously a sign. This Lif person apparently doesn't want a response from a weak sister."*

Deciding she was done with her soul space, Sam tapped her foot on the edge of the rune under her bed and vanished.

***

Nara and Lupie had waited two days in the cave, hoping Sam would wake up. They knew Sam was still alive because she was still active in their party menu, although Nara was now the party leader and Sam's status menu was locked.

On the morning of the third day, they decided to move from the cave to the forest as more and more cave monsters were finding their campsite. It was more of a nuisance than a problem, thanks to how many levels they acquired from defeating the Matriarch. But Nara could see it becoming a problem if she and Lupie had to keep protecting Sam.

It was now the night of the third day. They had traveled all day with Sam held securely in front of Nara by blood tentacles as she rode Lupie. The Bloodmorph enjoyed having Nara as a rider, thanks to the frequent ear scratches and neck rubs she received from the Tenarian. They made camp about a kilometer from the cave entrance in a densely wooded forest area, and Nara had just received a safe zone notification.

Nara sighed and relaxed a little at the familiar chime and message. The cave had too many high-level stealth predators for them to make a safe zone, so getting the notification was a welcome relief. She handed Lupie twenty kilograms of wolf steaks, thankful she still had access to Sam's inventory. After Lupie's tummy was taken care of, Nara assumed her now customary position, leaning against the giant Bloodmorph's side with Sam's unconscious body beside her. Listening to the deep, soothing sounds of the huge wolf beast's breathing, Nara munched on her own steak, staring at their small campfire. Not having anything else to do, Nara checked her status while she ate.

Nara Evander; *[Naris Blight]*
Race: Tenarian; Mortal; [Level 30]; *Soul Bound Blight [Level ??]*
Class: Sorceress [Level 16]; *Mana Reaper [Level 28]*
Title(s): A Grade Above; Mass Destruction

Health: 1245
Stamina: 828
Mana: 206849; *[??????]*

Attributes:
STR – 29 *[??]*
VIT – 74 *[??]*

END – 38 ***[??]***
AGL – 102 ***[??]***
INT – 82 ***[??]***
Free Attribute Points 0.

Abilities: 2/4
Mana Sense [Level 11]
[Mana Siphon; Level 49]

Class Skills: 1/7
Replicate [Level 8]

Racial/General Skills: 3/7
Archery; Expert; [Level 3]
Identify [Level 7]
Mana Drain [Level 29]

Class Spells: 2/5
Magic Bolt [Level 13]
Cleanse [Level 4]

Racial/General Spells: 1/5
Charm [Level 3]

Resistance(s):
Pain [Level 15]
Poison [Level 4]
Magic [Level 31]

She had gained ten levels in her race and twelve in her class. The levels and titles almost made the fight worth it…almost. She rechecked the title descriptions.

Title: A Grade Above
You have defeated a foe a grade above your own. A feat rarely achieved in the multiverse. For this achievement, you have been granted the title A Grade Above. Plus 15% to all base stats. Additional positive effects may occur when fighting enemies 50 levels or greater above your own.

Title: Mass Destruction

By using your knowledge of the flora in your immediate surroundings, you caused a sequence of events that resulted in the death of over 1,000 of your foes in less than 60 seconds. For this achievement of ingenuity, you have been granted the title of Mass Destruction. Plus 5% to your intelligence stat. Additional rare information may become available when identifying flora.

Nara was happy to see her archery skill had reached expert level, allowing her to coat standard arrows with magic and make them slightly more powerful. Also, her magic bolt at level thirteen required much less mana to cast, which was good because she wanted to wait to take any mana from Lupie. Nara knew it shouldn't happen but didn't want to take the chance that Lupie's mana would change her class to something else while they were still in the forest. Thinking of Lupie, Nara remembered she had given her permission to level up and assign her free points as she saw fit. She checked the Bloodmorph's stat sheet in their party interface to see what she had done with her points.

The Defeated [Summon of S.A.M.]
Race: Lupine Bloodmorph; Elite; Unique [Level 15]
Class: Bloodmorph [Level 17]
Blessing(s): Void Touched [Epic]
Title(s): A Grade Above; Death Runner

Health: 6678
Stamina: 4299
Mana: 2818

Attributes:
STR – 83
VIT – 326
END – 186
AGL – 121
INT – 67
WIS – 145

Abilities: 2/10
Blood Manipulation
Void Compatibility

Class Skills: 2/7

Blood Recovery [Level 17]
Void Coating [Level 3]

Racial/General Skills: 3/7
Final Push [Level 11]
Identify [Level 2]
Stealth [Level 6]

Class Spells: 3/5
Blood Harvest [Level 5]
Blood Spike [Level 7]
Void Spike [Level 6]

Racial/General Spells:
Howl [Level 5]

Resistance(s):
Void Magic [Level 27]
Blood Magic [Level 56]

Nara whistled, and the calming sounds of Lupie's slow breathing halted for a moment before resuming when Nara made no other sounds for a while. *"Damn, she's strong."* Nara was glad she was on their side. She had heard stories about summons killing their summoners, but Lupie had been helpful. Nara had noted her status went from friendly to adoring when she had dumped out the pile of whitling bodies for her to drain before they fought the Matriarch. The status had remained, and they were in a safe zone together, which showed Nara that Lupie was not a threat.

Reaching to her side, Nara scratched the Bloodmorph's fur just where she liked it, thinking, *"With her blood armor retracted, she's not much different than a normal wolf. Well, except she would probably beat out a Great Timberwolf in the size category...and could probably take down anything below level seventy-five in this forest."*

Just then, Sam groaned, and Lupie and Nara jerked in surprise! Nara quickly grabbed her friend's hand, and Lupie brought her head around, sniffing at the Pathfinder expectantly.

***

Sam was moving through the now familiar tunnel between her soul and reality, but there was no exit when she entered her core at the end. There was no hole in her core for her mind to access. *"Please tell me I don't have to blow another hole in my core to get out of here! It looks like it is all better now!"* She whined to herself, floating in the mixture of arcane and Void mana swirling around her. Then, a brilliant thought struck her, and she called out as loud as she could, "Naris! Cut open my soul core!" She hoped her real body would say the words or she was close enough to reality for her party chat to function. *"Assuming I'm still in their party..."*

Sam waited for something to happen; she didn't know what she hoped for but figured she would know when it happened. After a few minutes with no change, she started yelling again, even going as far as pounding on the inside of her core with her fists. She was reluctant to use her own mana to cut her core open. Her logic was that in her one and only experience with a damaged core, the wounds inflicted by Naris healed, but the wound from her own magic had not. Hours went by, but no help came. Sam finally formed a blade construct from her void magic and was about to stab it into the side of her core when the notebook vibrated in her pocket.

Dismissing the blade, Sam quickly pulled the book out, and again, it shot from her hand to hover in front of her, opening to a blank page. Words started appearing on the page, and Sam fist-pumped in elation, "Yes! Thank you, whoever you are—" She stared at the page in surprise, "Well fuck you too then!" Snatching the book in front of her, she slammed it shut and stuffed it in her pocket, grumbling.

The message read, "Thank you for the entertainment, sister. It is hard to believe we were all as dumb and weak as you once. We suggest you try pulling on one of your mind core tendrils above you and returning to yourself via that channel. Of course, as always, your path is your own, so you may disregard our suggestion and cut your way out of your soul if you choose. In fact, it would be much more entertaining to watch, so do that instead. – The Collective"

Still grumbling, Sam grabbed one of the hundreds of mana channels protruding slightly into the top of her core. Instantly, she felt the connection to her mind and disappeared from her soul core with a thought.

-END